The Prey Bites Back

A Jesse Watson Mystery

Ann Mullen

This book is a work of fiction. Any characters portrayed, living or dead, are imaginary. Any resemblance to actual persons is completely coincidental. Any places, business establishments, locales, events, or incidents in this book are the product of the author's imagination, or used fictitiously.

Afton Ridge Publishing
271 Entry Run Road
Stanardsville, Virginia 22973

Printed in the United States of America
Land of the free, home of the brave.

ISBN 13: 978-0-9909860-0-3

LCCN: 2015904494

Also by Ann Mullen

Jesse Watson Mystery Series:

What You See
South River Incident
A Crying Shame
Middle River Murders
Greene County Killer
Death on the Bella Constance
All About the Money

Short Story Collection:
Lunch Break Shorts

This book is dedicated to

Norman Slezak

body shop—*n*. a shop where bodies of automotive vehicles are repaired, manufactured, etc.

—*Webster's Dictionary*

Chapter 1

When most folks tell stories of their RV experiences, there always seems to be something disastrous that happened along the way—a flat tire, engine problems, somebody getting left behind at a rest stop or gas station by mistake—you name it; I've heard it all.

So, we did our best to prepare ourselves in advance. We discussed all the things that could go wrong and made a pact that whatever happened, we were going to take it in stride and enjoy ourselves. We had money, guns, cell phones and a satellite phone. What else did we need?

Billy had rented a Winnebago fully equipped with everything we needed, and we were just going to get on the bus and go. No destination. No timeline.

Hello. My name is Jesse Watson Blackhawk. Years ago, I moved with my parents to Stanardsville, a little town in the beautiful mountains of Virginia, got a job working for a private investigator, and then married him. Billy Blackhawk and I have been together now for almost ten years.

Dad died shortly after we moved here, and then a while later, my mom Minnie found Eddie. They were married in a triple ceremony at Chief Sam and Sarah's house along with my sister, Claire, and her guy

Randy Morgan, and Billy's brother, Jonathan, and his fiancée, Lu Ann Knotts. It was a huge celebration done up in grand Cherokee style. But the party was over, the newlyweds were off on their honeymoons, and we were still out of a job.

Let me explain.

Not long after I hooked up with Billy, I got my P.I. license and the two of us set out together to dig into peoples' lives. It was our job to get the dirt and we did it very well using pretty much any means we found necessary as long as it was legal… mostly.

Unfortunately, we crossed the line a few times and Greene County Sheriff Wake Hudson finally called us out on it. We reached an agreement with him that would keep me and Billy out of jail for our dirty deeds by promising to take a hiatus from work for six months.

But not to worry, we came up with a backup plan. Mom and Eddie were going to take our place when they got back from their honeymoon. They were going to do our snooping for us. We had to keep the business going.

Billy and I live in Charlottesville, Virginia, on the Blackhawk Compound in the same house he once lived in with his first wife, but that's okay by me. We have two children, Maisy and Ethan, who are attended to by Billy's cousin Helene, the best nanny in the world. We also have two dogs and a strange cat, making us the typical family.

Since we were temporarily unemployed, we decided to take a long vacation and see America. What else was there to do if we couldn't work?

I knew we were going to have a great time and hopefully there wouldn't be too many horror tales to tell, but low and behold, we hit a snafu right from the get-go.

We couldn't get Athena on the bus. She had always hated riding in cars, so why did I think this was going to be any different? After twenty minutes of chasing her around the bus, the yard, and through the house, I was about ready to give up. The kids were getting cranky, Billy was frustrated, and Spice Cat wasn't happy at all about being in a cat carrier—which was only temporary until everyone was inside and the bus got on the road.

Although it was the end of October, the weather was still hot and humid at times. Wiping the sweat from my brow, I glared down at Athena and Thor. They had been acting like rats trying to find high ground in a flood.

I yelled, "Get on the bus or we're going to the vet!" I emphasized the word vet.

Both of them ceased their running around, stopped and looked at each other. I swear, if they could've shrieked liked people do, they would have. A minute later, both were on the bus looking for a place to claim as their own.

It was a minor glitch to start, but now we were on our way, and after an hour on the road, everyone had settled in. It was going to be a good trip.

Three weeks later, after days of sightseeing and stopping at every tourist trap there was from Charlottesville to Denver, the thrill was gone. I'd had enough. I was ready to go back home and get to work.

We were sitting in a roadside diner on the outskirts of Denver eating yummy hamburgers when I looked at Billy and said, "I've had about as much fun as I can stand. I'm ready to go home. I've put on five pounds and there's no more room on the bus for souvenirs."

Billy looked hurt.

"Aren't you having a good time, `ge ya? I thought you loved eating out and stopping at all those quaint little shops."

"Of course she's having a good time," Helene said as she wiped catsup from the corner of Ethan's mouth. "She's just had enough. So have I. It feels weird being on vacation for so long… and you two have been spending money like drunken sailors on shore leave. It's time to pull the plug on this party."

We talked, laughed, and joked as the bus carried us back home. That all stopped when a young punk tried to carjack the Winnebago at a gas station in Topeka, Kansas. He made it a half mile down the road before the cops stopped him. The guy was barely twenty years old and said he only did it on a dare. What an idiot. Who in their right mind would ever think they could make a getaway in a Winnebago?

Fortunately, our kids weren't on the bus, but the dogs and cat were. The cops said the guy was trying to fight off the dogs and the hissing cat sitting on the dashboard when they pulled him over. The young man couldn't get out of the bus fast enough. They arrested him without incident, but after it was over, I told Billy to remind me to never visit Kansas again.

"You can't blame the great state of Kansas for what one criminal does. The scenery's beautiful and the people seem to be so nice."

Helene popped up and said, "Except for the kid who tried to steal our bus. He wasn't such a nice person. What if the children had been on the bus?"

Billy didn't have a response, but I knew what he was thinking. He would've gone after the guy, even if he had to steal the car on the other side of the gas pump to do it.

"Kansas was the name of that guy who tried to kill my mother," I added. "No more Kansas for me, thank you very much."

And wouldn't you know it? Just before we reached the Kansas state line, about ready to leave that fine state behind, the skies turned dark and a wall cloud appeared on the horizon. Way off to our left, a funnel cloud was well on its way to touching down. The tornado was behind us, but it could be on us any minute.

Poor visibility, gusting winds, and heavy rain made it almost impossible for Billy to control the bus. Then the hail started. A minute later, a bicycle came careening through the air like a rocket, slamming into the passenger side and knocking the mirror off in its wake. The mirror disappeared into the black abyss. Much to our relief, the tornado disappeared before it caught up to us, but it had been a mighty close call.

After the initial shock wears off, being carjacked gives you plenty of fodder for conversations, and almost being sucked up into a tornado really ups the ante for things to talk about.

"Now we can tell our friends about our bus jacking," Helene said, chuckling. "Who would ever believe…"

"And what about that tornado?" I added. "That was about the scariest thing I've ever been through. The whole time I kept thinking about Dorothy in The Wizard of Oz."

"So was I," Helene agreed, chuckling. "I kept waiting for a house to fall on us."

Then, while we were cruising through Kentucky in the middle of the night, Billy hit a deer.

I freaked out and Helene had a spaz attack when we saw the poor thing lying in the road, squirming and kicking in agony.

So, Billy did the right thing. He shot the deer and dragged the carcass off the road into a field.

Try explaining that one to a state trooper when he pulls up and sees a man in his headlights, covered in blood up to his elbows, coming out of a field. That was another exciting experience.

We had a fun time from Charlottesville to Denver, but once we turned around and headed home, the trip back left a lot to be desired.

Bus jacking, tornado, hitting a deer—what next? I kept asking myself that question over and over. I couldn't shake the feeling that something bigger and worse was about to happen.

The answer came all too soon with a single phone call.

We had just pulled into the rest area on I-64 for one last stretch when Billy's cell phone went off. It was a 9-1-1 from Jonathan. Billy said little, and when the conversation was over, he turned to us and simply stated, "My mother is in the hospital. We must go."

Like zombies, we sat motionless, doing a steady seventy-five in a Winnebago all the way to Charlottesville, slowing down for nothing.

Once we reached the Hydraulic Road exit, Billy eased off the gas pedal and kept it that way until we reached Martha Jefferson Hospital. He had said little the whole time, but I could feel his pain, and I could see it in his eyes. His mother was seriously ill and the doctors were doing their best to find out why.

Billy is a Cherokee Indian. They feel things differently than we do. They cover their pain. We shout it from the rooftops. We cry out loud. They suffer in silence.

I was numb. I knew there was something wrong with Sarah. Her health had been declining over the past few months, but nobody had talked about it. I just didn't know it was that bad. I should've seen it coming. All the signs were there.

Our stop at the hospital was brief. Billy had gone in to see his mother, but she was out of it and didn't even know who he was. She was hallucinating and screaming at anyone who got near her.

Once we got home, everything seemed so gloomy.

The house was dark, the sky was overcast, and a strong wind was blowing in from the northeast. A storm was brewing.

"Are you okay?" I asked Billy as we stepped out of the Winnebago. "What can I do? I want to help, but I don't know…"

"I am fine, `ge ya. We must carry on. When we finish here, I must go be with my father. He will need my comfort."

"Sarah's going to pull through this, Billy. I know she will. She's strong…"

"I fear the worst," he said softly. "She did not look well at all. She is pale. Her words did not make sense. "

Contractions. When Billy didn't use them, he was in Cherokee mode. This was something I had learned early on about him.

I expected the dogs to knock us down trying to get off the bus, but instead, they quietly followed Helene into the house. Neither one let out a single bark. Neither one tried to run off into the woods. That was a strange, rare occurrence. It was as if they were sad, too.

Spice Cat was… well… Spice Cat. His main concern was his next meal and finding a spot to lounge.

We took the children in the house, got them settled, and then went back to the bus to finish the daunting task of unloading our belongings. When I'd carried in the last bag of gifts and set it on the kitchen table, the bag fell over, spilling out the silk scarf I had chosen for Sarah. I picked it up, looked at Billy, and then started crying.

Normally, he would be right by my side the minute the tears came, but not this time. This time, he was in his own world.

I didn't say anything when he picked up his cell phone and walked outside. He would talk to me about his mother when he was ready.

Helene had disappeared.

Like a robot, I put the dirty clothes in the laundry room, the clean ones where they belonged, and then restocked the cabinets with the left-over canned goods and food from the bus. I grabbed up the bags of gifts and took them to the hall closet, crying the whole time.

Unlike Billy, I had to get it out. I finished my tasks and then went to the kitchen to make a pot of coffee. Coffee always seemed to help, no matter what the problem was.

My cell phone buzzed and then played a tune I had recently set for my mother—a nifty little number from James Garner's TV series, *Rockford Files*. Now that Mom was deep into the snooping business, I found it only fitting.

"Hello, Mom," I said in a low, sad tone. "I've been crying, so don't mind me."

"I understand," Mom replied, sympathetically. "We're all praying for Sarah. Did the doctor say what they've found out? The last I heard, Chief Sam said she'd been acting strange and then she just flipped out… went off the reservation."

"Billy said she's in another world, Mom."

"Oh, my word. I didn't know. I saw her early this morning and she seemed okay. I mean, she was a little out of it, but she could carry on a conversation… somewhat. Now that I think about it..."

"What do you mean, somewhat?"

"She acted like…"

"Like what, Mom?"

"Well… she said some weird stuff. She talked about her kids as if they were still little. She was angry at Chief Sam because he wouldn't let the boys play in the snow. Then, she looked at me and asked me if I wanted to go to the mall. I just figured it was the drugs they were giving her. What else could it be?"

"Maybe she had a stroke."

"No, she didn't. I asked the doctor."

"I can't explain it, Mom. Sarah has always been as sharp as a tack. Smart as a whip... as they say."

"I know. That's what surprises me. She didn't seem herself, but I figured it would pass when she started getting better. At least she didn't have a stroke. That would've been terrible."

"I can't get Billy to talk about his mother. At first, when I asked how she was, all he said was that she was not well. He has really shut himself out from the rest of us... emotionally."

"Give him a little time, honey. He's probably in shock after seeing his mother acting crazy. He's use to her being the sane one in the family. He always said she was the one who held everything and everyone together. Now she's falling apart and he can't handle it. Men handle these things differently than we do. You know that."

"The last few hours have been bad. Billy's gone silent. You know what that means. When he stops talking, I get freaked out."

"He's not getting ready to kill someone, is he?"

I laughed at Mom's silliness.

"Not today, Mom, but the day isn't over."

"Sarah will get better and then he'll come out of it. He'll pull himself together and be back to his old self in no time."

"I made a fresh pot of coffee. Yum... yum. Want some?"

"If that's an invite, we'll be right over. Is that all right?"

"Yes, please do come over. I need someone to talk to. Billy's outside on his cell phone, the kids are napping, Helene's wandered off, and even the dogs are nowhere to be seen, not to mention Spice Cat. I have no idea where he is. That's okay though. I'm sure we'll see his pretty little face when you least expect it. He has a way of sneaking up on you."

"Maybe we can talk about the case," Mom added. "It might give you a chance to think about something different other than worrying about Sarah. I've… we've come up with some interesting stuff that I know you're going to want to hear about."

"I doubt if I'll be able to concentrate. I just can't get my mind off poor Sarah." I took a deep breath. "It's so sad, Mom."

"I know, honey."

"Billy didn't want us to go see her until he'd had a chance to figure out what was going on. I think he just needed some time with her alone, so I didn't argue. This is just so weird. Sarah has got to get better."

"Chief Sam said she'd been acting a little strange, but it got worse right after the big wedding shindig. I hope it wasn't too much for her. I mean—three couples getting married at the same time at her house was a lot for her to take on. I'd hate to think it was our fault. I'd never forgive myself if we were the ones who brought all this on. Maybe it put too much strain on her."

"No way, Mom. Sarah loves throwing big parties and she's good at it. It wasn't that, I'm certain."

"I sure hope not."

Mom and Eddie arrived an hour later. By then, the kids were up, Helene was fixing dinner, and Billy was still outside.

After a quick shower, I was sitting at the kitchen table, drinking coffee. Helene had added a shot of bourbon to my cup.

"I just talked with Billy," Mom said, walking over to the table. She gave me a hug and then moved on to the kids, giving each a hug and a kiss. Eddie did the same.

"He's holding up well," she said, and then smiled. "I figured he'd be a head case by now. Says he's going to see the chief in a little bit. I guess he's psyching himself out, so he can see his father without falling apart. Most men can't stand to show a little emotion sometimes. They think it makes them look like a sissy."

My mother's a fine, semi-old-fashioned (but getting more in-tune with each passing day, thanks to Billy and me) Southern lady who doesn't smoke, drink or curse, and she has God on her side. And... she's not judgmental. They don't come much better than that. I would say we were a bad influence on her, but that would be a lie. She likes the work we do and loves getting involved in our cases.

"Has there been any further word on Sarah's condition?" Eddie asked. "She seemed fine the last time we saw her, well, more like her old self."

"Can I get y'all some coffee?" Helene asked from the kitchen. "I'm making spaghetti for dinner in case anyone's hungry. Care to stay?"

Eddie walked over and showed Helene a covered dish.

"Minnie made a casserole. I think its tuna fish."

He opened the refrigerator door and placed the dish inside.

"Maybe you can have it tomorrow night."

The front door opened and Billy walked in.

Billy's six-three, a muscular one-eighty-five, and has long, shiny coal black hair (with a few gray strands), and he's very good looking… but today wasn't one of his best. He looked ragged, and it hurt me so to see him like that.

I wanted to rush to his side, wrap my arms around him and tell him not to worry, but I knew it wouldn't do any good. He was going to struggle until his mother got better.

Some people are intimidated by Billy. Just the fact that he's an Indian sometimes scares the crap out of them. They act as if they expect him to pull out a hatchet any minute and whack off their heads. They just don't know him like I do. He wouldn't use a hatchet when he has a perfectly good gun to do the job. Men fear him, and women adore him. Luckily, I'm the one who snagged him. I still don't know why he picked me when he could have any woman he wanted.

Me… I'm a head shorter; one-thirty five on a good day, and my brown, shoulder length hair has a mind of its own. I might not have the size, but I can hold my own in a gunfight. Maybe that's what Billy found so attractive about me.

We do have a slight age difference. He's thirteen years older than I am. He's older and wiser. We make a good couple.

"I'm going to take a shower and then I'm going to see my father."

He looked around the room and then leaned over and kissed my forehead.

"I see you've already taken a shower. You look good."

He turned and walked out.

"Contractions," I said softly. "He's back to using contractions. I knew he'd get it together. He's one tough dude."

Mom and Helene smiled.

Eddie looked confused.

"If Billy talks stiff English, he's not in a good way or he's really unhappy about something," Mom explained to Eddie. "Yeah, when he gets like that, it kinda reminds me of those Indians in an old cowboy western."

"Helene, coffee for everyone!" I said, plastering a smile across my face and trying to relax.

Mom sat down next to me and whispered, "I need to tell you something about Sarah."

"No need to whisper, Minnie," Helene said, sitting a cup of coffee down in front of her. "There aren't any secrets in this family."

"What about Sarah?" I asked. "Does it have something to do with the case?"

"Sort of," Mom replied. "I think it might."

"This case—we're talking about a body shop, right? What could she possibly have to do with a body shop? Did she have a fender bender or something? Hey… maybe she hit her head. Maybe that's why she's been acting so strange. That could've been her problem all along."

"You're getting off-track, Jesse."

"We are talking about a car body shop, right?"

"Not exactly. This shop isn't for cars."

I looked at Mom, and then at Eddie.

"Okay, then what other kind of body shop are we talking about? I'm slightly confused."

"It's called The Body Shop, and it's a shop for the body. Like a body makeover place—a spa for the soul. It's a high class club where rich women go to get their bodies and heads straight."

"Oh... that kind of place. Hmm..."

"You almost have to be rich just to be able to pay their fee. I'm telling you, Jesse, you gotta see this joint. I didn't even know places like this existed until now."

"I can imagine. There's something out there for everyone. Whatever you want, you can find. Besides, spas have been around forever. What's different about this one, other than the name? Which is, by the way, rather catchy, wouldn't you say?"

"You'd be surprised at how many women join these spas. I'm glad they can afford it, but I sure can't... or maybe it's just that I wouldn't spend that kind of money on something so frivolous, when I could go home and soak in my own hot bath. I can rub lotion on my own body. I don't need to pay someone to do it."

"Oh, Lord. Now you're getting off-track, Mom. Tell me about this place and what Sarah has to do with it... in two words or less."

"Sarah joined a couple of months ago and talked me into joining when Eddie and I got home from our honeymoon, which was spectacular, by the way. Anyway, I wanted to get information about the club and what better way to do it than to join? Besides, I can always use a little pampering, and believe me, this is the right place to get pampered."

"But I thought you just said you wouldn't go to a spa."

"This is different. It's a job, not playtime. Anyway, here's the deal.

The fee is five thousand dollars a year! Can you believe it? But on the plus side, you get a five-day free trial before you have to pay. They're very selective. Savannah said they run background checks on everyone. She's a member, too."

"Moving right along," I said, motioning for Mom to get to the point.

"On my second visit I had a session with a nutritionist and was given a goodie bag to take home. I guess by then they know they have you hooked. Anyway, I was in Sarah's bedroom getting her ID out of her purse for Chief Sam when I noticed her goodie bag sitting empty on the dresser. So, nosy me, I went to her bathroom and picked up the bottle of shampoo. Mine smelled so good, I wanted to check hers out. I opened the bottle, took a whiff, and almost gagged. It smelled rancid. Now, that didn't seem normal. Maybe it had poison in it."

"What?"

"I'm serious."

"Maybe it had gotten old, Mom."

Billy walked back into the kitchen and went over to the coffee pot. He looked refreshed.

"We'll talk about this later," I whispered. "I'm sure Sarah's illness has nothing to do with a bottle of shampoo, Mom."

"But what if there's a connection?" Mom whispered back. "It could happen, you know. She washes her hair and the poison seeps in through her scalp. It sounds farfetched, but I've heard of stranger ways to poison someone. I mean, we all know that poison can be absorbed through the skin, so why not put poison in shampoo? Who would ever suspect poison to be in a bottle of shampoo?"

"You have a good imagination, Mom."

"What if I'm right, Jesse? This could get bad. Imagine what the Blackhawk men would do if they found out that their mother had been poisoned by a bottle of shampoo and almost died. They'd be on the war path. Heads would roll... or maybe scalps. To me, if it is true, it wouldn't matter whether it was heads or scalps."

I looked at Mom from the corner of my eye, brushing aside the idea of poison shampoo, and said, “I’m not so sure about your shampoo theory, but yeah, if you’re right, that would be bad. Right now, I’m thinking that bad is when you take a long vacation and come home to find your mother in the hospital, headed for the loony bin. Now, that’s really bad.” I paused for a second, and then added, “And if the two happen to be connected, bad would take on a whole new meaning.”

I had no idea at the time how close Mom was to the truth, but we all were about to find out.

Trouble was headed our way. Bad trouble.

Chapter 2

A day later, Sarah had fully recovered and was released from the hospital. Doctor Bryant discovered the cause of her illness had come from a mix-up in her blood pressure medication. After examining the bottle, he found her prescribed Atenolol pills mixed in with another type of pill—Panatral. Tox reports confirmed it.

Panatral can cause a whole host of problems when taken in large doses, and it seems that Sarah had been taking the highest dosage available. By the time the tests came back, she was on the brink of insanity. Once the medication was stopped, Sarah recovered quickly.

How the mix-up happened was anybody's guess. The pharmacist said he never filled a prescription for Panatral and had no idea how they got in her bottle. Sarah, of course, never suspected she was taking anything other than her Atenolol.

Billy and I would find out how this happened to her, but for right now, we were just glad to have her back home and feeling like her old self again.

In fact, she was feeling so good, she wanted to throw a party to celebrate her recovery. She wanted everyone to know that she was fine and she wasn't crazy. So, the next night the family gathered at her house for dinner.

The party came to a halt when Beth announced that she was in labor and the baby was coming right then. There was no time to make it to the hospital.

Billy's sister Beth and her husband Adam had suffered through two miscarriages, but this time they were going to get to experience childbirth—the good old-fashioned way.

Chief Sam delivered their twins—a boy and a girl—on the pool table in the den less than twenty minutes after Beth's announcement.

Holding both babies in his arms, Chief Sam showed them to us with pride. "Meet Sammy and Sarah Jane." A tear slid down his cheek, the first I'd even seen. So, of course, me being me, I cried.

The paramedics were called to take mother and babies to the hospital and then the party resumed. After all that excitement, the booze really flowed. Billy was well on his way to getting intoxicated.

This was the second time today I'd seen something I'd never seen before—Chief Sam's tear and Billy getting drunk. Billy never got drunk, at least not that I could ever tell, and I'm his wife, so when Mom pulled me aside to talk, I kept one eye on him.

"Her name is Dakota Stone," Mom whispered.

"Who are you talking about?"

"The woman who runs The Body Shop. Actually, she owns it."

"Are we back on that again? Can we pick up on this later? I just can't go there right now."

I looked up and caught Billy swaying. It was time to take him home, while I still could. If he went down, I'd never be able to get him in or out of the car without help.

"Excuse me, Mom. I have to take my husband home."

"He has had a bit to drink, hasn't he? Wow! He's really got a buzz going on. Look at him. He looks a bit unsteady. You better get him home before he passes out. I've never seen him like this before."

"Me, either. Having his mother almost die took a big toll on him." I kissed Mom on the cheek, and then went to fetch my husband.

Surprisingly, he turned out to be more agreeable about leaving than I had expected. I guess my lie about having a headache worked. I said the first thing that came to mind. I didn't know what else to do. Billy crawled into the 4Runner and laid his head back. He was almost asleep by the time we got to the end of the driveway. Four minutes later, he was undressed and crawling into bed. Good thing we lived so close to family, otherwise he would've been sleeping in the car.

"He really tied one on, didn't he?" Helene stated more than asked as we stood by the bed. "Billy never drinks to excess. He's going to regret it in the morning."

"No doubt. At least he behaved. He didn't do anything embarrassing. If that had been me, there's no telling what I would've said or done. I can embarrass the best of them."

"Yeah," Helene said, snickering. "I've seen you in rare form."

"Not funny. How's the kids?"

"Asleep."

"Thanks for bringing them home. I hate that you had to leave."

"Hey, that's what I do. I take care of the kids and sometimes you and Billy." She grinned. "Your mother called. I told her you'd call her back."

"Lord, help me," I groaned. "I'm not in the mood to talk about work. I know that's what she wants. Her and her poison shampoo theory."

"It might be important. Minnie and Eddie are pretty good at this snooping business. She told me what they've uncovered so far. She thinks that body shop is just a cover."

"A cover for what?"

"Murder!" she said with gusto. "Go stretch out in the den, and I'll bring you a glass of iced tea. Call your mother."

"Put some bourbon in that iced tea. I'm going to need it."

Our house is pretty big now. A lot bigger than it was when I first moved in. Back then, it had a couple of bedrooms upstairs with a bathroom and a master bedroom downstairs with a bathroom. The living room, kitchen, and dining room were all one room. There was a laundry room off the back of the kitchen. Now, well, let's just say, if we add another room, we'll probably have to get a hotel license. Families grow, and we needed more space.

My favorite room is the den at the back of the house. That's the place we all gather at the end of the day. The sixty-some inch widescreen TV is a real plus. I love to watch television. It relaxes me, and I really needed to relax now. I picked up the remote, turned on the TV, and then called my mother on my cell. I stretched out in a lounger and waited. I was happy when my drink arrived.

"Hello," Mom said after the first ring. "I'm so glad you called. How's Billy doing?"

"He's asleep."

She started talking and didn't let up. I just sat and listened half-heartedly, until she said something that really got my attention.

"Mae Bridges' husband was a rich investment banker until six months ago when he was shot down on Main Street in Charlottesville. The police have no leads, no eyewitnesses, so the case has pretty much gone cold."

"Call Mae and tell her to meet us at the office in the morning at eight. I want to talk to her."

"Let me call her right now and make sure that's a good time for her. I'll call you right back."

Mom hung up on me without another word. Five minutes later, she called back.

"We're on. Mae said she'd be there promptly at eight, so I'll see you in the morning."

I tossed the cell phone on the coffee table and took a long drink of my tea, but one gulp was about all I could handle. It was awfully strong and my stomach dared me to put more of that stuff in it. I got up, walked to the kitchen, and dumped the rest of the tea down the drain.

"I'm going to bed," I told Helene. "If you're up early, will you make sure to wake me? I have to meet my mother in the office at eight."

"What about Billy?"

"If he's not awake, let him sleep in. He needs to sleep it off. He really tied one on last night, so he'll probably be a real bear when he wakes up."

"Billy a bear? Never."

I went to check on the kids, gave them both a kiss, and then tiptoed into our bedroom in the dark so I wouldn't wake Billy. Once I stripped out of my clothes, I started feeling amorous. I longed for him to take me in his arms and make passionate love to me for hours. On the other hand, he would probably smell like a brewery.

I thought about it for a split second and decided I didn't care how he smelled. I wanted him. But he was in a deep sleep and didn't budge when I slipped under the covers… naked and hot, forgetting about everything else. So what if he didn't brush his teeth before he collapsed in bed? I could handle it. I scooted up close and slowly caressed his body, hoping he would respond to my touch. Weeks with your family in a Winnebago doesn't allow for much lovemaking, so I was ready for a wild, head-banging night of hard core sex with the man I loved… but that wasn't going to happen. Sleep was all I was going to get.

Monday morning I awoke to the sound of thunder. I looked over at Billy, who was still sound asleep, and checked to make sure he was breathing. I wanted to take a shower, but when I saw a flash of lightning, I gave up on that idea.

"What a way to start the day," I said to Helene as I walked into the kitchen. "Coffee. I need coffee."

I went to the counter and poured a cup while Athena shadowed me.

"What is it, girl?" I asked as I bent down to pat her head.

"You know she's scared to death of thunder and lightning. I think we should get her some tranquilizers. I'm sure Adam would give us some. Want me to call his office?"

"No, he's got his hands full now, but maybe you could get in touch with him later. He's a vet. He'll advise us on what to do."

"Drugs… that's the answer. I've talked to him before about Athena and her fear of storms. He offered to give us something then, but I said I'd have to talk to you first. Then, I forgot. Why don't you stop by his office after your meeting? I'm sure they will give you something. We don't want Athena to have a nervous breakdown."

I looked down and saw Athena shaking. I rubbed her soft coat and said, "Do I need to take you to a psychiatrist to help you work through your storm fears and riding in cars? We live in a modern world with modern medicine. Maybe all you need is a good doggy tranquilizer."

She started barking, twitching, and jumping around. I had to grab her and hold her to quiet her down.

"Shh," I said. "You're going to wake Billy."

"Too late for that," Billy said, walking over to the coffee pot looking sexy as ever. "My head feels like it's going to explode, and this thunder isn't helping. Geez, I think I'm seeing stars."

"That's what happens when you drink too much," Helene said. "You'll probably feel like crap all day, but the good news is, you'll be like new by tomorrow."

"Tomorrow's a long way off. I'll never make it."

Helene laughed.

"Yes, you will. All you have to do is get through today."

I walked over and kissed him… and he didn't smell like a brewery. Maybe I should've tried harder last night. I ran my hand around his back and then slowly down his butt. He looked at me and managed a smile, but that was about all.

"I feel rough," he said, kissing me on the cheek. He walked over to the table and sat down. "Remind me to never drink again. Aren't the kids up yet?"

Helene handed him a cup of coffee. "Not yet. It's only five-thirty. Give them time and they'll be up and ready to get into something."

Suddenly, a flash of lightning lit up the whole room, followed by a loud clap of thunder erupting overhead.

Athena took off running down the hall to safety… wherever that was this time around.

"That was close," Helene said, looking at me. "Maybe you should cancel your meeting."

"What meeting?" Billy asked, glancing at me. "What you got up your sleeve, `ge ya, and why didn't you tell me?"

"You've been out of it, that's why I haven't said anything. Why don't you go back to bed and sleep off your hangover. I got this one."

He pushed aside his cup of coffee and said, "Maybe I should. My head's killing me and my stomach doesn't feel much better. I feel like I'm going to puke."

"Here," Helene said, offering him a glass of tomato juice and two aspirins.

"Wash the aspirin down with the tomato juice. Great antidote for a hangover."

Billy tossed back the aspirin, downed the juice, and then stood up.

"Wake me when it's time for dinner." He looked at me. "Whatever you got going on, stay out of trouble. I don't feel like bailing you out of jail, and if Sheriff Hudson…"

"Don't worry about me. I'll keep it clean. I promise."

"God. I feel like I'm going to die," Billy said and then stopped. He dropped his head.

I rushed to him and engulfed him in my arms.

"It's okay, Billy. You're entitled to feel sad. I think you've held up pretty good considering. All of you have, especially Chief Sam. Your mother almost died, but she didn't, and she's going to be fine. We need to be happy about that."

Helene walked over and gave Billy a hug.

"You'll feel better as soon as you find out how Sarah got a hold of the wrong pills. I know that's what's bothering you."

"Someone at the drug store made a mistake," I added. "I know they said it wasn't their fault, but I'm sure it's probably happened before.

People make mistakes. There's nothing we can do about it, except try to make sure it doesn't happen again."

Billy forced a smile.

"Yeah, you're both right. I'll get to the bottom of this if it's the last thing I do." He hesitated for a second, and then said, "Sorry, but I gotta go lie down."

He turned and headed straight to the bathroom down the hall.

"That's not the…"

"Let him go, Jesse. He said he felt like he had to puke. That's what the bathroom's for. You sure don't want him getting sick in the bed. That would be gross. Yuck."

"Yes, it would."

"You remember what that's like, don't you?"

"Boy, do I ever."

Visions of my head hanging in the toilet flashed through my mind.

"But I never threw up in bed. That's a nasty thought. Thanks for putting that picture in my head, Helene."

"You might want to get an early start," she suggested. "Who knows what it's like out there? This storm came up in the middle of the night and it's still going strong. The roads are probably flooded in some places. I'll be surprised if your mother can even get out. South River Road floods at the drop of a hat. You might want to give her a call."

Just then, I heard my cell phone playing Mom's tune.

"Where's my phone?"

I followed the sound to the den where I had left it last night. I picked it up and said, "Hello, Mom."

"My power's out, Jesse, so I had to call you on my cell and the battery's about dead. Eddie said that South River Road is flooded. I can't make it out."

"Stay put, Mom. I'll handle it. I'll call you later."

I ended the call and then went to the bedroom to get dressed. I grabbed an umbrella at the door on my way out, which Helene quickly snatched from me, asking if I wanted to be a human lightning rod.

She handed me a baseball cap and said, "It won't keep you as dry, but at least I won't have to worry about you getting struck by lightning. Now go and be careful. It's going to be a nightmare out there."

The roads were flooded in some of the low lying areas, but not so bad that I couldn't navigate them in my 4Runner. I loved my Toyota SUV. It could go almost anywhere, and to prove it, I've taken it through some pretty treacherous places. During one of my more adventurous moments, I drove it across South River in a low spot just to see if it would make it. It did, but I won't ever do that again unless I absolutely have to.

I took the back way to the office, avoiding the traffic on Rt. 29, and made it there in no time flat. I was praising myself when I pulled into the parking lot of Blackhawk & Blackhawk Investigations, until I hit a slick spot. It was all I could do to keep from plowing through the double glass doors of the building. The 4Runner seemed to have a mind of its own, but fortunately, it stopped in time to keep me from turning into windshield pizza. My hands were shaking when I walked into the office.

"Need a cup of coffee?" Lila Grayce asked as she took my purse and then helped me with my jacket. "I just made a fresh pot."

Lila Grayce is our office manager… and lifesaver.

"No thanks," I replied, shaking the rain off me. "It's pouring out there."

"And it's supposed to be like this all day."

I looked around the office, and started to ask about our client when the door alarm chimes went off. The front door opened and in walked a short, heavyset, black woman with big hair. She was wet all over.

"You must be Mae Bridges," I said, extending my hand. "I'm Jesse Watson Blackhawk. It's good to finally meet you."

I looked back at Lila, but before I could say anything, she came over and helped Mae out of her wet things, asking about her interest in a cup of coffee.

Mae shook my hand, and then said to Lila, "A cup of coffee would be nice. Thank you." Then, she turned to me and said, "I bet I can read your mind."

"I hope not. I keep some pretty bad stuff hidden there. You wouldn't want to visit that place."

She laughed out loud and said, "I like you already. Your mom said I would, and she was right. She also said that I could trust you."

"You can. Tell me your darkest secrets and I'll take them to my grave… unless I'm tortured. If that happens, you're on your own."

"Have you ever been tortured?"

"Physically… no, mentally… all the time. In my line of work, crawling out of bed in the morning can be torture. Traffic can be torture, especially on a day like this."

"Murder can be torture," she said. "Especially on the ones left behind."

"Why don't we sit down," I said, pointing to an overstuffed sofa.

She looked around the room as if she was checking it out to make sure no one else was there.

"Oh, don't worry," I assured her. "We'll have our privacy. There's no one here but the three of us."

We both sat down and waited until Lila had placed the coffee on the table in front of us. When she walked away, I said to Mae, "So… tell me about your problem."

"Let me just say how glad I am that Sarah is going to be okay. I was really worried about her for a while."

"You know Billy's mother?"

"I know all the Blackhawks. They do their banking with us, or they did with my husband before he was murdered. Now, someone else handles their accounts."

"Tell me about your husband."

Mae told me all about her husband and how much she loved him. They had a great life together until Dakota Stone killed him.

"If she didn't kill him, she had someone do it just as sure as I'm sitting here drinking coffee with you."

"Explain."

"Look at me," she started. "I'm short and fat, my hair is a disaster, my complexion sucks, and I'm black. Black people don't usually get into snazzy joints like The Body Shop. But… I have a lot of money, and money will open a lot of doors. They say money can't buy happiness. Well that might be so, but it sure can buy a lot of other things... like becoming a member of a fancy place like The Body Shop. They sure didn't mind taking my money."

"I hate to admit it, but you're right about that. Money is power."

"Dakota Stone welcomed me with opened arms and acted like we'd been best friends forever. I don't trust people like that. Something didn't seem right about her, but I dismissed the feeling, thinking maybe I was just being too judgmental. Then one day something happened, and that's when I realized there was a devious side to Dakota Stone and everyone working at The Body Shop."

"And that would be what?"

"Don't get me wrong. The Body Shop is a fancy joint. The place is gorgeous. They have a fabulous spa and gym, a masseuse, a nutritionist, and even a psychologist on staff. I was impressed with how nice the place was. They really know how to pamper a woman."

"My mother said the same thing."

"I felt revived after my first visit. And then, on my third visit, I had a session with Olivia Swales, the psychologist. Everyone talks to the psychologist by their third visit. It's part of the program. They not only want to fix your body, but they also want to fix your mind... so they claim. Well, they are pretty good at the body aspect, but the part about your mind, that's another story. I didn't like her sticking her nose in my private life."

"Isn't that what they're supposed to do? How can they help you if you don't let them get to know you?"

"That's just it. I didn't need help. I was happy with myself and my life. After only a few sessions with her, I felt worse about everything... and I couldn't shake that eerie feeling that I had. I knew something wasn't right. It was like she wanted me to have problems with my husband or kids, or anyone for that matter."

"What was the event you mentioned?"

"I remember the day as vividly as if it were yesterday. I had just had a massage when Dakota approached me and asked me why I hadn't had a session with Olivia lately. I told her that I didn't need one. I was fine. She said I didn't look fine. She said I looked sad, and she was worried about me. She wanted me to see Olivia right away, so I did, just to get her off my back. Olivia wanted to know how it was going in my marriage. Did my husband treat me badly? She said I had all the signs—withdrawn, unhappy, scared, and a bunch of other malarkey."

"How did you react to her insinuations?"

"At first, I was shocked, and then I got angry. My husband was the kindest person you'd ever meet. Nathaniel wouldn't hurt a fly. So, I decided to fix her wagon. I lied. I told her that my husband had a bad temper and was so mean to me that I'd have him killed if I could. I was flabbergasted when Olivia said there were ways to get rid of a bad husband and then asked me if I wanted to know more."

"Maybe she meant..."

"I know what she meant, and so do you. But I kept my cool and said yes just to see what she'd say. She told me she knew someone who could dispose of my husband—for a price—and the incident would never lead back to me."

"What did you say to that?"

"I told her that I'd think about it. I wasn't ever going back there, so what did it matter? A week later, my husband was dead. I'm not proud of what I did. I want you to know that upfront. My lies probably got my husband killed. I'm so sorry for what I did. I just hate myself."

"I know you're not a bad person, Mae. I can see that. Be honest with me. Did you give her money to kill your husband?"

"No way!" Mae said, shocked at my question. "I didn't want my husband dead, so why would I pay someone to kill him? You have to believe me! I want Nathaniel back, but that's not going to happen. They killed him, and now he's gone forever! They have to pay."

"You're not responsible for your husband's death, so don't blame yourself because of a few lies you told to a crazy woman. It was foolish of you, but I understand why you did it. Sometimes you'll say anything just to get them to shut up."

I tried to make her feel better by letting her know I understood her behavior. I changed the subject.

"What did you tell the police? I know they questioned you. The spouse is always the first suspect."

"I had an alibi. I was at my sister's house in Cleveland. But… there is that matter of the tips. That would look bad for me if the cops ever found out. That's why I told them I had no idea who would want my husband dead when they asked."

"What tips?"

"Two weeks after Nathaniel's death, I got a call from Dakota. She said I hadn't tipped any of her employees, and tips were expected. Mine totaled twenty thousand dollars, and it would be wise to settle my account in cash, or my membership would be canceled. What she really meant was that she would cancel me—as in killing me off. She had my husband killed and she wanted her payment. They're all criminals."

"And you paid her."

"What else could I do? I was scared not to pay. She had already killed my husband. What next, my daughter, Marsha? I took the cash from the safe, paid her, and never went back again. I haven't heard a word from her since, but I haven't forgotten what she did. I might not be able to go to the police, but there're other ways to settle a debt. She owes me her life for taking my husband's. I want all of them tortured and then killed, but I'll settle for killed. That's right. I want them dead. Dakota

Stone and Olivia Swales. Both of them. Dead as a corpse. Name your price. Everyone has a price."

"Sorry, Mae. Can't help you there."

I told Mae that if she tried to hire a hit man, she'd be the one who would wind up in prison, and most likely, Dakota and Olivia would never be brought to justice for their crimes. I hoped she took me seriously, but Mae Bridges was a woman with revenge in mind.

This was not going to bode well for anyone.

Chapter 3

I assured Mae that she had come to the right place for help in bringing the two women to justice, and promised to call her with updates. We had a lot of digging to do.

Before she left, I made her swear to give up her quest for a hit man. She agreed to my demand.

Lila and I stood at the front door, looking through the glass as we watched Mae battle her way through the pouring rain to her car.

The wind was whipping up, blowing leaves and debris through the air. Scary lightning flashed overhead and thunder boomed repeatedly.

"This is a dangerous storm," I said. "Hurry up, Mae! Get in the car."

"Jesse, you worry too much," Lila said as she patted me on the back. "She'll be fine. She's almost there. See, she's got her hand on the car door…"

Once again, lightning flashed and thunder exploded in the air like a bomb, rattling the windows.

Seconds later, another bolt of lightning shot down from the sky and hit Mae's car. It all happened so fast, we froze.

Mae shook for a few seconds, and then dropped to the ground, her hand still stuck to the door handle.

"Oh, my God!" I screamed. "Call 9-1-1, Lila."

I grabbed for the doorknob, ready to run to Mae's aid, but Lila put a stop to that.

"It's too late for her, Jesse. Stay put. I'll call 9-1-1."

"But she needs our help!"

"You want to end up like her?"

"No, but…"

"Then do what I say. Don't go out there. I'll call for help."

Lila made the call while I stood at the door and stared at Mae's motionless body crumpled up on the cold, wet pavement.

Thunder and lightning continued as if nothing had happened. I watched in horror as Mother Nature continued her rampage.

Mae never moved.

There was no doubt in my mind that she was dead.

I thought about how awful it was to die like that, but death doesn't give you a warning.

"The ambulance is on the way," Lila said, joining me at the door. "They should be here real soon. Our emergency services are the best."

In a matter of a couple of minutes, an ambulance showed up, followed by another, three police cars, and then a fire truck. Red lights and sirens filled the parking lot.

It was a welcomed sight, although a little too late. Mae Bridges was dead. I knew it the second the bolt of lightning hit the car. Her hand was stuck like glue on the door handle. She couldn't pull away to safety.

My stomach felt like hamburger in a grinder. I didn't know whether I was going to throw up or suffer a severe case of diarrhea, but something was going on down there.

Lila handed me a glass of water and a little pink pill.

"What's this?"

"Xanax. Take it."

"Did you take one?"

"No. I took two."

With the storm raging outside, there was no way either one of us were going anywhere for a while.

I tossed the pill back and chased it down with the water. I was unaware at the time that Xanax could make you feel so good. Before long, I was floating on a cloud.

"Why haven't the cops questioned us yet about what we saw?" I asked, feeling a little fuzzy. My eyes seemed to have a hard time focusing. "God, Lila, what's in that pill? I'm really stoned. I feel like I just smoked a joint of some really good weed."

"What do you know about weed, Jesse?"

I rolled my eyes and said, "Oh, Lila. Don't tell me you've never smoked pot before."

"Once, and that was enough for me."

We looked back at the scene unfolding in front of us.

"Back to my question. Why haven't the cops paid us a visit? You know they see us watching them."

"Why would they? Once they assess the scene, they'll know what happened." She looked me up and down. "You might want to go into Billy's office and take a nap. You're beginning to act a little loopy."

"I'm fine. Am I slurring my words? Wow! I want more of these pills! They work great for stress."

"That's how it starts, and then you get hooked."

"You're not hooked, are you, Lila? I don't want to have to worry about you. Look what happened to Mae when I worried about her. She died."

"I think you have a buzz. You need to lie down."

She didn't usher me to Billy's office, but instead, walked me over to the couch in the waiting room, and then insisted that I lay down.

I dozed off as soon as I sprawled out on the comfortable sofa. According to the wall clock, two hours had passed by the time I woke up.

"What happened? I feel weird."

"You crashed."

"Crashed into what?"

"You don't remember?"

I sat there for a moment, waiting for the fog in my head to lift. The sight of Mae being struck by lightning came back to me all too real.

"Oh, how awful! I remember everything now. Poor Mae is dead."

"Actually, she isn't dead."

"She's not? Oh, thank goodness!"

"Don't be so happy just yet. It might've been better for her if she had died."

"How can you say that?"

"I ran out before the cops left and asked about her condition. They said she was barely alive, but at least she was alive. Detective Downey said the outlook wasn't good. Most folks don't survive a lightning strike and the ones who do, suffer severe after affects."

"Like what?"

"Burns, memory loss, heart and liver problems. You name it. The list is long."

"I need to get to the hospital."

I got up on wobbly legs and walked over to the front door.

"Look. The storm's just about over. I can go outside now." I looked back at Lila. "Call Adam's office for me. I need to get some drugs for Athena. She freaks out during a storm, so Helene suggested I get her some tranks. Hey, I wonder if I can give her a Xanax."

"I'm not sure. I know there are some people pills you can give animals, but I don't think Xanax is one of them. I could be wrong. I'll call Adam for you. He'll give you something safe for her to take."

Lila walked off, made the call, and then returned carrying a can of soda.

"Here. Drink this. You'll feel much better if you do."

"Why?"

"You need to re-hydrate. Tranquilizers take it out of you. You need to drink a lot of liquids. And don't drink any alcohol today. It intensifies the effect of the drug—in a bad way."

I took the can of soda, popped the tab, and took a long drink as I walked back to the sofa to sit down.

"Hmm. Good. I didn't realize how thirsty I was."

"Adam wasn't at the office, but the woman I talked with said she'd pull Athena's chart and have something ready for you when you got there. Helene and your mother both called. Helene was worried, and your mother wanted you to know that they still couldn't get out. The bridge is flooded over. Oh, and Billy's still in bed. I guess the stress really wore him out."

"He needs to recover from getting drunk yesterday."

Lila raised her eyebrows.

"That's unusual for him. I've never known Billy to drink much. In fact, I've rarely seen him drink at all."

"Well, he did yesterday. He had so much to drink, I thought he was going to fall down and pass out. Luckily, he didn't. We made it home, and he went straight to bed."

"I can see why he got drunk. He's still upset about his mother."

There was a lull in the conversation.

"I better get on home. I wanna take a shower before I go see Mae at the hospital."

"I'll be glad to drive you anywhere you want to go. That pill hasn't worn off yet, and the label says not to drive when taking them. You don't want me to have to worry about you, do you? The same thing that happened to Mae might happen to you... if I start worrying."

We both laughed, but not at Mae.

"I think I can manage. I feel fine."

When I stood up, I began to feel woozy again. I sat back down on the sofa and said, "Maybe you should drive me home."

"I'll get my purse."

We left the office, stopped at the vet, and then headed home.

The roads were littered with trash and debris from the storm. Even though the storm had passed, accidents were still being worked. But all in all, it wasn't as bad as it could've been… well… except for Mae.

Mae Bridges—I hated having to tell Mom about what happened to her. She'd be devastated. She believed Mae's accusations and wanted justice. My old mom Minnie would never be in the middle of something like this, but my new mom Minnie is a real go-getter. She has a knack when it comes to getting at the truth. Why did I ever think she might not be able to slink around in the shadows like a regular P.I.? She can, and she's good at it. So is Eddie. No one suspects two little old folks.

My fear was: If Mae's story was accurate, Dakota Stone and Olivia Swales could be a threat to anyone who nosed around in their business, or got in their way—the kind of threat that leaves one dead. The Body Shop. Just the name gave me visions of rusty cars, banged up fenders, and spray paint... not a spa for everything your body and brain wants, needs, and has to have.

I needed to learn more about Mae and Nathaniel Bridges, and their daughter Marsha. After that, I wanted to see The Body Shop for myself, inside and out.

Just a few miles from home, I asked Lila for her cell phone. The battery was just about dead in mine. She handed it over. I clicked on the image of a camera, the screen came up, and then I turned around backwards and took several shots of the SUV behind us… discreetly as I could. Immediately, I emailed the images to my computer at home and to Billy's cell phone.

"What was that all about, Jesse? You're freaking me out. Is someone following us?"

Lila was quickly coming unglued by my actions.

"Calm down, Lila. Act as if nothing's wrong."

I pulled my 9 MM from my purse and was on the ready. My paranoia was in high gear. Death does that to me.

"Just keep on driving and don't look back."

"Okay," she replied, fear in her voice.

Lila made a right turn onto Bear Mountain Road, but fortunately, the SUV didn't follow.

"Geez, Jesse," Lila said as she finally exhaled. "You scared the crap out of me. I thought we were under attack. I could see our bodies lying in the middle of the road with bullet holes in our heads, and blood pooling all around us."

"That image will be with me for a while. Thanks, Lila. Not that I don't have enough bad ones back there as it is. What's one more?"

My plan was to go home, check on everyone, and then call my mother, but I didn't get a chance to do the latter. Mom's canary yellow 4Runner was parked in the driveway. The flood waters on South River Road must've receded.

Lila pulled up next to Mom's car, looked at me and said, "I'll be right beside you when you tell Minnie about Mae."

We got out of the car, walked up on the porch, and then into the house, all in slow motion. I had a real heavy feeling in my heart.

Billy, Helene, Eddie, and Mom were sitting at the kitchen table going through files, the kids and the dogs were playing on the floor in the living room, and Spice Cat was napping happily on the kitchen counter. I let that one go. I was too stressed to worry about a cat on the counter, dropping hair and dander all over the place.

I was glad I took that pill, or I'd probably be having a full-blown panic attack right about now. The anticipation of having to tell Mom about Mae, and the cat on the counter thing, just about did me in.

I have this hang-up about animals and their bodies being anywhere near my food. Counters and table tops are off limits for our four-legged friends... and Spice Cat knows that. Guess he thought Helene was going to protect him from me.

Right this minute, he was the least of my worries.

They all jumped up and greeted us, sans cat. Billy gave me a quick kiss on the lips, and then stared into my eyes, warmly. He was telling me everything was okay. He was himself again. My heart melted and my anxiety fled. I kissed the kids, patted the dogs, and then shooed the cat off the counter.

Mom was holding up a sheet of paper. “You have to see this, Jesse,” she said. “I told you Mae was right. There’s something funny about that place and those wicked women who run it.”

I handed Helene the bag containing the bottle of pills.

“These are for Athena. Lock them up somewhere, and never give her more than one at a time.”

“Will do,” She replied. She looked at Lila. “Would you like some coffee?”

“No, thank you.” Lila looked over at me. “I should get back to the office.”

“Go ahead. I’ll get my car later. Thanks for the lift.”

No one asked about my car.

After Lila left, I began my account of the storm, my office visit, and Mae’s badly-timed departure, but Mom stopped me before I could finish.

“We already know the whole story,” she interrupted. “I called the hospital, and Mae isn’t dead. That’s what counts.”

“Whew,” I said, relieved. “I’m so glad to hear that. I knew you’d be upset about her. I even expected you to cry. I’m glad you didn’t.”

“I am upset about her being struck by lightning, but I can’t do anything about it. That’s in God’s hands now. I’m concentrating on righting a wrong. Snooping on people and fixing things. Getting justice for Mae and her husband is what I want. Dakota Stone and Olivia Swales are killers. All we have to do is get the evidence.”

“I’m sure we can do that,” I said, letting Mom know that she had our support. “If those women are guilty, we’ll find out.”

“The cops sure can’t seem to get anywhere on this case, and you know they must’ve questioned everyone who ever set eyes on Mae’s husband,” Mom continued. “Plus, the wife is always the first they go after. They accuse and harass them to no end. Oh, I’m sure they checked her inside and out. They know she was a member of The Body Shop. Perhaps they actually had the common sense to question the folks there. You know… check out the wife and all her associates… something like that. Hey, the first thing the cops probably did was check out her bank account to see if she'd recently withdrawn a large sum of money—hit man money."

Mom's head bobbed up and down and her eyebrows arched in the way they always do when she's sure she's gotten to the truth of the matter.

"Hmm… you'd think the cops could do better. I'm just glad people have us to rely on."

"She's got the bug," I said, looking at Billy. "She's a goner."

We smiled at each other… and it felt so good.

"What bug?" Mom asked, knowing the whole time what I'd meant.

"You know what she's talking about, Minnie," Helene joked. "You and Eddie are going to be another Jesse and Billy, just a little older. You've got the itch… the fever… and the nose for digging up the dirt. In other words, you're good at investigating. You know the right place to look and the right questions to ask. And you have something else going for you. You're both old. Folks trust old people."

"Geez, where have I heard that before?" Mom smiled.

Helene motioned to us.

"Everyone sit down and I'll fix some sandwiches."

"I am hungry," I said. "I missed breakfast and lunch."

"This'll be a late lunch," Helene said, grinning.

"By the way, I talked to Mae's daughter, Marsha," Mom jumped in. "She called me from the hospital. Nice girl. She sure loves her mama. Mae's pretty bad off."

"What did she say about Mae?"

"Mae's whole body is red like she has a real bad sunburn and in some places she has huge blisters. Unfortunately, if she survives, she might lose her hand. It's mangled because that's where the lightning entered her body. Her memory's gone, and her internal organs are messed up. The doctor says she's going to have a long recovery. Lightning strike victims don't usually live through it, but Mae's a fighter. She'll be okay. It'll just take a while. Don't know about the memory thing. Doc says that might take longer to come back… if ever. That's the long-term outlook. For the present, they just hope Mae doesn't suffer a heart attack and die. Her electrical system is whacked out, and that's bad on the heart. They're just not sure of anything right now. Only God knows."

"She can't have any visitors yet," Helene added.

"We'll do what we can," Billy said. "If Dakota Stone's a killer, she has to be stopped. When Mae does recover enough to know what's going on, we'll have this case solved."

"Y'all must know something I don't," I said, inquiring. "Where's the proof. Got any clues, hints, or ideas?"

Mom dropped a sheet of paper down in front of me, and said, "Here it is."

I looked over the document and discovered a very interesting and vital piece of information. There was no record whatsoever that Dakota Stone ever existed until four years ago when she opened her spa/killer/shop.

"How…"

"Billy said we could use his private computer." She pointed to the back where our home office was. "So, we did. After Eddie and I got back from our honeymoon, we went right to work. I joined that spa and started snooping. Eddie did the research. He's the one who found this." She pointed to the document.

I looked over at Billy. "You know what this means, don't you?"

"Dakota Stone is not who she says she is."

"So who is she?"

"If you like that," Eddie said, passing another piece of paper my way, "you're going to love this."

He went on to explain as I scanned the printout.

"Both women are using stolen social security numbers from dead women."

"How on earth did you get their social security numbers?"

"Computer." Eddie grinned. "If you know the right place to go, you can find out anything on the web."

"Now you're talking like a hacker," I said, shaking my head. "I hope you didn't leave any footprints."

"He knows the drill," Billy assured me.

Eddie continued.

"Olivia Swales is using the social security number of a woman who died five years ago in a car accident in Wilson, North Carolina, and Dakota's social security number belongs to a dead woman in South Carolina. In 2010, Dakota opened her shop and had to list her social security number on the business license, and I found Olivia's listed on a hospital admission form. She was admitted to UVA Hospital around the same time both women appeared in Charlottesville."

"And you feel there's a connection to their arrival time and Olivia's hospital stay."

"Yes, I do. And... I think it's odd that I can't find a single thing on either woman before 2010. It's as if they didn't exist until four years ago. Four years ago is when they set up residence in our fair city. Go figure."

"I'm no private eye," Helene said, placing food down in front of us, "but even I know that when someone changes their identity, they're either running from someone or something. Changing one's identity is one thing, but stealing someone's social security number is something else. It's against the law."

"Precisely," Billy agreed, picking up his sandwich. "All we have to do is find out who these women really are."

"How hard can that be?" I asked, knowing that Billy had his ways. He could find out anything he wanted to. That's what he does. That's what we both do. Get dirt. I looked at Mom. "You can take me to The Body Shop as your guest. That's a start."

"I can't do that," Mom said as if she was scared. She picked up her sandwich and bit into it.

"Why not? They won't know what we're up to."

"That's what you think. They know it all. We had to fill out paperwork when we joined. They want to know about you, your family, and your friends—so they can help you and make you better. That's what Dakota said when I asked her about all the questions. I felt like it was an invasion of my privacy, but I didn't tell her that." Mom frowned. "I listed you as one of my daughters—the private investigator one. I had to. I knew she'd find out the truth anyway, so I told her what she wanted to know. Sorry. I guess that was a mistake. I should've omitted a few details."

"Ah, possibly not," I replied. "It might work to our advantage. When it involves murder, people get paranoid, and when they get paranoid, they make mistakes. Having her know what I do might trip her up."

"Let's just hope Dakota Stone doesn't get mad," Mom said. "Mad could be dangerous. Dakota isn't the kind of woman who lets people push her around. I could tell that as soon as I laid eyes on her. She has that superior air about her."

"We won't push. We'll snoop."

"Hey, wait a minute," Helene said. "This Stone woman investigates every client, right? So what's the big deal? No matter what kind of job a person has, it has nothing to do with wanting a day at the killer spa joint. Right?"

Everyone laughed at her reference to The Body Shop.

"Stone has no idea you even know Mae Bridges. Correct, Minnie?" Helene didn't wait for a response. "Look. All you have to do is go back like nothing's wrong, and take Jesse as your guest. Make a big deal about how distraught you both are over Sarah's insanity episode, and tell her you need to be pampered." She glanced over at Billy. "No disrespect to your mother, Billy."

"It would be the truth," Billy replied. "Minnie and Jesse were distraught and now they need a little R&R. I think it's a good cover. We just won't tell my mother about the insanity part."

"So… Jesse," Helene said, slyly. "What happened to your car?"

"Ah, I thought you'd never ask. It's at the office."

"I figured that. Why?"

"I'm on drugs and can't drive."

"Got any more?" Helene smiled, and then looked at Mom.

Mom rolled her eyes.

"On a more serious note," I said to everyone. "We're all clear on the details of this case so far, right?" They shook their heads in agreement. "Including the part about Mae giving them the twenty thousand dollars in cash?"

"We know about the money," Mom said. "That doesn't make her guilty of anything. She just wanted to get those killer women off her back. She was scared."

"Okay," was all I said, and then the conversation moved on.

Billy held up his cell phone. "What's this all about?"

I looked at the photos I'd sent him from Lila's phone and said, "I thought we were being followed, so I took pictures of the SUV just in case we got murdered. Guess I was wrong. We made a turn, but they didn't follow. Xanax hallucination."

"I'll run the license plate just to be sure," Billy said. "We'll start in the morning. Tomorrow, we go after Dakota Stone."

"Time to misbehave!" I added with zeal.

"Let's hit hard," Mom agreed with eagerness. "Time to scrape off the scab and pour alcohol on the wound."

"Take no prisoners," Eddie said, and then saluted Billy. "They all go down!"

Neither Mom nor I mentioned anything about the stinky smelling shampoo from Dakota's shop she found in Sarah's bathroom.

Mom was convinced it was tainted and possibly connected to Sarah's insanity episode.

I was convinced that Mom needed more on the job training, but I would check it out. If nothing else, I would at least take a whiff of the stuff.

However, I wasn't going to say a word to Billy. The last thing he needed was for us to suggest that his mother was poisoned by a bottle of bad shampoo.

To me, the whole idea was just too ludicrous.

Our plan was mapped out. Mom and I were going to be on the frontline, while Billy and Eddie watched our backs. We'd be safe with their help. Nothing bad was going to happen to us as long as Sheriff Hudson didn't get wind of our activities. He was my biggest concern. Billy and I had promised the sheriff we'd take a hiatus from our job and be good for six months. Even though we weren't really breaking our promise, we were definitely in a gray area… and black wasn't far off.

Regrettably, nothing gets by Sheriff Wake Hudson.

Chapter 4

Our plan hit a bump in the road from the start. First thing in the morning, Billy had to go over to Chief Sam's house after Jonathan called and said their dad was losing it and going off the reservation—an emotional backlash most likely brought on by almost losing his wife because of someone's incompetence. Now that the emergency was over, he wanted answers. That's what Billy said when he called to let me know how things were going. He said to go ahead with our visit to the spa, stay out of trouble, and don't do anything to get ourselves killed. He also said he had confidence in us to keep a level head… or Sheriff Hudson would have ours. I said goodbye and then called my mother.

"I was just getting ready to call you," Mom said. "We have a problem on this end. Eddie was out picking up branches from the storm, and he stepped in a hole and twisted his ankle. I told him to stop digging up those rocks unless he was going to take the time to fill the hole with dirt so something like this wouldn't happen. You'd be surprised at how many holes we have in the yard. The man just won't listen. He could do it with his foot at the same time he digs up the rock. One minute is all it would take. But does he listen to me? No. Now he's out of commission for a couple of days."

I figured those last sentences of hers were aimed at Eddie. I know my mother. "I hope he's all right."

"He's going to be fine, but he's not going anywhere."

"Then, we're really out of luck. Billy can't make it either. He's over at the chief's house. Chief Sam suffered a heavy dose of reality and he's not dealing with it well. Like us, he wants to know about those blood pressure pills and where they came from. He's obsessed with finding out. I can't blame him." I cleared my throat and continued. "With Eddie down and Billy out of the picture, we don't have any backup. Billy…"

"What's the big deal? They were just going to sit in the car and wait to see if we would come out alive." She chuckled. "I'm sorry for making a joke, but this is silly. We don't need them. We both have guns."

"Billy wouldn't approve. He thought we'd have Eddie with us. Remember the times I did something Billy didn't want me to, and it almost got me killed? Does the name Rose Hudgins ring a bell? How about my run-in with the Greene County killer?"

"This is different. We can handle it, Jesse. It's not as if they're going to kill us on our first visit." She chuckled again. "Carry an extra gun if it'll make you feel better."

"They don't pat you down?" I joked.

"Nope, no searching and no metal detectors, but they do have cameras in every room. They think nobody knows, but I found them all. So… what do you say?"

"Let's go spend a few hours getting catered to and we can case the joint at the same time. What about Eddie? Will he be all right by himself?"

"He's stretched out with an icepack on his ankle, and I dragged out an old pair of crutches. He'll be fine. See… he's shaking his head."

"Do you still have that bottle of shampoo?"

"You bet. Why?"

"Bring it with you. I want to ask the nutritionist why it smells so bad. What's her name?"

"I don't remember, but she's not one of them, Jesse. She gives out goody bags and asks you if you have any questions. That's it. She's not real bright, either. She's just a peon."

"Let's see if we can cause a stir over some stinky shampoo."

That turned out to be an understatement.

An hour later, we were in my black 4Runner on our way to The Body Shop. Traffic was the same as usual, but at least the weather was nice. The sun was out and there were no signs of rain, thunder, or deadly lightning.

The Body Shop was located on Rt. 29 across the street from a furniture store. The brick building was enhanced by tall columns, fancy exterior lights in the front, and a well-manicured landscape. Parking spaces were abundant. The name on the building was in gold cursive letters, making the place look rich. On the outside it was a good looking place, so I was sure the inside would be, too, but it was hard to tell. There were no windows and the only way to see in was at the entrance.

As soon as we entered the shop, we were greeted by a tall, bleached blond who had curves in all the right places, dressed in clothes that looked as if they cost a fortune. I know the heels did—I recognized the signature red soles of shoes by Christian Louboutin. She was holding an envelope.

"Hello, Dakota," Mom said, smiling. "This is my daughter, Jesse. She's my guest."

"I don't think so," Dakota said in an ugly manner. "Here's your check. Your membership has been canceled. I don't need your kind in my place. I'd like you both to leave the premises immediately." She shoved the envelope into Mom's hands. "Leave now, or I'll be forced to call the police."

I stepped in between Mom and Dakota.

"What's the reason for terminating my mother's membership? Don't like her taste in clothing?"

Dakota looked Mom up and down, and then said, "She could use a stylist, but no, that's not the reason." She loomed over me, getting in my face with a menacing glare. "Do you think I'm stupid? You think I don't know why you're here? I know all about you, Ms. Blackhawk and Blackhawk Investigations."

"What has my job got to do with spending a day at your spa?"

"Give me a break! I watch the news. I heard Mae's name and saw her being carted off in an ambulance. And guess what? In the background was your detective agency. I know she hired you to prove I murdered her husband. What a joke! Why would I kill her husband?"

"How do you know what we talked about? You weren't there."

"Mae rambled on about me killing her husband, and said that you were going to prove it. The nurse who heard her delirious rant is a friend of mine."

"So you racked that pea brain of yours and figured you'd better do some spin control before you wind up in jail for murder."

"Get out of my shop!"

"Did I hit a nerve, Dakota? Oh, that's right. Your name isn't really Dakota, is it? By the way, who were you before you stole someone's identity? Hey, you could go to jail for that. Then, there's the matter of the tainted bottle of shampoo. Do you give these out to all your clients, or just the special ones?" I looked at Mom and held out my hand. "Give me the bottle."

Mom handed me the bottle of shampoo.

I popped up the cap, stood, and then aimed it at Dakota. Before I realized what I was doing, I squeezed the bottle and squirted her with the stinky stuff. The shampoo splattered across the front of her blouse, ran down one arm, and then dripped on the marble floor.

I don't know what I was thinking, but I had to do something. I didn't want this to be my first and last visit without making an impression. Also, I didn't like the way she talked to my mama.

Caught by surprise, Dakota squealed and jumped back as she tried to wipe the gooey liquid from her shirt and arm. From her reaction, you'd think I had just doused her with acid, but I didn't see any smoke coming off her. If I'd had time to think about it logically, I guess I would've jumped back too if I was wearing an expensive blouse like hers.

Dakota spun around, fast tracked it to her desk, and picked up the telephone.

"Don't bother, Dakota No-Name No-Person. We're leaving." I grabbed Mom by the arm, but hesitated. "I thought Mae Bridges was just a sad, grieving widow looking for someone to blame for her husband's death, but I don't anymore. I think you killed her husband, and if I find out you did, you won't be able to run far enough or fast enough to get away from me. Have a great day. Enjoy it, because you won't be having too many of those anymore. Trust me." I looked at Mom. "Come on," I said. "Let's get out of this rat infested dump."

"You're going to be sorry!" Dakota yelled at us as we fled.

Both of us were laughing and shaking when we got to my car.

"That didn't go as I expected," Mom said as soon as she got in the car and fastened her seatbelt. "Burn rubber, Jesse. You know she called the cops. You did ruin her designer blouse." Mom chuckled and then broke out laughing. "You think she'll bill you for it?"

I laughed right along with Mom.

"I bet I blew her mind when I told her we knew about the stolen social security number."

"No," Mom assured me. "It was when you tossed the shampoo on her."

We both enjoyed a good laughing marathon.

When we finally got ourselves under control, Mom said, "We're on her hit list now. Remember what you said about running scared? I can promise you that she's really running scared right about now. She's probably planning our demise as we speak."

"She's probably packing her clothes. She can't kill us all."

"What are we going to tell Billy? He's not going to like what we did."

Before I realized it we were almost to Ruckersville when we should've been heading in the other direction. "I think we missed our turnaround," I said, looking out the window. "I was in such a hurry to make a get-away, I wasn't thinking about where I was going."

"We might as well stop at McDonald's and get one of their frozen coffees."

"That sounds good. Nothing like having a drink after a failed spying expedition."

"Yeah, I guess we didn't do so well on this one."

"We did just fine, Mom. It threw her off-guard when I told her about all the dirt we had on her. I bet the wheels are turning like a spinning top. Oh, she's packing up and heading out of town as fast as her designer shoes will take her."

"She had the upper hand. She's the one who caught us off-guard by confronting us as soon as we walked through the front door. We thought we were going to have the run of the place to do our snooping, but she put an end to that real quick."

"But we did rebound quite well, don't you think?"

"You did all the talking. I was too dumbfounded. I had no idea she was on to us. I froze when she stopped us in our tracks."

"You handled yourself perfectly. Besides, it doesn't matter. You're never going back to that place again… at least not through the front door." I quickly looked over and smiled at her. "Let's go get our Frappe Mochas. Inside or drive-thru?"

"Let's go inside. I'm hungry, and I want to sit down and relax. My nerves are shot. Dakota Stone terrifies me. We know too much about her, and now she knows we know. She's coming after us. I can feel it."

"We're not the only ones who know, and she knows that, too. No… she's running."

"Running where?"

"Away. Change her identity again. She's obviously done it before. Why else would she be using a stolen social security number?"

"The more I think about it, the more scared I am. She might really be a killer, just like Mae said, and if she's killed before, she'll do it again. They say it gets easier after the first time. I think she's capable of it, don't you? Did you see the way she glared at you when you accused her of killing Mae's husband? That was downright spooky. Those eyes of hers bore right through you. She's wicked, Jesse."

We pulled into the Ruckersville's McDonald's, and barely had time to get out of the car when a Greene County deputy car blocked me in from the rear. Deputy Cole James got out of the cruiser and walked over to us.

"Hello, Cole," Mom said, greeting him in her usual adoring manner. She liked Cole a lot. She just didn't like him when he dated my sister, Claire. Ah, but that was moons ago and water under the boat.

"If you wanted my attention, you got it," I said to Cole. "You blocked me in. I think it's illegal to park there."

Deputy James walked up to me, pulled out a set of handcuffs, and told me to put my hands behind my back.

"You're under arrest for assault," he said, emotionless as he slapped on the cuffs. "You have the right to remain silent, and I suggest you do." He looked over at Mom. "I'm sorry, Minnie. I'm just doing my job."

"Don't apologize to her," I said, furious. "Apologize to me! Have you lost your mind? You're embarrassing my mother. What's this all about, Cole? I didn't do anything wrong. We were just getting something to eat."

Cole leaned over close to my ear and said, "What's the matter with you, Jesse? You know the sheriff has his eye on you and Billy." He reached down and removed my snub-nosed thirty eight from its ankle holster. "He's hot. You should've seen him when the call came in. I thought he was going to have a stroke. I've never heard him cuss before." He looked over at Mom and said, "Minnie, you need to call Russ Shank." He looked back at me.

"Who was Jesse supposed to have assaulted, Cole?" Mom asked as if she didn't know. "We've been together all day. I'm her alibi."

"No offense, Minnie, but you're lucky I don't arrest you, too. You were with her at the time of the assault… and you know exactly what I'm talking about. Have you taken to lying, Minnie? That's not like you."

"Alleged assault," Mom corrected him. "Where's your proof?"

"And who did I assault?" I demanded. "I haven't beaten up anyone lately."

"Dakota Stone. She called in an assault, and then e-mailed a video of the assault to the Sheriff's Office. She demanded that we arrest you, and after the sheriff saw the video, he sent his men out to pick you up. He said we could arrest you with extreme prejudice. You're lucky I'm the one who found you instead of one of the other deputies. You don't have many friends in the Greene County Sheriff's Office."

"That's not funny, Cole," Mom said, bitterly. "What video?"

"The video where Jesse throws some kind of liquid on the woman." Cole pulled out his Smart phone, slid his finger across the screen, and up popped my face. "Ah… the wireless highway. Don't you just love it?"

Mom and I watched the short video that showed me squirting Dakota. Those two seconds was all that was on the video. Nothing else.

"It's been edited!" I claimed. "Where's the rest?"

"This is all that matters, Jesse," Cole replied.

"But it was only shampoo!" Mom exclaimed.

"Don't say anything else," I said to Mom. "Call Russ. Ah, crap, call Billy, too. It's not as if he doesn't have enough on his plate already." I looked over at Cole and snarled.

"Yeah," Cole said. "I'm so glad Sarah's okay. Mom and I were worried about her."

"That's funny," I snapped. "I didn't see either one of you at the homecoming celebration."

Cole leaned in close and whispered, "Did you ever stop to think that maybe we weren't invited?"

"You didn't mention Savannah. You two break up already?" I asked hatefully as Cole led me to the squad car. I don't know why I was taking my frustration out on him, but I couldn't stop. "Gee wiz, who in my circle are you going to hook up with next? My mother? Oh, no, that's right, she's married. What about my brother? He's not married, yet."

"Now you're being ridiculous, Jesse."

"You just hate me for choosing Billy over you, don't you? That's why you're doing this. You like getting back at me."

"Are you drunk? Stop saying stuff you don't mean. What we had is over. We've both moved on. I'm happy with my life and so are you. Let it go."

I was saying things that were only half-true, but I wanted to lash out at him.

"Where're the keys to your car? I can't leave your mother stranded out here. The sheriff would have my badge. He really likes her."

I handed the keys to him.

He glared at me as he put his hand on my head to keep me from hitting the car doorframe when he put me in his patrol car.

"Yeah, the sheriff likes and respects your mother. You… not so much. I'd think by now you would've learned that you don't want to make an enemy of him. That's your problem, Jesse. You don't learn from your mistakes."

He slammed the car door and then walked over and gave Mom the keys.

"I'll be just fine. You just take care of my daughter." She waved to me and then got back into the 4Runner.

"No Frappe Mochas for us today," I said to Cole when he climbed into the cruiser. "Too bad. I was looking forward to something sweet."

As we left the parking lot, Cole looked straight ahead and said, "This is no joke, Jesse. You could do jail time. It might not be much, but I guess that depends on how much Sheriff Hudson wants to press the issue. You did break your promise, and he's not real happy. He's out for blood… your blood. Your best bet is to hope Dakota Stone decides not to press charges. So far, that doesn't appear to be on your list of options. But then again, even if she drops the charges, you'll have to win over the sheriff with your charming personality and hope he's in a forgiving mood. I don't see that happening either." Cole laughed. "No, that's just not going to happen."

"She's a killer, Cole."

"I don't want to hear it, Jesse. I told you to exercise your right to shut up, now do it. Anything you say to me will have to go in my report. You don't want that. You could be digging a hole you won't be able to get out of. Please, for your own sake, shut up!"

After I was processed, I spent the next two hours in silence, which was very hard for me to do. I sat in my jail cell, letting my imagination run wild, and waited for Sheriff Hudson to come in and read me the riot act, and for Billy to come save me. And… where was my lawyer?

A female deputy walked up to my cell carrying a tray of food.

"I'm Deputy Rager. Deputy James said he arrested you getting out of your car at McDonald's, so I figured you might need something to eat."

"Thanks," I said eagerly. "I'm starving." I stepped back against the wall to let her know I wasn't a threat. "I don't want you to pull out your nightstick and beat me to a pulp. I'm sure the sheriff would like that."

She opened the cell door, set the tray down on the cot, and then backed out of the cell.

"We carry tasers now. It's more effective." Once the cell door was closed, she added, "The sheriff is a good man. I think you know him well enough to know he wouldn't let that happen… and we wouldn't do it. We only resort to physical violence when nothing else works. Look around you." She motioned with a wave of her arm. "He was kind enough to put you in our special cell."

"This is a special cell?"

"Yes, it is. It's normally used for violent, high profile criminals or high profile white collar suspects. Ones that can't be kept in general population. You have your own toilet in that little cubby over there." She pointed to a room no bigger than a dollhouse. "It ain't much, but you'll have some privacy if you need to use the john. And you have a private hallway here." She pointed to the short hallway. "The door locks automatically. You need one of these to open it." She grabbed the magnetic card attached to a recoiling string on her belt and held it out for me to see. She let the card go and it snapped back into place. "Nobody's going to bother you in here."

I sat down on the cot, removed the napkin covering the food, and took a whiff. "Hmm. This smells good. I love chicken."

"One of the deputies was having lunch at Blue Ridge Café, so I asked him to pick up something for you. We don't usually feed detainees because they're not here long. They're sent to Orange."

"That's mighty nice of you to think of me." I took a big bite out of the chicken leg and then said, "Give my compliments to the chef. This is so good."

"I'll be sure to pass your message along."

"It's been over two hours, Deputy Rager. When can I get out? Is my lawyer here yet? How about my husband?"

"So far, no one has come for you. It's just you, me, and two other deputies. Everyone else is out in the field. It's been a real hectic day, what with that double homicide over in Ruckersville. You didn't kill anyone, did you?"

"Not today." I joked.

"You're funny."

"I'm sure you know why I'm in jail, deputy."

I think the deputy tired of me. "I'd better get back to work, Mrs. Blackhawk."

"You can call me Jesse." I was trying to get her to warm up to me by being nice. I didn't need anymore enemies. "It's creeping me out being in jail all alone. Solitary confinement is a real drag. And another thing, I regret my earlier attitude towards you. I'm sorry. It's just that…"

"What?" Deputy Rager asked. "You can tell me."

"I've been bad. I made a promise to the sheriff, and I didn't keep it.

I know I did wrong by going back on my word, but I had to go talk to that woman in person. She gave my mama some bad shampoo, and all I wanted to do was make things right. I get so tired of people cheating people. You sell someone an inferior product, you should be held accountable. You need to replace it or give the customer a refund. Don't you think so?"

"Yes, I do," Deputy Rager said. "But I think you went about it the wrong way."

"Perhaps I did. Maybe I should've…"

She cut me off. "I'm sure you can work it out with Sheriff Hudson when he gets back. You didn't mean to hurt that woman, did you?"

Smart deputy—she thought she was questioning me without my ever suspecting a thing. But I'm smarter than she thinks. She wasn't getting anything out of me that I didn't want to give.

"I didn't hurt her. All I did was try to return a rancid bottle of shampoo. That video doesn't tell the whole story. I just wanted to get a refund for my mother. You know how moms are. They don't want to make waves. The woman made me mad when she said insulting things to my mom, so I squirted her with her own rotten shampoo."

Realizing she was wasting her time, Deputy Rager excused herself and walked away. As she reached the door, she called out, "Eat your food. It's going to be a while before you get to see the sheriff."

"That's right. He's handling a homicide. Who got killed?"

"Sorry. Can't give out that information." Then, she was gone.

Time seemed to stand still. No one had come to help me out, and I was feeling sorry for myself.

"Where is everyone?" I yelled down the hallway, but no one answered me.

Two more hours had passed, according to the digital wall clock over the exit door. That's when I realized why people have killed themselves in jail. It's a horrible, lonely place; add that to someone's who's already severely depressed and you got yourself a recipe for disaster.

Another hour passed, and then another. By then, I was ready to slam my head up against the wall.

"Let me out of here," I screamed as loud as I could.

That's when I noticed a small camera in the upper left hand corner of the ceiling. Why hadn't I seen it earlier? So, they've been watching me the whole time, I thought to myself. Well, I'll give them something to see. I started banging my head against the bars and screaming nonsense about killing myself. I figured that would get their attention.

It must have, because the door opened and Deputy Rager walked back in. She took the ring of keys and opened the cell door.

"Sheriff Hudson wants to see you before we transport you to Orange County Regional Jail."

"What? Why am I being transferred to Orange? I'm not a criminal!" I was on the verge of a spastic tantrum. "You can't do this!"

"You've been charged with assault. That's a felony."

"But…"

The deputy gripped my arm and led me down the hallway. She opened the door, took me to the sheriff's office, and then presented me to the king. I walked in to see Sheriff Hudson sitting behind his desk… and... Billy and Mom sitting in chairs across from him. The sheriff stood up and said, "Sit down, Jesse. We need to talk. Actually, I'm going to talk, and you're going to listen."

I looked over at Mom and Billy.

"Don't look at them for help. They're just as guilty as you are."

I sat down in the chair next to Billy, placed my hand in his, and then murmured, "I'm sorry. Please don't be mad at me." I looked up at the sheriff and said, "Do whatever you want to do with me, but leave them out of this. I'm the one to blame. All of this was my fault."

"Yes, it is," Sheriff Hudson said. "And now you have to pay for what you did."

I had fouled up big time. I was going to be transferred to Orange County Regional Jail, then to court, and then to prison. My kids were going to grow up without a mother. I cried.

I've always said that Billy and I were just a footstep away from jail, but this time it was for real. I was going to prison—and that's where I was going to die. Escape was not in my future. I had to take my licks… like it, or not.

Busted over a bottle of shampoo. What was the world coming to?

Chapter 5

Sheriff Hudson placed his hands on his desk, leaned forward and said, "What do you have to say for yourself? And don't tell me you didn't do anything wrong, because we both know that's a lie." Before I could explain, he silenced me with a wave of his hand. "Never mind. I don't want to hear it. If you ever go near Dakota Stone again, I'll have my guys come after you, and it won't be pleasant. I promise you that!"

I was shocked. I thought for sure this was the end for me. I just knew the sheriff wanted to lock me up and throw away the key, but he wasn't going to. He was letting me off with a stiff warning.

I dried my tears with the back of my hand and said a silent prayer of thanks to the man upstairs. I was going home!

Mom and Billy still hadn't said a word.

Taking a cue from them, I remained silent. I wanted to ask the sheriff why he had kept me in jail so long, but I didn't. I knew the best thing I could do was let him have his say. And have his say, he did.

"I told both of you that I would lock you up if you broke our agreement," Sheriff Hudson began.

"But..." I started to say, but was silenced by the sheriff again.

"Stop! Don't say a word. You're going to sit there and listen and you're going to keep your mouth shut." He gave me a hard stare, and then continued. "You're lucky that Dakota Stone is such an agreeable person. She won't press assault charges if you pay for her blouse and leave her alone. That means no calls, no stalking, no nothing. Do I make myself clear? Don't say anything, just nod your head and at least pretend you understand what I'm saying."

I nodded in agreement.

"The cost of the blouse is a hundred and twenty-five dollars. Billy has already given me a check, which I will give to Ms. Stone."

Whew! What a relief. I was getting off with a slap on the wrist and a measly hundred and twenty-five dollars. It was my lucky day. God had answered my prayers. That's what I thought until Sheriff Hudson spoke again.

"How did it feel to sit in jail?"

"It wasn't so bad." I lied. I should've said it was awful, instead of trying to be so macho.

"Good, because you're going to spend the night here."

"What?" I said, jumping up out of the chair. "But you said Stone wasn't pressing charges."

"Sit down! That's right. She's not."

"Then why do I have to spend the night in jail?" I sat back down. My knees were getting weak.

"Well, since you didn't mind being in jail, I guess you haven't learned anything, because if you had, you wouldn't want to go back. I want you to know what it's like to be incarcerated and have your freedom stripped from you, because the next time I find out that you're back at it again before our agreement is up, you won't be so lucky. You'll be facing hard time. Judges take obstruction of justice charges very seriously. Five to ten. Does that mean anything to you?"

I swallowed hard.

"I thought so," he said, and then looked over at Billy. "I'm going to give you ten minutes with your wife. You'll be able to pick her up tomorrow afternoon at six o'clock."

"Six o'clock!" I jumped up out of my chair again. " That's ridiculous! You can't do this to me. Where's my lawyer?"

Sheriff Hudson raised one eyebrow. "Want to make it two nights?"

Billy reached up, grabbed my hand, and then pulled me back down in my chair.

"Say nothing, `ge ya."

The sheriff continued with, "Unfortunately, you won't be staying in our presidential suite. Got a real dangerous guy in there. So, you'll be put in with the general population. You'll have a cell to yourself, unless we get overcrowded. Then, you'll have to share." The sheriff shifted gears. "Nights are our busiest time. We get our fair share of hookers, drunks, thieves, killers, rapists…"

"I get the message."

"No, I don't think you do."

The sheriff walked out from behind his desk over to me.

"You know Jesse, I really don't want to do this, but I don't have a choice. I purposely kept you in jail for six hours, with the consent of your husband, hoping you'd get the message, but you didn't. You're laughing behind my back."

"You're locking me up because you think I'm laughing at you? That's not legal. You know that."

"Neither was that agreement you signed. I'm doing you a favor, so shut up, do your time, and then go home to your family. You won't get another break from me. This is the end of the line. My patience is gone."

He turned and looked at Billy. "Say goodbye to your wife. I'll be outside."

The sheriff walked out of the room.

"I'm so sorry, Billy," I said as soon as the sheriff left. "I couldn't help myself. That b…"

Mom spoke up for the first time. "This is my fault."

"No, it's not, Mom. I'm a big girl, but I should've known better. I think Mae is right, and we have to do something."

I looked back at Billy.

"You let him keep me in jail? Why?"

"I had to. I wasn't given much of a choice. Spend the night here and don't make waves, Jesse. I'll be back for you tomorrow, and then we'll go after Dakota Stone."

"Tell her about the SUV, Billy," Mom said.

"What SUV?"

"The one that was following you the other day," Billy answered. "It's registered to The Body Shop."

"Hmm," I said. "That puts a whole new slant on everything."

"It sure does," Mom added. "That Stone woman has been having someone follow Mae, that's why you were being followed. What does that tell you?"

"That she has something to hide."

"I'm going home," Billy said. "I don't want you to misbehave. Just keep quiet until this is over. Do the time and get it over with."

"I'm sorry, Billy. I'll try to be good.... if I don't die in here first."

The sheriff popped his head back into the room and said, "Okay, folks. Time's up."

I hugged Billy and Mom and then watched as they were led out. It was a scary and sad moment. I felt as if I'd never see them again.

"Don't look at me like that," Sheriff Hudson said, leading me to the cell. "You brought it on yourself. You're lucky I like you and Billy, or I'd be having you carted off to Orange so you could spend the night there."

After he locked me up, he turned and said, "I knew Billy would keep his word, but I had my doubts about you. I see now that I was right. I'll be watching you closer in the future. I don't want Billy to suffer because you can't stay out of trouble."

At least I'm not going to Orange County Regional Jail, I thought to myself. That would be very bad. I could get lost and never be heard from again. I was so relieved. I'd do my time and never return to this place again. I silently said thanks to the man upstairs.

"Thank you, Lord. I promise to be good if you let me live through the night."

As soon as the sun went down, the criminals started rolling in. First, they put a drunk in the cell next to mine and all he did was puke, fart, and then pee on floor. The sounds made me gag, and I was so glad when they released him. Regrettably, the next one locked up was a drunken woman in her late thirties. She, too, puked, farted, and peed on herself. It wasn't pretty.

"What you in for?" she asked me after she got her bodily functions somewhat under control.

"I killed a drunk."

She didn't say anything else to me after that. If she wasn't sober before, she was now. She scurried over to the corner of her cell and stayed there until she was let go.

A janitor came in after the woman's release and cleaned up after her and the previous drunkard.

What a yucky job. Nothing like pee and vomit to turn one's stomach. I was glad I didn't have to clean up the mess.

I stretched out on the cot, hoping no bed bugs or other infesting critters would attack me. The smell of urine and puke wouldn't allow me to sleep, so when Deputy Rager walked up to my cell, I was so glad for the distraction.

"I'm getting off duty soon and I was wondering if you wanted something to eat before I leave. I can call one of the deputies on patrol and see if he'll get you something."

"How can anyone eat in a place like this? The smell alone is obnoxious. It's so gross."

"Sheriff Hudson said to make sure you had dinner."

"I'll pass, but thanks anyway. You've been very nice to me. I really do appreciate it."

"Well, it's not as if you're a real criminal, but if you don't do what the sheriff says…"

"I know. I know. I've been…"

A ruckus was going on down the hall, so I jumped off the cot to have a look. Two deputies were dragging an unruly man toward my cell.

"What the…"

"Step back, ma'am," Deputy Rager said. "We got us a repeat offender here. He's crazy and won't hesitate to grab at you through the bars." She looked at the man and said, "How many times do you have to be locked up Percy, before you stop beating your wife?"

The man had been drinking. I could smell alcohol on him when he passed my cell.

"I didn't beat up nobody," he yelled. "Let me go!"

The deputies opened the cell and shoved the guy in. Percy stumbled back and fell. A deputy slammed the cell door and said, "You're lucky I didn't beat the crap out of you like you did your wife."

"I didn't beat up my old lady, and she ain't pressing no charges against me, so let me outta here! You can't do this to me. I got rights."

"You got nothing," Deputy Rager said to the man. "You're lucky Mabel didn't crack you over the head with a frying pan. Percy, one of these days, after she's finally had enough of your abuse, she's going to take a shotgun to you. Is that what you want?"

Percy jumped up, leaped at the cell door, and then spit on Deputy Rager. Glad to say, his spit hit her shirt and not her face.

His actions angered me to no end. I yelled over at him, "You're lucky these bars separate us old man, otherwise I'd be on you like flies on s..."

"Ah, shut up," he yelled back. "What's a puny little punk like you gonna do to me? You couldn't beat up nobody."

He laughed at me.

Deputy Rager hushed him when she said, "You better watch out, Percy. That puny woman over there is a serial killer. She's been on the loose for years, killed over twenty some people before she ended up here in our jail. Now we got her locked up, and she ain't happy. You better stay away from them bars, because she'll grab you and kill you with her mind. She's evil. She knows black magic. She'll put a spell on you. Make you wish you'd never met her."

The old man shut up.

Deputy Rager turned to me and smiled.

I winked at her.

"I'll bring you a bag of chips and a Pepsi," she said. "Think you can eat that?"

"That'll be good," I replied.

I walked over to the bars separating Percy and me, grabbed them and shook them as hard as I could.

"Hurry up, deputy. I might have to grab a piece of this old man's arm. I'm real hungry."

The look on Percy's face was worth a million bucks. He was terrified beyond belief.

Deputy Rager laughed when she left and was still laughing when she returned with my snack.

"I brought you a Twinkie to go with your chips. It's the best I can offer."

"Thanks, deputy," I replied, looking over at Percy's cell. "I'm so hungry I could chew that man's leg off."

"No problem," she said and then started to walk away.

"What?" Percy yelled. "I don't get nothing?"

"Come on over here, Percy," I said to him. "I'll give you something you won't soon forget."

"Stay away from her, Percy," the deputy called back to him. "She'll take off your arm. She's a real psycho. She don't care who you are. Did I tell you that she eats her victims? Yeah, she was eating some guy's arm when we caught her."

That was it. Percy cringed in a corner, never said another word, and was glad when they came for him. He was going to Orange.

"Wife beaters don't fare well over at Orange," a deputy said to Percy, trying to scare him as he led him out. "You might just get a taste of what's it's like to be on the receiving end of a good butt-kicking."

"I don't care," Percy replied, quickly. "I just want to get away from that crazy woman." He pointed to me. "She eats people. Did you know that? She even said she wanted to eat my arm."

"Liar!" I snarled at him.

The deputy just smiled.

I ate most of my snack, drank all of my Pepsi, and then lay back down on the cot. It was going to be a long night. I wondered who the next person would be to occupy the cell next to mine. I didn't have to wait long. They brought in two teenage girls who had been picked up for stealing a car and taking it for a joyride. The car belonged to one of the girl's parents, but that didn't matter. They were arrested and was going to be held until a parent could come get them. I heard the deputy giving them a lecture.

I rolled over on my side with my back to them and snickered when the deputy warned the two girls to stay away from the serial killer in the next cell.

I'll make it. This isn't so bad, I thought. That was, until they brought in a tall, well-built man who had eyes like Charles Manson, and put him in the cell the two girls had occupied earlier. He was one scary looking dude. The deputy on duty didn't have to warn me to stay away from him. I had no intentions of getting anywhere near that man.

"What you in for?" the creepy guy asked me.

"Killed a few people," I replied.

That lie had intimidated others before, so why not this time?

"Got caught eating a man's arm."

"You're a liar," Manson eyes shot back. "I bet you got snagged for reckless driving or something stupid like that. Maybe shoplifting? You're about as dangerous as a flea."

I didn't say anything. I was too scared to go back and forth with this guy. He could've been a decent looking guy if he didn't have those eerie eyes—the eyes of a killer.

"Hey, I was a tad busy today. Didn't have time for food, so I'm really hungry. Got anything left to eat over there?"

"Just part of a Twinkie," I replied, scared out of my wits.

I picked up the half-eaten Twinkie and was about ready to toss it through the bars.

"Don't throw it!" he insisted. "It might fall on the floor. Just hand it to me through the bars."

I hesitated.

"Come on," eerie eyes pleaded. "I won't hurt you. What can I do to you through these bars? Please. I'm starving."

I got up from the cot and walked up to the cell bars. I wasn't about to get too close, so I stretched out my arm and handed the Twinkie to the guy through the bars.

In a flash, he grabbed my arm and jerked me to him.

I could smell his sour breath.

Then he poked his other arm through, grabbed the back of my head, and slammed my face into the cell bars. I pulled back, but he had too much of a hold on me. He slammed my face into the bars again and again.

The pain was excruciating. I was sure I was going to die this time. The last thing I remembered before passing out was the unbearable smell of the man's sour breath. It smelled like meat gone bad.

I woke up in the hospital with a headache and blurry vision. I couldn't see what my face looked like, but when the memories of what had happened to me flashed back, I figured it was pretty bad. How many times had that man slammed my face into those bars? Two? Three?

"She's coming around," I heard my mother say. "Billy!"

"Just lay still," Billy said, taking hold of my hand. "That guy beat you up pretty bad. The sheriff said he smashed your face into the cell bars.

You have eight stitches in your forehead and a black eye."

"Thank goodness they have cameras in that place," Mom added. "A few minutes later, and you'd be dead. Thank God those deputies acted so fast. Five minutes later would've been too late."

"I know, Mom," I replied, half alert. "My throat is so dry. Can you get me some water? I feel like I'm going to choke."

"Sure, honey," she replied. "I'll get you a glass." Mom stepped out of the room and then returned with a plastic pitcher and glass. "Here, Jesse."

I took the glass of water and guzzled it down. "What time is it?"

"It's five in the morning," Billy answered. "You've been here for a couple of hours. Do you remember what happened to you?"

"Yeah. Everything's coming back to me. Who was that guy? Why did he do this to me?"

"Some people are just bad, Jesse," Sheriff Hudson said as he walked into the room. "Guys like him don't need a reason."

"I'm not talking to you ever again," I said, angrily. "Go away."

"I'm so sorry this happened, Jesse. I never intended…"

"You wanted to teach me a lesson and you did. I don't want to ever go to jail again. You got your wish, Sheriff. Now go away and leave me alone. I don't want to ever see your face again."

"I wanted to teach you a lesson, but not like this."

"Oh, yeah? Is that so? See, I figured you put him in there so he could rough me up. You wanted me to know how bad it was to be locked up. You win. Now I know."

"You have it all wrong," Sheriff Hudson said. "I don't know him. We picked him up over at Sal's for being disorderly in public. Jesse, I would never do this to you or anyone else."

"You're lying! You planted him there to harass me, but he went too far. He smashed my face in… and… oh, Lord… he had the worst breath. Smelled like rotten meat. Next time you do this to someone, get the guy to brush his teeth and gargle first."

"Sorry about the bad breath, but I don't control people's hygiene, and as far as the assault on you, I'm going to reprimand my deputies."

"No! You can't do that. It wasn't their fault. I never should've gone near that guy." I took another sip of water. "Your deputies saved my life. I owe them a big thanks, and so do you. Not a reprimand."

"I'm glad you're going to be all right."

"So who was the creep that beat my face in? One day I'd like to return the favor."

Sheriff Hudson didn't answer my question, but instead said, "I'm not making excuses, but my deputies at the station house were overloaded with work. They caught the attack on screen just when you hit the floor, but missed what led up to it. As I said, they had their hands full. So, after viewing the playback, it's hard to tell who started the altercation. The guy said that you're the one who stuck your arm through the bars first, and he's claiming it was an unprovoked attack."

"Are you nuts?" I shrieked. "He attacked me! Look at this mug!" I demanded, pointing to my face. "Does this look like an unprovoked attack? I gave the guy my leftover Twinkie, and this is what I got in return."

"You can file an assault charge against him if you want to, but until my guy analyzes the video, I can't arrest him. He hasn't filed charges against you yet, so—"

"He's not going to," I said, sarcastically. "He'll wait for another opportunity to…"

A memory of the last thing the guy said to me flashed back.

"Next time, I'm going to kill you."

"Oh, man! The last thing he said to me was that the next time he was going to kill me."

I hesitated and then asked again, "What's his name, sheriff? I have a right to know."

"Gavin Preston."

Mom and Billy glanced at each other with a freaky look on their faces, and then stared at the sheriff. I could tell they knew something, but it wasn't something they wanted to share.

A nurse walked in and said, "Sheriff, you have an urgent call." She motioned to him. "You can take it at the nurse's station right over there."

"I'll be right back," he said. "Don't go anywhere."

"As if I can," I yelled to him as he was walking out of the room.

I looked at Mom and Billy.

"Was he trying to make a joke? Because if he was, it wasn't funny."

"Give him a break," Mom said. "He's devastated over this. He didn't want you to get hurt. It was a bad call on his part. That's all."

"Tell that to my battered face. I need a mirror. Give me yours, Mom. No need to put it off. It must be bad. My face hurts something fierce. Giving birth was less painful."

Mom handed over her compact.

I opened it and held the mirror out far enough to get a glimpse of my entire face. What stared back at me wasn't pretty. I looked as if I had gotten into a fight with a meat grinder, and it had won.

"Geez, Louise! I can't go out in public like this. I look like Frankenstein's bride."

"It's not that bad," Mom said. "Who cares what your face looks like anyway? You're going to be okay. That's what's important."

"I'm not going back to jail," I stated, emphatically. "I don't care what Sheriff Hudson says. I think I've done my time. He got his point across."

Sheriff Wake Hudson walked back into the room in time to hear what I had said.

I looked at him and repeated my intent. "I mean it! I'm not going back! I don't care what you say. I've paid my dues. I could've died in there. I almost did."

The sheriff held up his hand and said, "You're free to go out and wreak havoc on the world again. Just remember what I said. Keep your promise, so you won't wind up in my jail again. I don't think my nerves can handle it. I'm pretty sure I'm on my way to having a nervous breakdown as it is. I don't need any more stress."

"You're just full of jokes, aren't you? I almost die in your jail and you joke about it."

"What I meant was…"

"I know what you meant. You're not going to make me go back and serve the rest of my time because you want to cover your butt. What would the public think if this ever got out?"

The sheriff turned to Billy and said, "Since she's not going to give me a chance to explain, I guess I'll tell you."

He went on to give us the bad news.

"Gavin Preston has been released."

"What?" I screamed. "You let him go after what he did to me? Have you lost your mind? Nurse! I need a Valium!"

Sheriff Hudson turned to me and said, "Calm down, Jesse. His lawyer got him out. Due process. We had to let him go. I'm sorry for what happened to you. If you'd like to press charges…"

"One thing is for sure, Sheriff Hudson—I don't want to ever go to jail again. If I have to go the straight and narrow, I will. Jail ain't for me."

I could see the relieved look on the sheriff's face, and it was heartfelt. He actually did care.

"You're not going to have to worry about my lawless behavior anymore, Sheriff Hudson. I've learned my lesson, and I'm not even going to hold this against you. It wasn't your fault. I realize that now."

I didn't blame the sheriff anymore, but the rest was a lie. I wasn't going to let this one go.

Before the sheriff walked out of the room, he turned and said, "I'll check on you later."

"I won't be here!" I said to thin air, and then turned back to Mom and Billy. "Get me out of this place. It's payback time!"

I never expected my day to turn out like this, but now that it had, I was even more determined to get to the truth. I was going to find every dirty little secret The Body Shop had… and I was going after Gavin Preston. I was going to draw blood.

CHAPTER 6

IT WAS DAYLIGHT BEFORE we left the hospital. I was not happy, in pain, and wanted payback. I would have my face-to-face with Gavin Preston, and the next time we met, he'd be the one who'd be sorry—sorry he ever hurt me. Somehow, I would do to his body what he had done to my face.

"Gavin Preston is Dakota Stone's driver," Billy said on the ride home from the hospital.

"I knew you were holding something back! I figured there had to be a reason the guy smashed in my face. Why didn't you tell the sheriff?"

"And let him know that we were investigating the Stone woman?" Billy grunted. "We made a deal, remember? One more slip-up and we're going to jail. He let you slide on this one. Next time he won't let it go. We have to play it clean."

"Dakota knew you were in jail," Mom added. "She had you arrested and then sent her henchman in to rough you up. What better way to get to you? She's a smart and dangerous woman. I told both of you that."

"Yeah, but… she had to have known they could link Preston to her. He is her driver. What was she thinking?"

"It doesn't matter. Besides, she'd say it was a coincidence… that she has no control over what he does off the job. That's what I'd say if it were me."

"You know, something isn't right about Preston. His breath smelled like rotten chicken mixed with a spoonful of molasses and dog poop. How gross is that?"

No one responded, as if his breath had nothing to do with anything. Maybe it didn't, but if he ever came near me again, I'd smell that rancid odor way ahead of time.

"There's more bad news," Mom sadly said, resisting the urge to cry as her eyes watered up. "That urgent call the sheriff got was to tell him that Mae was dead."

"How did you find out?"

"Bad news travels fast. Mae was murdered, suffocated with a pillow. The pillow was still on her face when the nurse rushed in to check on her. Seems Mae managed to press the call button before she died. We just found out, but didn't want to tell you—"

"Stop! I can't take anymore bad news."

I felt like crying, but I was all cried out. Mae was dead, and I had a pretty good idea who had killed her. It was obvious that the blood trail would lead straight to Dakota's front door. I had to close my eyes to shut out all the death happening around me.

By the time we reached our house, the latest round of painkillers had kicked in and I had fallen asleep. A bump in the driveway woke me, and after seeing two black Hummers parked out front, I was wide-awake.

I glanced over at Billy and thought about how much I loved him. Even after eight years of marriage, I was still attracted to him just as much as I was when we first met. He was handsome, strong and loving, and he had integrity. That means a lot to a woman. I laid my head back for a minute and let the images of his naked body flow through my mind like a slideshow. My sexual urges were getting ready to go into hyper-drive again… but my body laughed at the idea.

Billy parked next to Mom's yellow canary, and then the three of us got out and headed for the house.

"Are we having a powwow?" I asked, walking in the door. "Is this a welcome home party or a black ops meeting?"

"All of the above," Jonathan replied, walking to the door to greet us. "We're glad you're home, and we're getting ready to go silent. Mae's murder changed everything."

"It's the same thing as circling the wagons," Mom explained as if I hadn't heard that phrase before.

The smile on Billy's face was such a relief. Since his mother's illness, he had been in a dark place, but now he was back and ready for action!

Helene, the dogs, and another man stood by the dining room table.

The man was an extremely well-built, square-shouldered, chiseled jawed black man.

Including Billy, I was now standing in the middle of three men who looked as if they could flatten you with their thumb.

Athena and Thor were so glad to see me that they almost licked me to death... slobbering all over the place.

I smiled, instead of telling them to get down like I normally do.

After a few caresses, they got bored and ran off to their food bowls, forgetting about me.

A dog's love is unlike any other. All they want is affection and food. They had gotten their affection, now it was time for food.

No one said anything about the way my face looked. Not even Helene. I guess she'd seen worse since she'd been living with us, and from the look of the guys around me, I knew they had. I could just tell. They probably put my injuries in the same category as a mosquito bite.

"It's been done," Jonathan said to Billy. "Lu Ann has the children. They'll be safe. Mason and Gator are on the job."

"My children?"

I looked around and then back to Billy.

"Where are the kids?"

"Jonathan just told you they were with Lu Ann. They're safe, so don't worry."

I looked over at Jonathan. "Mason and Gator? Who are they?"

"The murder of Mae Bridges brought this to a whole new level," Billy said before Jonathan could respond to my question. "It proves there's something to what she told us about Dakota Stone. Why else was she murdered? People are getting bumped off one by one, and we're not going to let it go any further. Dakota Stone's reign of terror stops here."

"I'll fix something to drink," Helene said. "Coffee, tea, or booze?"

She scanned the faces in the room, and then excused herself as if she didn't want to hear me go into another one of my rages.

"It's seven o'clock, Helene," Mom shot back. "Who wants booze this early in the morning?"

"I can't believe Mae's dead, but I should've seen it coming. She was right to be terrified of Dakota Stone and her buddies. They tried to kill me and failed, and then they went after Mae and succeeded. I'm sorry about Mae. Next time Gavin Preston comes after me, I'll be ready… and I'm going to pay him back for killing Mae."

I soon learned that Gator and Mason were part of Jonathan's covert team of guys who had done battle together in more ways than one. I knew of Jonathan's past, and if these guys were his pals, we had a real fighting force on our side. But what did we need with them? We could handle the Stone woman and her killer friends.

"I need to sit down," I said, walking over to the kitchen table with Mom by my side. We both took a seat and looked up at the men in the room.

"What a bunch of scary looking dudes," I said. "I'd hate to meet either one of you in a dark alley—you included." I looked over at Billy.

They laughed.

I shivered with doubt, fear, and anxiety.

I figured Dakota Stone was the ringleader and Olivia Swales was just another one of her patsies in crime just like Gavin Preston—except that Preston was the killer in the group.

These guys were here to bring them down.

I was wondering when Jonathan was going to introduce the big, black hulk to us, and then, as if to read my mind, he looked over and said, "Oh, this is my comrade, Shark. He's the one you really have to look out for. He'll chop off your head in a heartbeat."

Jonathan made a sweep across his throat with his hand to emphasize his point.

My mouth dropped after sizing the man up. He was a mammoth, bodybuilding type guy, six-two, and weighed at least one-ninety, and not an ounce of it was fat. His head was shaved and he was dressed neck-to-toe in black—black T-shirt, black pants, and black boots, the same as Jonathan. They both had a tiny gadget in one ear, and strapped to their belts was a cell phone, gun, and some kind of device I'd never seen before. Perhaps it was a ray gun. They had everything else. I learned later that their gear also included knives in their boots and rocket launchers in their Hummers.

"Shark… is that your first or last name?"

"Only one name is necessary, Mrs. Blackhawk," Shark replied in such a way that I half expected him to salute me.

His build, mannerisms, and speech made me think of Denzel Washington, only a much, much larger version… with no hair. He had to have been a Marine in his other life. He was disciplined and tough. I remember hearing that Marines were once called Devil Dogs. Now I can see why. Shark was like a Pit Bull on steroids. Extremely dangerous.

On the flip side, did I mention he was good looking, or that he had muscles that bulged with each movement? He was every man's nightmare. Every woman's dream.

"Please, call me Jesse," I replied in a soft voice.

I wasn't flirting, just trying to ease the tension in the room. So many alpha males in one place was overwhelming and very intimidating.

"Mrs. Blackhawk is too formal if we're going to kill people together. We're a team, right?"

I looked at Billy for confirmation.

You see, I knew that if Billy and Jonathan brought in this badass guy, he expected me to sit this one out, but I wasn't about to do that, and I told him so.

"I would never leave you out, `ge ya," Billy said, winked, and then looked at everyone else. Then, he focused his attention on Jonathan, waiting for him to dole out orders.

Jonathan took command and said, "Shark, I want you to take Minnie to her house…"

"What?" Mom asked.

He looked at Mom.

"He's going home with you so you can pack a few things and then come back here. It's the only way we can keep you safe. He'll help you with Eddie."

"Hold on," I interrupted. "What am I missing?"

Jonathan reached over, grabbed the folder that had been sitting on the counter, and then handed it to me.

I opened it, looked at some of the paperwork and sucked in my breath. I looked over at Billy.

"When did you find out about the others?"

"Just last night," he replied. "Jonathan had to do some serious digging before he pieced it together. Nobody, not even the cops made the connection that there have been two other men that were murdered, and the one thing they all had in common was that their wives belonged to the same spa. Guess that never came up."

"Figures," Helene sneered. "A simple connection and the cops still couldn't get it right. You did good, Jonathan."

"Actually, Lu Ann's the one who came up with the connection. She's the criminal profiler in the family. You wouldn't believe some of the stuff she can piece together. It's as if she sees into a killer's mind. Give her the details of the crime and she can tell you all about the suspect. Sometimes it's almost scary."

"I can't believe anything would scare you, Jonathan," Mom said, ever so lovingly.

She adored him and everyone in Billy's family. She made it a point to tell everyone she could that I was lucky to have married into a family like Billy's. They were the absolute best, so diverse in their careers, and so close and loving. On and on and on. Bless her kind heart.

"These deaths weren't just random acts of violence," I said, flipping through the pages in front of me. "One a year for the last three years. Hmm. She's been a busy gal."

"Mae swore Dakota was running a hit shop and not just a spa!" Mom added. "Not in those exact words, but that's what she meant. And now she's dead, and it wasn't the lightning that killed her."

Jonathan reached over and pulled out a photo from the bottom of the file. "Here's an image of the person who was last seen leaving Mae's room before she died. It's not the best, it's a little fuzzy, but you can see the eyes. Maybe you'll recognize the face. A nightshift nurse didn't get a good look at him, but she definitely saw him walking out of Mae's room. I got this photo from a hospital camera, and don't ask me how."

I looked at the photo. It was grainy, but there was no doubt about who those eyes belonged to.

"It's him! It's Gavin Preston."

"We know," Jonathan said. "Just wanted to see if you concurred. This photo was captured an hour after he was released from jail, so he had the opportunity, and this picture proves it." He passed the photo to Mom. "Have you ever seen this guy before?"

"Oh, my Lord!" she exclaimed. "I think I might have passed him in the hallway at the hospital. Who could forget those menacing eyes?" She thought for a second. "Are you telling me he snuck into Mae's room and killed her while we were still at the hospital with Jesse?"

"According to the time stamp, it looks that way," Billy added.

"I can't believe he was that close to me again," I murmured. "He killed Mae right under our noses. He could've gotten to me if I'd been alone."

Mom cocked her head as if she was thinking about something, and then asked, "Shouldn't we give this information to the police? I mean, I think I saw him at the hospital, and we know he's connected to Dakota."

We all glanced back and forth at each other.

"Hmm…" I said. "A question we've come up against before."

It was the same question we had asked ourselves on a previous case. We made a wrong decision then, and it wound up landing me and Billy in hot water with the sheriff. If we'd just given Sheriff Hudson the gun when we found it, instead of holding onto it, our life would be as it was. We wouldn't be working on the sly, taking a chance we could land in the pokey for an indeterminate amount of time. We'd be out there kicking butt. Now we were reduced to sneaking around in the bushes like panthers waiting to pounce. But hey, isn't that the way we're supposed to operate?

"I'm sure they already know Preston was there," Jonathan said, looking over at the clock on the wall. "If we know, they know. We need to find out if Preston is in custody."

He motioned to Shark, who turned and walked outside.

"Where's he going?" I asked.

"He's going to check the status on Preston."

"Where? In the front yard?"

Jonathan chuckled, Shark smiled. "No, Jesse. We have a rather sophisticated setup in the Hummer. We can run a check on anyone, anywhere, in a matter of minutes."

Less than five minutes later, Shark returned. "They're looking for him in connection with the murder of Mae Bridges, but he hasn't been picked up yet."

"It's your call, Billy," Jonathan said. "We're here to protect and serve right?" He looked over at Mom. "You might want to leave the room, Minnie, because I'm getting ready to get down and dirty. You might not want to hear what I have in mind."

"I can handle anything you throw at me," she replied with confidence. "I think I'll stay. Gavin Preston almost killed Jesse, so I'm pretty much in agreement with whatever you want to do. I'm tired of bad guys trying to kill off my loved ones. So, fire away."

Jonathan looked back at Billy. "Why don't you let us go out and whack him? Save us a lot of time and trouble." He chuckled. "We'll dispose of his body, and I guarantee you his remains will never be found."

"What remains?" Shark jokingly asked. "We don't leave anything behind... nothing."

Shark had a deep voice that carried a lot of force. He reminded me of a guy I'd seen in a movie once. The only difference was that he didn't have the bulging belly, and he definitely wasn't overweight. He was as strong as an ox.

Mom flinched and said, "You mean, kill him?"

"That would be my guess," Helene said, adding to the conversation.

"We'd burn in Hell!" Mom squealed. "We can't just kill him in cold blood. I won't be a part of it. I say we turn our information over to the cops and let them take care of the problem. The evidence is right here in black and white." She looked at Billy and then at Jonathan. "We're not killers!" She shook her head in disbelief. "Maybe I should've left the room when I was told to."

"Oh don't act so surprised, Minnie," Helene said. "What do you think these guys do? Use harsh language? No. They terminate for a cause."

"What the hell does that mean, Helene?" Mom shot back, angrily.

You'd think someone had just hit the pause button on real life, because everyone's mouth dropped opened and stayed that way. Well, except for the terminate-for-a-cause guy. He was more baffled at our reaction than he was at Mom's use of a curse word. He didn't get it. You see, my mother never, ever cussed. She hated the use of foul language, so for her to come back with the h-word used in that way, was a real shocker. It surely got our attention.

"I'm so sorry," Mom said, her tone remorseful. "I never talk like that, but sometimes you can't control what comes out of your mouth when you're in shock." She looked around the room, going from one face to another. "If murder is what you have in mind, I'm leaving now." Billy started to say something, but she stopped him. "I'll go home, lock all my doors, and sleep with a gun, but I won't stand by and watch you commit murder. I'm sorry. I just can't do it." She looked at Jonathan. "I know I said I'd go along with whatever you had in mind, but that didn't include murder."

It was time for some damage control, and we all knew it.

"Minnie," Jonathan said as he walked over to her and put his arm around her shoulders ever so gently. "We're guys. We talk trash. It's just our way of getting through a mission. We're not going to kill anyone." He looked at Shark who immediately shook his head in agreement, and then he looked back at Mom. "We kill for God and Country, no one else."

Shark, the scariest looking one in the bunch, went over to Mom and spoke softly in his deep voice to her. "Don't let Jonathan fool you, Minnie. May I call you Minnie?" She shook her head submissively. "We're just pussycats." He slowly reached out and took her hand in his. "We're here to protect you. We know Gavin Preston is a killer. He's still out there and he's a threat to your family as long as he is. He tried to kill your daughter. Don't you want us to get him off the streets? We won't bump him off. I swear to God." He put his other hand to his heart as if he was making a promise to the man upstairs.

What a sight to see—Mom being consoled by the most unlikely person in the room—a big black guy whose body was made of steel and had a name that conjured up images of being ripped to shreds and then eaten alive. Shark… that should tell you something.

Jonathan's buddies weren't the kind who tried to appease a person; they used brute force instead. Yet, here was this guy, who could make you pee your pants just by looking at you, calming Mom's fears.

It was at that point I realized Shark was a man to be reckoned with. He could charm you and make you believe anything, but underneath that façade was a killing machine. But don't get me wrong. He's one of the good guys.

"I don't want anyone murdered," Mom said to Shark. "I want us to solve this case without killing anyone—unless it's in self-defense—and I want those criminals behind bars."

"Then let us do our job," Shark pleaded. "We'll be good boys, I promise. Don't let anyone fool you. We're tough, but we're not murderers. We're lean, mean, fighting machines." He gave Mom a sheepish, beaming grin, showing a mouth full of pearly whites.

"I've heard that one before," Mom snickered. "You're not so tough after all, are you, Mr. Shark? You guys were just pulling my leg. Shame on you! You scared me half to death."

"It's just Shark," he said to her. "But you can call me anything you want, Minnie."

"Shark is fine," she replied. "I like that name. Scary, but cool."

Her fear that we had all turned into murderous lunatics was now gone, thanks to the smooth-talking ways of a roughneck called Shark. He'd won her over.

Mom pointed her finger at Jonathan and admonished him. "Don't you ever play a trick like that on me again, Jonathan Blackhawk! I believed you!"

"All right," Billy said as he picked up the paperwork and slid it back into the folder. "Here's how it's going to play out."

We milled around him, waiting for instructions.

I knew that whatever he was about to say was going to be sugar-coated for Mom's benefit. She could play the role of private investigator, but she'd only go so far.

Billy looked at Jonathan and said, "The first thing we need to do is send someone over to pick up Eddie. I don't like the idea that he's laid up and by himself."

Jonathan motioned to Shark, knowing that Mom had warmed up to him, and said, "Is it okay if Shark takes you, Minnie?"

"I'm ready. Where's my purse?"

After Mom and her new buddy Shark left, we got down to the nitty-gritty.

"We're not turning any of this information over to the sheriff." Billy looked at me. "It proves we're not on hiatus, and there's the question of how we obtained it." He handed the file to Helene. "Would you mind putting this on my desk?"

Helene took the folder and replied, "Sure, but when I get back I'm going to fix breakfast. Y'all need to eat. Can't kill someone on an empty stomach." She walked away laughing at herself, proud of coming up with such a smart, timely remark.

"I'm starving," Jonathan said. "Gotta eat something before I go out and kill someone." Then he winked at me.

"As if it would hurt you to miss a meal," Helene wisecracked from down the hall, and then broke out in laughter. She yelled back, "I take that back. I need both my arms." After that one, she laughed so hard I thought she was going to choke.

We took a seat at the table and sat down with the idea that Billy would continue discussing his plan, but I had ideas of my own. I spoke up first.

"We know we're going after Gavin if the police don't have him locked up already. We'll torture him in some secluded bunker, and then we might just put him out of his misery if need be."

"We're not going to kill him, Jesse," Jonathan chuckled. "We'll dump him off naked and penniless in some third world country. He'll never get back to the states."

"That's a relief," I said. "I'm all for putting as much distance between us and him as possible. Dump him in Afghanistan for all I care. I would like to rough him up a little first. You know—payback."

"If this isn't a nice conversation to have at breakfast," Helene said while placing steaming cups of coffee in front of us. "Do I get to punch him a few times?"

"Wouldn't it be cheaper and quicker to just dump him off the top of a mountain?" I asked Jonathan.

Helene walked back to the kitchen. "Breakfast will be ready soon. Gotta feed these killers before I lose a limb."

Billy cracked up first, and the rest of us followed.

We had just finished breakfast when Athena and Thor barreled through the doggie door in the laundry room, barking and snarling. When they reached the table, they stopped, sniffed the air, and then went to the front door and sat down. Thor whimpered. Athena started howling like a wolf.

"I was wondering where you guys were, but now I wish you had stayed there. What's wrong with you two?" I had to yell to drown them out. "Stop it!"

They ignored me until the house phone rang. They stopped barking and sat staunch, their eyes glued to it.

"Thank you," I said to them as I got up to answer the call. "It's a little hard to talk above that racket." I picked up the portable phone and before I could say anything, I heard Mom's voice in the background, crying and screaming.

My heart skipped a beat. "Mom! Mom!" I cried out. Panic was strangling me. "Are you all right? Mom! Someone answer me!"

Finally, Shark spoke into the phone. "This is Shark, Jesse. Eddie's been attacked, but he's going to be okay. Your mom isn't taking it well. She's a little upset at the moment."

"I can tell. She keeps screaming something about killing someone. Is she talking about Gavin Preston? Has he been there? Did he beat up Eddie? That son-of-a…"

"I need to talk to Jonathan," Shark demanded. "Put him on the phone… please."

Mom kept screaming in the background, "Kill him! Kill him! Shark, you have to stop him! I want that man dead! Kill him!"

Shark tried to calm her down, but it wasn't working. She was outraged and out of control.

I knew exactly what had happened and what she wanted. She wanted Gavin Preston dead. Anger can change everything. Now she was the one who wanted revenge.

Chapter 7

Eddie had been watching TV, his leg propped up with a pillow, a glass of iced tea in his hand, when he heard someone at the back door. He figured it was Mom, so he didn't try to get up. When he finally turned around to look, the man was standing there with his hand raised. He cold-cocked Eddie up side the head, dragged him from the chair, and pinned him to the floor.

Eddie's in his late sixties, served his country for four years in the Army, and after that went on to serve citizens as a police officer. He retired several years ago and now spends his time serving my mother. At least that's what he tells people when they ask what he used to do for a living. He's not a large man. Age does that to a person. He's about five-eight and weighs around a hundred seventy pounds, almost the same as my mother, except she's a few inches shorter, weighing in at about one-fifty. Since neither one has size and strength going for them, they have to rely on their wits and the 9MM Billy had provided for each of them. Neither weapon was close by when Eddie was attacked.

The intruder knocked Eddie around, but didn't batter him as badly as he could have. He wanted this beating to be a lesson to the rest of us. He told Eddie to call off the dogs, or next time, he'd kill him and his busybody old lady. It happened so fast, the only thing Eddie could remember about the man was that he was big with awful breath and evil eyes.

Mom was angrier than I'd ever seen. She kept saying that if they had arrived twenty minutes sooner, they would've caught the man in the act. Instead, they got there just as Eddie was being loaded into the ambulance.

It seems the guy dialed 9-1-1 and then tossed the phone on the floor next to Eddie and said, "Better get help before you die of old age." Mighty nice of him.

Our crew congregated in the hospital waiting area, quietly discussing our next move. Shark and Mom were with Eddie, the kids were safe—that's the first call Billy made when we found out about Eddie's attack—and Gavin Preston was still out there, most likely planning how much more damage he could inflict upon us.

Jonathan's cell beeped and he excused himself, walked over to the nurse's station, and then returned with a woman wearing scrubs.

"You can use this room." She pointed to a door with the letter B on it. "I'll send in a grief counselor."

"That won't be necessary," Jonathan said, leading us into the room and then closing the door. He hit the speaker key on his cell and said, "Lu Ann has been doing some digging on Preston. Go ahead Lu Ann."

Everyone stood and listened.

"Here's what I have on Preston. He was physically abused as a child by his father, who happened to have the misfortune of falling on his chainsaw and decapitating himself when Preston was seventeen."

"Oh, my," Helene said. "That's awful."

"But well deserved if he beat his son," I added.

"Yes, it is," Lu Ann continued. "This incident is what we'd call a stressor—an event that sets someone off. But there's nothing in Preston's background that would indicate his father's death had any ill effects on him. He lived the straight and narrow for fifteen years, and then his mother killed herself. He cherished his mother, so if there ever was a stressor, this would be it. A couple of years after his mother's death, he went to work for Dakota."

"Such a tragic story."

"The one thing we know for sure is that two days ago he started smashing in faces. All we have to go on is Mae Bridges' accusations that Dakota killed her husband, or either got Preston to do it. Remember, this is a woman who said she wanted her husband dead, and then paid money after he was killed."

"But Mae wasn't serious," I said. "She was just playing along."

"Mighty dangerous game, don't you think?" Lu Ann said. "Who would do something so stupid? Would you?"

"No, I wouldn't."

"Maybe he's a latent serial killer," Helene added. "He could've had it in him all along and now it's coming to the surface."

"He's not a serial killer," Lu Ann replied. "If he were a serial killer there would have been signs of it in his past... trouble in school, torturing of small animals, fighting... juvenile stuff. There's nothing like that in Preston's past. If anything, he was a good kid."

"Then perhaps he's just a hit man for Dakota," Billy said. "You said his mother's death was a stressor. That could've gotten him started, made him susceptible to outside influences, especially when money's involved. What about his financial status?"

"According to his bank account, he deposits five hundred a week, and thanks to Gator's hacking ability, we now know Preston lives high on the hog. Has a fancy condo, wears designer clothes, and eats at all the best restaurants."

"Blood money," I retorted.

"No police record," Lu Ann continued. "Clean as a whistle, that is, until Sheriff Hudson locked him up on that disorderly charge."

"What about his health?" I asked. "His breath was awful. He must be sick or something. I've never smelled..."

"Ah, the bad breath," Lu Ann said. "Seems he has a stomach ulcer. His medical record says he's been seeing a doctor for the ulcer and diabetes. He's also had plenty of dental work—a couple root canals and crowns, lots of fillings. Since it seems he has had dental issues, maybe he had an abscessed tooth. That could account for his bad breath."

"Well, whatever his health problems are," I said, "his breath is rank. I mean it really stinks."

"Could be the ulcers," Lu Ann offered. "Perhaps Dakota makes him use mouthwash and eat breath mints before they have sex."

"Ah, they're lovers," I added. "That makes sense. She uses sex to get him to do what she wants."

"Sex… and the money," Lu Ann replied. "He came from a family who barely scraped by. Now look at him. He has it all—money, job, and sex with a beautiful woman."

"Who pays him to kill people," Helene added.

"Maybe," Lu Ann remarked. "Gator's been digging into her background, but he isn't having much luck, just like y'all. There seems to be nothing on her life before she moved to Charlottesville. We need a fingerprint or a DNA sample."

"That shouldn't be too hard," Shark said. "We can search her house."

"She lives at The Body Shop," Lu Ann said. "So does Olivia Swales. Can't dig up anything on Olivia either. Stolen social security numbers is all we have on them. They've gone to great lengths to cover their tracks. Even a DNA sample and a fingerprint might not do us any good, but it wouldn't hurt to try." Lu Ann paused and then said, "If Preston is Dakota's hit man, why didn't he kill Jesse and Eddie? He had the chance. Hit men don't play around. They don't warn their victims by making threats. They kill and then get out."

"Maybe she just wanted to scare us really bad," I said.

"Here's something else. Y'all think Preston killed Mae Bridges, but the nurse at the hospital told the police that a nurse had gone in Mae's room just before she saw the man leaving. She didn't recognize the nurse.

That nurse could've been Dakota Stone in disguise. Perhaps, the only thing Preston is guilty of is being stupid."

"Lu Ann, I'm confused," Helene said. "Is he a hit man, serial killer, or just a guy who got involved with the wrong woman? We need to know, and your answers aren't pinpointing it down for us. What kind of profile is this?"

"I'm just telling you what I've come up with on Preston. It's not like you see on TV, Helene. Profilers base their profile on facts and information they piece together, along with some gut instinct. But here, all we have is a man with a clean background until he got locked up and then beat up a couple of people, and two women with no background."

"What is your gut telling you?" Helene asked. "Because I'd sure like to know."

"What we can be sure of is that Preston viciously attacked Jesse and Eddie, and that proves he's a bad, dangerous man."

"Our guys will put him in the dirt," I said.

"We can handle that," Jonathan said. He looked over at Billy. "Just say the word."

"Whatever you plan to do," Lu Ann warned, "do it fast, before Preston's assaults escalate into something worse. He could be coming unhinged."

"So, he's not a killer yet, he just likes to beat up people. Is that what you're saying?"

"I think Dakota killed those men, he knows about it, and maybe he likes it. Most likely, it's some kind of release for him."

"Dakota?" I said, having my doubts. "She's too prim and proper…"

"Anyone can pull off a murder in a crowd," Lu Ann interrupted. "A gunshot goes off and people scatter. The only one left is the dead person, and no one saw a thing."

"What about cameras?" Helene asked. "They're everywhere nowadays."

"There're always blind spots," Lu Ann replied.

A knock at the door startled us.

"Gotta hang up," Jonathan said. "I'll call you back."

Billy opened the door and Mom and Shark walked in.

"I came out and y'all were gone," she said. "You scared me. I thought you had left us here by ourselves."

"How's Eddie?" I asked. "Is he going to be all right?"

"Preston went easy on him. It could've been much worse. His face is busted up and he has bruises on his body, but no broken bones, no internal damage."

"So now he looks like me," I said, jokingly. Then a thought hit me. "Is he alone?"

"Just for a minute…"

Jonathan looked at Shark and said, "Go!"

Mom let go of Shark's shirt and he quickly took off.

"Can Eddie leave the hospital?" Billy asked, looking at Mom. "We need to get out of here."

"Yes, as soon as they finish the paperwork."

"Let's go get him out of here!" Jonathan demanded.

Mom had a strange look on her face, but didn't hesitate to move when Billy grabbed her hand.

"Y'all are really scaring me now," she said. "Is my Eddie still in danger?"

"We all are, Mom. We need to get to safety and stay there until the guys can find Preston."

We briskly walked the corridor in a tight little group, until we reached Eddie. Shark had already gotten Eddie into a wheelchair and was heading toward us.

"Where are you taking him?" a nurse asked. "He can't leave without the doctor's…"

Dr. Bryant walked up just in time. "It's okay, Miss Fowler. I'll handle this."

"Sorry, Doc," Billy said. "But we have to leave right now."

"Someone in danger again?"

He didn't wait for an answer. If trouble was close by, he wanted us out of his emergency room.

"Go ahead and leave," he replied. "I'll handle the paperwork." He looked over at Eddie. "Aspirin ought to help out with the pain, but if not, get this filled." He handed the prescription slip to Mom and was about to say something else, but Shark escorted her and Eddie out before the doctor had a chance.

"Slow down, Shark. He's in a lot of pain," Mom demanded. She looked at him as he pushed the wheelchair a little too fast for her liking. "He could get hurt worse than he already is."

We didn't bother to wait for the SUVs to be brought around. We high-tailed it out into the parking lot. Shark, the behemoth, guarded our backs, while Billy and Jonathan carried Eddie. We were in a mad rush, making a fast dash to the cars. No one slowed down.

We were scrambling to get in the SUVs when a gunshot went off, dropping Shark to his knees.

"I'm all right!" Shark yelled. "Got me in the leg."

Billy and Jonathan grabbed him under his armpits, dragged him into the SUV, and after I jumped in, Jonathan slammed the door. I drove while Billy tended to Shark's leg wound. Eddie, Mom, Helene, and Jonathan followed us in the other vehicle.

Two black SUVs hauling butt down Rt. 29 gets everyone's attention. They must've thought we had the President of the United States in one of them, because they all got out of our way.

The shooter didn't pursue us. Gavin Preston had failed to kill his target again. What ever would Dakota say? I was still under the assumption that Preston was a hit man, but after listening to Lu Ann, I didn't know what to think anymore. Could Dakota Stone possibly be the killer?

I figured we'd head home and plan our strategy for capturing Gavin Preston, and then beating the truth out of him, but when we entered the Blackhawk Compound, Billy told me to turn into Jonathan's driveway.

"We can't go to Jonathan's house!" I said, looking back at him. "Our kids are there. What if Preston's following us?"

"We need to talk," Billy said, seriously. "There's something I've been meaning to tell you."

"And you're picking now to tell me? Right in the middle of outrunning bullets?"

This didn't sound good. Billy's tone meant only one thing—someone else had died—or so I thought.

"There's a bunker under Jonathan's hangar, and the Blackhawk property is now protected by laser beam security system."

"That's all?" I asked, relieved. "I thought you were going to tell me someone else had been murdered." It took a few seconds for Billy's confession to sink in. "I get the thing about the bunker. I suspected that all along." I glanced in the back seat at Billy again. "What I don't understand is the alien beam from outer space thingy. How does that work?" I couldn't help but laugh. "Do we have little green men in spaceships patrolling the compound?"

After what just happened, I wasn't thinking straight. If I had been, I would've known what Billy was talking about. Instead, I acted like an idiot, spouting off about spaceships and little green men. What a putz.

"I'm sorry, Billy. I'm not myself. People getting killed does that to me. When did you put in the system, and why didn't you tell me?"

"Months ago," Billy replied. "I didn't say anything because I didn't want to alarm everyone. After the bunker and hangar were complete, it was the next logical thing to do."

"How far does the beam go? All around the property?"

"Let's just say that we're covered."

"We're all safe in our tight little circle. Now we really can call this place a compound. It's a fortress. Where's the main location for the security system? In the bunker! Of course! That's the perfect place. I can't wait to see it!"

"You're not mad that I didn't tell you?"

"I didn't say that."

I drove down the hill behind the hangar as Billy instructed, and pulled up close to what appeared to be garage doors leading to a basement under the hangar. The doors automatically opened, and we filed in. The doors closed with a loud clank. I felt like I was in a James Bond movie. I'd seen bunkers like this before on TV, but had never been in a real one. It was amazing.

I stepped out of the Hummer and looked around. I expected the bunker to be a mass of cinderblocks, concrete and steel, drab in color and cold, but it wasn't. The garage floor was concrete like any other garage floor, but the walls had been finished off and painted a warm cream color, with dark stained baseboard trim that matched the interior doors. Once we went through the door on the left, the décor was also pleasing as if we were entering someone's house, not just a bunker. The walls were painted the same cream color as the garage and had the same trim. The only things missing were pictures hanging on the walls. I was going to ask Jonathan what he needed with a house when he had this place, but he was busy taking Shark somewhere. My guess was that he had a medical room down here. Everyone followed him. Billy was helping Eddie hobble along with Mom holding onto his shirt.

I seriously thought about calling Lila to get a Xanax for Mom, but I didn't want to drag her into our mess. Mom was scared and her husband had been brutalized. She could use a tranquilizer right about now. I pulled Helene over to the side and asked, "Got any drugs in that purse?"

"Just some aspirin," she replied. "Why?"

"Mom needs to be tranquilized. She's a wreck. Look at her. I've never seen her like this."

"On the ride over here Minnie said something to Jonathan about getting Eddie's prescription filled, but he told her not to worry because he had something for his pain at his Reboot Center, so maybe he has something for her."

"Reboot Center?"

"Seems he has a trauma room down here. They call it a Reboot Center because that's where they go to get fixed up and reboot. Kind of like a computer. Patch up and go back to work. Yeah, it seems Jonathan has everything you need right here to survive a nuclear attack."

"Hope he isn't expecting one."

"No," Helene replied. "He expects a collapse in the economy. What do you think he means by that, Jesse?"

"I don't want to think about it." And I didn't, so I brushed that thought aside. I had enough to worry about.

The second door on the left was the Reboot Center, it said so on a brass plate, and as we entered, I could see why Jonathan had named it that. The room was equipped with everything you'd see at an emergency room. It even had an x-ray machine overhead.

"Wow!" I said, impressed. "Who needs a hospital when you have this? All you need now is a doctor."

"That would be me," Jonathan said as he helped Shark up on the table.

Billy led Mom to a seat off to the side. "Sit here, Minnie. I need to help Jonathan."

Mom complied. The rest of us stood out of the way and watched as Jonathan and Billy helped Shark. Billy grabbed a pair of scissors and started cutting Shark's pants while Jonathan went to a cabinet and unlocked it. He grabbed a bottle of pills, walked over to Eddie, and offered him one for his pain.

"I'm okay," Eddie said, declining his offer. He looked at Mom. "Got anything for her in that cabinet? She's very distraught."

"I'm fine!" Mom said. "I don't need anything."

"Yes, she does," I agreed. "Unless you want her to flip out. Look at her hands. They're shaking like a leaf on a windy day."

Jonathan walked back to the cabinet and then returned with a different bottle. "They're very mild," he said to Mom. "I promise you won't get addicted. Just take one, okay?"

"If you say so." Mom took the pill and washed it down with the glass of water I'd fetched for her. "But if I start acting crazy, I don't want to hear a word about it."

Once Shark's pants had been cut, exposing the gunshot wound, Jonathan said, "Anyone with a weak stomach might want to leave now."

Blood was running from an open gash in Shark's leg. That was enough for me. I walked to the door and started to leave the room.

"Perhaps we all should leave," I said. "We'll go see the kids."

"Eddie can't walk and I'm not leaving him," Mom said.

"I'll be fine, Minnie," Eddie said. "I'll sit right here. Go with Jesse."

"Take a left," Jonathan said. "The hallway leads to the house basement."

I grabbed the doorknob and opened it at the same time the door across from us opened, and a man walked out.

The man didn't look like he belonged in Jonathan's group of butt-kicking, cutthroat, body smashing guys. Instead, he looked more like someone who manned the security system or ran errands. He was five-eight, weighed about one-sixty, and his muscles didn't bulge. And, he was Mexican. How destructive could he be considering his size? Another guy walked out behind him. He, too, was Mexican, same size, same dark, curly hair and dark skin. The only difference between the two that I could see was that one wore small, round glasses. Neither one looked like they could hurt a fly, but I've learned that looks can be deceiving. Perhaps, that was the case here.

Both men were speaking rapidly in Spanish, arms flailing, eyes bulging. I wasn't sure about anyone else, but I couldn't understand a word they were saying. However, the look on their faces was undeniable. Something urgent needed attention.

Jonathan stepped into the hallway. "Speak English," he said, and then went on to quickly introduce them to us. "Meet Gator and Mason. They monitor everything that goes on, but don't let their size fool you." Jonathan looked directly at me. "I know what you're thinking, but you're wrong. They're just as tough as the rest of us. They're fast and can snap a neck with the best of them."

"I didn't say anything."

"We've been monitoring Gavin Preston's cell phone location by GPS," Mason the guy with the glasses said. "He just pulled onto Bear Mountain Road."

"Intercept him," Jonathan commanded, motioning to Mason and Gator. "Bring him here."

Both men turned and took off down the hall to the garage.

Jonathan spun around to Billy and said, "Get them out of here. Take them to the house until I tell you everything is secure." He looked over at Eddie. "He can stay with us."

Billy rushed us down the hall as fast as he could. Mom didn't want to leave Eddie behind, but Billy assured her he would be in good hands.

"I want to be here when they catch Gavin Preston. I want to give him a piece of my mind," Mom said to Billy.

"You'll get your chance, but for now, we've got to get out of here, Minnie, so please move a little faster."

"The kids," I whispered to Billy as we climbed the basement steps to the house. "I hope they don't freak out when they see me. The last time I came home with a black eye, Maisy cried and Ethan looked at me funny."

"They know pain when they see it," Billy said. "You can't shield them from life, `ge ya. They can deal with a few bruises as long as they know you're still here. I have talked to both of them. They just want to see their mommy."

What a good man.

Twenty minutes later, Billy got a call on his cell phone. Mason the Mexican with glasses was on his way over to the house to guard Lu Ann and the kids while Gator, Jonathan, and a patched up Shark had Preston under control in the bunker. That's what Billy said when he got off the cell phone.

"Let's go!" Mom demanded, and was the first one to head to the door. "I have a few things to say to that man!"

"Wait a min…" Billy started to say, but was interrupted.

"Don't tell me to wait, Billy Blackhawk. You said I would get a chance to speak my peace, and I'm going to!"

"Mom, please don't go," I begged. "Let the guys handle him."

"I'm not going to do anything stupid. I just want to see the man who has caused us so much pain."

Helene got up and started to follow.

"Where do you think you're going?" Billy asked, defiantly.

"Hey, today I heard Minnie cuss for the first time ever. There's no way I'm going to miss this."

"Okay," Billy said, looking frustrated. "But everyone stays behind me. Am I clear?"

"Gotcha," Mom agreed. "You're the man. You lead the way."

"You don't have to worry about me," Helene said. "I don't want to get near that guy. I just want to hear Minnie cuss him out."

"I'm not going to cuss…"

"Come on," Billy interrupted. "If y'all are coming, let's go."

The four of us made our way down to the stairs and hallway to a different room.

"Here," Billy pointed. "They're in here."

The door clicked, and he opened it making sure the rest of us stayed behind him as he entered.

The room was completely empty, except for the chair Gavin Preston was sitting in. He was bound at the feet and his hands were tied behind his back. He had been beaten and looked pretty bad. Blood ran from his face. His head hung down in defeat. Jonathan and Shark stood on either side of him.

"How does it feel?" I asked, hatefully. "Not so good, huh?"

All of a sudden, Mom stepped out in front of us, pulled a small handgun from her purse, and then shot Gavin Preston in the foot.

"The Bible says an eye for an eye. That's for hurting Jesse and Eddie."

Gavin Preston screamed from the pain, and Mom had gotten her revenge.

Sometimes, you can only push a person so far, even a good-hearted one like my mother.

Chapter 8

MOM STUCK HER LITTLE HANDGUN back in her purse, slipped the straps of the purse back over her forearm and crossed her arms as if nothing had happened.

"What?" she asked, looking around the room. "He got exactly what he deserved."

I was dumbfounded, as was everyone else. My sweet, God-loving, Southern Baptist mother had turned into one of us. I guess a person can only handle but so much until they cross over to the other side.

"Hand it over, Minnie," Billy demanded, "before you shoot someone else."

"I can't believe you just shot the guy," Helene gushed. "You got more guts than ..."

I grabbed the purse from her, pulled out the gun and handed it to Billy. "Mom, have you lost your mind? Where'd you get this gun?"

"Your dad bought it for me when we moved here. It's only a twenty-two. It's a bee sting compared to the monsters you guys carry. Besides, I didn't want to kill him... just cause him pain like he caused you and Eddie. It's not as if I shot him with that big gun Billy gave me."

"Trust me, Mom. He's in pain. Look at him."

Out of the blue, Helene ran over and stomped the foot Mom had just shot, and then quickly backed away.

Gavin Preston squealed in agony and tried to lurch at her, but couldn't. All he managed to do was turn over the chair.

In one swift movement, Jonathan snatched him upright, drew back, and slapped him across the face. He then turned and said, "Maybe we should let the women have a go at him. We're not getting anywhere."

Mom stepped forward, but Jonathan held up his hand.

"I was just kidding, Minnie. Stay back. He looks like he's harmless in this condition, but he's not. If he got loose, he'd rip your guts out."

"Let him try. I got some pepper spray in my purse. I'll squirt his eyes out." She looked at me. "Give me back my purse, Jesse."

"What has gotten into you?" I asked, surprised at her behavior. "You're starting to act like… me."

Mom had never been violent to anyone in her whole life, so her actions were a shocker.

I dug around in her purse until I found the pepper spray, and then searched for more weapons. After the gun incident, it would not have surprised me to have found a knife hidden amongst her possessions. Finding nothing else, I removed the pepper spray, and handed the purse back to her.

She innocently took the purse, and before anyone had a chance to stop her, she lunged at Preston and smacked him across the face with it.

"Geez, Minnie," Shark said as he grabbed her and tried to pull her away from Preston. "Enough! I think you got your payback, don't you?"

Gavin spit blood at Mom and some landed on her arm.

"Aids!" she screamed. "I've got aids now!"

She leered at Gavin and said, "You'll pay for this young man. If I get aids, you're going to burn in Hell. God is going to get you for what you've done to people. You killed Mae!"

"I haven't killed anyone!" Gavin fired back. "You people are crazy!"

Mom wasn't herself. She was defiant and ready to do battle. She tussled with Shark, trying to free herself.

"Let me go, Shark! This man needs to be taught a lesson, and I'm the one who can do it. I'll show him what it's like to be on the receiving end of the stick."

"What stick?" Helene asked. "You don't have a stick, Minnie."

"This is like something out of a bad movie," I said, shaking my head. I looked at Shark. "Would you please escort Mom and Helene out of here before they get us all killed?"

Before leaving, Mom looked back at Gavin and said, "Go brush your teeth and gargle with some Lysol. Your breath smells worse than donkey do-do."

She laughed and then was led out of the room.

Once Mom and Helene were gone, we all looked at each other and smiled… well, except for Gavin Preston. He was in too much pain. Between Mom, Helene, and the guys, he'd been worked over. He moaned and groaned like a wounded animal.

"Wow, Jesse," Jonathan said. "Your mom has gone off her rocker. I've never seen her like this. Normally, she's so nice and quiet. What happened? I think I like her better this way. She's got spunk. She kinda reminds me of you."

"She's a spitfire all right," Billy added. "She sure surprised me. Maybe we should let her interrogate Mr. Preston."

He looked in Preston's direction.

"I bet she could do things to him that he's never had done before." He sneered at the man. "It's the quiet ones who are the most dangerous." Billy laughed. "Yep, we need to turn her loose on him."

"Phew!" I said, looking at Preston. "What's that smell? You need a bath, and that breath almost makes me gag."

The door clinked again and Shark walked back in.

"I left your mother and Helene with Gator. He'll keep them busy with all those monitors. They can see everything that's going on, and maybe at the same time he can talk them down. They're both wound up and I didn't think they needed to be around the kids." He looked at Jonathan. "What did you give her, man? That pill has made her crazy. Did you give one to Helene, too?"

"Oh, my God!" I said. "I forgot about the tranquilizer. What did you give her?"

"Tramadol," Jonathan replied. "It's a pain killer. Tranks make you feel hung over the next day, but a pain killer usually doesn't, so I gave her the pain killer. I didn't know it would affect her like that."

"Maybe you should leave the dispensing of medication to someone else," I joked, and then commented. "Mom obviously shouldn't take drugs. You see what they do to her."

"I think she did pretty good," Shark said, looking over at Preston's foot. "I like your mother."

"She can't see what's happening here, can she?" I asked. "I mean, if you guys plan to…"

"No, she can't," Jonathan replied. "So don't worry. Even if they want to see, they won't be able to. Besides," he pointed to Preston, "we got everything from him we could. He's sticking to his story. He says he didn't kill anyone, and get this, he said Dakota poisoned him."

"What?" I questioned, looking back at Preston. "He doesn't look dead to me. Guess the poison didn't work."

But actually, Preston didn't look too good. Underneath the bloody face, his skin had grown ashen, he drooled, and his head bobbed. Blood pooled around the foot that Mom had shot. He looked like he was just about done in. His moaning and groaning had slowed down and was now barely a whisper.

"Why would she poison him?" Billy asked. "They were lovers."

"They were," Shark said, "but that flame started to flicker quickly after Dakota asked him to kill Jesse and Minnie. He claims he was floored by her request, but he loved her, so he agreed to do it. He had a bad feeling, but he went along because he needed time to think."

"Time to think about what?" I asked.

"What he was going to do next. He said that after she asked him to kill you and your mother, it didn't take him but a minute to wonder if there was any truth to Mae Bridges' accusation. He now had his doubts about the woman he loved. Then, when he set out to kill you and Minnie, he just couldn't do it."

"I'm sure glad to hear that."

"He doesn't seem to have a problem with assaulting people, but when it comes to murder, he draws the line. He doesn't have the stomach for it. And he swears he didn't kill anybody's husband for Dakota."

"Wait a minute. He was going to kill my mother?"

"That's right."

"And Eddie? What about him?"

"A little icing on the cake," Jonathan interjected. "Eddie was in the wrong place at the wrong time. He got what your mother would've gotten if she'd been home."

He looked at Preston.

"What kind of man beats up on a little old lady? How sick is that?"

"What about me?"

Jonathan grinned, ignored my question and said, "I have to give him credit for one thing—he had a lot of nerve to think he could kill someone in jail and get away with it—stupid, but nervy. I don't think he'd make a good killer. His technique sucks."

"When he failed to kill his second target," Shark said, "Dakota was furious and called him incompetent and useless. That's when she told him she had poisoned him with antifreeze."

"She's one crazy woman."

"She told him she had made up a special bottle, and then set the bottle down in front of him to drink, which he did. She said she knew she had chosen the wrong man when he started asking questions about stuff that was none of his business, and when he botched killing Jesse and

Minnie, that was it. He had failed her, and now his time was up. She laughed at him as he walked out of the shop."

"I bet that really ticked him off."

"He panicked and came here to warn us. He now thinks she killed those men. He sure didn't do it. When I asked him why he took a shot at us in the hospital parking lot, he denied it. He was too sick by then. He could barely make it here. It had to be her. Dakota Stone is the killer."

We all turned back to look at Gavin Preston.

"Antifreeze?" I questioned. "Are you serious? How… I mean, wouldn't he be able to tell?"

"Antifreeze has a sweet smell and taste," Billy said. "Put some in a soda or a glass of wine and nobody would be the wiser."

"Is he dead?" I asked, nervously, noticing that Preston was sitting completely still with his head hung down off to the side, the crotch of his pants was wet all the way down his legs, and there was a poopy smell coming from his direction.

Everyone knows that when a person dies, the bladder and bowels are the first to let go.

After a moment of silence, Jonathan spoke, "He's dead."

"He was almost dead from the poison when he was captured," Shark added. "A man who is about ready to die usually tells the truth. He had nothing to hide anymore. He probably knew more, but didn't get around to telling us."

"What a mess," I said, turning away from him. "What are we going to do with his body?"

I turned and stared back at him.

His face was smeared with blood, gook seeped from his body, and the odor coming from him was worse than anything I'd ever smelled. He was a testament to the fact that death wasn't pretty—especially the kind of death he had experienced. He had been poisoned and then beaten up. Those were his last moments of life.

The thought of it made me sick. I was sure I was going to puke, but

I didn't. I managed to put that awful image of him out of my mind and move on.

"That's a good question," Billy said, pondering for a minute, and then he came back with, "He has no family, so I say we bury him somewhere. It would be the right thing to do."

A thought occurred to me, and a plan began formulating in my head.

"Why don't we take him to The Body Shop and leave him with Dakota? Let her explain his death. We can sneak in after dark, disable the alarm, dump the body, and then get out." I looked at Jonathan. "Are you the security alarm buster expert, too? You do everything else."

"Shark's our man," Jonathan said looking over at Shark. "But he's doped up. Shot him full of antibiotics and pain killers, and he needs to take a break."

"No way, man," Shark said. "I'm good to go. It was only a flesh wound. Nothing keeps me down for long."

"Actually, we don't need to do that," Jonathan said. "We have our computer geeks, Mason and Gator. They should be able to handle the alarm system from here. What was I thinking?"

"Do you think they can pull it off?" I asked. "I don't want to get caught again. Jail isn't my thing. I'm not going back."

I looked back over at Gavin and thought about Mom.

"Lord. What are we going to tell my mother? She'll never forgive herself for shooting him in the foot now that he's dead. She'll hate herself for what she did."

"Don't worry, `ge ya," Billy replied. "We'll tell her the truth. Dakota poisoned him and he died. We didn't kill him."

"We'd better do something fast. He's starting to get ripe. Hey, what about the bullet in his foot? I don't want it traced back to Mom when they find him."

"I'll take care of that," Shark said, looking around. "We need to wrap him in plastic before we dump him. We don't want any DNA left in the car. We'd get busted for sure. DNA sends people to prison."

"Speaking of car," I said. "What about his? What are we going to do with his car?"

"You let us worry about that," Jonathan replied, motioning to Shark, who then turned and walked out of the room.

"Wait a minute," I came back with. "His car should be parked at The Body Shop. You can't leave it in a parking lot somewhere, or abandoned on the road. When they find his body, the first thing they'll look for is his car, won't they?"

"His car doesn't matter. It's registered to the business. Anyone could be driving it. Trust me, they'll never find it. When we dispose of something, nobody ever finds it, whether it's a car or a body. It just so happens that we want Preston's body found, otherwise…" Jonathan's voice trailed off.

"Sometimes it scares me to think we're related, even if it's only by marriage," I said. "I hope you never get mad at me."

"Silly girl," Jonathan said. "I don't hurt women."

"I know this probably won't happen," I said, "but what if we get caught dumping his body?"

"We're not going to get caught."

"But just say we do. When the police question us, what are we going to tell them? That he walked to your house? How can we get the cops to believe our story, if we don't have the car?"

Billy looked at Jonathan. "She does have a point,"

"Our mission is to succeed, but…" Jonathan thought for a second, and then smiled. "Good girl, Jesse. I'm glad you brought up the subject of the car. We'll park it in Beth's garage. She won't mind, since she doesn't live there anyway."

"She'll never have to know."

"And if we need to produce the car as evidence, we'll be able to, and if not, we'll dispose of it later. Smart thinking, Jesse."

"Now that the problem with the car has been settled," Billy said, looking at me. "Let's go tell your mother about Preston."

Billy and I walked out of the room and went across the hall to the security center where Mom and Helene sat glued to the computers. They both rose when we walked in.

"Did you get the truth out of him?" Mom asked. "Or did he tell you more of his lies? He's a dirty, rotten…"

"He's dead, Mom."

"What?"

"I said he's dead, Mom."

Mom had a bewildered look on her face.

"How… what…"

She stopped for a second and then glared at us.

"Y'all didn't beat him to death, did you? Oh, my God! What have we done? We killed him, and I was the one who shot him in the foot."

"Of course we didn't kill him, Minnie," Billy said. "He was almost dead when he got here. Dakota poisoned him just like he said. Jonathan and Shark worked him over until they realized he was telling the truth about being poisoned. That's when they stopped and tried to get as much out of him as they could."

Helene made a good point when she asked, "If he was about ready to die and didn't have much time left, then why didn't he just call you? It surely would've saved time… since he didn't have much left."

"That's a good question," Billy said, "one I can't answer, but it's irrelevant now. What we have to do is get rid of the body and lay the blame at Dakota Stone's feet."

Mom didn't look so good. She was pale and seemed disoriented.

"Mom, are you all right?"

"I just need to sit down. I feel so bad about shooting the poor guy in the foot when he was so close to death."

"Don't feel too bad for the guy," I said. "Look at my face and remember what he did to me. Look at Eddie. Gavin Preston beat the crap out of him, too."

"I know, but..."

"He was going to kill you, too, Mom, so stop feeling sorry for the guy. I sure don't."

"Me? Why was he going to kill me?"

"Because he had a psychotic girlfriend who doesn't like your style in clothes," Helene said with a grin. "Oh, who knows, Minnie. The woman's nuts. We're after her, so she's going to do whatever it takes to survive, even if it means killing all of us."

Mom was deep in thought.

"Look, if it makes you feel any better, Minnie," Helene said, "I don't feel a bit sorry for the guy. He hurt Jesse and Eddie, and who knows what he would've done next? He just had the misfortune of getting poisoned. Dakota killed him, not us."

Billy put his arm around Mom and led her back over to the computer chair. "Sit down, Minnie," he said.

Gator got up from the computer screen and walked over to a water cooler to fetch a glass of water. He handed it to her when she sat down.

"Here, drink this, Minnie," he said. "It'll refresh you. I find that a drink makes me feel so much better after I've shot someone."

He chuckled, and after a gulp, so did Mom.

"You're such a comedian," she said to him, and then looked back at us. "He's so funny. He's been cracking us up with all his stories. Did you know that he used to be a sumo wrestler?"

I glanced at Gator, who was snickering, and then back to Mom.

"You don't believe that, do you, Mom? Look at him. He weighs less than I do. Sumo wrestlers are huge. Is he huge?"

"Well…"

Gator laughed out loud.

"I guess not," Mom murmured. "He sure fooled me."

"He didn't fool me," Helene boasted. "I knew he was making up all that stuff. No one escapes death that many times. He's a jokester."

"Some of my stories were true," Gator said, defending himself.

"Which ones?"

Billy interrupted their chitchat. "We have things to do, so I want everyone to stay here until we're finished."

"But Gavin Preston is dead," Mom said. "We're safe now. He's not going to hurt us anymore, so it's time to get back on the case and bring down Dakota."

"Yeah... well... he's never been the real problem," Billy explained. "Oh, he was ruthless when it came to cracking skulls, but he wasn't a killer. No, that title belongs to Dakota Stone, and it's time she got her due. We're going after her, and we're going to get her."

"She killed those men, didn't she?" Helene asked.

"It sure looks that way," Billy replied. "And I'm betting she was the one who killed Mae. She dressed up like a nurse, went in and bumped her off, and then went her merry way. No one thinks anything about a nurse going into a patient's room. It was a perfect disguise."

"But Preston was at the hospital when Mae was murdered," I said. "We saw his face in the photo."

"Maybe he was Dakota's lookout," Helene suggested. "Yeah, he kept watch while Dakota killed Mae. It all makes sense now. Cunning woman."

"She just didn't plan on us being so smart," Mom added. Out of the blue, Mom looked up at me and said, "It's time to tell Billy about the shampoo. Maybe there really was something wrong with it. If Dakota is capable of murder, putting poison in a bottle of shampoo ought to be right up her alley."

I was hoping Mom would forget about the bottle of shampoo and her idea that it was tainted, but I was wrong. She had opened the flood gates and it was now time to come clean.

I looked up at Billy and said, "Mom thinks Dakota put poison in your mother's bottle of shampoo. I tried to tell her there was nothing wrong with the shampoo except the smell, but she's convinced otherwise. I was going to get it tested, but I forgot about it, what with my being in jail and all."

"You saw how Dakota reacted when you doused her with it," Mom said, defiantly. “She knew there was something wrong with it, because she was the one who put the poison in it. It was probably the kind of poison that’s absorbed through the skin. Yeah, that’s how it worked.”

“It wasn’t poisoned,” Billy said.

Surprised, I asked him how he knew about the shampoo.

“I’m an Indian,” Billy said. “I have excellent hearing. I heard you talking about it when you thought I wasn’t listening, and after your little fiasco with Dakota went down and you were thrown in jail, I went through your purse and took the bottle.”

“Oh, yeah... the bottle of shampoo. I forgot about it. I’m glad I didn’t toss it in the trash.”

“I gave it to my friend at the lab and she checked it out. She sent me a text a couple of hours ago and said it was clean. She explained that sometimes, because of equipment malfunction at the factory, the mixture isn’t just right and can cause the odor you smelled, especially if it’s dandruff shampoo… which is what Mom’s was.”

“Why didn’t you say something?”

“Why didn’t you?”

Hmm. Snared like a rabbit in a trap. What could I say?

I should’ve confided in Billy from the start, but I was afraid he’d go off if it turned out to be true. The Blackhawk boys would’ve taken matters into their hands and busted into Dakota’s shop, killing the evil witch on sight. They take care of their own. Kill one of them and you might as well have killed the President. They’d come after you with a vengeance, and wouldn’t stop until they got justice. I would’ve done the same thing. If someone killed my mother, they might as well have killed me, because I’d put their lights out and take great pleasure in doing so. I would… I was getting riled just thinking about it.

“Well, I sure am glad it wasn’t poisoned,” Mom said, interrupting my thoughts and bringing me back from that eerie place. “I’d hate to think she was poisoned. What a waste. Life is too short as it is.”

Relief washed over Mom’s face. She had obviously been visiting the same place I had—that place in the back of your mind where you never want to go because the Devil and all his disciples live there. They taunt you, trick you, and make you do things you don't want to do. However, the bad side of a person also dwells there—the side that can be so easily led astray. Yep, it's a mighty scary place. I go there often and not because I want to.

Jonathan walked in, closed the door, and said, "It's time to go."

He looked over at Mom.

"How's that pill working for you, Minnie?"

"What do you mean by that?"

"Ah… nothing. I was just wondering if you were okay. You had a bit of a tantrum earlier, and I thought you might be having side effects from the drug. That's all I was saying."

Mom rose from the chair and walked up to Jonathan.

"I have all my wits if that's what you're asking. I'm sane enough to know what's going on here, and I'm willing to help. You want me to drive, or hand you the ammo? I'm quite capable of doing both. I can even shoot Dakota if I have to. I can't watch if you're going to skin her alive, but I can hand you the knife."

"I don't think that will be necessary, Minnie," Billy interjected with a smile. "We'll handle everything from here on out. You just stay put and help Gator."

Billy looked over at Gator, and then back to Mom.

"We need all the eyes we can get."

Billy glanced at Helene for a second to let her know she was to stay as well.

"Mason's watching out for Lu Ann and the kids, and Eddie's resting in the trauma room. Right, Jonathan?" He looked over at Jonathan for assurance.

"Yeah," Jonathan agreed. "Eddie's resting."

"Is he alone?" Mom asked, looking at Jonathan. "What if…"

"He's safe, Minnie," Jonathan replied. "Nobody's getting in here.

You can go stay with him if you want to, but I can assure you he's all right. He's probably asleep by now."

"Did you give him one of those pills, too?"

"Yes, I did."

"I'm going to sit with my husband if anybody wants me." She glanced over at me. "Are you going with them?"

I didn't say anything, afraid of the lecture that was sure to follow, but instead of a sermon, Mom simply said, "Well, you'd better wear some of that black paint on your face, or you're going to stick out like a sore thumb."

We decided to wait until it got dark before venturing out on what was sure to be a very tricky mission. All kinds of things could go wrong when trying to dump a body, and if we got caught, we'd spend the rest of our lives in prison. But I knew that wasn't going to happen. These guys were pros. They'd done stuff like this before. For them, this was a cake walk.

After a quick meal, Billy and I were taken to the suit-up room where we could choose the proper attire for the night. The place was stocked with T-shirts, pants, boots, jackets, and socks—all in black. Everything was black, right down to the belts.

Once we had suited-up, it was time to gear-up. That's what Shark said when he led us to another room down the hall. The door made the same clicking noise as the rest, but instead of opening up, Shark had to slide a keycard over a dot on the wall. The door opened and he waved us in as if he were showing off his prized mare.

"Pick your weapon of choice."

A gun enthusiast would be in hog Heaven in a room like this. We had just stepped into an armory. Every weapon you could possibly imagine was stocked here, and not just one or two of each either. There were dozens of guns I'd never even seen before. It was a paradise of firearms.

"I want one of each," I said as I turned around to look back at Shark. When I did, I froze. There on the wall behind him was the gun of my dreams. "I want that one! I've always wanted to fire one of those."

Shark smiled and declared, "We have one in the Hummer already. We never leave home without it. Can you handle one of those?"

"Never had the chance."

He looked at Billy for approval, and then after a brief moment he looked back at me and said, "If we need it tonight, you're our man. But don't get your hopes up. That baby is our last resort and we only use it when all else fails."

I was beside myself. I'd never had the opportunity to even get close to a rocket launcher, let alone fire one. What if I couldn't do it? What if I shot it in the wrong direction and killed one of us, or all of us? I had a lot of what ifs, but I wasn't going to let that stop me. My self-esteem returned and I now knew I could handle it. I wouldn't let the guys down. If they trusted me with a weapon like this, I would come through for them. What am I talking about? We weren't going to blow up anything.

While everyone else was safely tucked away at Jonathan's fortress, the four of us were cruising down Rt. 29 with a dead guy wrapped in plastic in the back of the SUV. The fact that we had a body in the car didn't seem to faze the other three occupants, but me—I was terrified, not by the fact that I was about to become involved in a major crime, but because I didn't see anything wrong in what we were about to do. The guy was dead… and we weren't the ones who killed him. We were just going to give him a proper send off, and let the true villain take the blame.

What ever would Dakota do when she discovered his body? I'd love to see the look on her face.

Jonathan took the back way to The Body Shop. When he pulled up to the tree line at the far side of the parking lot, Gator's voice came through on the wireless gadget I had in my ear. He was telling us that he was ready to disable the alarm system. We were set to go.

My heart pounded in my chest like a drum in a marching band. I was sitting in a parking lot with Billy, Jonathan, Shark, and a dead man, getting ready to add to the list of laws we'd already broken. And getting caught this time would be bad… really bad. Having a dead body in your possession was a sure fire way to spend eternity in prison.

I silently prayed that everything would go as planned and we would be able to get away untouched, but sometimes things don't turn out like you want them to. There was a rock in the road, and we were about ready to trip over it.

Chapter 9

THE ONLY LIGHTS VISIBLE in the pitch black darkness were the ones in the front of the building. This aided us in our quest to slip in the back, dump the body, and then flee the scene. But lugging a dead body around is no easy feat. It took all three of the guys to haul it from the car to the drop point. My job was to hold open the door.

Once inside, we knew something was wrong. There wasn't a light on in the whole place, and after a quick search, not only did we discover there was no one home, it looked as if the occupants had moved out.

"Dakota doesn't live here anymore," I said after going from room to room in the upstairs living quarters. "There're only a few articles of clothing left in the closet. A woman like her would have a whole wardrobe full of nice clothes."

I aimed my flashlight over to the makeup vanity.

"A bottle of perfume and a hand mirror… you know she would've had more junk than that."

"They're on the run," Jonathan calmly replied.

"Yeah," Billy added. "Everything started falling apart especially after Dakota found out her boyfriend wasn't the man she thought he was. She knew he would eventually be her downfall, so she took care of the problem and then took off."

"I kind of feel sorry for Gavin," I said. "Not that I liked the guy or anything, but she used him and when he became a liability, she poisoned him. He's dead and now she's free to start all over again in a new place… new city." I glanced around at the guys in a room only lit by our flashlights. "We have to find her."

"We have to finish the mission," Shark said. "We need to clean up our mess."

"And how are we going to do that?" I asked, huddled next to Billy. "There's nothing to clean up but a dead body downstairs. Look around, Shark." I used my flashlight to scan the room again. "Everything looks normal. The furniture's still here. I mean, even the beds are made. The only thing missing is Dakota, Olivia, and some of their belongings. They left just enough behind to make people think everything was copasetic. When people start showing up tomorrow they'll just think the shop is closed, and after a week or so, somebody might call the police… or they might not. Gavin Preston's body could go unnoticed until he's nothing but a pile of bones."

"Oh, that's not going to happen," Shark said. He looked around at the three of us while holding his flashlight under his chin. "Anyone got a cigarette?"

"Are you kidding?" I asked. "You're going to take up smoking now?"

"We're going to torch the place," he said, and then chuckled at me.

"With a cigarette? Are you nuts?" I was confused. "A cigarette will take forever. Plus, you know they've done something to cigarettes. Now they'll go out if you lay them down and not puff on them. Why don't we just use the rocket launcher? I'll be more than glad to go get it and do the deed."

Shark laughed at me.

"We'll break off the filter. The tobacco will burn just fine without a filter. I don't smoke, but I have friends who've told me this. Ah… a slow burn will do the job. A rocket launcher will have the cops on our backs before we even get out of the parking lot. No… we need something slow and quiet."

"We'll set the fire up here on the second floor so that the place will be in flames before it reaches ground level, Jesse." Jonathan said. "That'll give the fire department plenty of time to respond, and the first thing they'll find is Preston's body. We'll leave it right by the back door."

"Okay," I said. "I have a pack of cigarettes in my purse. I do smoke on occasion."

"Where's your purse?"

"In the Hummer."

"Then go get `em."

"All right, but I'm not going to light it. I don't want my saliva on that cigarette. You know those crime scene guys can find a flake of skin floating in the air. They don't miss anything."

"Just trust me on this one, Jesse, and go get your cigarettes."

"By myself?"

Then I thought about how silly I must've sounded. The girly part of me was coming out, but being a sissy wasn't going to cut it with these guys. My stomach quivered.

When I first met Billy, I was basically a pencil-pushing secretary. That was a while ago. Life changes. Now I was in the middle of a cover-up that could come back and bite us all in the butt if I didn't get it together. I wasn't going to be the weak link.

"No problem," I said. "I'll be right back."

I turned, ran down the stairs, and then looked at Gavin Preston's plastic covered body as I passed it, heading to the back exit. I grabbed the doorknob, yanked opened the door, and came face to face with Dakota Stone. She was holding a trigger device in one hand, the kind used to set off a bomb, and a gun in the other.

"No!" I yelled as I lunged at her, trying to grab the little black gadget or the gun… whichever came first.

But she was too fast. She jumped backwards just enough to keep me from getting to her, and when I finally did manage to inch my way closer, she stuck the gun under my chin. I stopped and froze.

"You'll never get away with it," I said with a sinking feeling in my gut and a pang in my heart.

If that truly was a trigger device for a bomb and it went off … I didn't want to think about the outcome.

Oh, she would get away with it and I knew it. She'd kill us and then make her getaway. She'd be free to continue her murderous rampage, and the cops would blame us for Gavin Preston's death. They'd say we tried to blow up the place to cover our tracks, but failed and were killed by our own hands.

I could just see the headline in the paper—Murder Cover-up Gone Bad. Five Bodies Recovered.

Dakota laughed as she lowered the gun and started backing up.

"Fools, all of you! I had you guys pegged right from the start. I knew Gavin was coming to warn you, so I decided to let him. That is, if he didn't die first… which he didn't, so here you are, dumping his body and trying to pin it on me. Well, girlfriend, it's not going to work."

"Don't do it," I pleaded, inching closer. "We can work out something."

I was stalling for time. I was hoping the guys would start worrying and come looking for me, but they were nowhere in sight.

"Oh, yeah, and what do you have in mind? You gonna just pretend this never happened and let me go on my merry way? I don't think so. Why couldn't you just mind your own business and leave me alone? All I ever wanted to do was run my business and help other women feel good about themselves, but no, you were jealous and couldn't stand all my success."

"Jealous? What are you talking about? I'd never heard of you until I tried to return that bottle of shampoo. All you had to do was refund the money, and I would've left without incident."

"Liar. You'll say anything to save your pals. Unfortunately, that's out of your control."

"I'm not lying. If you'd done the right thing, it wouldn't have led to this. Don't you know anything about trying to keep the customers happy? A refund would've done the trick. That's all it would've taken."

I guess my talent for lying wasn't up to par, because Dakota wasn't buying any of it.

"You're a terrible liar, Jesse. Why would I give someone a refund for something I didn't charge them for? You know all that stuff came free with their membership. Tsk… tsk, Jesse. You just don't get it, do you? I knew everything about you right down to the size of your underwear before you showed up at my shop that day. I'm sure you were told that I do a background check on every new client. I don't let just anybody join my club. I'm very selective."

"Yeah, I know that now. You only want customers who need a hit man. That's what it's all about, isn't it? What happened to you that made you want to rid the world of all men? Why do you hate them so much? Let me guess. Your daddy abused you as a child."

"I knew you were going to be trouble."

She held out the hand holding the bomb trigger and pressed it.

I turned and looked at the building. My first instinct was to run inside, but I knew better. All I could do was wait for the explosion… and hope my guys would make it out alive before that happened. I had images of firemen sifting through the ashes, picking up their body parts.

Nothing happened. The bomb didn't go off.

I was so relieved, the only thing I could do was laugh out loud at Dakota. She wasn't so smart after all. She couldn't even blow up her own building.

I turned around to tell her so, but she was gone, vanished into the darkness.

In her haste to flee, she had dropped the detonator. I stared down at it, but refused to pick it up as if it would explode in my hands. Leave it there for the cops to find, I told myself.

I looked around. I didn't know what to do next. I was afraid to go back into the building and afraid not to, so I just stood there, my imagination running wild.

Seconds later, Billy and Jonathan came running out with Shark between them. He was limping and they were holding him up.

"Run!" Billy yelled.

So… I did. I ran straight for the Hummer, jumped in and turned the key. The SUV fired up and as soon as I heard the doors slam and knew everyone was inside, I took off.

"Is Shark all right?" I asked, looking over at Billy in the front seat and then glancing in the back. "Why is he limping like that?"

"Floor it!" Jonathan demanded. "And keep your eyes on the road. Shark's fine. His leg's bothering him a little, but he's tough."

"I thought you said it was a flesh wound. There's a big difference…"

"I lied a little."

"Oh, God…" I murmured. "He isn't going to die, is he?"

"We're all going to die if you don't get us out of here!"

"What…"

The explosion wasn't what I had expected. I thought it would've shaken the ground and lit up the sky like a massive fireball, but it didn't. It made a terrible racket, and you could tell there had been an explosion, but the sound was nothing louder than a couple of transformers going off. No windows blew out because there wasn't any in the brick building, except for the ones in the front, and they couldn't be seen from where we were.

I hated to think what it was like inside. It scared me half to death. I gripped the steering wheel harder.

"Pretty good driving there, Jesse," Shark said. "I was afraid you might lose it, what with you being so shaky and all. Good thing that wasn't as bad as it could've been."

"What just happened back there?" I asked looking out the rearview mirror. "And here I thought Dakota's bomb making ability was a bust. She pressed the button, but nothing happened."

"You mean she was here?" Billy asked. "When? Where'd she go?"

"Just before the explosion. As soon as I came out the door, she was standing there waiting. She pressed the detonator, I turned to look at the building, and when I turned around she'd vanished. I don't know where she went. I didn't see a car, so I don't know how she got away. I was too busy wondering if you guys were dead."

"That means she's still in town," Billy said. "She hasn't fled yet, so we might still be able to find her before she hightails it out of here."

"Why didn't the place go up in flames when she pressed the button?"

"The detonator activated a timer," Shark said. "That way she had plenty of time to escape before the bomb went off."

"How did y'all know there was a bomb in the building?" I asked.

"We didn't," Jonathan said. "Shark had a bad feeling and said we should get out. When he gets those feelings, I listen to him."

"I guess you don't need my cigarettes anymore," I said, smiling and still driving at a high rate of speed. "Sending me out to get cigarettes was a ruse, wasn't it? Y'all wanted me out of the building. I mean, it could've taken forever for a cigarette to get a good fire going. I should've known better. Next time just tell me the truth. If you thought there was something strange or dangerous going on, you should've told me. I'm not a baby."

Jonathan chuckled. "You didn't even want to go outside by yourself."

Yep, I knew that one was going to come back and haunt me, so I rebounded with, "Actually, I didn't want to leave y'all alone. I was afraid something bad would happen to you… and it almost did."

"I'll buy that. How about you, Billy?"

"Works for me."

"It was all too neat," Shark said. "I knew something wasn't right the minute I walked into the place. I could smell it."

"Smell what?"

"Death approaching."

"Hmm… that's scary… or maybe it's a good thing."

"You might want to slow down, Jesse," Billy said. "We're safe now."

I pulled up to the stop light at Rt. 29 and waited, my hands still shaking from our near death experience.

"That was close. We could've been killed back there." I hesitated and then added, "No one tells my mother how close we came to being dog meat."

Fire trucks raced down Rt. 29, passing us as we sat at the light.

"I'll feel better as soon as we get home," Jonathan said. "Then we'll be in the clear. There's no way the cops can tie us to this one. We'll go home and act as if nothing happened."

By the time we got back to Jonathan's house, the explosion was all over the news, and Mom was freaking out.

"I thought y'all were dead!"

Mom fussed as we climbed out of the SUV.

"It's all over the news. Channel 29 said they found a body stuffed in a dryer. Please tell me you didn't put Preston's body in the dryer. That's just too harsh even for you guys."

We almost did a double-take upon hearing Mom's news.

"A body in the dryer?" I asked. "Are you sure?" I scanned the faces of Billy, Jonathan, and Shark.

"Don't look at us." Billy said, and then looked over at Jonathan and Shark for confirmation. "We left Preston on the floor right where we dropped him when we got there. If they found a body in the dryer, it isn't Gavin Preston."

"Then who is it?"

"I don't know." Billy replied. "But I'd sure like to."

Mom looked at Shark who was now leaning against the Hummer.

"Shark, you don't look so good," she said. "Is your leg bothering you? You should go lie down. You've been shot, for Pete's sake. You should be in bed."

"I'm fine, Minnie," he assured her. "It's nothing more than a pin prick. All I need is a stiff drink. It's been a hectic day to say the least."

"Here," she took him by the arm and said, "I can help you there. Come with me and I'll fix you a tall one."

The two of them started walking down the hallway, Shark pretending to need Mom's help all the while. She stopped for a second and looked back at us.

"Y'all can come, too. No need to hang out in the garage. I mean, after all that hard work, I'm sure a drink is in order for everyone. Blowing up buildings and stuffing bodies in dryers can wear a person down. Y'all must be all dried out."

She chuckled to herself as she turned back to Shark.

They continued their walk down the corridor as Mom continued with her praise for a man who could kill a person with his pinky finger.

"Eddie's doing so much better thanks to you, Shark. You saved my husband's life, and for that, I'll be forever grateful. You're such a good man. How did you ever get into the business of killing people? Were you abused? I bet you were bullied in school, weren't you?" She didn't give him time to say anything. "Well… you don't have to worry about that anymore. You have us now."

The three of us tagged along behind them, scratching our heads, trying to figure out who the other body was. We didn't kill Gavin Preston and we surely didn't put a dead person in the dryer.

"Dakota did this," Billy said. "She's cleaning up after herself. She's gonna run, but she had to get rid of anyone who could be a witness. I'm willing to bet the body in the dryer is her cohort, Olivia Swales."

"But why kill Olivia?"

"Maybe she turned on Dakota, just like Preston did. Maybe Olivia wasn't party to Dakota's madness after all."

Jonathan laughed, and then said, "You just don't know who you can trust these days. People are strange."

Changing the subject, I said, "Is it me, or has anyone else noticed how weird my mom's been acting? I looked at Billy and then Jonathan. "Y'all know her. She's taking this rather calmly, don't you think?"

"It's probably the drug I gave her."

"No, it's not just that. She's been too accepting of our activities. Normally, she'd give us a hard time about everything we do that's not God's will—and you know what I mean."

"I think she's beginning to realize that everything we do is in the best interest of our family. We do what it takes to protect our own." Jonathan was being serious. "She knows we always do the right thing."

"That's what I mean. She also knows we skirt the law to get the job done, yet that doesn't seem to bother her anymore."

"Your mother has been through a lot since she met us," Jonathan said. "When you think about it, Jesse, she's been thrust into a whole new world unlike what she's been used to… and she's adapting."

"I hope you're right. She can adapt all she wants, but I'd hate to see my mother cross over to the dark side."

"To be truthful," Billy said, "I cracked up when she shot Preston in the foot."

The three of us smiled.

"Time to get out of this gear," Shark said to Mom. "You go tend to your husband and we'll see you in a minute."

"Okay, but don't be too long. I want to hear every detail."

Mom continued ahead as the four of us entered the armory. By the time we got out of our gear and had stepped back out into the hallway, we were met by Mason.

"We have a problem."

Mason had a disturbing look on his face.

"We have got company. Looks like Sheriff Hudson just pulled in with some of his guys. No sirens, no flashing lights, and that bothers me more than if they'd come in like a fire truck, horn a-tooting. You know this can't be good. Think fast, folks."

We quickly followed Mason to the computer room where we saw everything playing out on the screens. Sheriff Hudson had just stepped out of his SUV and was waiting for his deputies in the other two cars.

"What's he doing here?" I asked. "Isn't he out of his jurisdiction?"

"He's here to interrogate us about the explosion," Billy said. "The Body Shop is in Greene County. He has every right to be here. All we have to do is convince him that we've been here the whole time."

"We're going to get caught on this one, Billy," I said. "He's not stupid. He knows we were involved. But how? No one saw us, and no one can even prove we were even in the vicinity."

"Stoplight cameras," Mason said. "They'll get you every time."

"But can't you do something about it? Kill the cameras, or something?"

"It's a little too late for that." Mason looked over at Jonathan. "I'm sorry. I should've…"

"It's not your fault. You had your hands full. We just have to come up with a good reason for being in the wrong place at the wrong time. Anyone got any ideas?"

"Let me pull up the cameras and see exactly what they've seen."

Mason hit a few keystrokes and there we were sitting at the stoplight.

"All you can see is Billy and me. Thank God for tinted windows. We'll tell him we were out shopping. Christmas is coming up."

Jonathan and Billy both leaned over and kissed me on the cheek and Shark patted me on the back.

"I understand why you married this woman, Billy," Shark said. "She's a fast thinker... and quick on her feet."

"Does that mean I'm a good liar?"

"Pretty much so, but that's an attribute. Now let's head up to the house and intercept them before your mother gives them an earful. She's not happy about the fact her husband was beaten up, and her daughter was almost killed in the sheriff's jail cell. I'm afraid she might lose it and not know when to stop talking."

By the time the sheriff had gathered his men and was at the door, we were there waiting for them… and we were prepared.

We were all sitting in the living room as if we didn't have a care in the world. Well, except for Shark. He was hiding in a bedroom, and Mason and Gator were down in the bunker. We didn't want to have to explain their presence.

Jonathan answered the door with a big, fake smile on his face that noticeably faded when he saw Sheriff Hudson.

"Come on in. What's the problem, Sheriff?"

"Oh, I think you know," Sheriff Hudson said as he walked in followed by his men. He glanced around the room. "Looks like a nice, quiet family gathering, but I know better."

"What do you mean?" I asked in a pleasant manner, jumping up from the sofa. "That's exactly what it is. If you'd like to talk, I'd appreciate it if you didn't do it in front of my kids. Perhaps, this can wait. We just finished dinner and the kids are tired. We were just getting ready to leave."

"What makes you think this isn't a social call?"

"You don't make social calls, especially with all this much backup."

I looked at his deputies.

"You're here to accuse us of something, and I'd appreciate a little tact on your part in front of my children."

"Fair enough," the sheriff said. "I just have one question for you."

"Go ahead, ask your question, and then we're leaving."

"Where were you two hours ago?"

"Billy and I were out Christmas shopping."

"In full tactical gear?"

"It turns me on, and it freaks out people in the stores. I get a kick out of it, so Billy plays along. Something wrong with that?"

The sheriff smiled.

"And where did you go shopping? I'm sure we can pull up some footage from the stores or the mall to corroborate your story."

I giggled. "We never made it to the mall. We intended to, but things got a little amorous, so Billy and I…"

"I can see where this is headed. I thought you'd make it easy by being honest, but I can see that's not going to happen. You could save us all a lot of grief by just telling me what you know about the explosion at The Body Shop. I know you were there."

Billy stepped forward.

"Give us a minute, Sheriff." He then turned to Mom and said, "Minnie, why don't you and Helene take the kids to the kitchen for a cookie."

"A cookie? Are you sure?"

Mom seemed confused at first as to why Billy would allow sweets when he has always been very strict about the kids' sugar intake, but it didn't take her but a second to get the message.

Before she could react, Maisy stood, took Ethan by the hand and said, "Come on, Grandma. Maybe Aunt Lu Ann has apples. We love apples, don't we, Ethan?"

Ethan shook his head and smiled. "And oranges, too."

I was so proud of Maisy. She's almost eight, going on twenty, and she's smart as a whip. How she came to us as a baby is another story, and even though she knows she's adopted, she still loves us.

And… after all these years of seeing one of us come home battered and bruised, she knows that no matter what, we're on the right side.

So, when Billy says something so off the wall like allowing cookies, she knows he just wants them out of the room for their own sake. It was time for grown-up talk.

Billy turned to Eddie and said, "Eddie, you stay right there. I know you're in a lot of pain and you don't need to be walking around more than you have to."

Relieved, Eddie complied. I'm sure he wanted to hear what Billy had to say to Sheriff Hudson as much as the rest of us did. I, for one, had no idea he was going to tell the truth.

Once the kids were out of the room, Billy turned back to the sheriff and said, "Would you like to sit down, Sheriff Hudson? This could take a while. I'm going to tell you everything we know and everything we've done. It's time to just lay it all out there."

A face-off was coming and it looked as if both men were testing the waters.

"I'll stand, but thanks for the offer," the sheriff replied. "I'm going to give you a chance to tell your side of the story, so please do me the courtesy of telling me the straight truth this time. No leaving anything out. Convince me that none of you have done anything illegal… lately."

He turned his head and stared at each one of us separately before coming back to Billy.

"I see guilt on every face in this room. Who killed Gavin Preston?"

"Dakota Stone!" I blurted out. "She's the one you should be after." I pointed my finger at the sheriff. "Instead of harassing us, you should be out looking for her. She's behind everything. She even…"

Billy interrupted.

"Jesse, please sit down and let me handle this. "You're way too emotional to say anything without flipping out. We need to tell the sheriff everything we know if we want him to arrest the right person, instead of us."

"I guess I am a little bit emotional."

I turned and stared at the sheriff. "Look at my face and you'll see why, or better yet, have a look over at Eddie. I think this is the perfect time to get emotional. It sure isn't any fun being hounded and beaten up."

Actually, my little outburst was just a ploy to give Billy more time to think. He knows better than to try to shut me up. If I had something to say, it was coming out… and under no circumstances would he ever accuse me of being too emotional, at least not in front of anyone.

"This is how it is and what we know so far, Sheriff."

Billy started his account of what happened, while the rest of us held our breath.

"Jesse's right about Dakota Stone."

He glanced my way for a second, and then back to Sheriff Hudson.

"Gavin Preston came here to warn us about her just before he died."

"Gavin Preston came here to warn you about his lover? Yes, we know he was her lover."

Billy continued.

"She'd been slowly poisoning him once he was of no use to her. He had refused to maim or kill for her anymore, so she eliminated him. She even told him so at the last minute. She laughed when she said she had used antifreeze, and that he had never suspected for a minute. Well, by the time he found this out, it was too late. He didn't think he was going to recover. So, he tried to make things right. He came here and told us everything."

"And you believed him?"

"A dying man has no reason to lie."

"Okay. Say I believe you. Go on."

"I will tell you that we intercepted him and interrogated him slightly. We thought his arrival might be another attack on one of us. However, his interrogation was short-lived. He was already about dead because of the poison. He wanted us to take him back to the shop so he could die there, and put the blame where it belonged. Unfortunately, he died here before we could honor his wishes, but we did as he asked."

"Honor his wishes? Are you serious?"

"My people take great pride in honor. Don't yours?"

The sheriff was caught off-guard by Billy's frank and deliberate question. When honor is called into doubt, one tends to go blank—if only for a second.

"So… we wrapped him up and took him where he wanted to go."

"Jesus Christ!" The sheriff hesitated just long enough to regain his composure. "You just admitted to… Never mind. We'll get to that later. Why didn't you call the police when he died, instead of dumping his body? It makes you look mighty guilty. How can I believe you when it would be so easy for you to lie to cover your tracks?"

"Have you ever known me to tell a lie, Sheriff Hudson?"

Sheriff Hudson knew Billy wasn't a liar. Even if it meant trouble for himself, Billy would still tell the truth. It might not be the whole truth, but it wouldn't be a lie.

"Alerting the police to Preston's demise wasn't at the top of our list. We arrived at the shop, dropped off Gavin Preston, and then we had a look around."

"So you have been doing P.I. work? That really ticks me off. We had a signed agreement. You made a promise. You swore…"

"No, I wasn't working. I was protecting my family. The important thing is that you know Dakota Stone's a killer, and she's on the run. She blew up her own shop to cover her tracks."

"Oh, come on. You don't expect me to believe that, do you?"

"She confronted Jesse at the back entrance with the detonator in her hand. She, or most likely someone she hired, planted a bomb. She was expecting our visit. She tried to kill us."

"You really expect me to believe this crazy story, Billy? Give me a little credit."

"The woman has no past. Think about it. She runs a spa that caters to rich women, and some of these women hate their husbands. She's been known to approach at least one woman with the offer to kill the husband, and that husband is now dead. Who knows how many more she's had killed?"

Sheriff Hudson shook his head in disbelief. "You're telling me that Dakota Stone is a man-hater and for some reason she wants to kill off all bad men?"

Lu Ann spoke up.

"Sheriff, the profile fits. I believe the Stone woman was married to, or had a relationship with an abuser. She was most likely physically and mentally abused so badly that she had to do something to stop the abuse. Being abused does something awful to a person. I also believe she killed him, whoever it was, and she got such great relief from the act that she made it her goal to help other women in the same situation. She actually thinks she's doing them a favor. But now, her actions are out of control. She can't stop herself."

Lu Ann's good at her job. Sheriff Hudson knows it, and he has great respect for her work. He's mentioned this a few times after she was instrumental in helping to solve a few cases that he was involved in.

"After Jesse's incident in my jail, my office looked long and hard into this woman's background, especially when we discovered that Preston worked for her."

"I bet you didn't find out much about her since there's not much to find out."

"Don't bet on it, Lu Ann. We know a lot about her."

"Then you know she isn't who she claims to be," Jonathan said, speaking for the first time since Billy's announcement that we were going to tell our side of the story. The shock had worn off. "She's hiding from something, or someone."

"Yes, we know that too, but that doesn't make her a killer. People have been known to change their identities... for whatever reason. There's no law against that."

"Ah, come on, Sheriff Hudson," I said. "There's a law against stealing someone's identity. Why don't you arrest her for that? You know what's going on here. We admit to transporting a dead body. That's all we did. Suppose Preston hadn't died. All we would've been guilty of was giving a guy a lift back to work. The point is, we didn't kill anyone, and you know it. We've had our ups and downs in the past, but you know we're good people. So, I lied about the shopping trip. Big deal."

I looked over at Billy and then back to the sheriff.

"I didn't know we were going to share."

"I ought to arrest all of you right now just for getting in my way, but I'm not going to. You see, I'm the sheriff and I know everything."

He looked directly at me.

"I know a lie when I hear one… and I know the truth."

"So what do you want from us?" I glared back at him.

"I want you to stay out of my way and let me do my job! What you did was…"

"What we did was the right thing to do. We transported a body. That's all. You can't arrest us for that."

The sheriff walked over to me, and then kicked my foot with his.

The look of surprise was on everyone's face… except the cops.

"You just assaulted a police officer, right deputies?" He didn't even glance at his guys.

"Yeah, that's what I saw, Sheriff," one of them said.

"Me, too," the other agreed.

Sheriff Hudson kept his stare on me. "I could arrest you for that." He stepped closer to my face. "And here, all this time, I thought we were best friends."

Memories of the time when Sheriff Hudson saved my mom from a crazed killer came flooding back. I told him then that I'd be forever in his debt, and would love and worship him forever. I guess he's felt cheated since that day, and he'd have every reason to. He was right. I hadn't given the man the respect he deserved, and I surely haven't been a good girl like I promised to be. Old habits never cease. They just lie around and fester, waiting to resurface.

He stepped back and took a deep breath.

"I have a headache, and I'm tired." He rubbed his head.

"I can get you an aspirin," I butted in.

I guess I was feeling badly about the way I had treated him since the incident. He had saved my mother from certain death, and in return, I'd done nothing but drive him crazy. Or… maybe I was just trying to sound sincere.

"I don't want an aspirin! I want the truth!"

"We've told you the truth! You need to get your men out looking for that woman before she kills someone else… and next time, it'll probably be one of us. Time's running out, Sheriff Hudson."

That statement rang true. Before skipping town, Dakota had a few loose ends to tie up—us. We'd ruined her thriving business and put her on the run. She'd be out for revenge.

"If what you've told me turns out to be false, I'll have all of you in my jail by morning. If you've left out one little detail, you're done." He looked at me. "And that includes your mother."

"Leave her out of it," I demanded. "My mother knows nothing of this."

"Now, see…" Sheriff Hudson shook his head at me again. "I know that's a lie."

Billy waved me off.

"You have something to add, Billy? You say you didn't blow up a building and you didn't kill anyone, so what's left?"

"Sheriff, there is one other thing you need to know."

Oh, no! Billy was going to tell the sheriff that mom had shot Preston in the foot. It was one important thing that hadn't come up so far, and I wanted to keep it that way. After the explosion, there was probably nothing left of Preston anyway. The cops would never find out… would they?

"No, Billy, it's irrelevant."

"No need for secrets now."

"God…" the sheriff moaned.

I could tell by the look on his face that he didn't want to hear what was coming next. What else had we done that he didn't know about? I'm sure that's what he was asking himself.

"You always save the best for last. Jesse's begging you not to tell me, so it must be about her mother. What did Minnie do? Please don't tell me she shot somebody."

"As you know, Minnie hasn't taken this well. Jesse was brutalized in your jail and then Eddie was almost killed. At his age, there's no telling how long it'll take for him to be back to his old self."

Billy looked over at Eddie.

"No offense, Eddie, but you're not a kid anymore and you did take a pretty bad beating."

"None taken." Eddie smiled.

"Enough!" Sheriff Hudson said. "Where's this going, Billy? Did she shoot Gavin Preston? Is that what you're trying to tell me?"

He didn't give Billy a chance to say anything. He just shook his head in that usual manner of his.

"I'm going to have to arrest her."

He looked over at me.

"I blame you for this."

"Me? Why me?"

"Because you're the one who dragged her into your little criminal enterprises."

"I resent that!"

"And now she's gone and killed someone! I hope you're happy!"

"Stop!" Billy said, stepping between the sheriff and me as if he was trying to break up an argument between two kids. "Minnie didn't shoot Preston… well, she did, but it's not what you think. She shot him in the foot."

"What?"

"We gave her a trank, and she went temporarily insane," I said, defending my mother. "I'm sure you're well aware that no jury, if it came to that, would ever find my mother guilty… under the circumstances."

Surprisingly, the sheriff chuckled and stepped back.

"An eye for an eye, huh?"

"That's exactly what Mom said!" I smiled.

"You people are crazy."

"Does that mean you believe us?"

"What he's saying, Jesse," Billy surmised. "Video surveillance from somewhere picked up on us entering the building, and shortly afterwards, the building exploded. It's all on tape somewhere, right, Sheriff?"

"Correct."

"And in this video, it must show me and Dakota behind the building. It should also show her dropping the detonator and then running off."

"We have it. Forensics is checking for prints."

"You wanted to question us about the death of Gavin Preston, so you'd have a head's up," Jonathan added. "You'll know when the autopsy comes back whether or not we're lying. If we are, you'll be back for us, and if we're not… then what? By the time all the results are in, Dakota Stone and Olivia Swales will be in Brazil, setting up shop again. If you don't get a move on, she'll get away just like…"

"Just like Vera did," the sheriff admitted with a sad look on his face. "I was wrong then, but I won't be this time."

Vera was Savannah Kelley's housekeeper/assistant/friend, that is, until she turned out to be one of the bad guys. She slipped through the clutches of Sheriff Hudson and his deputies. Vera Brown was the one who got away. The sheriff would never forget that.

"I know y'all didn't bomb the building." He looked at Jonathan. "If you had, there wouldn't be anything left. Now that I'm somewhat convinced one of you didn't kill Preston, my efforts will be focused on finding Dakota Stone and Olivia Swales."

"It's about time!" I hissed. I started to tell the sheriff that we could prove part of our story, because we still had Preston's car, but thought better of it. He should've asked.

"One other thing," Sheriff Hudson said. "Where's the other guy?"

"He's resting from his wound," Mom said, walking into the room. "He's a good man. He saved Eddie's life, and he got shot in the leg trying to protect us."

"Mom!"

"She's talking about the incident in the hospital parking lot," Sheriff Hudson said, looking at me. "Like I said before—I'm the sheriff. I know everything. I need a name."

"Find out for yourself," Mom said. "We're not giving him up."

"Oh, Minnie. I already know who he is. I just wanted to see if you'd tell me the truth. I'm disappointed in you."

"I'm afraid it won't be the last time."

I chuckled and then tried to move onto another subject quickly.

"If you know so much then why haven't you caught the guy who shot at us?"

"Because he's dead, burned up in an explosion." After a second, the sheriff grinned. "I guess Preston said he didn't do anything, huh?"

"What does it matter now?" Billy asked. "What's done is done. You need to concentrate on apprehending the Stone woman and her side-kick."

"That's my plan, and I want all of you to stay out of it."

"But we can help," I said. "How many times have we come through for you?"

"Yeah, but at what cost? Bodies start piling up when you're around."

"Bull."

"You're like little kids fighting," Mom interrupted, looking at me and then at the sheriff. "Why don't you two play nice?" She stared back at the sheriff. "I think there might be something to what Jesse said a little while ago. That woman's coming back for one of us. She has to. It would be her ultimate revenge… to at least take one of us out."

"That thought crossed my mind," the sheriff said, and then looked over at me.

"See, Jesse, I do listen to you sometimes."

Then he looked at Billy and Jonathan.

"No one leaves your compound tonight. No helicopter rides, no grocery store visits… nothing. I'll post a couple of my men on the grounds… for your protection."

"We don't need your men," Jonathan said. "They'd be more useful to you on the streets."

"Oh, that's right," the sheriff replied. "I forgot you have this whole place hotwired and fortified. Pretty fancy setup you have. Like you're ready for the apocalypse. With a place like this, you don't need any outside help. I guess you got everything covered."

"Just can't keep a secret anymore, can you? Make a few upgrades and everybody hears about it. What's this world coming to?"

"Sorry, Jonathan, but I wouldn't be doing my job if I didn't post some guys. There's a possible threat of retaliation, and I know it. I have to do my best to make sure that doesn't happen."

"If you insist, but we can take care of our own."

"That's what I'm afraid of. I want this woman alive."

"Are you saying..."

"Let my guys do their jobs."

"I'm sorry to interrupt," Mom said, "but the kids need to go home. They're exhausted."

"I think we're finished for now," Sheriff Hudson said. He looked at Billy. "Take your family home, stay there, and be safe. My men will be on watch."

"And so will we," Jonathan added.

I raised my hand. "Whoa… wait a minute, Sheriff. That's it? You ask us a few questions and we answer them to your satisfaction somewhat, and then you just walk away? No way. It was too easy. Other than harassing us, what's the real reason you're here?"

From the look on Sheriff Hudson's face, he did have something left to say… something he dreaded talking about.

Somebody must've died.

Somebody we know.

"Let me take a stab at it. You have something very uncomfortable to tell us, but you're not going to, unless we ask, so… I'm going to ask. Who was the person they found in the dryer?"

"I was hoping you wouldn't ask, but since you did."

The sheriff paused as if he really hated to say what he was about to.

"I wanted to tell you before you heard it on the news."

"Who was it?"

"It was Savannah Kelley."

Chapter 10

The room took on an eerie silence. Everyone gasped at the news. With tears in her eyes, Mom asked the sheriff, "Is she… is she dead like they said on the news? They said the cops found a dead body in the clothes dryer."

Sheriff Hudson walked over to Mom, put his hand on her shoulder and said, "Don't believe everything you hear on the news, Minnie. I don't have an update, but the last I was told is that she's alive."

"Well, find out! You're the sheriff. You said you know everything, now make a call and find out how she's doing!"

There was no way he was going to get out of making that call. Mom would see to it. He wasn't leaving until he got an answer for her.

That was her way.

First, she'd ask, and if that didn't work (which it usually did), then she'd plead in her own special way, and… if that didn't work, she'd go into one of her lectures. I could see one coming on.

"You might as well take the time and make the call, Sheriff. You know how my mother is. Savannah is like a daughter to her, not the good one like me, but still…"

"Okay," Sheriff Hudson said as he pulled out his cell phone.

He looked up at Mom.

"I don't usually do this, but I'm going to for you, Minnie. I know how much you care about Savannah. That's why I didn't want to tell you. So… prepare yourself. The news might not be so good. I'll be right back."

He motioned to his men, and then the three of them walked outside.

"I'm shocked," I said, looking around at everyone. "How… why…"

"I have a theory," Lu Ann said, glancing over at Mom. "Isn't Savannah the one who first told you about The Body Shop?"

Mom hesitated for a second.

"She told Sarah about it, and then Sarah told me. I went there once, but I refused to pay that much money. My body can do just fine without that place."

"Savannah's friends come into the picture, and then trouble lands on Dakota Stone's doorstep. Minnie, you said Savannah told y'all that Dakota checks everyone out before they're allowed to join, right?"

"I don't remember if she told me or if it was…"

"My point is, most people have a small circle of close friends. Oh, they might know a lot of people, but there's only a few they consider real friends."

Lu Ann then spread her arms out as if to emphasize her point.

"You all are Savannah's circle of friends."

"I see what you mean," Mom said, looking around at our faces. "Private investigators, a bounty hunter, a profiler… and let's not forget Savannah's dating a Greene County deputy. All of her friends are in law enforcement or connected to law enforcement in one way or another."

"Yeah, but why Savannah Kelley?" Jonathan asked. "She's a famous writer. Killing her off would cause a real stink with the press. The cops would never give up chasing down her killer. The public wouldn't allow it. High profile people attract attention, and the media would demand answers. Why not pick one of us instead?"

"I know where Lu Ann's coming from," Billy said. "We're Savannah's friends, and when Mae Bridges came to us with her accusations, we started investigating The Body Shop."

"That's right," I said. "Savannah was the first one. She got Sarah to join, and then Sarah got my mom to join. Next thing you know, I show up. That's what got the ball rolling."

"In Dakota's mind, she traced the blame back to Savannah and tossed her in as an appetizer," Billy added. "She wanted us to know that she knew where it all started."

"But she was wrong."

"Not in her mind."

"Dakota Stone expected us to die in that building," Jonathan said. "We'd be blamed for everything. If it had gone as planned, she'd be at the Greene County Sheriff's Office right now, accusing us of murder and God only knows what else. She's an expert liar. Who would suspect that a fine, upstanding woman such as herself would be capable of doing such terrible things? Who would suspect her of murder? Then, she'd leave town, and start all over again. She'd be free to kill again and again. Once they start, they don't stop."

"But how did she know we'd go there?" I asked. "She knew Preston was going to die, and she might have even suspected, or known, he was coming to see us, but how did she know we'd dump his body at her shop once he was dead?"

"She's sharp," Lu Ann said. "I hate to say it, but she'd make a good profiler. I think she can read people well."

"You mean read their minds?" Mom asked. "Oh, come on, Lu Ann. You don't believe in…"

"No, I mean she's good at sizing up a person."

"All I can say is, I'm glad Shark got a bad feeling about that place when he did," Jonathan said, "otherwise, a few of us wouldn't be standing in this room right now."

"And thanks for a time-delayed bomb," I said. "I bet that really ticked her off. She should've gotten you to build it for her. It would've been a lot more powerful, and it would've gone off instantly. We'd all be history… and so would Dakota."

I laughed nervously for a second, and then added, "That wasn't even funny. I don't know why I said that."

Billy shook his head.

"She'll make a mistake. They always do."

Sheriff Hudson tapped on the door, and then walked in.

"All I can tell you for now is that Savannah's alive."

"Oh, thank God!" Mom said, relieved. "I'm so glad!"

"She's hurt pretty bad, Minnie. The doctors don't know if she'll make it, but they're doing their best to see to it that she does. That's all I know."

He looked around the room at us.

"I can't help but notice the silence and the look on your faces. Too much confidence. What changed in the ten minutes I was gone?"

Billy explained our suspicions, and for once, the sheriff said it made sense. The evidence was consistent with our story.

"We should be able to lift a fingerprint from the detonator."

"It'll be too late by the time the results come in," I said.

He ignored my remark again.

"Don't think any of you are off the hook for your part in this mess. Dumping a body and shooting someone in the foot."

He looked at Mom and said, "I can't believe you did that."

"I was insane at the time."

"What are we to do now?" I asked the sheriff. "We don't know where this woman is, or who she's coming after next. We can't just sit around and wait for her to show up."

"That's exactly what you're going to do."

Mom reacted as if she'd just come to a scary realization. "What about Savannah's son? Where is he? Is he all right?"

"We're looking for him."

"What? He's missing?"

Kaleb—the son of Savannah's dead husband's one night stand with his also dead secretary, killed by Savannah. But that's another story.

"Deputy James went to Savannah's house about four hours ago. He found blood on the kitchen floor, and Savannah and Kaleb were missing. Her car was still in the garage, and her purse was on the table. I'm hoping they won't find the boy's body in the rubble of that building. They're still sifting through the…"

Mom started crying.

I went to her, put my arm around her and said, "Don't cry, Mom. The sheriff and his men will find him. He's going to be okay."

"She's right, Minnie," Lu Ann said. "I don't think Dakota's a baby killer. She only hates men, not kids. She probably stashed him somewhere, but I don't think she killed him. She might've even dumped him at someone's house. If she doesn't want the kid to die, she'll leave him somewhere public. If she doesn't care, she could dump him out in the middle of nowhere."

The room went silent again, allowing Lu Ann's statement to sink in.

"You're a genius, Lu Ann!" Sheriff Hudson said. "Y'all could be a big help if you'd go home and have a look around, and call me if you find the boy. In the meantime, I'm going back to the scene."

"I thought you were going home."

"I was, but I guess that'll have to wait. I just got a call that needs my attention."

With that said, the sheriff left.

Billy and Jonathan stepped out of the room for a quick tête-à-tête. No one asked what they were doing. We just stood around waiting for their return. We all knew they were planning something, and once they'd come up with their plan, we'd hear about it.

Mom's tears had dried up and she was now on the verge of getting antsy. The news about Savannah had been devastating, and now that she knew she was alive, Mom would want to go see her. Unfortunately, that couldn't happen, unless…

Billy walked back into the room, followed by Helene and the kids.

"We're taking the children home," Billy said. "Minnie, you and Eddie will stay with us, where you'll be safe, and we can keep an eye on you."

He looked directly at her.

"You know why I'm saying this. You want to go see Savannah, but I can't let you."

Hmm… Mom didn't argue.

"Mason's going to your house to do a search. Do you need anything while he's there?"

"Not really." She smiled slightly. "We learned from you, Billy Blackhawk. We keep a bag in the car, and there's a pharmacy downstairs in case we run out of drugs. We have that room at your house, and we have more stuff there than we do in our bedroom at home."

She chuckled.

"And by the way, I am going to see Savannah."

"No, you're not."

That was all Billy had to say.

Mom backed down. She respected Billy and knew that if he was making a demand on her such as this, he had a very good reason, maybe one she didn't even know about.

"Helene, why don't you take the kids to the bunker? We'll be leaving here soon."

Helene promptly turned and did as he asked.

"We know Kaleb isn't at the compound," he continued once the kids were out of the room. "If she brought him here, it would've showed up on the monitors in the bunker when she broke the beam. Also, anytime the perimeter's broken, Jonathan gets a beep on his cell phone. Gator's going to… let's say… make adjustments to everyone's cell for security purposes. Minnie, I'll need your house key."

Mom walked over to the sofa, sifted through her purse, and then pulled out the set. She tried to get the key off, but those rings could be so difficult and she was really having a hard time with it.

Seeing her struggle, Billy walked over, held out his hand, and then got the key off the ring. He handed the set back to her.

"I know you're concerned about Savannah, but I have to think of our safety first. I'll personally take you to see her the minute the opportunity arises."

He winked at her… and Mom was appeased.

"Okay, folks, let's get going."

As we were leaving, Mom whispered to me. "Billy Blackhawk never listens to the cops. What's he got up his sleeve now?"

"I don't know, Mom, but I'll be the first one to find out, and then I'll let you know. I can promise you that."

Once we got back to the house, we did a search, and after finding nothing unusual… or Kaleb, we put the kids to bed.

Billy took the dogs out to have a look around the place.

"He could be anywhere," Helene said as she walked to the kitchen. "Anyone want coffee? I need something to help me sleep."

"Not me," Eddie said. "Coffee at this hour would keep me up all night, and I'm ready for bed. But I sure could use an aspirin."

"I'll get you a couple," Mom said as she went about doing so. She poured him a glass of milk and heated it in the microwave. "Here you go, honey."

Eddie tossed back the aspirins and chased them down with the warm milk.

"Warm milk. Yuck."

"You should give it a try sometime, Jesse," he said. "It helps me sleep. I don't know why, but it does." He looked at us, kissed Mom on the cheek, and headed for the stairs. "Don't wake me up unless a tornado strikes."

"I'll walk you up," Mom said, and then looked back at Helene and me. "Pour me a cup, and then we'll have a little girl's chat. I have a feeling this night is just getting started."

"Okay," I said. "You know where your room is."

Helene looked at me as Mom and Eddie headed upstairs.

"Drink this," she said, putting a cup of coffee down on the table in front of me. "I added a little something extra to warm your belly." Then, she winked at me.

"You're a lifesaver, Helene. What would I do without you?"

I was about ready to take a sip when I heard a wild animal noise, a crash, and then heard Mom screaming. I jumped up from the table, my heart pounding in my chest, and then ran up the stairs, taking them two at a time. When I reached the bedroom door, Spice Cat came scurrying out of the room.

"Is everything okay?"

"I'm sorry, Jesse. When I turned on the light, it must have scared the cat. He went flying off the bed, jumped on the dresser, and knocked over a bunch of stuff. I'm sorry I yelled. I wasn't expecting him, and he wasn't expecting to be disturbed."

"It's been a long day, Mom, and we're all a little on edge. Sorry about the cat. I'll wait by the door while you get Eddie settled in…just in case that tiger comes back." I snickered.

After I heard the squeak, I knew Eddie was in bed, so I peeked in to see what was taking Mom so long. She was standing by the dresser holding a picture.

"What is it, Mom?"

Mom turned around, her face ashen.

"I don't believe this."

"What is it?"

I crept into the room, hoping not to disturb Eddie, who was now lightly snoring, and had a look at the photo.

"Oh, my God! She's been here! She's been in our house!"

Panic set in when I saw the photo of Dakota and Olivia.

Mom and I stared at each other.

"Hit that panic button on your phone!" Mom cried. "Call Billy! We have trouble here! We need his protection!"

"It's on the kitchen table. Come on."

I grabbed her hand and the two of us hustled downstairs to the kitchen. I snatched up the cell phone and started tapping away as Mom and Helene stood and watched.

"What happened, Minnie?" Helene asked in a whisper. "What was all that racket about? Who's Jesse calling?"

Mom held out the framed photo to show her.

"That's Dakota Stone and Olivia Swales. What's this all about? Most importantly, Minnie, why do you have it?"

"She's been in our house!" I said—scared and mad at the same time. "I'm so nervous, I can't get this smart phone to be so smart. I hate these touch screens."

Frustrated, I threw the cell phone down on the table, went over and grabbed the wall phone receiver. I punched in Billy's number.

Wall phones… so outdated, but so useful sometimes. Although, this time, instead of ringing, all I got was static.

"House phone's acting up," I said, hanging up.

"Take a deep breath, and try your cell again."

Before I could do that, Billy and the dogs came in the back door.

The dogs were doing their thing—barking, jumping, and then finding their way to their dog bowls. Soon, they would be searching for a place to flop down.

"Helene, we need to give Athena one of those doggie downers," Billy said. "There's a storm coming. I haven't heard thunder yet, but I saw lightning off in the distance."

He stopped when he saw the looks on our faces.

"What is it?"

Mom held up the photo.

"This was in my room."

Billy pulled his Glock from its holster.

"Get your gun, Jesse!"

I ran over to the desk in the living room and snatched mine from my purse, ready to do battle when the time came.

"I'll get mine, too." Mom went for her purse.

"No, Minnie, we got this one." He looked at me. "You go upstairs and look for anything out of the ordinary. I'll check around down here."

Then, he looked over at Mom and Helene.

"Don't move. We need to know where you are. We don't want any accidents. No running about."

I guess Billy must've scared them, because they were huddled together and not moving when I left and headed upstairs.

After the search, I had come up empty-handed, but Billy found two more photos—one in the den, and one in our bedroom. All three photos were the same.

"What happened to that fancy security system we have? How did she manage to get in here without setting off an alarm?" I was beginning to have my doubts about the efficiency of our new protection.

"I don't know, but I'm sure going to find out."

He put his gun back in the holster and pulled out his cell phone.

"I'll call Jonathan, see what he's got."

Mom and Helene sat down at the table. I laid my gun next to my cell phone and coffee mug, and then sat down with them, waiting for Billy to make the call.

After listening to his conversation, we had a pretty good idea of what happened.

"Are you telling us that system can't tell the difference between a deer and a person?" Mom asked. "What good is it then?"

"Jonathan said a camera scan showed a couple of deer over by the woods close to the barn. The blip showed up right when the sheriff arrived, so Mason didn't think much of it, especially when he saw the two deer. Same thing had happened a couple times earlier, but it was deer then, too."

"So…she was here the same time the sheriff was," Mom said. "That was only an hour or so ago. Where is she now? Oh, Lord. She's probably still on the property."

"I want to know how she got in the house without setting off that alarm."

Helene pointed to the tiny box by the front door.

"That should've gone off, but it obviously didn't. There's a big malfunction in your system somewhere."

"The alarm wasn't set," Billy replied. "Someone forgot to set it when they left."

The three of us looked back and forth at each other, and then I said, "It doesn't matter now who forgot to set the alarm, Billy."

"It's too late to worry about who left the gate open after the cow gets out," Mom added. "Besides, that thing is so confusing. I figured as long as the green light was on, everything was okay."

"It confuses me, too," Helene agreed. "I'm with Minnie. I figured the same thing."

Billy walked over to the front door.

"Come here, ladies. I'm going to explain it to you again."

Mom and Helene got up and headed over to Billy while I sat at the table. They stared at me when I didn't move.

"I know how to work it," I said as I took another sip of coffee. "Don't need any lessons."

Billy went about explaining how to use the keypad once again and what each number represented.

"See this last row of numbers with this line and the image of a badge? Hit any one of those, and it summons the police, fire department, and rescue squad. It's set up like that in case you have a serious emergency."

"What does that blinking red light mean?" Mom asked. "It was green."

Billy looked back at the keypad.

"That means we've gone into lockdown mode. Y'all should be getting a text any minute now."

As soon as the words were out of his mouth, cell phones started beeping. I looked down at mine and hit the text image. “Mine says, ‘Lockdown Mode’. I guess you forgot to tell me about that one, Billy.”

“Mine says the same thing.”

“Same here,” Mom said. “I know it probably means there’s danger, but does it also mean we’re locked in the house? Can Jonathan lock everyone’s doors from his bunker?”

Billy chuckled.

“He could, but he won’t unless he actually sees someone lurking about. The text is a warning to lock everything up and be on the lookout for anything suspicious.”

We all turned to look when we heard someone coming down the stairs. It was Eddie, holding his cell phone in one hand, and rubbing his eyes with the other.

“I just got a strange text,” he said. “I was sound asleep, felt something licking my face, and when I opened my eyes, your cat was sitting on my chest. That’s when I heard the beep on my phone. The cat took off, so I reached over and picked it up. Am I missing something?”

Mom explained to Eddie what was happening. She even took him over to the alarm keypad and told him what Billy had just told us. “We’re in ‘Lockdown Mode’, so if you ever see this blinking red light and get a text, you know to lock up the house, and be on the lookout for trouble.”

Eddie looked over at Billy. “Do I need to go get my gun, stand watch, or something?”

“You need to go back to bed, honey,” Mom said. “You need your rest. Remember what the doctor said. You need to take it easy. You’re not a spring chicken anymore. Besides, Billy has everything under control, don’t you, Billy?”

Billy gave him the thumb’s up.

“We’re good here. Go back to bed, Eddie. If anything happens, I’ll let you know.”

Eddie looked at me. “That’s one smart cat you have, Jesse. He was trying to tell me something. Is he part Indian, too?” He chuckled and then headed for the stairs. "Wake me if something goes down."

"He's not my cat," I called to him as he was leaving. "Mom's the one who let him in to start with. He ought to be living with her."

"Oh, Jesse, you love that cat and you know it, but I'll be glad to take him home with me if that's what you want."

"He's yours."

"She's not serious, Minnie," Helene said. "And besides, the kids would have a fit."

I looked up at Billy.

"Why didn't you tell Eddie about the breach?"

"There's nothing he can do. He's too injured to put up much of a fight, so why worry him? We have enough guns in this house to keep an army at bay. We're good."

"My money says she's still on the property… and she's watching us," Helene said. "I bet she's out there right now, waiting for the right time to come in here and kill us all in our sleep."

"Don't be ridiculous," Mom came back with. "She's long gone, isn't she, Billy?"

"We're not sure. That's why Shark and Jonathan are out doing recon. I should hear something soon."

"Shark!" Mom exclaimed. "He's such a teddy bear! Don't you just love him? I know I sure do. Wonderful guy. Just wonderful."

I looked at Billy, and then back to Mom.

"Shark's a good man as long as he's on your side, but just remember what it is he does for a living. He has Jonathan's military training, and if he's after you, you're going to die. He has skills you wouldn't want to know about. You do realize that, don't you, Mom?"

"I'm no fool, Jesse. I know who Shark is and what he does. I also know about Billy and Jonathan and the rest of the Blackhawk crew. I know what they can do, and I love them just the same. It's a different world we're living in now. Things change, and we have to change with it. We have to adapt. I'm adapting."

"I'm glad you brought that up, Minnie." Billy looked at me and then back to Mom. "While you're adapting, maybe you should consider adapting to a change in your life."

"What do you mean?"

"We've been trying to get you to move in with us for a long time, but we know you like to have your independence, so Jesse and I picked out a parcel of land on the backside of our property close to that huge cherry tree you love so much, and we want to give it to you. The Blackhawk boys will build you a house, any kind you want. Just say the word."

I knew Mom would be surprised by Billy's offer, but after all we've been through in the last eight years or so, and the lifestyle we've lived, I was hoping she might agree now. It would be best for everyone. She'd be living on the family compound where she'd be safe, and she'd be surrounded by her family.

"That's a mighty tempting offer, Billy, but I already have a house, and I like my home."

"I know you do, Minnie, and no one's saying you have to get rid of it. You can sell it, or keep it and rent it out. It's all up to you." He smiled at her. "It's time for a change, don't you think?"

I grinned. I could see Billy was winning her over.

"Let me think about it," Mom said. "I have to talk with Eddie, see what he has to say."

I jumped up, ran over, and hugged her.

"I'm so glad, Mom!"

"I haven't said yes, yet." She looked at Billy. "If I do agree, you will sell me the land, and I will pay the Blackhawk boys to build it."

"I will give you the land, the Blackhawk boys will build you house, and you can pay for the materials. How does that sound?"

"Like I'm not going to win this discussion."

"We all win," Helene said. "No offense to Billy, but if Geneva and Eli can live on the compound, so can Minnie and Eddie. At least all of us like them."

I chuckled. "Enough… I was wrong about Geneva. She wasn't the money-grabbing villain I thought she was… and they are Maisy's biological grandparents." I looked at Mom. "You're the only one of the grandparents who doesn't live here. Think about that. Those two poor kids going without Grandma Minnie and Grandpa Eddie."

"You're being silly, Jesse. They see us all the time."

"We'll build you a nice, big home with extra bedrooms, in case Claire or Jack wants to bring their families for a visit. You'll have plenty of room for them to stay with you, if you want," I said, trying to encourage her along. "We'll put in lots of windows upstairs, so you'll have a fantastic panoramic view. Wouldn't that be great? It's so beautiful there when that cherry tree blooms."

"If I was going to move, I wouldn't pick a house that had an upstairs. We're getting too old to be climbing those stairs every day."

"No upstairs… then how about one with a Cathedral ceiling?" Helene was doing her bit to encourage Mom. "Yeah, and a split-level on each side for bedrooms."

She looked at Billy.

"Would that be called a tri-level?"

"I like that idea, Helene," I added. "Who says you can't have plenty of room if you don't have a second story?"

"I kinda like it, too," Mom said. "But I'm still going to have to discuss this with Eddie."

"Eddie loves you, Mom. He'll do anything you want."

"As soon as this mess with Dakota Stone is over, we'll get started," Billy chimed in. "We'll have you in your new home by Christmas."

"Good luck on that," Mom said. "You won't even be able to lay the foundation pretty soon. It'll be too cold. Winter is just around the corner. There's no time."

"You leave it to me, and I'll make it happen. You made the right choice, Minnie."

Billy walked over and gave her a hug.

"Welcome to the reservation."

Lightning reared its ugly head and the room lit up like a solar flare. A clap of thunder silenced us all. It was a loud, rumbling noise that seemed to go on forever.

Athena came running up to us from wherever she'd been hiding, and started prancing around. When she finally stopped, she just stood there trembling.

Billy looked at Helene.

"Did you give her one of those pills?"

"Yes, I did as soon as you asked me to."

"This might be a two-pill moment. I have a feeling this storm's going to be worse than the last, and you know how bad that one was."

"Yeah, Mae got struck by lightning."

For a moment, I had visions of Dakota Stone sneaking around, looking for ways to kill us… and then getting struck by lightning. Wouldn't that be ironic?

I had no idea how quickly my thoughts were going to turn into reality.

Chapter 11

THE RAIN WAS steadily coming down, but that wasn't bothering any of us as much as the dangerous lightning. The thunder, although loud, was tolerable, but that lightning was a real killer.

"The guys shouldn't be out in this mess," Mom said. "It's too dangerous. With all these trees around, no one should be out there. If Dakota's still hanging around, then she's crazy."

Billy leaned over the table and took a picture of one of the photos of Dakota and Olivia with his cell phone.

"I'm going to send this to Mason and get him to check your house for one. You never know. She might've been there, too."

"Why would she go to my house?"

"She's sending us a message. She wants us to know that she can get to any one of us at any time."

"I just don't get it, Billy," I said. "Why leave something so incriminating? It proves she's been in our house."

"She's trying to intimidate us, so we'll leave her alone. She thinks that if she causes enough fear, we'll back off, but I've got a surprise for her. She's going down."

We sat at the table, drinking coffee, and waiting to hear back from someone. If the storm hadn't come up, Billy would be out there searching with the guys, but since it had, he wouldn't leave us by ourselves.

"I'm worried about Jonathan and the guys," Mom said. "Call someone and see what's going on. I won't be able to sleep until I know they're home, safe and sound."

To appease Mom, Billy picked up his cell phone to make the call, but as he held it in his hand, it rang. He looked at the screen and said, "It's Mason."

All of us started asking questions at the same time, so he got up from the table and walked down the hall.

When he came back, he said, "Mason found the same photo on your dresser, Minnie."

Mom gasped.

"The good news is, Kaleb has been found and he's all right."

Billy looked at Mom.

"She left him at your house."

He waited for the news to sink in, and then added, "Mason said he's surprised the kid wasn't hurt, because he got into a few things."

"Like what?"

"Mainly, the cabinet under your sink."

"That's where I keep my cleaning supplies. Please tell me he didn't drink any of that stuff."

"No, he didn't, but he found the booze. An empty bottle lay on the kitchen floor, and Mason said he smelled of bourbon when he found him in your closet."

"He's only three years old, right?" I asked.

"No, he's four," Mom replied. "Just old enough to get into something he shouldn't."

"Mason called the sheriff the minute he found Kaleb. The rescue squad came out, picked him up and took him to the hospital to have him checked out."

"What's going to happen to him? Savannah's in the hospital, so who will look after the boy?"

"As soon as they give him a clean bill of health, Cole will be taking him home with him."

"Bless his heart," Mom said. "Cole's a good man."

"Yes, he is," Billy said. "I'm just wondering where Kaleb was when Cole went by the house earlier."

"He could've been hiding under the bed for all we know. I'm sure he was scared. Who knows what that woman did to him? She could've terrorized the poor kid."

"He's been found and he's going to be all right. We know he'll be safe with Cole."

"Yeah," Helene said. "If you can't be safe with a deputy, then who can you be safe with? Cole knows how to take care of Kaleb. I just hope Savannah survives to be with her son."

Billy's cell phone went off again and he automatically got up and started walking down the hall.

The three of us wanted to hear the conversation, so Helene told Mom to go listen, but Mom refused.

"He'll tell us when he gets back. Don't be so impatient."

In the meantime, in between the thunder, we could hear the sound of sirens. They seemed to be getting louder and louder.

Helene, Mom, and I stared at each other, wondering if the cops were coming here.

After what seemed like an eternity, Billy walked back into the room.

We waited with baited breath to hear what he had to say.

"That was Jonathan, and those sirens you hear are coming this way. We've had a fatality on the property over by the stable at Mom's house. A woman was struck and killed by lightning, and it wasn't Dakota Stone."

"Well, then who was it?"

"We don't know, yet, but Gator and Lu Ann are looking into it. Jonathan sent them a picture of her face from his cell phone, and he sent one to me. She looks pretty bad, but if anyone wants to have a look… maybe one of you will recognize her. I have to warn you that it's rather ugly. Jonathan thinks she must've been leaning up against a tree or sitting under it when it when lightning struck the tree. She got thrown a few feet. Her body's mangled, that's why he just sent a pic of the face, which has some pretty bad burns."

Before we had the opportunity to have a look, Billy's cell went off.

A few seconds later, he said to us, "Lu Ann went to The Body Shop website and she's pretty sure the woman is Nancy Woodward, the nutritionist."

"That's her name!" Mom said. "I couldn't remember it before, but now that you've said it, I remember. I can't believe it was her. She's such a nitwit. I'm sorry to be so rude for saying that, but the woman ain't real bright. I can't believe she's part of Dakota's gang."

"Oh, she's the best kind. She's expendable."

"She might've planted those photos, Billy, but I don't think she could pull off a kidnapping. She's just not smart enough."

"Don't be so sure, Minnie. It doesn't take a lot of brains to snatch and grab, just speed and the element of surprise. Stick a gun in someone's face and they'll usually cooperate, especially when a child's involved."

Helene waved her hand.

"I'll bet that Nancy woman did it all—the kidnapping and that stupid photo-planting stunt. If she's as dimwitted as Minnie says she is, she'd make the perfect patsy, and we all know patsies can do a lot of harm before they stumble over their own feet. Leaving those photos… I'm still trying to figure out what that was all about."

Billy smiled.

"Oh, I know what it's about. Dakota was leaving a calling card. She wanted us to have something to remember her by while she's sitting on a beach in California… or wherever it is she's headed to next."

I added my opinion.

"Dakota isn't the kind of woman who gets her hands dirty, nor would she take a chance of getting arrested for such a petty crime as trespassing. She gets her underlings to do her dirty work. If they don't live up to her expectations, she gets rid of them… like she did Gavin Preston. Nancy Woodward was nobody to her, but I bet she didn't plan on this."

"She won't care."

"No, she won't."

"I bet it sure put a snag in her plans. Perhaps, Nancy Woodward wasn't finished. She might've had other orders to carry out."

"I guess Dakota will just have to do it herself."

My cell phone vibrated and then rang. I looked down at the screen and then back up at Billy.

"The Body Shop."

"Answer it. I'll see if Gator can trace the call."

He walked over to the kitchen and whispered into his phone.

I put my finger to my lips, touched the answer icon, and then hit speaker. I also hit the record button.

"Jesse Blackhawk here. What can I do for you, Dakota? Want me to go out and kill someone for you?"

"My, aren't we cheerful?" she replied. "No, not today. I just wanted to say goodbye and tell you what an experience it was to have known you and your family."

"I hope it was pleasant."

"How's Eddie doing, by the way? That old man must be pretty strong to survive that kind of beating. Most men his age would've died."

"Oh, he'll live to fight another day, and so will I, but thanks for your concern. It's so touching."

"I told Gavin to kill your mother, but he let me down. He let me down in so many ways. What'll you do with a man who isn't committed?"

Mom's face was getting redder by the minute. I knew she was about ready to grab the phone and scream at the woman, so I held up my hand to keep her from saying or doing anything. She slumped back in her chair and didn't say a word. She knew how important this call could be.

“Preston wasn’t a bad guy until he met you. You poison everyone with your insanity. What’s wrong with you? Did your father sexually abuse you as a child?”

I was trying my best to rile her, but she remained unflappable.

“Poor Nancy. Too bad she was too stupid to get out of the storm. What do you do with someone who’s smart enough to do all the things she’s done for you, yet too dumb to get out of the rain? I tried with her, I really did.”

“How do you know what happened to her? She was only found thirty minutes ago.”

“Jesse, you’re so naïve. I know everything. I do have a police scanner. Doesn’t everyone?”

She laughed.

“I know about your security system, which I must say is very impressive.”

“Then you knew she’d get caught.”

“Not if the timing was right, and it was. I didn’t, however, expect her to go and get killed.”

“I guess that means you’d better leave town in a hurry.”

“I know about your friend Savannah.”

“What about Savannah, other than the fact that you stuffed her in your dryer?”

“That was unfortunate, but necessary.”

“We found the kid.”

“Of course you did. I told Nancy to leave him, but she wouldn’t. She was afraid he’d hurt himself if he was left alone, so she took him too. I made her take him back. He was getting on my nerves. All that crying…”

“You’re a sick b…”

“Your ex-boyfriend, Deputy Cole James, murdered Savannah’s husband. Did you know that?”

“You’re such a liar. He killed McCoy in self-defense.”

“Yeah, that’s what they all say, but she knows what really happened.

Why don't you take a minute and ask your dear friend to tell you the truth about what her new boyfriend did to her husband?"

"I don't have to. I know what happened. You're just trying to stir up trouble, but it won't work. You've misjudged me. I'm not as gullible as you think."

"Don't you just hate Cole for dumping you for Savannah?"

"It didn't play out that way and you know it."

"Did you know Billy was seeing his ex-wife, Ruth?"

For a second, that was like a slap in the face. Anytime someone tells you your husband is cheating on you, it hits a nerve. I bit my lip and remained calm. I knew she was lying about that little tidbit. She was trying to turn us against each other.

"Yeah, we've got a threesome going on. Can we talk about something else? You're starting to bore me."

Helene snickered, and I gave her the evil eye.

"Thanks for the photos. I'll remember you always."

"You want to know why I am the way I am, don't you?"

"It's not top on the list of my priorities, but if you need to tell me, I'm listening."

Billy waved and gave me the thumb's up. They had traced the call and we now knew where she was. He mouthed the words, "Omni Hotel, Charlottesville."

"We could talk more, if you'd like. I can come to the Omni, or you can come here."

"God, it's about time your trace went through. I was beginning to think I'd have to talk to you all day. No, I'll have to pass, perhaps another time."

"Say hello to your girlfriend, Olivia, for me. I didn't know you were a lesbian, but hey, that doesn't bother me if you like women instead of men. To each his own—isn't that what they say?"

I thought I heard someone in the background say something, and then Dakota laughed.

"My girlfriend's waiting on me, so I'm going to have to say goodbye. I'll check up on you in a few months… after we get settled in."

She disconnected before I could say anything else.

I looked around at everyone.

"I recorded her confessing to a whole bunch of crimes, but it won't mean a thing if she's not apprehended. We have to catch her before she makes her getaway. She's good at changing her identity. She'll go into the abyss and never be heard from again."

Billy picked up my cell phone.

"What are you doing?"

"I'm sending this recording to Sheriff Hudson. If he had any doubts about who killed Preston, this should clear it up. I just hope he doesn't believe the part about Cole. We know she was lying."

I didn't want to say it, but I felt compelled to.

"Billy, I had some doubts about what happened that day, too, and it wasn't because I was jealous or anything. Those days are long gone. If you send that recording, it just might light a fire under the sheriff's butt and cause Cole a whole lot of grief he doesn't deserve. You might want to rethink that text."

"I knew she was a lesbian," Helene said, giggling. "That's why she hates men."

"You did not!"

"Come on, Minnie. Don't tell me you didn't think the same thing."

"She's not a lesbian, Helene." I said.

"She said she was."

"No, she didn't, she laughed, remember?"

"Yeah, so what?"

"Coming out of the closet or being exposed, isn't something someone laughs about. I think there's a side to this story we haven't considered. Maybe we've been looking at this all wrong. I was thinking about a movie I saw where two women meet on a plane, talk about how they hate their husbands, and then make a pact to kill them off. They don't know each other, so there's no connection between the two. Dakota kills off Olivia's husband, and in return, Olivia kills off Dakota's husband. Then, the two hook up and run off together."

"Hmm… now that's a thought."

"There's no information on either one of them that goes any further back than five years ago. It's as if their lives started then. I say, what happened five years ago?"

Billy smiled.

"That's my `ge ya. I think you might have something there."

"Yeah, but it's going to be hard to track down. We don't know where they lived at the time they met. We don't even know what state they lived in. They could've come from Canada for all we know. It'd be like looking for a needle in a haystack."

Billy handed my cell phone to me.

"Call her back and see if she answers."

"And if she does, what do you want me to say to her?"

"Oh, I don't know…"

Billy paced while trying to come up with something, and then he stopped.

"Lie to her. Tell her we have Nancy's cell phone. If she takes the bait, I'm sure you'll be able to put a spin on the story."

Helene got up, walked to the kitchen to refill her cup, and then looked back at us.

"If she answers, tell her that our guy is tracking the GPS in her car… that he locked on it when he traced her cell phone to the hotel. He hacked into their cameras, and saw her get in her car. Boom! She's busted."

Mom grinned.

"Forget about telling her we have Nancy's cell phone. Tell her that Nancy didn't die."

"Ah, you ladies are so devious."

Billy smiled again, and then looked back at me.

"Make the call, Jesse. We don't have a thing to lose."

Billy's cell phone beeped, signaling an incoming text. After reading the message, he laughed, and then looked over at Helene.

"You should be a detective. Gator did exactly what you just said."

"You mean you can actually do that?"

"Yep, but it means hacking into DMV to get the VIN number, and then hacking into the carmaker for the GPS code. Easy as pie, if you know what you're doing, but you have to be really good not to get caught. Gator and Mason are two of the best hackers you'll ever meet. She's on I-64 heading east."

"I'd love to be able to do that."

"Do what, Helene, be a hacker?"

"Yeah, Minnie, just think of how much fun that would be."

"With my luck, I'd get caught and wind up at Gitmo, getting tortured by two big, burley military men."

Helene laughed so hard at Mom, coffee shot out of her nose. After she regained her composure, she wiped her face and was still chuckling when she asked her how she knew about Gitmo.

"I watch the news. I know all about that place."

"All right, everybody be quiet. I'm calling Dakota."

Billy got another text and stopped me.

"Hold off a minute. Let's see what we have here first. Hmm… Dakota jacked a car from the hotel parking lot. Gator says it's registered to one of the guests."

"How does he know that," Mom asked. "Did he hack into the hotel's computer, too?"

"Yes, he sure did. The car wasn't registered to The Body Shop, so he compared the owner's name to the guest list at the hotel. The car belongs to Ray Forester—a white Toyota Camry. I told you he was good."

"I got plenty to tell her now, so can I make the call, or is there anything else?"

"Go ahead."

"She won't answer," Helene said, recovering from her coffee blast. "She's probably already dumped the phone."

I made the call, and much to everyone's surprise, Dakota answered.

"Hello, Jesse. I sure didn't expect to hear from you so soon. What can I do for you?"

"First thing you might want to do is dump the stolen car. Ray Forester wants his white Toyota Camry back."

We heard a noise in the background like a glove box being opened, and then papers being shuffled around.

"Got you thinking, haven't I? By the way, how's the weather on I-64? Is it still storming there? It sure is here. I'm telling you, this storm is the worst I've seen in a long time. It's a real killer, but fortunately for Nancy, it didn't kill her. That's right, she's still alive. I can't wait to hear what she has to tell the cops. My… my… what a mess you left behind. She's going to lead them straight to you."

"I'll be way gone by then."

"Oh, honey, she's already awake. She took an indirect hit and was revived. You can thank Jonathan for that. He gave her CPR until the ambulance arrived. Just thought you'd like to know."

"You're lying."

"You might want to send one of your buddies over to UVA Hospital and have her killed. Oh, that's right, you don't have any friends left except Olivia Swales. You killed off all the rest. Well… except me."

"We're not friends."

"We're not? Now that hurts my feelings. I thought we were pals, best buds and all."

We heard some kind of racket, tires screeching, and then the line went dead. I disconnected and looked around at everyone.

"Sounds to me like she tossed the phone out the window. I guess she didn't like what I had to say. That's too bad. I'll miss our conversations." I rolled my eyes.

"And those tires we heard squealing was probably her getting off the interstate," Billy said. "I bet she's on her way to UVA Hospital to tie up loose ends. Good going, `ge ya."

He kissed my forehead.

"You put doubts in her mind about Nancy being dead, and now she can't flee while there's still a witness left behind. She has to kill Nancy Woodward. I told you she'd make a mistake. When she comes back, the cops will be waiting for her."

"Throwing her cell phone out the window was pretty stupid." Mom rubbed her forehead. "I don't get it. Why didn't she just call the hospital and find out the truth? That's all she had to do."

Helene looked at Mom.

"The hospital won't give out that information over the phone, Minnie. No… she has to go there to find out anything. I think Billy's right. She's coming back to tie up loose ends. If Nancy had died, she'd be free and clear to make a run for it, but now that she thinks Nancy might be alive, she has to do something to shut her up. She's coming back to kill her."

Billy picked up his cell phone.

"I'm going to call Sheriff Hudson and tell him about Dakota calling Jesse… and I'm also going to tell him she's on I-64."

He looked around at the three of us.

"He'll want to know how we knew she was on I-64, so I'm going to say she told Jesse. We don't want to tell him the whole truth about this one. It wouldn't play well for any of us."

I smiled and said, "Tell him she's driving a white Toyota, and that she bragged about stealing it from the parking lot of the Omni Hotel where she's been hiding."

"Before I call the sheriff, I have one thing to do first."

Billy lay his phone down, picked up mine, and made a call to Jonathan.

"Hack into Jesse's phone and retrieve her recorded calls. That's right… yes… permanently delete them from her phone. Okay… that's fine. Do whatever it is you do. Yeah… I'm getting ready to call the sheriff and tell him where she is. I will. I'll let you know."

When the call was complete, Billy handed me the phone and said, "It's done. The calls you recorded have been downloaded to a secure place in Jonathan's system, and deleted from your phone."

Mom rubbed her eyes.

"Hurry up and call the sheriff, Billy. I need to know if it's safe for me to go to bed. I'm bushed."

Billy called the sheriff, put the phone on speaker, and then laid it on the table.

"I hope you have something for me, Blackhawk. I'm pretty busy at the moment."

"Then, I'll get right to the point. Dakota Stone called Jesse about thirty minutes ago. She told her she was on I-64 in a white Toyota, heading east. She's making a run for it like we said she would."

"Why would she tell Jesse that, unless it was a lie to throw us off-track?"

"She might be lying, but I don't think so. You know how Jesse can be when it comes to riling someone up. Dakota didn't stand a chance against my woman."

"I agree there."

I smiled.

"Dakota bragged about stealing the car from the Omni, where she'd been staying. However, she got quite upset when Jesse told her that Nancy Woodward wasn't dead. She's coming back, Sheriff."

"But Nancy Woodward is dead."

"Yeah, and Dakota heard that on your police scanner, but Jesse convinced her that the initial report was wrong, and Nancy is still alive."

"All right, Billy. I'll check it out, but you'd better be right. The State Police don't take kindly to wild goose chases, and neither do I. Waste our time and people die."

"I don't think it'll be a waste of time, Sheriff."

"Okay… I'll contact Captain Trainum and let him know she might be coming his way."

"Who?"

"Your old pal, Frank Trainum."

My sister, Claire, and I were the first to meet Frank Trainum a few years ago when her scumbag ex-husband, Carl, kidnapped her kids and took them to D.C. to the house where they had lived. In the middle of the night, Billy and his brothers rescued the kids and brought them home safely, and then Carl mysteriously disappeared, leaving a dead body in his basement. Claire and I found the body. That was our introduction to Detective Frank Trainum. He didn't particularly care for me, but that changed somewhat when he fell in love with a woman named Alexandra and moved to Charlottesville.

"What happened to Captain Mealphall?"

"Misfortune. His guys botched a big case and someone had to take the fall, so he was asked to retire. That better not happen to me, Blackhawk. If this turns out to be a load of crock, I'm not going to be happy. Get my drift? I plan on being re-elected in the next election, and you'd better not mess it up for me by…"

"Just check it out, Sheriff."

The call ended abruptly when the sheriff disconnected. Billy looked at us. "I guess all we can do now is wait and see what happens next. I sure hope they catch her, because if they don't, the sheriff's going to be out for blood."

"Do you hear that?" I asked, looking around at everyone.

"Hear what?" Helene stood up, walked over to the kitchen sink, and set her empty cup down. "I don't hear anything."

"That's just it. I don't either. I don't hear thunder anymore. I guess that means the storm has passed." I got up from the table, walked over to the front door, and opened it to look outside. "Yep, and the rain has quit, too. It sure is getting cold out there." I closed the door. "Maybe it's going to snow. Nah, it's too early for snow."

"Don't bet on it. Here in the mountains it can start snowing at any time. Remember the year it snowed before Halloween?"

"I'm going to bed. I'm beat." Helene walked back over to the table. "How about you, Minnie? I know you're tired. It's been a very long day."

Mom got up to leave, but stopped.

"Hey, the red light isn't on anymore. It's green now."

We all looked at the keypad, and a second later, Billy's cell phone rang. "Hey, Jonathan, I see the red light is off. What's going on? Okay. Let me put you on speaker phone, so I don't have to repeat myself. The women are ready for bed, and so am I."

Billy looked at us and said, "Wait, don't leave just yet. Jonathan has some news. Go ahead, Jonathan."

"You're not going to believe this, but the cops just busted the psycho twins. According to State Police, the driver, psycho twin number one, Dakota Stone, threw her cell phone out the window doing almost eighty on the interstate, and it hit the windshield of the car beside her. The man in the car lost control, and slammed into her, forcing her car into the guardrail. After that, it was like a domino effect."

Mom, Helene, and I were dumbfounded. We just stood there with our mouths hanging open. The news didn't seem to faze Billy. It was as if he expected that it would end badly for Dakota and Olivia.

"How did you find out?"

"The dot on the screen stopped moving, and usually when someone stops on the interstate that means they've either had a flat tire or an accident. No one just stops on the interstate without a reason, unless they're a fool, so I called my state trooper buddy, Wally, and he filled me in on what happened. No fatalities, but seven people were being transported to either UVA or Martha Jefferson Hospital… and two of those seven folks are our psycho twins—Dakota Stone and Olivia Swales. Wally said they don't think the Swales woman's going to make it. She's pretty bad off."

"At least they're not going to be able to hurt anyone anymore. I hope the cops handcuff them to their beds."

"I'm sure they will, Minnie."

"Oh, God, I'm going to get blamed for this."

"You? What did you do, Jesse?"

"I was the person she was talking to just before she threw the phone out the window."

When I said I was going to get the blame, I didn't mean by the cops, but by Dakota. If she survived and Olivia didn't, she would hate me even more, and be determined to get revenge. All I could do was hope the cops put her away for a long time, but if they didn't, my nightmare was just beginning. She would come after me with everything she had, and I feared that my family would suffer the fallout. The best way to get back at a person is to hurt someone they love.

"You don't have anything to worry about, Jesse. She's finished. She stole a car and caused an accident, and if anyone dies, she could be held accountable. Once the cops start digging around, I'm sure they'll find something else to charge her with. She's been a very bad girl, and Sheriff Hudson knows it. He won't quit until he gets his answers. I think we can all sleep well tonight."

"I hope you're right, Jonathan, but if they cut her loose, she'll be coming after me. How am I going to sleep knowing that? If she wants retribution, someone in our family might die other than me."

"Forget about her. All is well."

Unfortunately, I had a nagging feeling that all was not well and never would be as long as Dakota Stone was still alive.

Chapter 12

I tossed and turned all night long, and when I did get some sleep, Dakota's face haunted my dreams. I knew that if she was released from the hospital and wasn't taken to jail, she'd be heading my way, coming after me or Billy or Mom, or worst, my children. She wasn't going to run again until she had gotten even with me.

It was still dark when I woke up covered in sweat, drenched with the strong odor of fear. Everyone was still asleep, so I jumped in the shower, and was in the kitchen making coffee when Helene walked in.

"You're up mighty early this morning, Jesse. Couldn't sleep?"

"I had nightmares about Dakota all night. It was awful. I can't wait to find out what happened to her. I sure hope Sheriff Hudson has her in his jail. I'll sleep better knowing that she isn't out running around killing people."

"Jonathan said she was taken to UVA or Martha Jefferson. I would think the Charlottesville Police would be in charge of her arrest. Why don't you give Captain Trainum a call? He's your buddy, isn't he?"

"Somewhat... but if I call him this early in the morning, he won't be for long."

An hour later, the house came to life. Everyone, except Billy, was awake and ready for breakfast. The kitchen was buzzing with chatter when he walked in dressed in a white T-shirt and lounging pants, his long, dark hair hanging loosely down his back, still damp from his shower.

"Don't you look handsome," I said as I jumped up and gave him a kiss. "I hope I didn't keep you awake last night. I didn't sleep well."

"No, you didn't. I went out the minute my head hit the pillow, and slept like a baby." He looked around the kitchen table. "Good morning, everyone."

He went over and kissed Maisy and Ethan, and then told Ethan to stop feeding his bacon to the dogs.

"But they like it, Daddy."

"I'm sure they do, son, but it's not good for them. That's why they eat dog food. It's made just for them and has all the nutrition they need. Bacon clogs their arteries."

"What about us?" Maisy chimed in. "Should we be eating bacon?"

"Probably not." Billy chuckled, while making his way over to the coffee pot. "Probably not."

As I poured his coffee, I noticed something weird. The marble bowl with its little masher thingy that Helene used to grind up herbs or whatever else she needed to mash, had a small mound of white powder in it. The first thing I thought of was cocaine. I poked Billy, pointed to it, and whispered, "Is that what I think it is?"

He looked at the bowl, licked his finger as if he was going to taste it, but I stopped him.

"No, please. We don't know what it is. It could be anything… it could be poison."

He got Helene's attention and waved her over. He pointed to the bowl. "Do you know what this is?"

"It's Athena's doggie downer. I can't get her to take the pill, so I mash it up, scrape it onto a slice of cheese, ball up the cheese, and then she woofs it down. Geez, with all the commotion, I guess I forgot to give it to her. I'm sorry." She smiled after a second. "What did you think it was?"

Billy and I looked at each other and grinned.

"We thought it might be cocaine, a present left by Nancy when she paid us that visit."

"I'll put the lid on it and clamp it shut. Athena might need it today. The weatherman predicts another storm starting about midday. He called it 'thunder snow', and said we could get a few inches out of it."

"Thunder snow? Never heard of it. Sometimes, I think they make that junk up."

"No, it's for real, Grandpa Eddie." Maisy explained. "It's like getting a thunderstorm with lightning and everything, except instead of rain, it snows. I think it sounds cool."

"Global warming."

"That's right, Grandma. I read about it in class. Mrs. Baker also said we've been polluting our planet. She said we should recycle more, and that people shouldn't throw their trash out their car window. Then, she told us about this commercial where this Indian guy is crying because the river has trash floating in it."

The breakfast conversation started with global warming and ended with designer clothes, the adults avoiding any discussion of what the day might hold.

When the kids finished eating, Helene took them to get cleaned up, leaving us to plan our next move.

"I need to check in with Jonathan for an update, then we'll go from there. If Dakota and Olivia are in custody, I think it'll be safe for Minnie and Eddie to go home and pack up their stuff. Just the essentials, Minnie."

He looked at Mom.

"And before you argue with me about it, I want you to stay with us until your house is finished. We're going to get on that right away."

"But..."

"No buts, Mom. It's the only way you can be safe. Even if those women are in jail, they might get out. We can't take any chances."

Mom looked as if she was going to protest, but she didn't.

"If that's what you want, Billy."

"It is." He looked at Eddie. "I hope you don't mind, but we can't protect you if you're going to be living out there in the middle of nowhere. You have no security, and your neighbors live too far apart to be of any help."

"I agree. Minnie and I talked about it this morning, and I like your idea, but we're not going to let you do it for free. You're giving us the land, so we want to pay for the materials and your time."

"We're family. You can pay for the materials, but you won't pay us for our time."

"Case closed," I said, beaming with joy. "I'm so happy, and the kids will love having y'all so close by."

"All right, here goes. I'll put it on speaker, so nobody misses anything." Billy pulled out his cell phone and punched in Jonathan's number. "What have I missed, brother?"

"Olivia Swales died last night, and Dakota went crazy when she found out. They've been keeping her sedated. She's strapped and handcuffed to the bed."

"What about injuries?"

"Minor. They were going to release her to the police, until she went nuts."

"What about Savannah? Have you heard how she's doing?" Mom asked.

"Minnie… she's not doing so well. She was knocked out and then drugged before she was even put in the dryer. The explosion… well, it busted both eardrums, and she has burns from the blast heat. The one good thing I can tell you is that she doesn't have any broken bones."

"How much?"

"How much, what?"

"How much skin was burned off? If it was only a little, she should be all right, but if it was a lot..."

"It wasn't a little." Jonathan paused. "She can't have visitors, Minnie. I know you want to see her, but you can't just yet."

Mom sighed.

"Recovery will take time, Mom." I hugged her. "All you can do is pray for Savannah, and hope she gets better soon."

Jonathan spoke again. "Dakota could be faking her craziness. She managed to be lucid enough to call her lawyer. Thanks to Gator, I got to hear the conversation. I think she's just smart enough to pull off this insanity thing. She almost had me believing her story."

"Who's her lawyer?"

"Russell Shank."

"She's smart, that's what she is." I winched at the thought. "Oh, God. Russell's the best. He'll get her off, and then who knows what'll happen next. We're doomed. She'll go free, and the rest of us will go straight to jail. No passing go."

"So far, all they can charge her with is reckless endangerment for throwing her cell phone out the window and causing an accident, and reckless driving. The man and woman in the other car came out of it okay. They're both fine, just a little shaken up, and they've already given their account of the accident to the police. Don't you just love a good eyewitness? Anyway, I had a chat with our friend, Captain Frank Trainum. You know he got Josh Mealphall's job, right?"

"Yeah, we know."

"Trainum said they fingerprinted both women, and if Dakota's print shows up on that detonator, there'll be a string of charges to follow. She'll do hard time. Olivia died, so she's in the clear. They can't do anything to a dead person."

"I don't know about that. She might end up being the fall guy for Dakota. With Swales dead, Dakota can blame her for everything. When Gavin Preston's autopsy comes back, they'll know the cause of death was poison, but Dakota can say Olivia did it."

"Dakota will say nothing. Even though Preston was poisoned, there's no evidence linking her to his death, only our word, and hearsay won't cut it. He told us she poisoned him, but where's the proof?"

"Hey, are they allowed to fingerprint you without your consent?" Mom asked. "Don't you have to be under arrest or something?"

"Mom, they can do anything they want."

"Actually, Jesse, there is a protocol, but since Swales is dead and Dakota is under arrest, they have every right."

"Good! Maybe now we'll find out just who this Dakota woman really is. I'm sure she's been fingerprinted before."

"Maybe not, Minnie. Some people go their whole lives without ever being fingerprinted."

"What about her footprints? Hospitals have been taking footprints of newborns ever since I can remember. Perhaps they can match up…"

"Hmm… now that's a thought, but I don't know if footprints are like fingerprints. With fingerprints, no two are alike. They'll all different. I don't know how it works with footprints, and as far as I know, footprint patterns may change as a person ages. In theory, it sounds like a good idea, but I've never known anyone to be caught based on their footprints as an infant. But hey, with the technology we have now, nothing would surprise me."

"Is there any way Dakota might escape from the hospital?"

"No way, Billy. She's handcuffed to the bed, and there're two police officers stationed at the door. The only way she's leaving the hospital is in handcuffs, escorted by Trainum's men. She's not going anywhere… at least not yet. Once she's in jail, it'll be up to Russell to obtain her release, and that might prove to be a hard sell. There'll be no bail for a woman who has been using the social security number of a dead woman for the last five years. That's a big, red flag. The D.A. will eat this case up. She'll be indicted and the rest will be up to the judge."

"Does that mean we'll be safe to go on with our lives?"

"It looks that way, Minnie, but you can count on us to keep our eyes opened. The minute anything changes, we'll let you know."

"Well, folks," Billy said. "It looks like this case is closed."

"The only way this case will be closed is when that woman is in prison. I won't feel safe until then."

"Don't worry, Minnie. We'll make sure nothing happens to you or Eddie… or anyone else in this family."

"By the way, Jonathan, how are Sarah and Chief Sam doing?"

"They're doing fine. Great, as a matter of fact. Mom seems to be her old self again, and Dad's… well, he's just Dad. Why do you ask? You got something on your mind you want to share?"

"I was wondering what Nancy Woodward was doing so close to your folk's house? Why didn't she leave after she planted the photos, unless she wasn't finished?"

"Wow, pretty good, Minnie. I know why Billy and Jesse want you working with them. It never occurred to me that she had more work to do. I thought she was just trying to find a place to hide until the storm passed, but…"

Billy frowned and asked, "You got something else, Jonathan?"

"The police recovered a baggie of cocaine from her purse, more than one person's usual stash, unless they have a heavy cocaine addiction… and lots of money."

Billy and I looked at each other.

"Hold on a minute, Jonathan."

Billy walked to the kitchen and checked out the white powder that was supposed to be the mashed up pill for Athena.

"I thought that was a lot of powder for one pill. It's cocaine."

He dumped the powder down the sink and turned on the water, rinsing the bowl afterwards.

"What's the matter?" Jonathan asked.

"Billy just found cocaine in the bowl where Athena's doggie pill was supposed to be. Helene mashes it up and wraps it in cheese, so she can get Athena to take it. Athena has a hard time swallowing pills."

Mom's eyes widened. "I wonder if she planted cocaine in my house, too. Oh, Lord, we could be arrested."

"I can see where this is headed. Let me get off the phone and call my friend, Rex, and get him to bring out his K9. If there're any drugs present, that dog can find them. I'll get back with you."

Jonathan disconnected.

"That's a scary thought," Eddie said.

"What is?" Helene asked, walking into the room with the kids. "What did I miss?"

"Being arrested for something you didn't do."

"It happens all the time. If you ask anyone in jail, they'll tell you they're innocent. Isn't that right, Billy?"

Billy nodded in agreement, and then asked Mom to take the kids to the den.

Without hesitation, Mom and Eddie gladly led the children out. They looked almost relieved to be leaving the room and away from all the talk about murder, drugs, and psycho women.

Once they were gone, Billy filled Helene in on the conversation with Jonathan.

"Olivia Swales is dead, and Dakota Stone is handcuffed to her hospital bed. She'll be going to jail as soon as she's released."

I added, "Jonathan said she was pulling an insanity stunt, acting all crazy and everything. They strapped her to the bed, and then slapped on the handcuffs. It sure made my day to hear that."

Billy continued to tell Helene the entire story, ending with, "That white stuff in Athena's bowl wasn't her pill, it was cocaine. Jonathan's getting a buddy to bring his K9 dog to check everyone's house. We don't know how much she planted before she got killed, but she still had plenty left on her. We now think Mom and Dad's house might've been hit by her, too."

Helene smiled and said to me, "If you hadn't ticked off Dakota, she would've never thrown her phone out the window, caused that accident, and then gotten caught. Ironic how things work out, isn't it?"

"I don't want to take the credit. With credit, comes blame. Next thing you know, Sheriff Hudson will be showing up at my door with a warrant, arresting me for contributing to a crime, or something stupid like that. No… I take no credit."

Helene started clearing the table. "What are we going to do next? I mean, do we go on about our business as usual, or do we wait around to see what that crazy woman will do next?"

"She's done in, so we move on," Billy said as he walked over to the front window. "Looks like rain. Maybe we're going to get some of that thunder snow you were talking about."

"Are you making fun of me, Billy Blackhawk?"

He walked over and gave Helene a hug.

"You know I would never do that." Then, he laughed. "It sure feels good to laugh again. Dakota Stone has plucked my last nerve… as Minnie would say."

Helene and I started laughing and couldn't stop. I think our joyous moment had a lot to do with relief. There was no longer anything to fear from Dakota Stone. We all knew there'd be some blowback from Sheriff Hudson for the part we played, but we'd survive.

Mom rushed into the room, followed by Eddie, the kids, and the dogs, and then she said, "Have y'all gone nuts? We can hear you all the way back in the den. What's so funny?"

"Ah, Mom, we're just glad the case is closed. Billy's nerves have been plucked."

That got everyone laughing and the dogs barking, but all soon ceased when we heard a loud clap of thunder overhead. Athena yelped as if she'd been hit with a stick. A moment later, she was shivering and twitching, so much so that you could hear her toenails scratching on the hardwood floor.

"Time for a pill. Follow me, girl."

Helene went to the kitchen and took down the bottle of pills from the cabinet. A minute later, she fed the pill she had wrapped in a slice of cheese to Athena, and not to leave Thor out, gave him a slice, minus the pill.

Mom clapped her hands and the kids' eyes lit up when she said, "How about a bowl of ice cream? We need to celebrate!"

"It's too early in the morning for ice cream."

"You didn't object last night when we gave the kids a cookie before bedtime, Billy. Besides, it's never too early for ice cream, is it kids?"

I winked at Billy. "You've created a monster, and just think… she'll be right next door soon."

Billy threw his hands up as if to surrender as Mom and the kids made their way to the kitchen.

Over a bowl of ice cream, we discussed the day's plans. Billy was going to get Shark to go with Mom and Eddie to pack up a few things, and Helene would stay home with the children.

"We don't know what this thunder snow is going to do…" Billy was cut off before he could finish.

"Yes, we do. I checked the weather while we were in the den. Channel 29 says the snow's going to start in this afternoon and we're going to see significant accumulation by nightfall. The thunder isn't going to last long."

"Minnie, you don't trust the weather channel, do you?" Helene got up to collect bowls from those who had finished their ice cream. "You said they never get it right."

"I don't trust the national weather channel, but if Norm Spruce says it's going to snow ten inches, I believe him. He's not an actor like those people you see on TV, he's a real meteorologist."

"He said we were going to get ten inches?"

"No, he said eight to ten, but that's just an estimate. He said we could get more or less. It's hard to predict exactly, but he says we will get snow."

"That's a contradiction in itself, Minnie. What Norm's saying is, they don't know. The sun could come out and get up to eighty today."

Billy chuckled and said, "I don't think so, Helene. Okay… where was I? Oh, yeah. Rex and K9 Suzy are coming, so someone needs to be here. That's you, Helene. It goes without saying that I don't want the kids to go anywhere, what with a mutant storm coming, so you, the kids, and the dogs can stay home and wait for Rex. Jesse and I will go visit our friend at the hospital."

"Savannah?"

"No, Minnie, but we'll check on her while we're there, and then give you an update. Don't you worry, we'll call you as soon as we find out anything. I know you're concerned about her."

"I'm really worried, Billy. Please call me the minute you hear anything, okay?"

"We will, Mom." I glanced at Billy. "What about the cops at the entrance? Are they still there, and more importantly, can we leave the compound? Sheriff Hudson said…"

"Our restriction applied to last night." Billy grinned. "I got a text from Jonathan saying all is clear."

"Daddy, why does the sheriff pick on you and Mom? He tells you when you can and can't leave the house. I thought this was the land of the free. That doesn't sound like freedom to me."

"Ah, Maisy…"

There are some things we don't tell our children, and one of them being the extent of our questionable behavior, and what happens when we don't live up to our promises.

"He does it for our safety," I said. "He's the sheriff. His job is to protect people, so if he says to stay home, we stay home."

Maisy wasn't buying my cover-up, but said nothing. She knew the truth, and her question was her way of saying we were being pushed around by the sheriff. We were, but we had deserved it. I'm sure she knew that, too.

Billy's a Cherokee Indian and the Cherokees believe in teaching their children how to hunt, survive off the land, and think for themselves. He had taught Maisy well. At the age of six, they were out in the backyard shooting targets with a rifle. Of course, I protested, but then gave up when I realized I was wasting my time. When she was almost seven, they came home with two rabbits, and she had been the one to make the kill. Billy was so proud, and I was just glad they made it back home alive.

Hunting, using a knife, and roughing it in the woods, especially with all the bears and wild animals around, gave me plenty of restless moments, but the part about Maisy learning to think for herself made it all worthwhile. Now, all I had to do was survive the trauma one more time. Soon it would be Ethan's turn.

"Sometimes we have to do things we don't like, but it's for our own good." Mom winked at Maisy.

Eddie glanced out the front window and said, "There're a couple of cars coming up the driveway, a black Hummer, and I think the other one might be a cop car."

It was Shark, Rex and his German shepherd, K9 Suzy.

The first thing Rex said after being introduced was, "Jonathan says you have a cat. You might want to lock him up. K9 Suzy loves cats, but they don't seem to care for her."

"I can see why." Helene went over and grabbed the kids by the hand, getting them out of their chairs, and then stepping back. "She looks intimidating… as if she could chew you to pieces."

"Ah… not to worry." Rex bent down and patted her head. "She loves kids. She's just like any other dog, except that she has a job to do." He looked at Maisy and Ethan. "She sniffs out stuff for people. She's friendly. You can pet her if you want to."

Both of them delighted in doing so, and K9 Suzy was just like he said. She was charming and playful. Rex, on the other hand, looked more intimidating to me than his dog. He was a replica of most cops around here—tall, handsome, and built for the kill. He looked to be about thirty-five, and I was surprised when he said he'd been doing this for almost thirty years, ever since he got out of the police academy. That would make him about forty-eight, but he sure didn't look his age. I told him so.

"Thanks, Jesse, but to be honest, I've seen my share of dogfights."

With that said, K9 Suzy started barking.

"That's my cue, so where's the cat?"

The pill had kicked in and Athena had been lying by the fireplace without a care in the world, with Thor for company. Thor, on the other hand, had lain still too long. He had been reserved and didn't approach… until K9 Suzy barked. Once she had made her presence known, Thor wanted to do the love dance. She was having none of him, and took off down the hallway.

"Find your cat," Rex called out.

The search was on to find Spice Cat after everyone had confirmed that he hadn't been seen all morning. Even Shark, who had said little, helped. We searched the house and came up with nothing, and by that time, K9 Suzy had finished her job. She, too, had found nothing.

Helene looked down at Spice's food bowl. "He ate most of his food, so he's probably outside. That's why y'all put in that doggie door, and he takes advantage of it. He's out there getting into something right now. He's fine. He'll come home when he's ready."

Thor moaned and groaned when Rex and K9 Suzy left. He was in love and heartbroken after being snubbed. Thor has always been a whiner, but he'd get over it after a few days of being a crybaby and seeking consolation from everyone. Then, he'd find something else to whine about. It was his way.

Maisy took Ethan's hand, and then motioned to Thor. "Come on, Thor. You can watch TV with us and cry on my shoulder." She smiled back at us before leaving the room.

Shark, Mom and Eddie were the next to go, leaving in two separate vehicles—Shark in the black Hummer, and Mom and Eddie in her canary yellow 4Runner.

"Billy, we should ask Mom to get rid of that car. It sticks out like a bad knee scrape. She needs a more generic color, something black or dark blue that looks like all the other cars on the road. She can't do surveillance work in that thing."

"She has been."

"And I've never liked it. You're the one who taught me to be discreet. How can anyone be discreet when they drive a big, bright yellow banana?"

"We just convinced her to move out of her house. We can't ask her to get rid of her car. Besides, she loves that car. She calls it her grandma mobile. Where's this coming from, `ge ya? You never said anything before."

"Hey, you can let her use your old Mercury to do surveillance. Nobody pays attention to that car. They like new, shiny ones, not something that looks like poor people own it. They think it has a disease and they want to get as far away from it as they can."

I was pacing the floor.

"And where's that darn cat? If he goes out and gets himself killed, the children will be devastated."

Billy looked at me as if he was trying to figure out what had come over me in the last few minutes. He could tell something was wrong. He stepped in front of me, stopping me in my tracks, and then put his arm around me.

"What is it, `ge ya? You're not acting like yourself."

Helene wiped her hands on the kitchen towel and said, "She's nervous, Billy. All that stuff you said about everything being all right and the case being closed… well… she has her doubts… and frankly, so do I."

We had no idea that soon our doubts would prove to have merit. Things were not all right, and the case was far from being closed.

Chapter 13

The weatherman had hit his mark this time. The front brought in streaks of lightning, followed by thunder that rolled and cracked overhead. Then the snow started falling. Once the snow came, the thunder and lightning faded away, much to my relief. Nothing scared me more than lightning. I'd seen its power and destructive force and what it could do to anyone in its path. I had refused to go out in it, delaying us from going to the hospital as planned. I wanted to know the status of Dakota Stone and Savannah Kelley just as much as anyone, but I put my curiosity on the back burner. I couldn't bring myself to step outside until the lightning had completely quit, and now that it had, it was time to go.

Billy and I were getting ready to leave when I heard the cat meowing in the utility room.

"Ah, he's back. That little rascal. He's probably covered with snow." I went to check on him.

Spice Cat was indeed covered with snow, right down to his soaking wet paws. I grabbed a towel and started wiping him. That's when I discovered it.

"Billy, come here! Spice Cat has something stuck in his paw."

Billy examined Spice's paw, and then chuckled.

"It's just a bur, Jesse. He's been out in the woods again." He gently removed it and showed it to me. "See, nothing but a little old bur." He rubbed Spice's head. "You do manage to get into everything, don't you?" He ran his hand down the length of Spice's back, and then stopped. "What's this, little fellow?"

I laughed and said, "He doesn't look so little when he gets his winter coat. I wouldn't be surprised what you'd find in there."

Billy slid something off Spice Cat's tail and held it up for me to see.

"It's a wedding band. Now that's odd. Someone put it on him. There's no way he could've done this to himself. It's as if someone slid it on his tail like you would when placing it on a person's finger. We were meant to find the ring."

"If I remember right, the last time anyone saw Spice Cat was last night when he woke up Eddie. I wonder if he had it on him then. Do you think Nancy did this when she was lurking about?"

"She could have. What other explanation is there?"

Billy looked closer at the ring.

"There's an inscription and date on the inside—R & D 4ever 2008. Hmm…"

The wheels started spinning in my head as I counted off the years.

"That was… six years ago. You think the D could stand for Dakota? I bet she's married, or was, and this was her wedding ring. She's been leaving us clues. Why can't we piece them together?"

"I think we just did." He stood and called to Helene. "Grab me a sandwich bag, would you please?" He looked back at me. "She just made it easier for us to trace this ring."

"How so?"

"Tracing a plain gold wedding band would be almost impossible if it didn't have an inscription, but this one does. We'll trace the scriber. It might take a while, but it's not impossible. Jewelers keep good records."

Helene grabbed a plastic bag from the kitchen cabinet and brought it to him and asked, "What you got there, Billy?"

"I think it might be Dakota Stone's wedding band. Guess she doesn't want it anymore." He dropped the ring in the bag, zipped it up, and then shoved the bag in the pocket of his jeans. "We'll drop this off at Jonathan's and get him to run a trace on it."

I looked over at Helene to explain.

"It has an inscription on the inside—R & D 4ever 2008. Six years ago. The timeline fits. Billy says we might be able to get a trace on it."

"I guess the D stands for Dakota. Very good! It's about time we got something on her we can use. Boy was she ever stupid."

"Wow! Déjà vu! This reminds me of the time Athena and Thor dragged home that severed hand with that big fat diamond ring on the finger. Creepy. Remember that, Billy?"

"Of course I do. I remember it quite well. Y'all had a fit when I wanted to put it in the freezer to preserve trace evidence."

"Yeah, and after you put it in the freezer, you kicked the refrigerator for emphasis. Freaked us out." I glanced at Helene. "You should've seen the look on Mom and Claire's faces. At first, they were startled because they were already scared, and then the idea of a body part being put in the freezer just grossed them out. When I think about it now, it's funny, but it sure wasn't funny back then."

"I bet."

Spice Cat had given us all the time he was going to. He shook as if to throw off any snow I might've missed, and then walked out of the room, leaving a trail of damp paw prints behind.

I walked over to the back door, unhooked the latch holding the doggie door to the opening in place, slid it down, and then locked it.

"I don't want the dogs or Spice Cat to be able to go outside without one of us knowing about it. This is the only way to make sure they don't. The dogs will bark if they need to go do their thing, and Spice Cat has a litter box, so we're covered."

Helene shook her head. "A cat isn't like a dog. Spice Cat has always been able to come and go as he pleases. You change that and he might show you his displeasure by peeing on the carpet… your clothes… the sofa. Cat pee smell is nasty, and it's hard to wash out."

"He'll get over it. Besides, it won't be for long."

Billy put his hand on my shoulder.

"Okay, the doggie dog stays closed if it'll make you feel better, but you gotta snap out of it. Focus. You're letting your fear take over, and that's not good."

"Yeah, I guess you're right. My anxiety's kicking into overdrive. Where're my crazy pills? I need to chill out."

"I'll go get you one."

Helene turned, walked out and was back before I had a chance to tell her that I didn't need a pill. I was fine, just a little jumpy. I had heart palpitations, but they, too, would pass. I had places to go. Then, I thought about it and decided that this might be the right time for a pill, before my anxiety gets out of control and I have a full-blown panic attack. I took the pill, tossed it back, and then chased it with a glass of water.

"I'm good. Let's go. This pill ought to kick in just about the time we get to the hospital. Who knows what'll I say or do, but at least I'll be calm. I might be zoned out, but I won't be anxious."

Helene rolled her eyes. "I can't imagine you'd do anything to embarrass Billy." She was still laughing when she walked out.

"You're not funny, Helene. I know how to act. I got everything under control, even when I am crazy, right Billy?" I didn't wait for him to agree. "Grab your coat. I'm ready."

The snow was already an inch deep when we pulled out of the driveway, and according to the weatherman on the radio, there would be plenty more of it to come. Before it quit, we could get as much as a foot. By nightfall the roads would be treacherous, and people were being warned to stay off the roads for their own safety.

"He's not talking to us," I said, pointing to the radio. "You can't stop a Dodge Ram truck."

"Yep, this baby will take us through anything. She's tough."

Billy patted the dashboard, and then leaned over and kissed me.

"Keep your eyes on the road, Injun Joe. I no wanna die."

"Me no wanna die either."

Twenty minutes later, Billy pulled into the UVA Hospital parking garage, and as always, we had to search for a parking spot. We finally found one on the third level next to a black, Lincoln Town Car.

"It looks like Russell's here. That's his car. I recognize it by the license plate."

"Yeah, you know it's gotta be a lawyer's car when the plate says SUE EM."

"Thank God for elevators," I said as we entered. "I got a little buzz going on. I don't think I could stand a flight of stairs. It'd wear me out."

"You're not getting old on me, are you, `ge ya?"

"Never." I grabbed him and gave him a sexy, lingering kiss. "Nope, not me. Do I kiss like I'm old?"

He didn't say anything; instead, he took me in his arms and kissed me passionately, stirring my emotions and jacking up my sex drive.

"It's been a while since we've done anything naughty. Want to go back to the truck?"

"We could be naughty right here."

"I don't think so."

I kissed him again, egging him on. We were locked in an embrace, his hands caressing my body and mine doing the same to his when the elevator door opened.

Facing a group of people, I said, "We just got married."

They smiled and wished us well.

Billy smiled back, and then whispered to me, "You're terrible."

"I know. Don't you just love me even after all this time?"

"I sure do. Come on."

"What about the truck? Not interested?"

"Later. Business first."

"Who are you, and what have you done with my husband?"

We were walking to the entrance of the hospital when Billy felt his pants' pocket, and then said, "I forgot to stop by Jonathan's and drop off the ring."

"Call him. He doesn't need to see the ring to run a trace on it, does he?"

"In fact, no he wouldn't. I'll give him a call and see what he can find out for us."

Billy pulled out his cell phone, called Jonathan, and gave him the information. He put the cell phone back in his pocket.

"He isn't holding out much hope, but he's going to give it a try. Finding the owner of this ring could prove to be a long, painstaking job, unless he gets lucky."

The hospital was a buzz of chaos. The snow had caused numerous accidents, and victims were being brought in one right after the other. It was non-stop. Hospital staff was running around shouting orders, while others were wheeling patients to different destinations for treatment.

Billy walked up to the woman manning the desk and asked about Dakota Stone, and was told that she couldn't have visitors. Then he asked about Savannah.

"Are you family?"

"Yes, she's my wife's sister." He pointed to me as the lies flowed. "We were told that she's awake now, and my wife wants to see her. It's been such a trying time for us since this happened. We've all been so worried."

The lady punched keys on the computer, and then said, "Room three-sixteen."

Billy grabbed my hand and we speedily headed to the elevator.

When we got to Savannah's room, there was a policeman standing at her door. After a brief conversation with the officer, he allowed us to enter.

Savannah looked awful. She was covered in bandages and her face was badly burned. Her hair had been singed off to the roots. But she was alive… and awake.

"Come on in," she said in a barely audible voice. "Don't let… my looks fool you. The doctor says… I'm going to be okay. I'm lucky… to be alive."

Russell Shank was sitting in a chair by her bedside. He'd once had a crush on Savannah, but it was short-lived, like all of his past crushes. However, she was one of the few he had kept on as a friend. He stood when we walked into the room, held out his hand to Billy and then to me, and asked us how we were doing.

"We're doing well. How about yourself?"

We exchanged a little small talk, and then Savannah spoke up. Her voice sounded scratchy.

"The doctor said I was lucky the firefighter got to me… when he did. The dryer had protected me… from the flames… but the heat was unbearable. I had to get out. I balled up… and gave the door a kick… crawled out… and that's when the flames got me. God… this has been a nightmare. I hurt… all over."

I walked over closer and lightly touched her shoulder.

"You survived. That's what counts. It'll take a little time to get back to normal, but then everything will be all right."

"When I came to this morning… all I could think about was Kaleb." She looked at Russell. "Russell told me… that Cole's taking care of him. Have you seen him?"

"No, but if Cole's taking care of him, I'm sure he's fine."

"I was so afraid he'd… died in the explosion." She looked back at Russell. "I don't remember much… after that woman knocked me out. I remember waking up… and realizing I was in a dryer… and then I heard an explosion. I panicked when it… started getting so hot."

Savannah closed her eyes and dozed off.

"She's in and out of it," Russell whispered.

"Has Cole been here?"

"He came earlier this morning, but she was still unconscious. He'll be back, I'm sure."

"We hear you're Dakota Stone's attorney."

"She's crazy, Billy, but everyone deserves representation. They have her up in the psychiatric ward. She'll be lucky if she isn't permanently committed to a nut house. She has a lot of issues."

"You can say that again. We're still trying to find out who she really is. You know she isn't who she says she is, don't you?"

Russell had a strange look on his face when he asked, "What are you talking about, Billy?"

Billy explained what we knew of the woman and all that had transpired since we'd met her, ending with saying that she was a danger to our family.

"She's out for blood."

I added my account by saying, "I was talking to her on the cell phone when she had the accident. She's going to blame me for the death of Olivia Swales, and she'll be looking for revenge. She has to be stopped."

"I think she has been. She's handcuffed to her bed, and the minute the doctor says she can go, Captain Trainum's hauling her off to jail. I talked with him this morning."

"Did he tell you what the charges were?"

"The list is long, but at the top of it is murder. Gavin Preston's body was autopsied this morning. I spoke with the medical examiner and he said the COD was poison, but there's no way they can lay this on the Stone woman without proof that she actually did it. Trainum's hoping to pull a few rabbits out of his hat."

I smiled and said, "Meet the rabbits."

"What?"

"Just before he died, Gavin Preston told us that she poisoned him with antifreeze."

"Hearsay. Prove it."

"Don't tell me you believe that woman."

"I didn't say I believed her. All I said was prove it."

He looked at Billy.

"Without proof, she's going to walk on the murder charge, if one is even filed. Trainum knows it. He's scrounging for evidence, but as it stands right now, he won't be able to charge her with murder. He's threatening to, hoping to get a confession out of her, but that's not going to happen. And if he does get a confession, I'll file a diminished capacity claim."

"I don't believe it. You're taking her side."

"Look… I'm just telling you like it is. She'll get a slap on the wrist for the accident, but without hard evidence, she'll walk. I'm just doing my job. When she called me, I had no idea how deep this went. She paid me a retainer, so legally, I can't back out now. The judge would have my butt. I could lose my license to practice law."

"She's not mentally incompetent. She knows exactly what she's doing. She's acting."

"That may well be, but if she is, she's doing a good job. She's got the doctors convinced. Heck, she even had me convinced. That's why she's in the psych unit. So… that's where this is headed. No evidence, no conviction." He winked at us. "Get the evidence, or walk away."

"How are we supposed to do that?"

"I don't know. Snoop around. That's what you guys do best. Bring something to the table, or she walks. Find the container laced with antifreeze… with her fingerprints on it."

"Yeah, right, I'm sure that went up in flames when the bomb went off."

"Not necessarily." Russell hesitated. "Talk to Jonathan's wife. She's a profiler. She could probably give you some insight as to where the evidence might be, if there is any. A serial killer always keeps something from their victims. Maybe she has something in her suitcase."

"You think she's a serial killer?"

"I didn't say that. I'm just giving you a place to start. Talk to Lu Ann."

"You know more than you're telling us."

"She's my client. I can't divulge aspects of the case, unless it comes out in court. Do your job, and let me do mine."

"She's confessed something to you, hasn't she?"

"That's all I can tell you. The rest is confidential and was said under extreme duress. She wasn't coherent when she was brought in to the hospital. When I first talked to her, all she did was rant. Half of what she said is suspect. I'm going to talk with her again after I leave Savannah, but I won't be able to share."

"Well… thanks for the advice, Russell." Billy looked at me, and then shook Russell's hand. "I'm glad I'm not in your shoes. I imagine this is hard on you, what with us being friends and all. You do what you have to, and we'll do the same. No hard feelings."

"Glad to hear it."

"Tell Savannah that Minnie will probably come see her now that she can have visitors. She's been worried sick about her."

"I'll be sure to tell her."

Billy and I turned and walked out of the room.

"What next, kemosabe? Where do we go from here?"

"To the truck first. We have a date, remember?"

"Oh, you bad boy."

The wind had picked up and the snow had gotten heavier. Once we were seated in the truck, Billy started it and then sat there for a minute, thinking.

"What's on your mind? What happened to our date?" I looked around at the people getting in and out of their cars. "I guess we'll have to wait. Too many people around."

"I was thinking about what Russell said about finding the evidence."

"And…"

"Something Preston said has got me wondering."

"Wondering about what?"

"If I told you that I had been giving you wine with poison in it, and then I set the bottle down in front of you, what's the first thing you would do?"

I thought for a second.

"I'd grab the bottle and head for the hospital."

"Exactly, but Preston didn't go to the hospital, he was way too sick by that time. He knew it was too late to save himself, so he came to us. He wanted to do the right thing. I think the bottle might be in his car."

"And we still have the car, don't we?"

"We certainly do."

Billy put the truck in gear, backed out of the parking space, and drove to the garage exit. Once he paid the parking fee, we were on our way back home. The going was slow, and I was getting antsy.

"Can't you drive any faster?"

"I could, but I'd rather make it back alive."

He wiped the inside of the windshield with his hand, and then reached over to turn up the defroster. When he looked back up, the traffic had come to a stop. He had to slam on the brakes to keep from running into the car in front of us. The truck skidded, but finally came to a halt just in time.

He wiped his forehead with his hand and said, "I need to slow down. That was close."

"We're crawling as it is, Billy." I reached over and touched his leg. "You're doing fine. If I'd been driving, I probably would've hit that car. We're excited because we think Preston took the wine bottle and it might be in his car, but it might not be, so forget about being in a hurry. Preston's SUV might not have anything in it at all. I'm sorry I tried to rush you. I should know better."

"We never searched it."

"I'll call Jonathan and ask him if anyone searched Preston's car."

I took out my cell phone and hit the speed dial number for Jonathan.

A minute later, I disconnected and said, "The car wasn't searched. Jonathan's meeting us at Beth's with her house key."

It took us forty minutes to make the twenty minute drive. The snow was still coming down harder than ever, and as predicted, the roads had been a mess. When we pulled up to Beth's house, Jonathan was already in the garage waiting for us.

"Have you searched the car?"

"No, I just got here."

Jonathan aimed the keypad, hit the button, and unlocked the doors and the hatchback.

"What are you looking for?"

"A bottle of wine."

Chapter 14

The bottle we were looking for lay on the floorboard of the passenger side, wedged underneath the seat. The pieces of the puzzle were starting to fall together, and we now had the evidence we needed to put Dakota Stone in prison for the murder of Gavin Preston. Without thinking, I went to grab the bottle.

"Don't touch it!" Jonathan yelled, and then grabbed my arm. "You need a pair of gloves. Fingerprints, remember?"

He reached in his pocket and pulled out two pairs of latex gloves and handed us a pair. "I'm sorry, Jesse. I didn't mean to yell at you, but we don't need for the boys in the lab to find your prints on that bottle. You could be implicated, and we sure don't want that to happen. Are you okay?" He hugged me. "I'm just looking after you."

"I know you are. I don't know what's wrong with me. I know better than to touch evidence. I guess I was just too excited to think straight." I looked at Billy. "What do we do now?"

"We call the sheriff."

"He never asked us where Preston's car was. I mean, we already told him Preston came to us, so why didn't he ask about the car?"

"I don't know, but I wasn't about to bring it up. I knew he'd get to it sooner or later. He's got a lot going on, just like we have. Let's look a little closer before we call in the cavalry."

The SUV was clean. The only thing we found was the wine bottle, but that was all we needed to bring down Dakota Stone. She was going to fry for killing Gavin Preston.

Jonathan looked at Billy and said, "So who do we call, Sheriff Hudson or Captain Trainum?"

"I say we call both." I had recovered from the shock of having Jonathan yell at me. "We don't want to leave anyone out. They might think we're hiding something."

Billy winked at me. "Oh, that time has come and gone. We have been hiding something—this car. I guess we'll have to answer for that also."

"It'll be worth it. I mean, what can they do to us? We solved their case for them."

"I don't think they'll see it that way."

"Oh, come on, Billy, they're not going to do anything to us. They'll see it as a gift on our part. We came up with the murder weapon… so to speak."

"A gift?" Jonathan laughed. "They'll see it as withholding evidence, so be prepared for repercussions. I hear trouble knocking at the door."

He put his hand to his ear.

I looked around, listening for the sound of someone knocking, and then realized he was speaking metaphorically.

"You had me going there for a minute, Jonathan. I'm out of it. Must have been that pill I took. You know, lasting effects."

"Perhaps you should stay away from drugs, Jesse. Your mind ain't on the job."

Jonathan was right. My mind was somewhere else, but I didn't know exactly where. I was a wee bit light-headed and feeling very carefree. I glanced over at Billy, thinking how sexy he was and how much I wanted to be alone with him. I wanted his naked body, his lips, his hands…

"Oh, God! All I can think about is sex. It has to be a side effect from that pill. It's an aphrodisiac! I get all warm and fuzzy just thinking about crawling in the sack with my man."

Billy slipped up close and snuggled me.

"You don't hear me complaining. I like it!"

Jonathan pulled out his cell phone and said, "Geez… get a room."

"Wait! Don't make that call yet. I just thought of something. Shouldn't we move the car back to your house, Jonathan? That way we can say it was in the backyard the whole time, if someone should ask. At least this will be one charge they can't pin on us. The car would have been in plain sight the whole time. We didn't try to dispose of it."

"I was just thinking the same thing. We'll look guilty as sin if the sheriff sees this car in Beth's garage. Let's do it. It'll be one less thing we have to explain." He looked at Billy. "I'll drive Preston's car, you drive mine, and Jesse can drive your truck."

We moved the SUV back to Jonathan's house, parked it out back, and waited a half-hour so the snow could accumulate on it as if it had never moved. Then, Jonathan made the call.

"Hmm… voice mail. Sheriff Hudson, this is Jonathan Blackhawk. We have physical evidence that proves Dakota Stone killed Gavin Preston. Come to my house as soon as you get this message. I'm also alerting Captain Trainum. Thanks."

He looked back at us.

"One more phone call to make." He touched the screen and waited. "Voice mail again. Where is everybody? Hello, Captain Trainum, this is Jonathan Blackhawk. You need to get over here. If you forgot where my house is, just follow the Greene County police cars. We'll be waiting."

Jonathan put his cell phone back in his pocket.

"It's done, now all we have to do is wait. Shall we go inside where it's warm?"

The three of us slipped off the latex gloves and shoved them in our pockets. We walked through the garage, down the long hallway, and to the den where Lu Ann was sitting, watching TV.

"Ah, you're back." She got up, walked over to Jonathan, and gave him a kiss. "Is everything all right? You had me worried there for a minute."

"The cops will be here soon." Jonathan went on to explain about finding the wine bottle. "We brought the SUV back. We didn't want the cops to think we moved it."

"That was smart. It'd be a little hard to explain why it was sitting in Beth's garage."

"Yeah, we thought about that, so we brought it back."

"Let's go to the kitchen and I'll fix some coffee."

We followed Lu Ann to the kitchen, took off our coats, and then sat down at the table. We talked about how this was going to go down, but in all honesty, no one knew how Sheriff Hudson was going to take the news.

"When he finds out Preston's car has been sitting in your backyard all this time, he's not going to be happy, and when we show him the wine bottle, he's really going to be mad."

"Maybe not," Lu Ann said. "He'll be glad to finally have the evidence he needs. Oh, he might be mad at first, but he'll get over it."

"That's what I said, Lu Ann. If it wasn't for us, he'd still be spinning his wheels."

"Well, I wouldn't tell him that, Jesse. You know they don't like it when someone else does their job for them. They see it as interfering—obstruction of justice. He's liable to lock you up."

"I'm ready for him. I can handle anything he throws my way… and if he gives me a hard time, I'm going to sock him… and Frank Trainum, too! I'm tired of them pushing me around. I'm going to give them a piece of my mind."

"No, you're not, Jesse. You don't have much to spare right now." Jonathan looked at Billy. "Maybe you should take her home. I can handle this one."

I was getting riled up. "You're out of your mind. I'm not going anywhere. Why do y'all always try to shut me out? I'm a big girl. I'm not afraid of the cops. If anything, they should be afraid of me. I'm dangerous, too… when I want to be."

"Your mouth is going to get you arrested. I'm taking you home and putting you to bed."

Lu Ann looked at my eyes. "What did you take? You're not acting like your old self."

"That's just it. She is acting like herself… on drugs."

"No wonder she's acting like she's drunk." Lu Ann looked at me. "Maybe you should go splash some water on your face. You'll feel better. Come with me. I'll take you to the bathroom."

"I kinda do feel a little drunk, but I think I can make it to the bathroom by myself."

I got up and hurried to the bathroom. I thought for sure I was going to puke before I got there, but I didn't. I went to the sink, turned on the facet, and splattered my face with the cool water. After I was convinced I could hold it together, I walked out of the bathroom and went back to the kitchen. I saw Jonathan and Billy standing at the front window.

"They're here," Billy called out.

I walked over and stood between them.

"I don't like the looks of this, brother," Jonathan said.

"Me, either. I don't think they're too happy with us."

Cop cars were flying up the driveway, driving with a vengeance, skidding sideways with their lights flashing and sirens blasting. They were in a real hurry, and most likely, ready to do battle.

"They'll get over it, and we'll be rid of Dakota Stone once and for all…and we'll be free to go on about our business."

"Yeah, in about five to ten years."

"That's not funny. Is he serious, Billy?" I looked from Billy to Jonathan. "Tell me you're not serious."

"I'm not serious, but this isn't going to go smoothly. I can promise you that. Who do you think can yell the loudest, Billy? Sheriff Hudson or Captain Trainum?"

"I'd say they're both about even."

Sheriff Hudson yelled to his men and motioned for them to follow him as he made his way through the accumulating snow to the front door. He rang the doorbell, and when Jonathan opened the door and let him in, I whispered, "And the yelling begins…"

I smiled at the sheriff.

"You can wipe that smile off your face, Mrs. Blackhawk. This isn't a social call." He looked at Jonathan and then at Billy. "Okay, what's this all about? Got another dead body for me?"

He looked at his men and said, "Okay, search the house."

"Whoa… wait a minute." Jonathan stepped in front of the line of deputies. "There's nothing in here to see. It's in the backyard." He looked at the sheriff. "Unless you have a search warrant, your men aren't going to traipse through my house."

Sheriff Hudson motioned for his men to halt, and then turned back to Jonathan.

"Show me what you got, and this better be good. You dragged me away from…"

I walked over to the sheriff.

"Shouldn't we wait for Captain Trainum? This is his jurisdiction, isn't it?"

"He's not coming. He has his hands full with…" The sheriff paused.

"With what?"

"That's none of your business, Mrs. Blackhawk. I'm in charge here, so show me what you got. I don't have all day."

"Are you mad at me? What's with this Mrs. Blackhawk? I thought we were on a first name basis."

The sheriff gave me a stern look.

"Now you're starting to tick me off, Jesse." He emphasized my name. "Okay, so what's in the backyard?"

"Evidence."

The sheriff didn't say a word, instead he motioned to his men.

They all turned and headed out the front door to the backyard behind him, not missing a step.

We grabbed our coats and followed.

"Whose car is this?" After a second, he shook his head and sighed. "This is the car Gavin Preston was driving, isn't it?"

"Yes, it is, Sheriff Hudson, but before you go off the deep end, there's something you need to see."

Billy led him over to the passenger side of the car and pointed to the wine bottle on the floorboard.

"I'm sure you'll find Dakota Stone's fingerprints on the bottle and antifreeze residue on the inside. Here's the evidence you need to put that woman away. This proves she killed Gavin Preston."

The sheriff signaled to one of his men.

"Bag it, tag it, and get it to forensics. Take Peters with you and make sure you maintain chain of custody protocol."

His deputy complied.

The sheriff looked back at the three of us.

"My… my… my. How convenient. Where'd you get the bottle? I know you didn't get it from The Body Shop. You couldn't get in. It's still a crime scene."

Jonathan grinned and said, "Give us a little credit, Sheriff Hudson. The bottle has been there the whole time. Nobody noticed because it was stuck under the seat, and even if we'd seen it, we wouldn't have thought anything of it at the time."

Billy held up his hand.

"Okay… we made a bad judgment call when we moved the body. We admit that, but you can't let your anger at us stop you from getting to the truth." He pointed to the bottle again. "There's your proof."

"Yeah," I added. "We found the proof, so you owe us."

The sheriff's face turned blood red and the shouting started.

"I owe you nothing! You're renegades, all of you! This time you've gone too far! I'm sick and tired of trying to keep you out of jail! I'm done with covering your butts! All you do is give me grief!" He turned and walked around the car. A phone call later, he returned and started in on us again. "I called a tow truck, and you better hope those forensic guys don't find one hair from either one of you in that car, because if they do…" He looked directly at me. "You better start making arrangements. You'll need someone to take care of your kids while you're in prison."

Sheriff Hudson was madder than I'd ever seen, and this time he was serious about sending us up the river. We'd crossed the line so many times he'd just plain had enough. The only way to save ourselves was to convince him that we were doing the right thing. We just went about it wrong. He knew we lied about Preston asking us to take him back to The Body Shop. Heck, even I wouldn't fall for that one. We moved the dead body to lay blame on someone else, and now we were offering up the murder weapon. I could see why he was aggravated. If I could get him to calm down, perhaps we could keep things under control, and stay out of jail. I had to convince him to see the situation from our perspective.

Sheriff Hudson was an old softie when it came to crying women, so I brought out the big guns. I started crying.

"I can't believe you'd do that to me. My kids need their mother, and now you're going to put me in jail because Dakota Stone killed Gavin Preston. You're an awful man."

Billy walked over and put his arms around me. I buried my face in his jacket and cried harder.

"We're going to jail, Billy. Our kids are going to grow up without us, all because of that man." I pointed to the sheriff. My nose was running and I'd cried so hard that I was getting the hiccups.

I looked at the sheriff.

"I confess. I did it all. Just keep my mama out of jail… please. She's innocent."

I couldn't read the look on Sheriff Hudson's face, and that really bothered me. Was he buying any of this, or was I wasting my time? I had to keep trying.

I ran over to him, threw myself in his arms and pleaded, "Please don't send my mama to jail, I beg of you. Put me in jail instead. I'll confess to whatever you want, but just leave my mama alone."

The sheriff gently pushed me away.

"You had me right up to the point where you said you'd confess to anything. I know you better than that. Wipe your face. You look like a mess."

He pulled out a handkerchief and handed it to me.

"Go over there and stand by your husband before I slap the cuffs on you right here."

I took the handkerchief, wiped my tears and my nose, and then handed it back to him.

"Keep it."

"Thank you. My mama always said you could tell a man was raised right if he carried a handkerchief." I whimpered and wiped my nose again. "I'll get her to wash it for you and return it. By then, I guess I'll be in jail."

I let loose again with the tears.

The sheriff held up his hand like a traffic cop and said, "Stop."

That one word said it all, but from the look on his face, the sheriff had already turned his thoughts to something else. Hopefully, he was rationalizing the situation, or maybe coming to grips with the pickle we were in—all of us, including him. We had played our part in this mess, but he had failed to look for the car, or even ask about it.

He turned and paced back and forth, looking at the SUV… and hopefully, thinking about the implications of what had transpired here.

The sheriff walked over to me and shook his finger in my face.

"I didn't buy your little crying tantrum for a second. I know you can turn those tears on and off like a water facet, so… no, it didn't work on me… but it did calm me down watching you do your routine. I almost enjoyed it. Tell me, how long would you have cried to get your way? An hour? Two?"

He shook his head and chuckled. Then he paced as he talked.

"I don't know what to do with you people. I know you're not killers. Why do you always have to get in my way? You lie to me. You take advantage of my leniency. If it hadn't been for me," he pointed to Billy and me, "you two would've gone to jail for that stunt you played in the Flo Garner case."

He stopped pacing and stared at us.

"I saved you both from doing time, and how do you repay me? You lie to me again, over and over, that's what you do."

The sheriff looked directly at Billy and said, "You gave me your word. Doesn't that mean anything to you? You swore you would take a hiatus, not work, not get in my way, but did you? No, you didn't."

He waved his arms around, and then looked back at Billy.

"What am I supposed to do about this? I sure hope you have something up your sleeve, because I'm at a loss. If you had just done what you were supposed to do, you wouldn't be in the mess you're in."

"Sheriff…"

"Let me finish. I forgot about the car. I admit it."

He looked back at me.

"I was more concerned with finding a killer, and… I didn't want to be the one to tell your mother about Savannah. Your mom's a good woman, and I knew it would upset her. Unlike you, she would've cried real tears. I hate being the bearer of bad news. I was hoping y'all didn't know about the body in the dryer, but I should've known better. That threw me."

The wind was whipping up the snow and blowing it in our faces. The air was so cold.

The sheriff had been good to us. There were times when he could've arrested us, but he didn't. We had helped him more than once, so he gave us a little leeway. Unless something changed, this time was going to be different. We had pushed him to the breaking point. Something had to give, so I tried to fix things with him by saying, "It seems to me that you did ask about Preston's car, but then something happened, and you never got your answer."

Billy agreed.

"Yep, Sheriff, that's how I remember it, too."

The sheriff laughed.

"That's a downright lie. God, now you're lying to protect me. Well, I don't need your help."

Jonathan stepped in and added, "You must be confused, Sheriff Hudson. At the time, we all were."

I couldn't contain myself any longer.

"So we're all a bunch of liars!" I said. "Big deal! Who cares about that? We need to concentrate on the here and now. You have the evidence, Sheriff. That's what matters. Now go and arrest Dakota Stone. Isn't that what this is all about? Finding Gavin Preston's killer?"

A tow truck from Crumpler's Towing Service showed up and hauled the SUV away, leaving us standing out in the snow, wondering what was going to happen next. Was the sheriff going to arrest us, and if so, on what charge? I had to know. I walked over to him.

"Are you going to arrest us?"

"Not today, but then again, the day isn't over."

Jonathan's cell phone rang, and he excused himself to take the call. When he returned, he had a strange look on his face.

"What's going on?"

"The bomb at The Body Shop was more bark than bite. Oh, there was a loud explosion, lots of smoke and some fire, but the fire department got it under control quickly. Thank goodness, otherwise Savannah would be dead."

"What else?"

"Dakota Stone had a wall safe, and it's still intact."

Jonathan looked over at the sheriff and said, "I guess you forgot to mention that."

"It's an ongoing investigation, and I don't share," Sheriff Hudson replied.

"That's the problem," I said. "Nobody shares. That's the second time today someone has said the same thing. Maybe if more people shared, we wouldn't have so much trouble getting to the truth."

Jonathan looked back to us and said, "She left her journal behind, and according to it, she's been a very bad woman. It contains names, dates and the amount of money paid to her. That can only mean one thing. She kept a record of payoffs from women—that had nothing to do with getting a body makeover."

I gasped, and then looked at the sheriff.

"You knew and you said nothing?"

Billy moved closer and said, "Sheriff, if she left her journal behind, she wanted someone to find it. She's taunting us. She's laughing at our perceived stupidity. I mean, that's how she sees us… as stupid. She's rubbing our faces in it. She's so sure she's going to get away with her crimes. Why else would she leave it? She thinks she's invincible."

"I guess she didn't plan on having a wreck on the interstate." The sheriff looked in my direction. "We have you to thank for that."

"Don't think you're going to blame me for that, too, along with everything else. I wasn't even there. All I did was talk to the woman. It's not my fault she got so mad she threw the phone out the window. That was all her doing."

"You never let anyone finish, do you? You always have to have the last word. Actually, what I was going to say, if you had given me time, was good for you, Jesse. Whatever you said to her did the trick. She lost her cool, and because of that, she's lying in a hospital bed wearing her new jewelry—silver handcuffs."

"Glad I could be of service. I'm just so relieved that nobody died in the wreck."

"Olivia Swales did."

"I was talking about the other motorists. I'm sorry about Olivia, but that wasn't my fault either. She's another death you can lay at Dakota Stone's feet. Olivia would still be alive if it wasn't for that crazy woman."

"Actually, according to her doctor, she is crazy, but I guess you know that already… since you tried to pay her a visit this morning."

"We went to see Savannah, not her."

"Now see, there you go lying again. Can't you, just for once, tell me the truth?"

"You're right. I did want to see her. I wanted her to come back at me with everything she had, so I could laugh in her face. I wanted to go get her so riled up that she'd slice her wrists with her new bracelets. Are you happy now?"

"At least you're being honest for a change."

"I'm curious about something, Sheriff."

He groaned.

"What is it, Jesse?"

"What's going to happen to those women who paid to have their husbands killed? They broke a few laws there. Conspiracy to commit murder. Solicitation to commit murder. You gonna throw them in the pokey… right next to Dakota Stone? Now... wouldn't that be priceless. I'd love to hear that conversation. You gonna let me listen in? What do you say?"

"No comment."

The sheriff signaled to the rest of his remaining deputies to move out.

As they began to leave, he started walking to his Greene County Sheriff SUV.

"Hey, where you going? We're not finished."

He stopped and turned back to me.

"Oh, Miss Jesse, you have no idea how finished we are."

He opened the car door to get in.

"Wait a minute, Sheriff Hudson," Billy called to him.

He walked up to the sheriff, pulled the plastic baggie out of his pocket, and then handed it to him.

"Our cat was wearing this wedding band on his tail this morning, and I'm sure he didn't put it there. You might find the inscription interesting. If you come by the house, we have some framed photos of Dakota and Olivia you might also want to see. There's more. We found coke in the dog's pill bowl."

"Pill bowl? Never mind." He took the baggie. "What did you do with the coke?"

"What do you think? I poured it down the sink. We thought there might be more around, so Jonathan got a K9 out to do a search. So far, our house is clean. I don't know about the rest, yet."

"Yes, we do." Jonathan walked up with his cell phone in hand. "I just got a text from… well… it said all houses had been searched and all were clear, except Minnie's. The dog found coke in a glass bowl in the refrigerator." He looked up at the sheriff. "Nancy Woodward had a bag of coke in her purse. She must've been spreading it round, but had to quit when she got struck by lightning." He looked at Billy. "Next stop was going to be Mom and Dad's house."

"My mom is going to go nuts when she hears this," I said.

"She already knows. She was still there when Rex and K9 Suzy showed up. You know your mother, she wasn't about to leave."

The sheriff stepped forward. "Where's the coke?"

"Shark has it. I told him not to dump it. When I heard Nancy Woodward had coke in her purse, I figured we'd find more since Billy found some at his house. I guess it blew his mind when he found it. His first response was to pour it down the sink and wash out the bowl, so we had nothing. Now your guys can test it to see if it's the same. I'm sure it is."

"Get your guy to bring it in. I'll let my guys know he's coming. Since I'm already here, I'm going to follow Billy and Jesse back to their house to get the photos."

He looked at us.

"Ready to go? I haven't got all day."

Billy and I got in his truck and headed home with Sheriff Hudson following close behind.

There was now four inches of snow on the ground, and just making a path through it up to the steps of our house was a chore. My fingers and toes were freezing and my legs were stiff by the time I got inside. I was just glad the thunder and lightning had quit earlier.

"Ah… it's so nice and warm in here!" I shook off the snow and then pulled off my coat. "Come on in, Sheriff. Take off your coat and thaw out by the fire." I walked over to the fireplace and turned my back to it. "Feels so good."

Helene came out of the den and walked up to us.

"I thought you might appreciate a good fire. The kids helped me. Ethan's taking a nap, so try to keep it down to a roar. Maisy's in her room on the computer." She looked at the sheriff. "Nice to see you again, Sheriff Hudson. Would you like a cup of coffee? I got a fresh pot in the kitchen."

"Thanks, but I'm in a hurry."

"You're always in a hurry. If you don't slow down you're going to have a heart attack. One cup won't hurt you, and from the way you look, I'd say you could use a timeout."

The sheriff smiled.

"Why not? Thanks to Jesse and Billy, I don't get much free time to relax. I better take a minute and have a break before I keel over."

"They can be right trying at times, can't they? Have a seat at the kitchen table and I'll bring you a cup." She looked at us. "You, too."

We sat at the table and waited for Helene to bring the coffee.

"If you're wondering where those picture are, they're on top of the refrigerator," Helene said. "The kids kept asking about them."

She set the cups down, walked over to the refrigerator, and returned with the photos. "Vain, ain't she?"

"You put them in a zip-lock bag. Very good."

"I learn fast." She looked at the sheriff. "You know we handled them, so you're going to find our prints on them."

"I figured as much. Couldn't be helped."

The sheriff finished his coffee and stood up.

"Thanks for the coffee, Helene."

He turned to leave, but stopped and looked back at Billy and me.

"We'll talk later about… you know what."

Then he was gone.

We sure did. There'd be more questions for us to answer before this party was over. Sheriff Hudson would be back, or either he'd call and tell us to come in to make a statement. That's when he'd tell us our fate. It's happened that way before.

"Minnie called and said they had to drop off the coke at the Sheriff's Office. They should be back soon."

"What's she been doing? They should've been back hours ago. I told her to pack a few things, not the whole house."

Billy took his empty coffee mug over to the sink.

"You know your mother. Everything's essential to her. I bet she was hot when K9 Suzy found that stuff in her refrigerator. I can just imagine her reaction. Did you manage to get a word in on that conversation?"

"Not hardly. She was irate, and you know we're going to hear all about it when she gets back."

Maisy walked in and was surprised to see us at home. She greeted us with her beautiful smile and wanted hugs.

"I missed y'all." She looked up at me. "Your face is starting to look better, Mom. Does it still hurt?"

"A little. I…"

Before I could finish, she turned to Billy.

"I need some help with my computer, Dad. It keeps locking up on me. I've rebooted it twice, but nothing I do seems to work."

She looked back at me. "I Googled K9 Suzy. Did you know she has her own website? She's amazing."

"Ah…"

"Will you look at my computer, Dad, before someone calls and you have to leave again?"

"Sure, honey, lead the way." Billy grinned back at us when Maisy grabbed his hand. "I'm your man. I can fix anything." The two of them went to investigate the computer crisis.

Helene and I listened to Maisy's constant chatter as they made their way to her room.

"She's growing up so fast. I remember when the only problem she had was keeping the dogs from knocking over her teacup set. She'd sit at her little table with her dolls and serve them make-believe tea in plastic teacups. Oh, those where the days."

"Wait until she discovers boys." Helene turned and walked back to the kitchen.

A rumble of thunder rolled overhead.

"Not again." I walked over to the sink, stood beside Helene, and looked out the window. Sure enough, a streak of lightning flashed across the sky.

"I thought that part was over," I said. "I'd never heard of thunder snow, until you said something."

"Hey, Maisy knows more about it than I do. It was news to me. The first I heard about it was this morning from the weatherman."

"Maybe I should Google it."

We shared a laugh, until Athena blew into the kitchen, feet sliding on the floor, and then coming to a halt after bumping into the cabinet. Her barking brought Thor, who still had on his whiney face.

"All we need now is the cat."

"Ah… he got out again. I'm sorry. I opened the door to let the dogs out, and he scooted right by me before I could grab him."

"He'll be back."

I went to the utility room and unlocked the flap to the doggie door. When I returned, Helene was fumbling around in the cabinet.

Athena's barking grew more intense as Helene grabbed the bottle of pills and started preparing one for her.

"Hush, Athena. You're going to wake Ethan. I'm working as fast as I can." She looked at me. "She needs her medication."

"You gave her one this morning. Can she have another so soon?" I picked up the bottle and read the instructions on the label.

"It's been four hours." Helene pointed to the label. "It says one pill every four hours as needed… and she needs it. I might just mash another one for later. I don't think this storm is going to move out for a while."

My cell phone rang.

"Got to be Mom. That's her ring tone."

I hustled over to the rack by the door and pulled the phone from my coat pocket.

"Hello, Mother. Where are you?"

"I'm at the Sheriff's Office. We brought in the cocaine, and now they won't let us leave… and they locked up Shark."

"What? Why?"

"Shark got a little unruly. He bumped into one of the deputies and the guy said he pushed him. Bumping and pushing isn't the same thing. Shark's not the kind of man who takes to having someone get up in his face. I think the deputy, who looks like he just graduated from high school, was doing it on purpose. You know how those young ones are. They slap on a badge and think they're God… until they're confronted with someone like Shark. Guys like Shark are usually a real eye-opener for a new kid like Deputy Doolittle."

"Oh, come on, Mom, that's not his real name, is it?"

"Honest to God, Jesse. I feel bad for the kid having a name like that. You know the children must've teased him all the way through school."

"Maybe that's why he became a cop… to help put a stop to bullying. Come on, Mom. I'm sure there's just been some kind of mix-up. The sheriff said he was going to let his guys know you were coming."

"Well, he must've forgotten, because they were clueless. They weren't real happy when Shark walked into the Sheriff Office with that cannon strapped to his hip, and when they asked him if he had more weapons, he pulled a knife from his boot, the taser from his belt, and a tootsie roll pop from his pocket. Deputy Doolittle said that wasn't a weapon and he laughed. Shark looked down at the kid and said it was if you're shoving it down someone's throat. The deputy jumped back like he'd been stung by a bee."

I chuckled and said, "He had."

"They treated us like criminals when Shark tossed that bag of coke up on the counter, and I heard someone say something about possession. What was that all about? They didn't catch us with the stuff. We brought it in. Anyway, you've never seen anyone move so fast. Two other deputies ran out and surrounded him. Now they have him sitting in a holding cell. Deputy Della said it was for his protection, but I think they were afraid Shark might hurt one of them." Mom's voice lowered to a whisper. "I don't think they know what to do with us. We told them we were here to bring in evidence—the cocaine—but they acted like we were drug dealers or something."

"Where's Eddie?"

"He's sitting on the bench next to me. They didn't put us in jail, but they told us to wait here, and I can tell you one thing, these seats aren't comfortable. Eddie's back's hurting him already. Jesse, you have to do something. Call Sheriff Hudson and tell him I said he better fix this mess. Here we were trying to be good citizens, and what do we get for our efforts… nothing but trouble."

"I'll call him now, Mom, and then I'll call you right back. Just sit tight for a minute."

She disconnected.

I called the sheriff and got his voice mail, so I called Captain Trainum, hoping he might know why the sheriff wasn't answering his calls, or where he was. I thought they might be together. If Trainum didn't know, I was going to ask him if he could handle the problem. Sheriff Hudson had once told me the neighboring police departments worked together, so there shouldn't be any reason why Trainum couldn't help me out.

"He's standing right next to me, Jesse," Trainum said when I asked him if he knew where Sheriff Hudson was. "Here, talk to him."

"What is it, Jesse?"

"Did you forget something… like telling your deputies that my mother was coming in with the coke? She's fit to be tied. Your guys threw Shark in a cell."

"Why did my deputy put Shark in a cell? There're no outstanding warrants on him."

"Well… Shark did come in fully loaded, if you know what I mean, and I think he spooked Deputy Doolittle. Mom said your deputy got in Shark's face, and Shark may have bumped him, but he didn't push him like the deputy said. Mom saw the whole thing, and that's her account of what happened. Your deputy overreacted."

"If it isn't one thing or another with your family. How could such a simple act turn into such chaos?" Sheriff Hudson was silent for a second. "Tell your mother I'll take care of it immediately and that I apologize. I forgot to call my guys. I'm so sorry."

"I thought you might be at the hospital and had your phone turned off."

"That rule doesn't apply to us. We don't ever turn our phones off."

"So… why are you at the hospital? Stone didn't escape, did she?"

"I'll make the call, Jesse, but I have to go now. I have important business to handle."

"One more thing before you hang up, Sheriff. You need to check your cell phone. It keeps going straight to voice mail."

"Darn."

"You rat. You've been screening my calls. That's not a good idea, Sheriff Hudson. You never know when it could be important… like it is now."

"Jesse, with you, everything's important. I told you I'd take care of it, and I will." He ended the call.

I looked up at Helene and said, "He disconnected without even saying goodbye."

"I wonder why, Jesse. You and Billy have been a thorn in his side ever since you met. We all have to some degree. No wonder he screens your calls."

"One day something's going to happen, and he'll wish he hadn't screened my call. Then he'll really be sorry, but by then, it'll be too late. Mark my word."

My cell phone rang, and it was Mom saying they were on their way home. Sheriff Hudson had fixed the problem, and the deputy was going to get a stern lecture for his unacceptable behavior. She was content. She asked the sheriff not to be too hard on the young guy. He was doing his best and was still learning.

When I managed to get a word in, I told her about Savannah, and about finding the wine bottle in Gavin Preston's car. She had no response to the wine bottle, but she was thrilled to hear about Savannah.

"Change of plans." She was talking to Eddie. "We're going to the hospital. Savannah's going to be all right, and I want to see her. Look Jesse, I need to hang up, so I can call Shark and tell him we're going to UVA Hospital. I think he's still a little ticked off at that deputy. He's driving so fast, it's all Eddie can do to keep up with him."

"Shark might have other obligations, Mom, but his job was to get you there and back in one piece."

"He doesn't have to go with us. He can…"

"Yes, he does. His job isn't over until you're safely back at home. I guess you could call him your bodyguard on a mission."

Mom liked the idea of having a bodyguard—especially someone like Shark. She started to go into a tribute to the man, but I had to cut her off.

"Mom, you need to call Shark. We can talk when you get home. Go to the hospital if Shark says it's okay. He won't let you go without him, so do what he tells you."

When Mom said goodbye, I knew where her next stop would be.

Shark, a force of a man to be reckoned with, had a soft spot in his heart for Mom… so they were going where she wanted to go.

"That was fast. Sheriff must've gotten on the horn the minute after he hung up on me."

"I guess he's scared of your mama, too."

"No, he's not. He respects her. Too bad he doesn't respect me. Oh, well… I'm going to check on Ethan, and then see if Billy has made any progress with Maisy's computer. I'm sure he has."

I walked down the hall and looked in on Ethan, who was enjoying a peaceful slumber, and then went to Maisy's room. I stood by the door and watched as the two of them laughed and carried on the way a father and daughter should every chance they get.

Maisy looked up when she saw me standing at the door.

"Dad fixed it, Mom. It had a worm." She looked back at Billy and giggled.

"A worm, huh? Did it eat up your hard drive?"

Maisy giggled again and said, "No, Dad killed it."

"Yeah, we had a problem when the lightning started back up. The wireless reception was erratic, but I managed to save the day." He kissed Maisy on the head. "Okay, I'm done here, unless you need more of my expertise."

"No, I'm good for now, Dad. Thanks for the help. I need to get back on Facebook. My friend Julie said she was going to post a pic of her brother. I want to check him out."

Billy got up and walked over to me.

"I'm not even going to ask." He rolled his eyes. "Did I miss anything in the last hour?"

I filled him in.

"There's no telling when Mom and Eddie will get back. You know she's going to stay at the hospital as long as they'll let her, and Eddie will do whatever she wants. That's okay. She has her bodyguard, Shark, there to protect her."

Billy smiled and said, "Shark isn't fond of hospitals."

"Yeah, but he's fond of my mother. Who isn't?"

The thunder and lightning had slowly moved out again, but the snow continued to fall, carrying with it strong winds that whipped through the trees, bending them with their gusts, and blowing snow everywhere. The temperature gauge on the kitchen windowsill read ten degrees. The snow would remain until the temperature rose, which could be a while.

Because of the weather, Billy and I decided to stay home and hang out with our kids, something we didn't get to do as much as we'd like. Our job kept us on the go, so when we got a chance to be with them, we took it. I wasn't the best when it came to playing games, but I was good at watching TV. It was safe here, and unless something major arose, we weren't going anywhere. The cops had Dakota, and all was well... until Mom called an hour later. She was crying so hard, she couldn't talk.

Shark came on the phone and said, "Jesse, you need to come to the hospital. Eddie had a heart attack, and your mom's hysterical. I tried to calm her down, but it's not working. She needs you."

"I'll be right there."

I disconnected and told Billy to grab his coat.

"We gotta go to the hospital. Eddie had a heart attack." I looked at Helene. "I'll call you when we find out how he's doing. You know the drill. Keep the doors locked."

I grabbed my coat and purse while Billy set the alarm.

All the way to the hospital, I kept asking myself what else could possibly go wrong. Right when everything seemed to be going well, something else would happen to upset our lives. With us, the action never seemed to stop.

When Billy and I first got together, being a P.I. was fun, exciting, and adventurous, but now, it had become scary and dangerous. Our cases always seemed to find a way into our private life, our home, our family. The fun had worn thin a while ago, and the danger had grown too vast. Had I gotten old, or had reality finally set in?

An event was about to unfold that would put my doubts to rest. Danger had arrived, and it was knocking on our door.

Chapter 15

Eddie was in the ER at UVA Hospital, and the doctors were still running tests on him when we got there. Mom was standing in the hallway, waiting to hear something, her eyes red and teary. Shark stood by her side, his big arm wrapped around her tiny shoulders.

"I don't know what happened. One minute he was fine, and the next, he was on the floor clutching his chest. Oh, Jesse, he can't die. He just can't! I don't know what I'd do without him."

"He's going to be fine, Mom. I'm sure. He's getting the best care possible. The doctors know what they're doing. He'll be sitting up smiling at you in no time."

"You think so, Jesse? You think he'll be all right?"

"I'm sure he will. Let's go sit in the waiting room, Mom. There's nothing you can do until the doctor finishes. By then, we'll know more about Eddie's condition and what they're going to do to fix it."

I wasn't sure about anything, but I wasn't about to tell my mother that. She was already worried out of her mind, and I wasn't going to add to her worries by saying I had no idea what was going to happen to Eddie. She needed my encouragement, so I stood by her side, and kept my fingers crossed.

We sat in the waiting area as the minutes slowly ticked by. An hour passed, and we were still waiting as other patients came and went. There wasn't as much chaos as there was earlier today, so when I noticed the police scrounging the hallways, I asked Billy if something was happening.

"Look, Billy, the cops are everywhere. What's going on? They act like they're searching for someone. Maybe there's a patient on the loose. As big as this hospital is, I wouldn't be surprised if they lost someone."

"I think calling in the cops would be a last resort… unless the patient that's missing was one who was in custody and had escaped."

We glared at each other.

"You don't think Dakota Stone escaped, do you? I mean, she's handcuffed to the bed. How could she get loose?"

Billy shook his head.

"Nah, it's not her. There's no way she could've gotten out of those cuffs. Not unless she's Houdini. It's probably nothing, Jesse. The hospital's always busy and it's not unusual to see a lot of cops hanging around, filling out reports or the like."

"Look over there, Billy." I pointed to the entrance. The cops are checking everyone out as they leave. I'm telling you, something's going on. I have a bad feeling about this."

Shark stood. "I'll check around. See what all the fuss is."

He walked down the hall, turned the corner, and then disappeared. A few minutes later, he returned.

"Some kid wandered off from his mother, but they found him."

Mom dabbed her eyes with a tissue.

"That explains why there're so many cops here," she said. "When a child goes missing, they jump right on it. When little kids get lost, they can't find their way back like adults can. They might've thought the child had been abducted."

Finally, after waiting for almost two hours, an intern walked out of the ER and called Mom's last name. He talked and looked at his laptop at the same time.

"Mr. Wilson had an anxiety attack, but he's going to be fine. He's been given a mild sedative, and Dr. Bryant has written a prescription for Diazepam. Your husband has the paperwork. Please make sure he reads and follows the instructions. If you have any questions, call your family physician, or if his symptoms worsen, bring him back to the hospital."

"You're sure he didn't have a heart attack? He had really bad chest pains."

"An anxiety attack mimics a heart attack in some cases. You were right to bring him to the hospital. Chest pain shouldn't be ignored. Mr. Wilson should be out shortly."

The intern turned and walked back through the ER doors.

"Well, I was going to tell him we were already here when it happened, but he didn't give me a chance. I guess it really doesn't matter as long…"

The ER doors swung open and Eddie walked out, carrying a hand full of folded up paperwork. Mom ran up and threw her arms around him.

"I'm so glad you're all right. I was worried sick. I thought you were going to die."

"I feel so silly."

I walked over and hugged Eddie.

"No, no, don't say that," I said. "There's nothing silly about chest pain. Mom thought you were having a heart attack. I'm just glad you were already at the hospital." I smiled, and then winked at Eddie. "If you fall out in the hospital, there's no waiting line."

Mom grinned and said, "That's true. You should've seen how fast they reacted when Eddie went down. I said he had chest pain, and before you know it, they had him up on a stretcher and were pushing him down the hall. I don't know why they wouldn't let me go with him."

Billy touched Mom's hand. "Chest pain isn't like getting a cut stitched up, Minnie. Something could go wrong, and you'd just be in the way. No offense, but family members have a tendency to get loony when they think their loved one is going to die. See, if you got all crazy on them, they'd have to sedate you, and that would take time away from their patient. It's a good policy."

"Yeah, I guess you're right, Billy. I never thought of it that way." She looked back at Eddie. "You ready to go? I know I am."

"What about Savannah? I thought you wanted to see her," Eddie said as took her hand. "I'm doing good. It wasn't a heart attack, and the doctor said I'm fit as a fiddle, so if you want to go see her, I'm willing." He chuckled. "We're already here."

Mom glanced around at us with a questioning look on her face.

Shark walked over and smiled down at Mom.

"If you want to go see your friend and Eddie feels up to it, I'll go with you, Minnie. It's the least I can do before hitting the road. My job here is almost done. They got that bad woman locked up, and everybody's safe now. This one's over, and you won't need me much longer."

"I'll hate to see you leave, Shark," Eddie said, holding out his hand. "I liked having you around. It's been interesting, to say the least. Oh, and thanks for being there when we needed you. You've been a big comfort to Minnie throughout all this, and I'm not just talking about what happened to me here." He leaned over and whispered. "I think she has a crush on you, but that's okay. I know who she really loves."

It was nice to see two men joke and carry on over my mom. The attention was just what she needed. The stress lines faded from her face, and the laugh lines took their rightful place.

"Well, he's not leaving yet, Eddie. You act as if he's leaving right this minute and this is goodbye." Mom looked back at Shark. "You ready to take us to see Savannah?"

"Your wish is my command."

Mom took the papers from Eddie and handed them to me.

"Would you get Eddie's prescription filled?" she asked. "He'll probably need one when we get home. We use the Wal-Mart pharmacy."

"Sure, I'll take care of it, Mom. You said home. Does that mean you're going back to your house or our house?"

"Our house is your house." She beamed as she grabbed Eddie and Shark by the hand and walked off. She glanced back and said, "See you later, alligator."

Billy and I hugged each other, smiling about how easily Mom could bounce back, change her tune, and then take control of the situation.

"She's a keeper."

"Yes, she is. I would say she's come out of her shell since we all hooked up with the Blackhawks, but the truth is, I don't think she ever was in a shell. She's just been reserved about her actions. She and my father never experienced the kind of life she's living now. Situations change and I think she's done a fine job of keeping up with the changes. Well… shall we go home, or see if we can get in to see Dakota?"

"Like Eddie told your mother—we're already here. Let's give it a shot. We got nothing to lose. Besides, we know what floor she's on. All we have to do is snoop around to find her room."

I knew something was wrong the minute we stepped out of the elevator and saw Sheriff Hudson and Captain Trainum standing in the hallway, surrounded by their men.

"Oh, my God! She's escaped, Billy!"

I started walking towards them in a hurry. "She's gone, isn't she?" I asked. "You said you had everything under control, but now she's gone."

Three deputies stepped out in front of us, stopping our approach, and then one of them said, "You can't be here. You're going to have to leave."

Waving his men off, Sheriff Hudson walked over. Captain Trainum followed.

"Go home, Billy. We'll find her. There's no way she could've gotten out of the hospital. Our guys are stationed at every entrance and exit. They have been since last night. She's not leaving this hospital."

Captain Trainum added his input. “This is a matter for the police. There’s nothing you can do, so let us do our job. Do what the sheriff said and go home.”

“She got out of her handcuffs!” I was furious. “You let her slip through your fingers, and now she’s gone. How long has it been?”

“That’s not important.”

“It most certainly is! How long?”

“About two hours.”

I looked at Billy.

“Two hours! Oh, Lord, she’s been gone for two hours! She could be anywhere by now. You know where she’s headed, Billy. She’s going to our house. She blames me for Olivia Swales’ death and wants revenge, and she’s not running until she gets it.” I looked back at the sheriff. “How did she get out of the handcuffs?”

“I can’t discuss this with you right now, Jesse. Just go home.”

“Did one of your men help her? Is that how she escaped? Did she pick the cuffs with a hairpin? What? I want to know!”

“If you must know, the deputy took the cuffs off so she could use the bathroom, and when she came out, she grabbed the telephone and hit him over the head.”

“Who was the deputy? I want to know who to blame after she kills one of us.”

“Don’t be ridiculous. It wasn’t his fault. He was just doing his job.”

“You actually think she’s still in the hospital somewhere? You’re nuts. She’s gone. If I were her, the first thing I’d do would be to find the locker room, break into a locker, and steal some clothes and car keys.”

Sheriff Hudson glared at me and said, “We checked the locker room. No one is missing anything.”

“As far as you know. What about the workers you couldn’t talk to? Like doctors or nurses who might be in surgery. It’s been two hours. Your men have combed this hospital for two hours and come up with nothing, and you still think she’s still here? I gave you more credit than that, Sheriff Hudson." I turned to Billy, "Let's get out of here. These guys got nothing."

Billy and I turned and fast-tracked it to the elevator.

"Stay out of this, Blackhawk!" the sheriff yelled.

We didn't pay attention to the sheriff's demand; instead, we got into the elevator and waited for the doors to close.

"As soon as we get out of this elevator, I'll call Shark and tell him to get Minnie and Eddie out of the hospital and take them to Jonathan's house. I don't want them going to our house just in case the Stone woman shows up."

The second we exited the elevator, heading to the entrance door of the hospital, Billy pulled out his cell phone and called Shark. Their conversation was brief. "Grab Minnie and Eddie and leave right now. Meet us at the entrance. We'll be waiting."

Five minutes later, the elevator door opened and Shark hustled Mom and Eddie out.

"What's all the hurry?" We heard her ask him. "I didn't get to see Savannah."

"Billy said to leave, so we're leaving. There he is, ask him."

Billy explained as we walked to the parking garage.

"Dakota Stone escaped, and Jesse and I think she might be headed to our house. We can't be sure, but we're not taking any chances. I want you and Eddie to follow Shark to Jonathan's."

Mom stopped in the middle of the crosswalk. "Are you serious? They let her get away?" Snow was blowing in her face, but that wasn't going to stop her rant. "You mean to tell me that a hundred cops couldn't keep their eyes on one little woman? How hard could it be? She's only one person. Incompetents, that's what they are!"

"Come on, Mom." I said as I grabbed her hand. "We don't know where she is. She could be hiding in the parking garage for all we know. We need to get to our cars and get outta here. I'm going to call Helene and tell her to grab the kids and head to Jonathan's house. I don't want them at the house in case she shows up."

We trekked through the snow to the garage, jumped in our cars, and pulled out. If Dakota Stone was hiding there, we didn't see her. The sheriff said there was no way she could've gotten out of the hospital without his men catching her, but obviously, that wasn't true. Stone was a smart and cunning person. She'd found a way to escape, and most likely, was coming after me.

As we brought up the rear, following Shark, Mom and Eddie, I looked over at Billy and said, "I can't believe she conked the deputy over the head and got away. These guys aren't small men. They're behemoths, strong, and well-trained. Why didn't he get up and go after her?"

"He got hit over the head with a telephone. It probably knocked him out."

"We need to call Helene and warn her… tell her to get out of the house. God, it's been two hours. I hope it's not too late."

I pulled out my cell phone to make the call, but it rang before I had a chance.

"Oh, good, it's Helene. Maybe she's checking in. I hope everything's all right." I touched the screen. "Helene, is everything okay?"

Helene's tone was unnerving and her reply floored me.

"What? Say that again."

I hit the speaker icon on my phone so Billy could hear.

"I think I just killed Dakota Stone."

Chapter 16

I thought for sure my hearing was playing tricks on me when Helene said she might have killed Dakota Stone. Helene? The most harm she had ever inflicted on anyone was to use harsh words, so to think she was capable of killing someone was inconceivable.

"I didn't mean to kill her, but I had to do something! I had to stop her! She just showed up at the front door! She was going to kill us! She said so!"

"We're five minutes from the house, Helene. Stay put, and keep the kids safe. We'll be right there."

I disconnected, sat there, staring straight ahead.

"I'm stunned. I don't know what to say." I glanced at Billy. "I guess we were right to be worried. My gut told me she was coming, but I was hoping I was wrong. All I've been able to think about was making it home before she got there."

"Why didn't you ask Helene what happened?"

"I wanted to, but she was too distraught, Billy. Couldn't you tell it by her voice? That must have been awful for her. No… she's got plenty of time to explain when we get there. I'm just hoping she can hold it together until we do. You know she's probably terrified."

We turned onto Bear Mountain Road and then separated from the others when we pulled into our driveway. Shark, Mom, and Eddie continued on to Jonathan's house as we followed the tire tracks in the snow to the front yard.

All the lights in the house were on, and a bright yellow 4Runner just like Mom's was parked beside Helene's car.

"Whoa! That can't be Mom's car. Am I hallucinating?"

"No, you're not. Dakota Stone had to get here some way. It's a coincidence that the car she commandeered was one like your mother's. Maybe Helene thought it was Minnie."

Billy parked the truck and we jumped out running, and then plowed through the front door. My heart was pounding out of my chest.

Helene met us, crying as she tried to talk.

"She's dead! I killed her! See…" She pointed to the dining room floor where Dakota Stone lay. "I saw the car and I thought it was Minnie, so I opened the door."

Billy took his coat off, tossed it on the table, and then put his hands on Helene's shoulders.

"Calm down, Helene," he said to her. "We're here now, and you're safe. It's over. Are the kids okay?"

"They're fine. I made them go stay in the den with the door closed."

Billy walked over to where Dakota lay by the dining room table, and checked for a pulse.

"How long has she been out?"

"About a half-hour. Is she dead?"

"No, she's not dead, but she's down."

I glanced over at the body on the floor, and then back to Billy.

"I'll go check on the kids."

I hurried down the hall to the den, opened the door and peeked in.

"Everybody okay in here?"

The dogs jumped up from their hiding places and started barking, while Maisy came over to the door. She turned to them and pointed.

"Be quiet and sit back down," she told them.

Athena and Thor dropped to the floor, obeying her command.

Maisy turned back to me and said, "Helene told us to go to the den and stay there, so we did. Is that bad lady still here?"

"How do you know she's a bad lady?"

"Because Helene yelled at us. She never yells at us. I might be just a kid, but I know when something's not right. I grabbed Ethan and we hid out here. I didn't know what else to do. I was scared."

"You did good, honey."

I looked over at Ethan who was asleep on the sofa, and then looked back at Maisy.

"You're safe and there's nothing to be afraid of. We're here now, but I'm going to need for you and Ethan to stay in the den just a little longer. Can you do that for me?"

"I'm hungry."

"I'll get Helene to fix sandwiches. Can you hold off for a little while?"

"Sure, Mom. You want me to close the door?"

"Please."

Maisy closed the door, and I headed back to the dining room, taking off my coat while I walked. I threw it across the back of the living room sofa, and then walked over and stood by Helene and Billy.

"That's Dakota Stone for sure," I said.

I looked down at the body in relief. My insides had been shaking ever since we learned of her escape, but now my fear was gone. Dakota wasn't dead, but at least she was incapacitated, sprawled out on the floor like a limp rag doll. I almost laughed when I saw the clothes she was wearing.

"I guess your high sense of fashion went out the window when you had to choose your wardrobe from the hospital locker room," I said to her even though I wasn't sure she could hear me. "I'm surprised that you would lower yourself to wear someone else's clothes."

Dakota was wearing a pair of black jogging pants, the old kind that were thick and bulky, a gray sweatshirt that had UVA in large letters on the front, and tennis shoes that were too big for her feet. A yellow ski jacket hung from the table chair, and a set of car keys lay on the table next to a cup and saucer.

I looked back at Billy.

"So… she's not dead," I said. "Too bad."

"No, but she's going to have a doozy of a headache when she wakes up. Helene fed her a cocktail of pain killers and doggie downers."

I had to laugh. "You did what, Helene? You drugged her with Athena's pills? Good for you."

Now that I knew the woman wasn't dead, I had to get in a last word. I stepped closer to the body and gave her a swift kick in the side.

"That's what you get for messing with my family!" I said.

I thought about kicking her again, but there's no satisfaction in beating someone when they're already down.

"And you might want to rethink that outfit. It doesn't do anything for you."

"I don't think she hears you, Jesse. She's been like that for a while. I tried to call you as soon as the body hit the floor, but you were at the hospital and all I got was your voice mail… until…"

I grabbed Helene's hand and led her over to the opposite side of table away from the body.

"Come on, Helene. I want you to sit down and tell me everything that happened." I looked back at Billy and winked. "We could use a good shot of whiskey right about now." I pointed to the body. "She's not going anywhere."

Billy fixed us a drink and set them down in front of us.

"I'm going to get the handcuffs," he said. "She's not getting away this time. I have a few questions for her."

"Then, you might want to think about getting some rope and tying her up. She's a crafty one. She might come to her senses and try to choke one of us. It wouldn't be hard. Catch one of us off-guard, come up from behind, and get one of us in a chokehold. She'd be strong enough with those handcuffs on. Don't you think so?"

Helene took a big gulp of whiskey and then sat the empty glass down.

"I like duct tape," she said. "Handcuff her, and then duct tape her to the chair."

Billy left the room and then returned with handcuffs and a roll of duct tape. He rolled Dakota over and handcuffed her hands behind her back, and then lifted her limp body off the floor to the chair. He grabbed the duct tape and taped her feet to the legs of the chair, and then ran the tape around her waist, securing her upper body. When he finished, he walked over to the kitchen counter, poured himself a whiskey, downed it, and then poured another.

"This is going to be a two-whiskey kind of day… maybe three. Anyone else?" he asked, holding up the bottle.

Helene raised her hand and said, "Hit me again."

I downed my drink and held up the glass. "Me, too."

"I don't think so, ge `ya. You took a tranquilizer earlier, and I don't want you to go into a coma and die from mixing drugs and alcohol."

"I see your point," I said, agreeing with him.

I put my glass down, turned to Helene and said, "Okay. Tell us what happened here today, and don't leave out anything."

Billy walked over and sat down, waiting to hear the rest of Helene's story. "I've heard most of it, but I'm listening. Go ahead, Helene. Tell Jesse what happened."

Helene began her account of Dakota's visit.

"I saw the yellow 4Runner pull up, so I thought it was Minnie. I walked over to the door, opened it, and then saw Dakota standing there holding Spice Cat by the scruff of the neck… and he wasn't happy. He meowed like he was in pain. I was afraid she'd choke him or something, so I invited her in. I know it was crazy, but I didn't know what to do. When she walked in, she dropped Spice Cat on the floor like he was a piece of dirty laundry. He howled and ran off. Then, she looked at me and asked me if I knew who she was. Of course I knew who she was, but I didn't say so. All I said was that you wouldn't like it if she hurt your cat. She laughed at me, and then pushed me back. She demanded to see you, but I told her you weren't here, so she said she'd wait. I figured if I didn't let on that I knew her, maybe we'd get out of this alive. That's when I yelled at the kids to go to the den and take the dogs with them."

"Yeah, Maisy said she knew something was wrong when you yelled at them."

"I never yell at them, and I still feel bad about it. That's no way to treat a child."

"Don't feel bad. You did the right thing. The kids will get over it. I'm just glad Maisy knew what to do. Most kids would've argued with you and made the situation worse. Go on with your story."

"Anyway… I figured I should act innocent and be polite. I asked her if she wanted a cup of tea while she waited, telling her I would love one. I told her she looked like the kind of person who would appreciate a good cup of tea. I also said that I had fresh mint. She liked that idea. I guess she is a tea drinker after all. I went to make the tea while she made herself comfortable at the table. I think she thought I was harmless. Boy, did I ever show her. When I put the kettle on to brew the tea, I noticed the mashed up doggie downers, and that's when I got the idea to put the drugs in her tea."

"She could've switched the cups on you. Did you think of that?"

"Of course I did. That's why I gave her the cup without the stuff in it. I knew she'd switch them on me, and when I turned my back, she did. Her mistake. You see, I dropped in a few of your tranquilizers, too. They dissolve easily. I topped off the tea with a mint leaf."

"How many pills did you give her?"

"Four, I think. I don't remember. They're only five milligrams each, so I didn't know how many it would take, and I didn't have much time to worry about it. I wanted to knock her out, or at least make her too woozy to do anything. Then, I could go get my gun."

"Where is your gun?"

"In my back pocket."

She pulled the small handgun out, laid it on the table and said, "I was going to be ready in case she woke up before y'all got here."

"I'm surprised you didn't tie her up."

"I didn't want to get that close. What if I hadn't given her enough? What if she woke up the minute I got near her? I panicked. My mind was racing and all I could think about was getting my gun. The minute she fell over, I knew the stuff had worked. She just flopped right over, and I was sure I'd given her too much. I just knew she was dead, but I still went and grabbed my gun… and then I called you. When I couldn't get you, I sat in the chair and held the gun on her. I'm glad I kept calling."

"What did she say to you? I know she must've said something."

"Not really. She treated me like I was beneath her and a waste of her precious time. She sat there, sipping her tea, saying nothing, until I couldn't stand it anymore. I was waiting for the pills to kick in, but the wait was driving me insane, so I tried to be civil. I told her that we might as well introduce ourselves since it might be a while before you got home. I offered to call you, but she said not to bother. I told her I was Helene, but before she could say anything, she closed her eyes and fell out. It seemed to take forever for the pills to kick in, but when they did, it happened so fast. Next thing I know, she's lying on the floor, out cold."

"I didn't know you were a tea drinker, Helene. I always thought you were a coffee fanatic."

"I fix coffee for y'all, and a lot of times I drink it, too, but tea is my favorite. And… there's something about tea that helps dissolve tablets. I learned that a while back when I was taking some medication. I had a hard time swallowing pills, so I'd just toss one in a cup of hot tea. Did the trick for me."

I got up from the table, walked over to Dakota, and then stared down at her.

"She isn't so tough anymore."

I grabbed her hair, jerked her head back, and then slapped her hard across the face.

Helene looked shocked by my actions.

"Hey… crazy lady," she said. "What are you doing? She's out. No need to beat her up."

"I'm not beating her up. I'm waking her up."

I walked over to the sink, filled a glass with water, and then walked back over to Dakota. When I threw the water in her face, she stirred and shook the water from her face.

Billy got up from the table, walked over and stood next to me.

"Let's liven up this party," he said. "Slap her again. I think she's coming around."

I slapped her once more.

Helene looked away. She wasn't accustomed to seeing someone get slapped around, but then her curiosity got the best of her and she looked back at us.

Dakota blinked a couple of times before opening her eyes. She tried to focus in on her surroundings. She glanced around, looked down at herself, and then looked back up at us. A moment later, she gave us an evil, stab-you-in-the-eye look. She looked like she was stone-drunk, but her words were cold sober.

"You're going to be sorry you ever met me."

I leaned over and whispered in her ear.

"We already are. We're sorry we ever laid eyes on you. You're a stone cold killer, but those days are over, Missy. You're all washed up. You're going to prison for the rest of your life... unless we kill you first. Yeah, I think I like the idea of snuffing you out better. Why waste the court's time?"

She closed her eyes and dropped her head. Then, she looked back up at me and said, "You're… crazy. I haven't… killed anyone."

I stepped back, crossed my arms, and let out a sigh.

"Now you see, Dakota, that's just not true. You're a killer, and you're the worst kind. You kill your friends, your lover, and people who trust you. You're heartless, and you have no remorse. I can see it in your eyes. You don't care about anyone but yourself."

I filled the glass again and tossed more water in her face.

She shook the water from her face and gasped for breath. She was starting to slowly come around. She opened her eyes, and then jerked back and forth in the chair. She was trying to break free of her restraints, cursing all the while.

"Is this coffee left over from this morning, Helene?" Billy asked.

"Yes, but I cut off the pot, so it's probably cold."

"That's the way I want it."

Billy walked over to the coffee pot, poured some into a cup, and then walked back over to Dakota. He grabbed her by the hair, jerked her head back, and poured the coffee in her mouth.

"Drink up," he said. "And if you spit it out, I'll just pour more in."

At first she spit out the coffee, and then coughed as if she was choking. Obviously, she had no desire to drink the cold coffee.

"Here we go again."

Billy poured more coffee in her mouth, still holding her head back, and she was forced to swallow it.

"That's better. Let's try again."

"Stop, Billy!" Helene said. "She's going to choke to death."

"I'm not going to let that happen. I'm trying to get some caffeine in her body, otherwise, she's going to be in for a long nap."

"I have an idea that might work better," Helene came back with. "Prozac… shove one of those pills down her throat and you'll have to pull her off the ceiling."

"What?" I said.

"When my husband died, the doctor put me on Prozac and Valium. The Valium worked, but the Prozac jacked me up so much, I refused to take anymore. I still have the bottle."

"Oh, yeah? Where's the bottle?"

"It's in my bathroom cabinet. I guess they're still good. It was the Valium that I was talking about putting in my tea."

"We don't need no pill," Billy said. "I can bring her around."

"Come on, Billy," I said. "Let's give her a pill. What's the worst that can happen? It'd be quicker."

"Wait a minute," Helene said. "What if she has a reaction to it?"

"Then maybe she'll do us all a favor... and die."

"We're going to pass on the pill," Billy said, "but thanks anyway, Helene. I think we'll stick with the coffee."

He poured the last of the coffee in her mouth, and she swallowed it again. Then, he walked back to the kitchen and refilled the cup.

I looked over at Helene.

"Maisy said she was hungry. Would you mind fixing the kids something to eat... maybe a sandwich?"

"But it's almost dinnertime," she said. "You want them to eat sandwiches before dinner?"

"Dinner might have to wait for a while," I said. "We're going to get the truth out of her before we do anything else."

Helene hesitated as if she couldn't grasp my illogical timing. She was watching us try to interrogate Dakota, and right in the middle, I ask her to go feed the kids. I'm sure she wondered whether I thought they would starve if she didn't give them something to eat right then.

"But I want to be here. I want to hear what she has to say... and I want to watch y'all slap her around. She deserves it and more."

She glared at Dakota with a menacing look.

"You might as well tell them what they want to know. Billy knows all kinds of ways of extracting information from a criminal like you… and it won't be fun. You don't stand a chance."

"You're not going to miss anything, so please go feed the kids," I said. "We'll try to hold off on the good stuff until you get back."

Helene went to the kitchen, mumbling under her breath.

"Yep, I'm gonna miss it all. Gotta fix sandwiches right this minute. Just can't wait."

She prepared the sandwiches and walked out, still mumbling to herself.

I called to her. "Come back when the kids finish eating. By then, we'll just be getting to the best part."

Helene picked up the pace.

Billy continued with the coffee, until Dakota put a stop to it.

"Enough. It's making me sick… to my… stomach." She leaned over, puked, and then pleaded for a washcloth.

Billy went to the kitchen, got a hand towel, and then dabbed her mouth. He tossed the towel on the dining room table and held up the cup.

"Ready?"

Dakota stared up at Billy with droopy eyes and said, "No… no more."

Billy stepped back.

"Just trying to wake you up."

I grabbed a chair from the table, turned it my way, and then straddled it. I scooted closer to Dakota and propped my arms up on the back of the chair.

"This is going to be long and ugly, unless you wanna skip the niceties and get down to business. It's your choice. You can tell us what we want to know, or Billy can beat it out of you. Myself… I don't care one way or the other, but before we turn you over to the sheriff, we're going to have our answers."

I leaned in.

"You're a bad person. You tried to have my mother killed. If you die in this chair, it won't hurt my feelings a bit."

I smiled wickedly at her as I lied.

"Your boyfriend, Gavin Preston died in this chair. Oh, we slapped him around a bit, and that was fun, but it was your poison that killed him. Anti-freeze, really? Don't you know that stuff shows up on a tox screen? What were you thinking… or did you just not care? I'm betting you thought you were going to get away… run from the devastation you caused… start a new life. That ain't gonna happen."

I was surprised when Billy reached down, pulled a knife from his boot, and then pressed the shiny blade up against her face.

"I going to ask you a question, and if you lie, I'm going to cut you. I'll start with your face."

Her droopy eyes widened.

I had to wonder if he really would. Could he do that? This wasn't the man I know. The man I know would never be so cruel. But then, I had to think about his actions. You see, most people fear Indians. They have a preconceived notion that they're all like the ones they used to see in the old westerns where the Indians kill the white man and then scalp him, women included. Maybe that's what Billy was doing. He was trying to bring back those memories of another time, and that old fear. I sat there and said nothing, waiting for Billy's question and her response. If she lied, what would he do then?

Dakota trembled, keeping her eye on the knife the whole time. She was awake now, and she didn't move an inch.

"It's over… I give up… what do you want to know?"

Tears ran down her face.

I mocked her.

"Ah, the woman cries," I said sarcastically. "I didn't know you had it in you, Dakota. Oh, that's right, your name isn't really Dakota, is it? What about your girlfriend, Olivia? What's her real name? Where did you come from? How many people have you killed?"

Dakota kept watch on the knife as sweat beaded on her forehead and then ran down her face, mingling with her tears.

"Make him… take the knife… from my face."

It was obvious that she wasn't going to be able to withstand a brutal interrogation. The thought of having her face scarred for life and her body being used as a punching bag must've gotten to her… or maybe, it was the idea that she might actually die where she sat… at the hands of an Indian prone to killing and scalping people. Yep, that last one must've done the trick.

Billy took the knife from her face, but held it close by.

"Instead of wasting my time with a bunch of questions, why don't you just tell us what turned you into a killer?" he asked. "You can start your story by telling us who you are. We'll go from there."

He grabbed a chair, sat down, and then crossed his legs, the knife still in his hand, resting on his lap.

"I'm waiting."

He leaned forward.

"And remember, the first time you lie to me, I'm cutting you. That ought to really wake you up. Yeah, you sure look awake now."

He waved the knife to validate his promise, and then slapped it across his legs.

Dakota jumped and almost tipped over the chair. She regained her composure somewhat and began her tale, knowing that if she lied, she was doomed to die… or so she thought. She was still doped up, but she managed to tell her story.

"Six years ago, I was married to a man that everyone loved. He was nice to everyone except me. Oh, he started out like the perfect husband, but it wasn't long before his dark side came out. He beat me… always screamed at me. I tolerated it. I didn't know what else to do. Then, one day he went too far."

Her tears dried up, and her eyes opened wider. She was slowly coming out of her stupor.

"We were on our way to visit his folks when he went ballistic after I told him that I wanted to spend more time with my sister. He hated her. He pulled the car off the road… got out and dragged me out of the car. He dragged me to the woods and started knocking me around. I was in shock. He'd been brutal… so many times, but this time was different. This was the end of the road for me, and I knew it when I looked into those dark, menacing, evil eyes. He'd snapped and was going to beat me to death. Finally, he hit me so hard he knocked me to the ground. The place was littered with trash, condoms… nasty junk. He jumped on me… raised his hand back… I grabbed the first thing I could… I cut his throat with a broken bottle. He fell on me, making a gurgling sound. I was covered in his blood. I sat there on that damp and nasty ground, trying to come to grips with what I had done."

"You were just defending yourself," Helene said, coming back into the room. She walked over to the sink and set the dishes down. "No one would blame you for that."

"Yes… they would. I know what happens in cases like these. I'd go to prison. Nobody would care that my husband beat me. No, all they'd see was a woman who murdered her husband. So, I called 9-1-1… said we'd been attacked by a hitchhiker my husband picked up. I told them the guy had killed my husband and was going to kill me. I screamed and cried for them to come save me. Then, I got in the car and drove off. Later, I dumped the car in a Wal-Mart parking lot. My sister and I disappeared. We took the money our folks left us… changed our looks… got a new identity."

"So… Olivia's your sister."

"Yes… but her name isn't Olivia… its Bernice. I'm Denise… Denise Sutton. You might've read something in the paper about me. They never found my body. The case went cold and off the radar. We laid low for over a year. They stopped looking, so we came here. The Body Shop was my idea."

Billy leaned back.

"Whose idea was it to start the killing?"

"Roger preyed on me like a hawk. Do you know what that's like? A hawk swoops down with razor sharp talons, snatches his prey by the neck, and squeezes until the prey is beaten… dead."

Helene walked over to her and said, "Ah… so… the prey bites back."

"Exactly. Why not? They deserved it. They beat their wives just like Roger beat me. Someone had to stop them… so I did. I made them pay for their crimes, and it made me feel good to do it. I helped those women."

I rolled my eyes and shook my head.

"You helped no one but yourself. You wanted to make every man pay for what your husband had done to you. You wanted revenge. You got a charge out of it. That's sick."

"That's right, I am sick."

Dakota was now more alert.

"Roger banged me up pretty bad. I was bruised, cut, you name it. Bernice got me to a doctor. He patched me up. Then, I had that nervous breakdown. Killing Roger made me sick. Bernice took me to see a psychiatrist, but I never told him that I killed my husband. Kept that one to myself. I wasn't that insane. Bernice told the doctor that Roger beat me and would kill me if he found me, so the doctor helped us out. Kept everything on the down-low. Things were going well, until you showed up. You caused me nothing but trouble. We were happy with our lives, and you took that away from me when you meddled in my business and killed my sister."

"You killed your sister, not me. You still don't see that, do you? It was your fault. Maybe you should go back and see that doctor again. You're nuts. You belong in a loony bin. You might've been an innocent victim when you killed Roger, but that ended when you started killing other people. You wanted payback. Now, you're going to get the needle."

Denise laughed at me in a wicked way.

"After what I just told you, you think any jury would convict me? I went crazy. My husband abused me… almost beat me to death. Drove me over the edge. My psychiatrist will testify to that. He knows how bad off I was."

"Yeah… but he didn't know you killed your husband. What do you think he'll have to say when he hears that?"

"He'll be shocked at first, but then he'll say he's not surprised. I was terrorized and had to defend myself. He's not going to throw me under the bus."

I laughed at her for thinking she was going to get away with what she had done.

"We'll see about that," I said. "Oh, by the way, my cat wants to thank you for the gift."

"What gift?"

"Why… your wedding band, of course. We're going to sell it for the gold and buy Spice a new collar. You know… one of those expensive ones."

I was making up some good lies, but she didn't care.

Helene grunted, and then asked, "What about Gavin Preston? Don't you feel the least bit of remorse for killing him? He was your boyfriend… lover, for God's sake. He was a good man until you came into his life."

"You didn't know him," Denise said. "Gavin was nobody. He let me down and deserved to die."

"Jesse's right, lady, you are crazy. You're never going to get away with killing Gavin and those other men. The evidence just keeps piling up against you. The sheriff has the wine bottle. He's going to find your prints on it."

"So what? My prints have been on a lot of wine bottles. That doesn't prove a thing. Catch me with the bottle in my hand and then you might have something."

"You need to pay for what you've done."

Helene's eyes narrowed, her anger building. She calmly walked over, picked up her handgun from the table, and aimed it at Denise's chest.

"You deserve to die. Your killing spree stops here."

No one said a word, and no one moved.

We stared at Helene as Denise sucked in her breath, fear seizing her body. She closed her eyes and waited for the inevitable, but the inevitable never came. Helene lowered the gun and placed it back on the table.

"I've always wanted to do that."

"Geez, Helene, you scared me half to death."

Billy dropped his knife on the table next to his coat, reached over, picked up the gun and tucked it in the waist of his pants.

"Don't ever do that again. I almost had a heart attack."

"Why? You thought I was going to shoot her, didn't you?"

"No, I was afraid you'd miss and hit one of us. You and Minnie with your handguns... I don't know whether to be afraid or happy."

Denise exhaled and looked down. The crotch of her pants was wet.

"See what you made me do? It's all your fault. Not only am I dressed in these hideous clothes, but now, I've peed on myself. I hope you're satisfied."

I had no sympathy for someone like her.

"Hmm… ain't that a pity. They're going to haul your pee-pee butt off to jail. Want me to call the crisis hotline?"

Billy pulled out his cell phone.

"Well… I guess this party's over. Time to call out the dogs. I hate to tell you this, Denise, but just because you had an abusive husband, it doesn't give you the right to kill people. "

Denise giggled like a little girl.

"And what are you going to tell the cops? That the three of you beat me into confessing to crimes I didn't commit? I'm not well, you know."

Helene spat at her. "I never touched you!"

I glared at her and said, "No, you're not well, Denise… Dakota… whatever your name is, but that won't matter when I play my phone recording of our conversation to the police. I think they'll find it very interesting. Hmm… and so incriminating."

Denise was furious. She started screaming at us, hurling accusations, saying ridiculous things, ranting about anything and everything—most of which was gibberish—all of which was lies. Either she was playing the crazy person card, or she was going down a long, dark road to nowhere. Maybe this time she was a real goner. She'd lost the only person she ever really cared about, and now she was alone. There was nothing left for her. If she wasn't a killer, I could almost feel sorry for her… but she was a killer.

When did the coin flip from being a victim to being a killer?

I wanted to ask her, but she wouldn't know. She was in her own little world now… or at least she seemed to be. She stopped hollering, became quiet, and looked as if she was spacing-out. Her eyes wandered in a freaky way and her head bobbed.

Was she a nut case, or was she acting? I couldn't tell.

"Ah, Billy, let me make that call to the sheriff," I said. "I just want to see if he'll answer me."

I grabbed my cell phone, touched the screen, and waited. After two rings, the call went to voice mail. I held my phone away from my face.

"See, he's doing it again. He's screening my calls."

Denise yelled out something crazy again.

"Shut up!" Helene screamed at her. "Someone please call the sheriff before that lunatic drives me insane! I can't stand it anymore! I should've shot her when I had the chance. Where's my gun?"

I called the sheriff's number again, but as usual, he didn't answer.

"Okay, that's it. He's ignoring me. I'm going to send him a 911 text, and see how he reacts to that. Hopefully, the text for help will get his attention."

I sent the text, and a few seconds later, Billy's cell phone rang.

"Ah, it's Sheriff Hudson."

"Guess he doesn't like talking to me."

Denise's ranting made it impossible for Billy to hear. He walked out of the room and down the hall.

I heard him say something about Denise, but that was about all I got from the conversation.

Helene walked over and showed me the screen of her cell phone.

"I Googled Denise Sutton, and look what I found. It says here that she disappeared in 2008 after being attacked by a hitchhiker. Her husband was killed and she's never been found… and neither has the hitchhiker."

"That's because I made him up, you idiot!"

Denise started humming. The tune sounded like one I'd heard in my childhood, but I couldn't place it.

"The sheriff ought to be here soon, Helene. Why don't you go stay with the kids until he arrives and takes away Miss Crazy over there?"

"It'd be my pleasure."

She looked over at Denise.

"I've had enough of her noise. She ain't right, you know. Why is she acting like that?"

"She's finished and she knows it. She thinks that if she acts crazy enough, she'll avoid death row."

I glared back at Denise.

"You might as well shut up. It's not going to work. Being crazy won't keep that needle out of your arm."

"You think she'll really get the death penalty?" Helene whispered.

"I don't know," I whispered back. "I just like tormenting her. At least she won't escape again. Once the sheriff locks her up, we won't have to worry anymore. She'll be out of our lives for good."

"I sure hope you're right. I'd hate to see her get away again."

"Yeah, she's done. You go sit with the kids and I'll keep an eye on Crazy Lady over there, okay?"

When Helene walked out of the room, Denise called me over.

"Jesse, come here. I've got something to tell you."

The last thing I wanted was to listen to more of her bull, but my curiosity made my feet move.

"What do you want? You got more lies to tell me?"

She grinned.

"Jesse, you're getting old. Maybe it's time you got yourself a new occupation before you get yourself or someone in your family killed. You're not cut out for this kind of work."

"Oh, I don't do so bad. I got you, didn't I?"

"I'll never see the inside of a prison."

She smirked, and then laughed out loud.

"You see, I know how this game is played. I can do crazy, and once the judge hears from my doctor, there's no way I'll stand trial. He'll send me to a psych hospital for evaluation, and I'll escape. You'll see. It's going to play out just like I said, and down the road, I'll come back for you and the rest of your crappy family."

I stared her in the face.

"Well, maybe I should save the system the cost of a trial."

I went to my purse and took out my gun. I aimed it at her.

"Yep, I could shoot you right now, and all of this would be over."

"Oh, yeah? I'm tied to a chair, and now you're going to shoot me. I don't think so. How would that look? You'd be the one going to jail."

"Actually, I'm just making sure you don't try anything stupid. I wasn't going to shoot you. I'd miss the trial, and I sure don't want to do that. I'm going to be around to see you fry."

"You were right about the shampoo."

"What?"

"A little skin irritant goes a long way. A dab of ammonia wreaks havoc on the scalp and you don't need much… itchy… scaly… yuck… nasty stuff. Burns the skin right off in patches. Oh, and those vitamins… it doesn't take much Panatral to drive a person insane. Did you know that? I picked up that little tidbit off the internet. Yep, that's right. That's why Billy's mother almost died. Too bad she didn't kick the bucket."

Billy came back to the room, walked over to Denise, and then slapped her across the face so hard, she and the chair went crashing to the floor.

"I heard what you said. That was for my mother."

Blood ran down the corner of her mouth as Billy snatched her back upright. He grabbed the hand towel off the table, wiped the blood from her mouth, and then handed it to me.

"DNA… just in case."

I took the towel, put it in a zip-lock bag, and then tossed it in the refrigerator. Of course, we no longer needed her DNA, but she didn't know that.

Billy's hands were trembling. Denise's confession about what she tried to do to his mother had gotten him riled, more so than I'd ever seen. It was all he could do to refrain from putting her down. If he ever wanted to kill someone, this was the time, and she was the one.

I touched Billy's arm.

"It's over. She can't hurt anyone anymore. Just think of the pleasure you're going to get out of knowing she's going to rot in a prison cell."

We heard the sirens before we saw the flashing lights. The sheriff was here to take Denise Sutton away. She would be locked up and never be able to cause trouble again.

I'm sure the relief showed on our faces when Sheriff Hudson and his deputies walked through the front door with their guns drawn.

His men surrounded Denise while Deputy Cole James guarded the door. She was not going to escape again.

Deputy Cole James was my ex-boyfriend, my sister's ex-boyfriend, and now Savannah Kelley's boyfriend. I harbored no hard feelings toward him. He had come into my life at just the right time, and faded into the background the same way. We had remained friends.

"Put your gun down, Jesse, before you shoot someone," the sheriff said as he lowered his weapon, walked over, and relieved me of mine. "The last thing we need is you with a gun."

"I was guarding our prisoner. I guess Billy filled you in on what happened here, huh? I told you she was coming to our house, didn't I? You were so sure she hadn't escaped the hospital, but you were wrong. She came here to kill me, and if anyone had gotten in her way, she would've killed them, too. She's a stone-cold killer, Sheriff. I can't wait for you to hear her story."

The sheriff looked around the room as one of his deputies removed the duct tape and pulled Denise up from the chair. Sheriff Hudson hesitated for a second.

"Whose knife is that on the table?" he asked.

"That's Billy's, why?"

"Where's her weapon?"

"What weapon? She didn't have one."

"How was she going to kill anyone without a weapon… talk you to death?"

"She tried to."

"What? Talk you to death?"

The deputy removed the handcuffs and handed them back to Billy, giving him a dirty look.

"Where'd you get these cuffs? Steal `em?"

"Bought `em off the home shopping network," Billy joked.

In the split second it took the deputy to pull out his cuffs, Denise lunged forward, grabbed the knife from the table and plunged it into Sheriff Hudson's back. One quick jab and he fell to the floor.

She stood there with the knife raised, blood dripping from the blade.

Deputy James fired one round, hitting her right between the eyes.

Her head snapped back and she went down in a flash. The party was truly over for Denise Sutton—a.k.a— Dakota Stone. She lay dead on the dining room floor.

I was shaking and overcome with panic. I squatted down on my knees and pressed my hand to the sheriff's back to stop the flow of blood as it soaked through the tear in his jacket. I had no idea how far the blade had gone in, but prayed it hadn't been deep enough to kill him.

"She didn't come here to kill anyone," the sheriff gasped. "She came here to be killed. No weapon."

"Shh… save your energy. The ambulance's on its way. You're going to be fine."

Sheriff Wake Hudson closed his eyes for the last time.

Epilogue

I sat on the floor, holding the sheriff's body, and crying. I thought about all the times we'd been at each other's throats, and regretted the part I had played. He was gone and I'd never be able to tell him how much I liked him… how much I admired him. He was a good man, and a good sheriff. He'd given me a run for my money, but I'd also given it right back.

Now… that was in the past. It was too late to tell him how I felt about him… how much I appreciated his saving my mother's life on that dark, stormy night, or that I knew he'd kept us out of jail when we should've been locked up. We'd done a few things… broken a few laws… done the stuff he wanted to do, but couldn't. What I wouldn't give to have one more chance to tell him how sorry I was for being such a pain in his butt, or for the times I had lied to him.

At least he died knowing Billy and I were the good guys. Of that, I was sure.

And then, he stirred.

I was so startled, I let go of him and fell back on my rear end, shock sucking the breath from my lungs. When I realized he wasn't dead, I grabbed him again and hugged him as tight as I could. I didn't want to let go. I was afraid if I did, he really would die on me.

"Hey, pressure to my wound, remember? You want me to die here on your floor?"

I released my grip and put my hand to his back. Blood was still flowing, still running from the tear in his jacket, but at least he was alive.

"You had me scared there for a minute, Sheriff. Thought you were dead."

"Never thought I'd see the day you'd have your arms wrapped around me. You got a thing for me, or something, Jesse? I always figured you did," he teased.

"Yeah, in your dreams, pal. Stop talking or I might just have to kill you myself."

We looked at each other and smiled.

I should've known the sheriff wasn't dead. When a person dies, the eyelids don't close. They stay open. It's not like you see in the movies. You can't run your fingers over a person's eyes to get them to stay closed. They just pop back open. When preparing a body for a funeral, the mortician glues the eyelids shut to keep them that way.

When notified that Sheriff Hudson was down, every emergency service for fifty miles or more came to the rescue. Two fire trucks even showed up. I guess he was right when he said they all stick together… have each other's backs, because they sure came through for him. He was prepped for transportation and on the move within minutes after their arrival.

An hour later, the medical examiner and the crime scene technicians had completed their tasks and were on their way, taking Denise Sutton's body with them. I was glad when the last one of them left. It had been a tense and frightful day.

After soaking up blood from the floor with paper towels and then mopping over the spot, Helene took to scrubbing the blood spatter and what looked like brain matter off the wall. It was a disgusting sight, one that I didn't want to ever see again, let alone be the one who cleaned up the mess. I gagged every time I looked at the wall.

"Billy, you might have to paint over this stain. I can't get it all out. I've wiped and wiped, but there's still a brown spot."

"Yeah, I kinda figured that. I've got some paint in the garage that ought to cover it."

He walked over to where I was standing by the sink.

"You okay, `ge ya? You haven't said much."

"I've been trying to wash his blood off me, but I can't get it out from under my fingernails." Tears rose in my eyes and promised to spill over. Once the first tear fell, the gate opened. "When I thought Wake was dead, I had that same sad, horrifying feeling like I had when Daniel died... as if I'd lost one of my own. It was awful, Billy. Then, I thought about my dad, and that empty feeling wouldn't go away."

"Here, let me help you." Billy reached down, grabbed a small brush from the cabinet, and then tenderly held my hand as he scrubbed under the fingernails. After doing the same to the other hand, he held both of my hands under the running water. The blood washed away.

I pulled a bunch of paper towels from the roll and started wiping. "Thanks, I needed that. You always know how to make me feel better." I hugged him, and then kissed him on the cheek.

My cell phone rang, and when I picked it up and looked at the screen, Sheriff Hudson's name appeared. "It's the sheriff! I don't believe it. What's he doing calling me? He should be in surgery."

Helene stopped what she was doing. "Answer it, Jesse! It might not be the sheriff. He could've died and someone's calling to tell us."

I frowned. "Don't say that! He's not dead, is he, Billy?"

"We won't know until you answer the call."

Nervously, I said, "Hello, this is Jesse. Is that you, Sheriff?"

His voice was raspy and he sounded as if he'd been drugged. "Yes, it's me. I called to say thanks. The doctor said what you did help to save my life. I could've bled out right there on your floor, but thanks to you,

I'll live to continue the fight."

"I hope you mean continue the fight of right and wrong and your police force, not the fight between me and you."

I could almost see the smile on his face.

"Yeah, that's what I mean." He coughed.

"Are you all right? You sound rough."

"Man... my shoulder's gonna hurt tomorrow, but for right now, they've got me doped up, and I'm not feeling any pain. They're going to fix me up and then send me home to recuperate, but I'll be seeing you soon."

"That sounds like a threat. You say thanks, and then leave me with that?"

"It wasn't a threat, but we do need to talk."

"Yeah, I guess we do. Just keep in mind that I saved your life. You owe me."

He coughed, laughed, and then disconnected.

Helene smiled and walked over to me. "See, Jesse, the sheriff likes you. He took the time to call to let you know he's okay. That says something."

"It's what he didn't say that bothers me." I looked at Billy. "He said he'd be seeing us soon. What do you think that means?"

"I think you know what it means, but don't worry, I don't think he's going to arrest us. You heard him. He said you helped save his life. He won't ever forget what you did for him."

Helene walked over to the front window. "Did you look outside? The emergency vehicles cleared a path in the snow all the way down the driveway. I guess that won't last long since it's still snowing. At least the thunder and lightning quit. Haven't heard a peep for a while."

I glanced over to the window, and then looked back at Billy. "I have this nagging feeling he's going to do something we won't like."

"As long as he doesn't arrest us, how bad could it be? We're tough. We can take it as long as he doesn't put us out of business."

We stared at each other.

"Hmm… so what do we do now? Where do we go from here?"

Billy raised his eyebrows and cocked his head. "We pick up the pieces and move on."

So… that's what we were going to do. The blood had been cleaned up, and everything appeared to be normal, except for the leftover tan discoloration on the wall that would have to be painted over. Blood spatter is a strange thing. You can never really get rid of it. You can scrub as hard as you can using every cleaning agent known to man, and you can paint over it, but it will always remain there, hidden in the background. Turn the lights off and spray Luminal, and the blood pattern will light up like a Christmas tree, regardless of any effort to cover over it. This brought to mind the other time we had to clean up a pool of blood. I was sure traces of that blood had seeped through the hardwood slats and would remain there indefinitely.

"Can we come out now?" Maisy stood in the hallway. "We heard a loud boom and Ethan's scared. He's crying, Mom." Ethan stood behind her, cowering.

The loud boom they had heard was obviously the gunshot that had put Denise Sutton down, not thunder like they had thought.

Helene went to her. "Bless your hearts. The storm's over, so there's nothing to be afraid of anymore. Come on, you two. I'm going to fix you some dinner."

Maisy and Ethan walked into the dining room followed by Athena and Thor, who were shaking almost as much as the kids.

Once we had soothed the kids' fears, Helene went about rustling up some grub, and then I walked to the hallway to call Mom. I filled her in on what had transpired here in the last couple of hours, and then told her she could come home. The threat was over and everyone was safe now.

A few minutes later, Mom and Eddie came rushing through the front door. They had their share of questions, but they were put on hold until dinner was over and the kids were put to bed. After the kids were out of the room, Mom and Eddie fired questions at us. They had missed the scene and wanted to know every detail.

Billy explained in length about what had gone down here, and when he had finished his account, Mom had a concerned look on her face.

"What about Sheriff Hudson?"

"He's going to be fine, Minnie. He already called to say thanks to Jesse for saving his life."

"That's not what I'm talking about, Billy Blackhawk, and you know it. I'm glad the sheriff's going to make it, but what happens when he recovers? Is he coming after us? Are we going to jail? I don't think I'd fare well in jail. As a matter of fact, we're thinking about giving up the snooping business. It's just too dangerous."

"That might be a good idea. I'm sorry we ever dragged you into it. You should be at home, playing with your grandchildren, not running around like a bunch of lunatics… like we do." Billy looked at me. "Perhaps it's time to change the way we operate."

Mom grinned.

"That's not going to happen. You can't change who you are, and you don't want to. You'll go on doing what you do, except maybe from now on you'll be a little bit more cautious about how you approach a situation. Stop taking so many chances. And… by the way, you didn't drag us into it. We volunteered, remember?"

I looked at Mom. "Well, your services are no longer needed. I have enough to worry about without having to worry about your safety."

Billy chuckled. "At this point, our future as private investigators is debatable. We might have to retire. We broke our agreement with the sheriff, committed a couple of questionable acts in the process, and have obstructed his justice. If we do manage to stay out of jail, I doubt very seriously Sheriff Hudson's gonna let us continue to practice. He'll have our licenses yanked."

"Can he do that?"

"He can't actually do it, but he can make it happen."

"What will you do then?"

"We are not without other talents." Billy smiled. "We'll come up with something."

I laughed. "Maybe Jonathan will put us on his payroll."

Mom glared at me.

"As bounty hunters? Are you nuts? No way—no how. I won't allow it, and I mean it! Jonathan's told me more freaky tales than I care to hear about. If you and Billy join up with him and start busting down doors, hunting for bail-jumpers or what not, Eddie and I will pack up and move to Florida. I won't stand by and watch you..."

"Easy, Mom. I wasn't serious. My body has taken enough beatings as it is. Besides, Jonathan doesn't just track down bail-jumpers. He has gone after some of the most violent criminals imaginable. Thanks, but no thanks. I'm still waiting for my face to get back to normal."

Billy got up from the table and walked to the kitchen. "I'm going to have a bourbon, straight up. Anybody interested?"

Like school children, we all raised our hands, and then waited for Billy to pour the drinks.

He wouldn't give me one, so I got up from the table, walked over to my purse, and pulled out a pack of cigarettes. I walked to the kitchen, turned on the stove fan, and lit up.

Mom turned up her nose. "Now, that's nasty. Do you have to smoke inside?" She looked at me with that evil look of hers. "I thought you quit."

"I did... four or five times. Sorry, Mom, but I'm a drug addict. Nicotine has a hold on me and is never going to let go."

"Malarkey. You could quit if you tried."

Billy poured another round, and then looked at me.

"Sorry, `ge ya. Drugs and alcohol don't mix. I say we all get a good night's sleep. Tomorrow's going to be a big day. Besides, they don't serve alcohol in jail."

Helene grunted. "That's not funny, Billy."

A third glass did the trick. We retired for the night.

By morning we were all moving a little slower. Perhaps that last glass of bourbon had been one glass too many. Helene handed out aspirin with the coffee to those who needed it.

"My head feels awful," Mom said. "Remind me to never drink anything ever again. All I want to do is go back to bed."

"Me, too, Minnie," Eddie added. "I feel like someone hit me upside the head with a hammer."

Helene, being her usual bouncy self, followed up the coffee with a glass of tomato juice.

"Hair of the dog. Drink up. You'll feel much better if you do."

"Don't need it, Helene. I feel fine. No hangover." Billy handed the glass back to her. "It takes more than three drinks to do me in. Remember, I'm heap, big warrior. I can drink you guys under the table, before it affects me."

I laughed. "Yeah, I've seen you in action."

Mom sniffed her glass of tomato juice. "What's in this? It smells like bourbon. I'm not drinking this junk." She pushed the glass aside.

"It's not bourbon, Minnie. Its a little concoction I put together, so drink up."

"It smells like bourbon."

"Everything's gonna smell like bourbon after last night. Trust me. There's no bourbon in it."

After we downed our tomato juice, Helene retrieved the glasses.

"Geez, Helene," I said. "You put Vodka in it."

"Yep, it's a real cure-all. Feel better already, don't you?"

Mom winced. "I think I'm going to puke."

"No, you're not, Minnie. You just think you are. You're going to feel better after you get some food in your belly."

Helene made oatmeal for everyone, explaining that it would be bland and it wouldn't upset our stomachs. She was right.

The snow had stopped falling sometime in the middle of the night, and the sun was now out doing its job of melting the white stuff. The weatherman warned of possible flooding due to the rising temperature expected today, and told everyone to be prepared. He said it could get ugly, but here in the mountains, that was part of everyday life.

We needed to put a halt to work and be on our best behavior for a little while, at least until we'd heard something from the sheriff, so we started our day out parked in front of the TV, watching the news while the kids played with the dogs in Maisy's bedroom.

Around ten-thirty, Jonathan called, and as usual, Billy put him on speaker so all of us could hear.

"You're on speaker, Jonathan. The whole crew's present. Tell us what you have."

"Shark, Gator, and Mason left. Their job's done, and now they're off on a new adventure. Can't tell you what or where. What can you do? You get good help, and then they up and move on." Jonathan laughed.

"But I didn't get a chance to say goodbye."

"Don't worry, Minnie. You'll see them again. Have y'all heard from Sheriff Hudson or Captain Trainum?"

"Nothing yet, brother. Have you been watching the news?"

"Yeah. Looks like the sheriff left you guys out of it. You got lucky on this one. The press won't be knocking down your door to hear your side of the story."

I added my thoughts to the conversation.

"There was no mention that Denise Sutton was shot and killed at our house. Maybe Sheriff Hudson and Captain Trainum wanted all the glory for catching a dangerous serial killer, or maybe, they didn't want to have to explain our part in it. It doesn't matter. I'm just glad not to be bothered. The press is like vultures circling a dead carcass. They never give up, and then they say or print whatever they want. Who needs that?"

"I just got a call from my friend about the wine bottle found in Preston's car. Negative for antifreeze. Positive for minute traces of arsenic."

"Arsenic? Who uses arsenic anymore? That was stupid."

"Here's something else for you. The guys searching Preston's car found a soda can shoved up under the driver's seat. Guess what they found in it?"

Billy raised his eyebrows. "Traces of antifreeze."

"Yep. Guess she tried everything in her bag of goodies. Oh… never did come up with anything on the wedding band, but I guess that's moot now."

"We've been watching the news, and they reported the capture and subsequent death of the suspect, but that's it. Very few specifics, and then they went on to reporting something else."

"By tonight, this will be old news, brother. When the cops want to keep something out of the news, they have people who make it happen. You know that."

"What you got going on there?"

"Nothing. Just hanging out around the house… waiting for the sheriff to come and arrest me."

"Same here."

"You know we're going down for this one, brother… don't you?"

"My feeling isn't good, but jail isn't part of that feeling. We made a few blunders, but so did the sheriff. I'll be sure to point that out when he pays us a visit. He didn't have his mind on his job, or he would've locked us up the minute he saw the video of us sneaking in The Body Shop. Perhaps the sheriff has something more serious on his plate than us right now."

"I think you might have something there. I've been picking up chatter about recent abductions in the area over the past few months, and the cops are up in arms over it. At first, they treated it as a missing person's case, you know runaways or the like, but now they're rethinking their stance because of the similarities. Lu Ann's been called in, so you know they must think they have a serial killer running around."

"You kill one, and another takes its place." Billy paused. "That was meant to be a joke. Listen. After all that's happened, the worst we'll get is community service. No doubt in my mind."

"Let's hope you're right, but whatever happens, we'll deal with it. Man, this has been a weird case. I kinda feel sorry for the woman."

"Save your pity. She made her choice. She didn't have to go on a killing rampage."

"Yeah, you're right. She chose to kill. She doesn't deserve my sympathy. She got away from her abusive husband. That should've been enough, but instead of being happy, she started getting revenge. When is that ever right?"

"Never."

"Wouldn't it be a trip if we all ended up in jail because of her? We'd be the ones who'd suffer the fallout of her insanity… just another one of her casualties. When does a person go from sane to insane?"

"That's a question for Lu Ann."

"Keep me informed." Jonathan disconnected.

The mood in the room had taken on an ominous feel. It was as if our life had been put on hold and would stay that way until we got the call… or a knock at the door. For the first time, our lives could easily change from something very good to something really, really bad. Jail could be part of our future. I knew it, and Billy knew it, but he said nothing of the sort, and tried to put our fears at rest.

"You all heard what I told Jonathan. This is all going to blow over soon, and we're going to be fine. Jesse and I might have to pick up trash off the side of the road for a few weeks," Billy looked at me and winked, "but that's okay. We've dealt with trash before. So… until we hear from the sheriff, we need to go about our business as usual."

Helene acted surprised.

"You mean, take on another case? Are you serious? You can't do it… I mean, you shouldn't do it. Not now."

"No, we're not taking on another case until we finish our business with the sheriff." Billy started to slowly pace around the dining room table with his hand on his chin.

I knew he was formulating something in his head. I'd seen that look many times.

"I've been thinking. If I was the sheriff and I really wanted to make someone suffer, I'd make them sweat it out. If he was going to throw any of us in jail, we'd be there right now. No… he's got plans for us. He's going to make us sweat it out for a couple of days, and then he's going to tell us what he wants. Like I said, we'll probably get community service."

Hmm… was Billy right or was he sugar coating the outcome? I just didn't know what to think. I prayed for the best, but…

"Community service, my a…" Helene refrained from finishing her sentence, knowing how much Mom hated profanity. "Wake up. If you think you're going to get a slap on the wrist, you're dreaming. Sheriff Hudson's going to throw the book at you. We need to face up to the fact that…"

"What about me? I shot Gavin Preston in the foot."

"If Billy's right, Minnie, you're going to be picking up trash right along with him and Jesse." Helene looked over at Eddie. "I guess we'll have to take care of the kids and do the housekeeping while they're out beautifying America. That is… if we're lucky."

Mom waved her off. "Stop being a downer, Helene. Jesse doesn't look worried, so I'm not either. If she didn't believe what Billy said, I'd know. We're going to be just fine. Besides, I don't mind picking up trash." Mom smiled at Billy. "It'll be worth it."

"We'll see about that."

Billy raised his hand and broke in.

"Enough. We're not going to argue. Since we're going to be homebound for a while, we're going to take advantage of our time. I'll talk to Lila at the office and tell her to continue screening cases and refer perspective clients to Larry Mayhew over in Greene County, unless something big comes along." He looked at me. "We can do a lot from home.

The computer is a magical thing." He looked over at Eddie. "Think you're up to making a sketch of your new home? You draw it, and Jonathan can make up the blueprints. It doesn't have to be perfect, just something to give him an idea of what you want. He'll do the rest."

"Sure, I'm game." Eddie looked at Mom. "Tell me what you want, Minnie, and I'll draw it."

Mom smiled. "I think it's a wonderful idea. It'll keep us busy until we have to start picking up trash." She looked at Helene and chuckled.

As the day wore on and there was no sign of Sheriff Hudson, the more I believed Billy had been right. He said the sheriff was going to make us sweat, and we were sweating. Even though we'd kept busy, we still had that underlying feeling of a disaster waiting to happen.

Dinner came and went, and when it was time for bed, we were more than glad to call it a day. We were exhausted. Stress does that to a person, and we'd all had our fair share of stress for one day.

By the time the lights went out, I was snuggled up close to Billy, waiting for a restful, uneventful sleep. My mind went from one scene to another, playing out the recent events, until finally, I closed my eyes and drifted off, sleeping peacefully throughout the night. No bad dreams. No one chasing me. I woke refreshed and ready to take on a new day. I heard the kids playing and the occasional bark of one of the dogs. I smelled food cooking. I crawled out of bed, got dressed, and then headed to the kitchen.

"You're up early," I said to Billy as I walked up and gave him a kiss. "Where is everybody?"

He handed me a cup of coffee.

"The kids are playing, waiting on their breakfast, and your Mom and Eddie are in the den still going over the plans for their new house."

"And I'm here." Helene waved as if I hadn't seen her. "Cooking breakfast. You hungry?"

"I'm starved."

Billy's cell phone rang.

"Hmm…it's Jonathan. Mighty early for him to be calling. I smell trouble."

"It's probably the bacon," Helene joked. "I burned a couple of slices."

Billy touched the screen.

"Hope you have good news for me."

"Not so much. They're here. Sheriff Hudson's SUV followed by a plain, white van… and wait… they're pulling into your driveway. Oh… I know what's happening here." Jonathan laughed. "You were right all along, brother. No jail. Call me."

The call ended.

Billy and I glared at each other.

"Why was he laughing?"

"I have no idea, but it must not be too serious, or he wouldn't be laughing. See… I told you everything was going to be all right."

I went over and looked out the window, my heart skipping a beat with every step. I looked back at Billy.

"It's the sheriff and Cole, and there's some guy getting out of the van. The guy's carrying a big, black suitcase thingy. You think our striped vests are in it? I mean, they have to wear those vests when they do highway cleanup, right?"

"Calm down, `ge ya. I think I know why Jonathan was laughing."

"Well, then please fill me in before I have a heart attack."

There was a loud knock at the door, and then the sheriff said, "Greene County Sheriff."

Billy gave me a wink, and then opened the door.

"Come on in, Sheriff Hudson. You look well, considering what you've been through. How about a cup of coffee?" He held out his hand to the sheriff.

The sheriff offered his hand and said, "We need to talk in private. I don't want to disturb your breakfast, but I have a busy day ahead of me."

"Yeah, I've heard."

"What have you heard?"

"About the abductions. I know every police department around must be frantic."

The sheriff started to say something, but Billy cut him off. "Helene, why don't you call everyone to breakfast? We'll be in the den."

Billy motioned to the sheriff. "Follow me."

When Mom passed the sheriff in the hallway, she didn't say a word. She just kept walking.

Once in the den, Billy closed the door, and then turned to the sheriff. "Who's your friend?"

I walked over to the recliner and sat down. My hands were shaking as I held my cup of coffee and waited to see what was going to happen. It was now down to the wire, and I was afraid we were about to be hung. Then, I realized that if we were going to be arrested, it would've happened the minute the sheriff walked in the door, so what was really going on here? I couldn't stand it any longer. I had to say something or explode.

"So… are you going to throw us in jail or not?"

"I wasn't planning on it, but if you want me to, I'm sure I can accommodate you."

"Why not? You've wanted to lock us up for as long as I can remember. What…"

Billy gave me a stern look.

"Jesse… let the sheriff talk." He looked back at the sheriff. "Shall we sit down and talk about why you're here."

"Sure we can, but I think you know why I'm here."

The sheriff and Cole sat down on the sofa while Billy waited for the other guy to sit.

"Have a seat, Billy." The sheriff pointed to the guy dressed in street clothes. "He has official business to attend to."

Billy sat down in the recliner next to mine.

By now, my heart was in my throat.

"God! Stop with the polite chitchat and get to the point!" I sneered at the sheriff. "You know I have anxiety! Are you trying to kill me?"

"I want to introduce you to Tommy. He's with our home monitoring system, and he's here to fit you with your new police jewelry."

"What jewelry? Is this a joke?"

Billy reached over and patted my hand. "Ankle bracelets, Jesse. Tracking devices." He looked at the sheriff. "Are we under house arrest or just tracking?"

"Both. You'll be under house arrest for thirty days and then you'll be tracked for an additional sixty days. I'm sure you know how the system works."

This was the last thing I had expected. I was shocked, but at the same time I was almost euphoric knowing we weren't going to jail. This is what Billy was about to tell me before he answered the door.

"House arrest ain't so bad, Billy. We can still go to work, right Sheriff?"

The sheriff laughed.

"You know the drill, Jesse. You're not going anywhere for thirty days, and then, when the thirty days are up, you'll be able to leave the house. Just remember, I'll know where you are every minute of the day for ninety days. I'll be like the pink elephant in the room. If you have a problem with this arrangement, there is another alternative."

Tommy pulled out a two-inch wide, black leather strap with a tiny box-like thing attached and proceeded to hook it around my ankle. The monitor beeped, and I was all set. It took all of five minutes.

Five minutes and now I would be confined to this house for thirty days. Would I go insane?

"What's the other alternative? I'm willing to pick up trash off the road. This thing already itches." I reached down and scratched around the bracelet for emphasis.

"The other alternative is, I arrest you and you go to prison—you, Billy, and Jonathan. How many times have I told you that obstruction of justice is a serious charge? Judges don't like it when you get in our way. You'll go down, and you'll go down hard. I don't want to see that happen, but I have to do something. And… there is that matter with your mother shooting Gavin Preston in the foot."

"Prove it. I made it up."

"Now… I knew you'd say that." The sheriff rubbed his forehead as if he could feel the headache that was coming. He looked back up at me. "Jesse, you're an instigator and a troublemaker. You're impulsive and irresponsible. Shame on you for dragging your mother into your little three-ring circus."

"Technically, she offered, so stop trying to make me feel bad." I looked at Tommy and then back to the sheriff. "You're not going to make my mother wear one of those things. No way. Put one on Helene instead. She won't mind."

The sheriff laughed again. "I'm not going to put one on your mother, so don't freak out. I know that anything she does wrong can be traced directly back to you."

"While under house arrest, all communications will be monitored." Tommy began his explanation of our boundaries and the few freedoms afforded us as he finished securing Billy's bracelet. "Doctor and dentist visits have to be verified."

He went on and on until I was about ready to nod off. I closed my eyes for just a second.

The sheriff coughed. "Are we boring you, Jesse?"

"I want to talk about what happened. I don't care about all these rules and regulations. I get it. I'm shackled to you for the next three months. I can live with that."

"Your inability to follow the rules and regulations is what got you where you are now." He looked over at Billy. "I blame her for allowing Minnie to get involved, but I blame you for breaking your promise. I might have to reassess my opinion of you and your word. Do the time and restore my faith."

I waved at the sheriff. "I'm still here."

"What do you want?"

"We all know the story, and the killer's dead. Case closed. What about the women who paid Dakota/Denise to kill their husbands? Are they going to be charged?"

"That's up to the D.A., but I wouldn't hold my breath. Conspiracy, solicitation of murder… can't build much of a case based on a name and dollar amount found in a book, especially when the accused solicitor is dead. Circumstantial at best. Next."

"Tell me about the video. You lied about seeing us, didn't you?"

"I must admit the video was rather poor. I saw two large men with ponytails and a big black guy with a slight limp, and then I saw this puny little girl acting all dressed up. I put two and two together and came up with you. Much to my surprise, you confirmed it that night at Jonathan's house."

"So what do you really have?"

"Little girl, you don't want to play this game with me."

Tommy closed his suitcase. "Ah, I'm done here, Sheriff Hudson. I can wait in my van until you're ready to leave, if you'd like."

Tommy was finished and so was our discussion.

Sheriff Hudson and Deputy James stood.

"We're right behind you, Tommy." The sheriff looked at me. "If you feel the need to talk, please don't call me. I can recommend a good therapist." He chuckled as he turned to leave. "You both might need one after a week of being locked up together. Don't kill each other. Now, I'm on my way to see Jonathan. Sometimes I just love my job."

It's amazing what something so small like a monitoring bracelet can do for your life. It kept Billy, Jonathan, and me out of jail. I don't know all the details or how the sheriff managed to pull this one off, but I don't care. I've learned my lesson. Never get caught.

A week later, Billy and I were sitting in the swing on the front porch, looking up at the stars, talking about how cold this winter was supposed to be, when the subject of the recent abductions came up.

"I have a theory. Want to hear it?"

"Sure, `ge ya. What is it?"

"The killer has a killing ground, a place where he takes his victims. Find the killing ground, and you find the killer. Reminds me of a case several years back. This guy was luring women off the road, claiming there was something wrong with their car. He snatches them up, and then they turn up dead, or never heard from again. Happens all the time."

"Unfortunately, we can't do anything. Look at us. We're stuck here for a while."

I laid my head on his shoulder. "I don't mind, do you?"

"Not one bit."

"You never know, Blackhawk and Blackhawk just might have another case to solve pretty soon. Ninety days isn't that long."

Shark showed up a few days later. He told Mom that he wanted to hang around and help with building her new house, claiming he didn't have anyone to kill at the moment and was available for the job.

She thought that was hilarious.

...to be continued.

Acknowledgements

I would like to express my deepest gratitude to my family for providing encouragement and support in the writing of The Prey Bites Back. My mother, Minnie Crumpler, as always, was there for me with a kind word and a pat on the back. My husband, Tom Mullen, never gave up on me even when I was cranky. Kudos to my children, Wendy Kantsios and Tommy Mullen. I know you got tired of hearing me talk about my book, but neither one of you ever complained. Thank you all.

Thanks so much to my proofreaders/editors, Billie Kerfoot, Ethyle Guiseppe, Norman Slezak, and Trish Eckstein. Without you, this book would have been a mess.

This book is dedicated to Norman Slezak. Thanks for putting a bug in my ear.

Look for Ann Mullen's next book:

Be Very Afraid

A Jesse Watson Mystery
Book #9

Visit Ann Mullen's website:
www.aftonridge.com

E-mail the author:
aftonridge@aol.com

Afton Ridge Publishing
271 Entry Run Road
Stanardsville, VA 22973
434-985-1957

A little something extra for your reading pleasure from my short story collection…

Lunch Break Shorts

Available on Kindle & Nook

Encounter

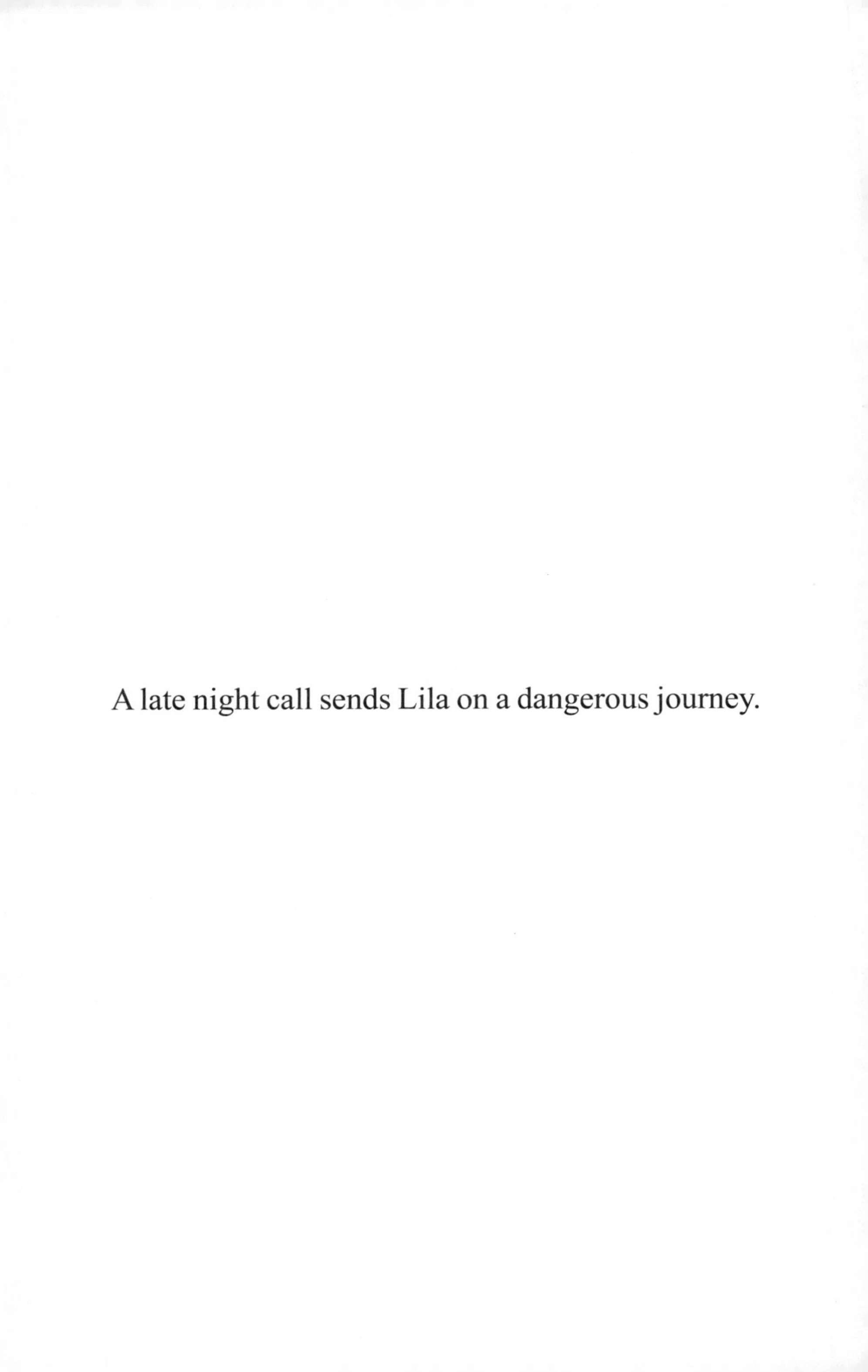
A late night call sends Lila on a dangerous journey.

Encounter

THE CALL CAME AROUND ONE in the morning and rousted me out of a peaceful slumber.

Aggravated by the intrusion, I snatched up the phone and blurted out, "I hope this is good. You woke me up."

I didn't need to check Caller ID. I recognized the ring tone.

Normally, I'm not such a grouchy person, but insomnia has dogged me for a while, so when I finally do get to fall asleep, I don't like being interrupted. I'm lucky if I get more than four or five hours, and that's on a good night. On the bad nights, a couple of hours are about all there is to my rest.

Sometimes I wonder how long my body will be able to keep it up before I totally collapse and never wake up again.

But... I'm still going, and I'm not dead yet.

To top off my bad mood, for days I've been having an uneasy feeling of doom; the feeling I get when bad things are about to happen.

So it wasn't a surprise when the news arrived, but I never expected to be awakened in the middle of the night to get it, or that it would involve a family member.

When I lived at home, bad news always seemed to come just before dinner. Every time someone died or was in a bad accident, the phone would ring right when my dad was saying grace.

Dad hated that. He liked to sit down at the table with his family for a little peace and quiet and he didn't like it when his meal was interrupted by a ringing phone.

Eventually, my mother discovered she could turn off the ringer. That made life a lot easier.

It's funny the thoughts that go through your head in that split-second just before the bad news is delivered.

My sister, Joshlyn, was on the other end of the phone, crying hysterically.

"You have to come home right away," she said. "Daddy had a heart attack! He's in ICU at Riverside Hospital. Intensive Care, Lila!"

"What?"

"You know what that means? He's dying, and those stupid doctors won't tell us anything. I know they think he's going to die. I just know it!"

"Did they tell you that?"

"No... they didn't say so, but you know they never tell you the whole truth. Lila… Lila… are you listening?"

"What…?" I asked as I rubbed my eyes and sat up in bed. "Of course I'm listening. I was asleep. Give me a few minutes to wake up."

"Okay," she said flippantly, her sobs now somewhat under control. "I'll give you time to wake up and then I'll call you back in ten minutes just to make sure you didn't go back to sleep."

"Don't be ridiculous, Joshlyn. I'm awake. My father had a heart attack, for Christ's sake. You don't think I'd go back to sleep, do you?"

"You don't have to be mad at me. I didn't do anything wrong."

Oh, geez. Here we go again.

Joshlyn paused for a few seconds, and then said, "Oh… is this one of your bad nights?" She paused again, and then spoke in a whisper. "I'm sorry you're having a bad night, Lila." She hesitated once more, and then she squealed, "But I'm having a bad night, too! My father is dying!"

"Stop it, Joshlyn!" I yelled back at her. "Don't go off on a tangent. Take a pill or something."

The line went silent. Nothing like telling someone to take a pill.

"I'm sorry," I said, trying to backtrack. "That was rude of me."

"Yes, it was," she said. "Sometimes you can be so mean to me."

"I'm never mean to you, Joshlyn, and you know it. I've always been a good sister. I've put up with your immature behavior..."

"See, there you go again, being mean to me."

"I'm not being mean. It's just that I'm tired and irritable, and you woke me up from what was almost the beginning of a restful night. Look, Dad's going to be fine. You'll see. I know you're upset and so am I, but we have to pull it together for him. We have to stay positive. How's Mom holding up?"

My twenty-two year old sister, Joshlyn, is ten years younger than me and still lives at home. She was spoiled as a child and is now suffering from immaturity and lack of ambition. Needless to say, she's inconsiderate, selfish, and has just about every kind of character flaw one could imagine. After several failed attempts at holding down a job, she has resigned herself to letting our parents take care of her. They, of course, are just glad to have her still living at home with them. I guess growing up wasn't part of the deal.

But she's my little sister and I love her, despite her lazy, lackadaisical ways. Sometimes she drives me insane when she acts like a child, and this was one of those times.

"You are coming home, aren't you?" she whined. "Daddy needs you. We all need you. Mom's falling apart."

"Sure, I am. I've just got a few things to do first. I have to…"

"Well… I'm sorry if this inconveniences you, but I thought you'd like to know about Daddy… before the funeral."

"Oh, don't be so melodramatic, Joshlyn. Dad's not going to die," I said, my patience wearing thin. I'd had about enough of her baby ways.

"How do you know?"

"I don't know for sure, but I'm hoping he's going to be fine. I'm praying he's going to be okay."

I had no idea how bad my dad's condition was, but if it was as critical as she was making it out to be, my mom would be the one on the other end of the phone. She wouldn't leave something this important to my sister. Joshlyn was such a drama queen and Mom knew it.

Dad probably had a case of indigestion. At least that's what I told myself so I wouldn't freak out.

Panic started slowly creeping in as I scanned the room, mentally preparing myself for what was going to happen in the next few hours.

What if Joshlyn was right? What if Mom was falling apart and couldn't handle making the call? Suppose my father really did have a heart attack and was on his death bed?

I would soon find out for myself.

Just in case my sister wasn't having one of her over-zealous moments, I was going to take the situation seriously. Later, if it turned out to be nothing, I could brow-beat her for upsetting me so, and then I'd take her out shopping. She'd love the shopping part and it would appease my conscience, because I fully intended to let her have it if she was getting me riled up for nothing.

"It'll take me an hour to pack, close up the cabin, and then get on the road. I'll be there in about three and a half hours."

"Three and a half hours? Are you for real? He could be dead…"

"I can't do any better than that, Joshlyn. I have to do the speed limit. I could go eighty and hope I manage to elude the police, but I'd be taking a big risk to save fifteen minutes. No thank you. I'm not going to do that. I'll be there as soon as I can."

"I don't know why you have to live so far away, and what's the deal with that cabin? Who lives in a cabin in the middle of nowhere?"

"You know why, Joshlyn, so don't bug me about it. I'll see you soon. I'm getting out of bed as we speak. Let me get off the phone and get ready."

"If you're not here in five hours, I'm calling the police."

"You can always call my cell if you're worried, but I promise to be there in a few hours just like I said I would. If I'm not, feel free to call in the National Guard. I'm hanging up now."

And I did. I cut her off and started getting ready for the trip. I knew she'd be calling me every fifteen minutes to check on my progress, so I hurried along.

I took a quick shower, made a cup of instant coffee in the microwave, and then pulled out my travel suitcase. I didn't know how long my visit was going to be, so I threw in a few of the basics: a sweater, a couple of T-shirts, two pairs of jeans, bras, underwear, socks, and at the last minute, I decided to include my little black dress and matching heels.

I had to be prepared just in case my father's condition was serious and took a turn for the worst. I surely didn't want that to happen, but I had to think ahead.

I filled my overnight tote with bathroom toiletries, and then set both bags down by the front door. After checking the windows to make sure they were locked, I set the alarm and left.

It was still dark outside and the temperature was bitter cold. By the time I had put my stuff in the car and reached the end of the long driveway, snow had started to fall.

"Now... isn't this just great," I said to myself as I turned on the windshield wipers and watched the snow quickly freeze and smear on the glass.

I turned on the defroster, but all it did was put out cold air. I turned it off and came to a stop. I sat there shivering and waiting for the car to warm up, while I chastised myself for not starting the car ahead of time.

This was not a good start to my trip and it made me wonder what else was going to go wrong.

For me, when a day starts out like this, it only gets worse. I know that to be a fact because I've had my share of bad days.

Actually, that's not completely true. My days had always been fairly happy ones filled with good friends and loving family… until about a year ago.

My name is Lila Jackson and I'm a reporter for the Charlottesville Reader. I mostly write human interest articles for the paper, but occasionally I get to do a story with a little meat to it—but not very often.

My trouble started last year when I wrote a piece about a new business that had opened a few months earlier.

Mike's Bar & Grill was supposed to be a place where people could get a good steak, a cold beer, and watch football on the overhead widescreen TV. There was no meat to this story, except what was served at the restaurant, until after the article ran. Calls started coming in claiming the establishment was a front for selling drugs.

As usual, I had checked the place out before I wrote the article. I'd eaten there several times and never saw anything that would substantiate the accusations.

I told my boss as much, but he wanted me to investigate further, so I did a follow-up visit. I wasn't expecting anything to pan out. It was a nice restaurant, the food was good, the place was clean, and the service was excellent. You couldn't beat that.

However, I've learned from past experiences that there was always going to be someone who had a complaint about something. I never thought a nice restaurant such as Mike's to be a hotbed for drug traffic.

Upon my return, I was greeted by the owner and then served a delicious meal. I stayed for over an hour and didn't see anything out of the ordinary.

There were no drugs being sold or used that I could see, so I left with the intention of returning again at a different time of day.

Two days later, I showed up for lunch and noticed the crowd was a lot different than they were the previous time I was there.

The place was filled with college students, and I was sure I smelled marijuana when I walked in.

Then later, I saw Mike slip a small packet to one of his customers, which made me a little sad. I was hoping the complaints were unfounded, but I was wrong.

Before I left, I called Mike over and asked him about what I had seen him do earlier and mentioned something about smelling marijuana.

Mike Grayson was a tall, handsome man in his early forties with a full head of brown curly hair that was neatly combed back out of his face, and from the look of his physique I could tell he worked out regularly.

He had been very pleasant until I laid that accusation on him. His face turned blood red; he threw his arms up in the air, and then started shouting obscenities at me before tossing me out.

I fled in tears; scared out of my wits by the way he blew up at me. I never expected that kind of reaction out of him, but I should have. What did I expect him to do after I had blindsided him like that?

I reported my findings to my boss and told him about Mike's reaction. I also let him know that Mike's outburst really scared me, but he assured me everything would be fine, and I had nothing to worry about. He said guys like that were all mouth.

If it turned out there was going to be trouble, I had the full weight of the paper behind me, he promised.

I joked and told him if there was any trouble, all I needed was a big, brawny guy to protect me.

He smiled, and that smile washed away some of my fear… but not all. I still had a little nagging feeling of fear left.

Barry is the kind of editor who always wants more, so he sent two other reporters to the bar and grill to dig a little deeper. I surely couldn't go back, and Barry would've never sent me knowing how intimidated I was by the man.

Robbie and Danny blended in well and hung out long enough to make friends with Mike. They went back twice before they managed to earn his trust and get him to come around.

On their last visit, they hit pay dirt. Robbie scored some Ecstasy from Mike, and Danny left with a bag of pot—confirming what the callers had said.

The drug activity was reported to the police and the cops started their surveillance on Mike's Bar & Grill, paying random visits and upsetting customers by their presence.

Against my better judgment, I wrote a follow-up story. I stated the obvious: Mike's Bar & Grill was a fine eating venue, with the exception of the drug activity.

Mike managed to elude getting busted, but his bar and grill suffered from the fallout. His business closed down a month later. He was an idiot. He should've known better.

By the time the follow-up article was published in the paper, my nerves were shot. I was scared of Mike, afraid he would want revenge against me for destroying his business. But I wasn't the one who was guilty. He did it to himself. I only wrote about it.

Shortly thereafter, my stomach started acting up and I suffered my first panic attack. I made it through the attack without going completely insane, but knowing I could have another one at any moment just added to my stress level.

Then, I started having bouts of insomnia. The first week I barely slept five hours a night and then it got even worse a month later when I started receiving those late night hang-ups.

Someone, who had blocked their number on Caller ID, would call at four in the morning, wake me, and then hang up. This went on for eight days before I finally said something to Barry about it. I told him that I suspected Mike, and he agreed. Who else would it be?

Barry immediately contacted his friend, a Charlottesville police officer, and told him what was happening.

His friend said they would do what they could to catch the caller, but before they could put their plan into action, the phone calls abruptly stopped. No more phone calls—no more trouble. That's how they saw it. But me, well, I still had my concerns.

A month passed, and then one afternoon I came home to my apartment and found a bouquet of dead flowers on the stoop in front of my door.

That incident was followed up a month later by cutouts of my articles that had been crossed out with a big red X, and left on the windshield of my car.

And finally, a decapitated squirrel in a box was left by my back door.

The no-headed squirrel was the one that finally sent me over the edge. I sunk into a deep hole like Alice, but unlike Alice in Wonderland, I was overcome by depression, not the Queen of Hearts or the Mad Hatter… and I wasn't chasing a rabbit. I was the one being chased.

To add to my misery, the whole time all of this was going on, I had an eerie, creepy feeling someone was watching me—and being watched was the scariest part of all.

I could deal with the no-headed squirrel, dead flowers, and defaced newspaper clippings, but I couldn't handle the fear of knowing someone was hiding in the bushes, watching my every move. It was creepy and spooky.

A stalker was after me and I knew it was only going to escalate.

I've written articles about stalkers and how they intimidate their victims, so I knew there was nothing the police could do unless they caught the culprit in the act. I couldn't prove it was Mike, but I could do what I had suggested in my articles to my readers: make a lifestyle change.

And so that's what I did.

I made sure I never went to work or left work at the same time every day. I stopped going out for lunch. I sold my little red BMW and bought a non-descript, black Toyota Camry.

Also, I moved out of my apartment into a cabin in the woods that Barry owned and rented to me dirt cheap.

And last but not least, I never went out at night alone again… until tonight. Tonight, I didn't have much choice.

I had changed my routine in a big way, and so far, it had paid off. My stalker no longer knew where to find me except at work, and I knew he wouldn't have the nerve to come after me there. That was a load off my mind.

Perhaps, Mike had given up.

The car finally warmed up and the defroster had done its job, so I pulled out of the driveway and headed out to see my father.

Snow was accumulating quickly and the back roads were a mess, but if I could make it out, the rest of the trip shouldn't be so bad. I dreaded the idea of having to slip and slide my way to Newport News, but I'd do what I had to do. Nothing would stop me from seeing my father.

Forty white-knuckled minutes of battling blowing snow and icy back rural roads, I finally made it out to Rt. 29.

My hands were shaking, I was sweating, and my heart was pounding so hard it was choking me. I had to find a place to pull over and collect myself.

I couldn't drive and have a panic attack at the same time.

There were very few cars on the road, and for Charlottesville that says a lot. Traffic congestion is the same here as it is anywhere else in a big city, so to have the road almost to myself was a nice surprise in what had otherwise been a very tense drive so far.

At the stoplight, I made a turn and pulled into the Best Buy parking lot. I sat there trying to calm my nerves as I listened to the weather report on the radio.

I should've checked out the weather before I started my trip, but after being dragged out of bed in the middle of the night and told my father had a heart attack, the weather was the last thing on my mind.

I should've guessed this wasn't going to be an easy trip the minute I saw the snow coming down, but I thought it was just a quick shower, a dusting that would be gone just as quickly as it had come in.

Regrettably, according to the radio, this was just the start of a slow moving system that was going to dump eight to ten inches of snow before letting up in the morning. The temperature wasn't expected to get above twenty degrees.

The storm had just hit, so if I was careful, I could make it to Newport News before the full brunt of it had done its damage. It'd be scary, but I could handle it.

After a few deep-breathing exercises, I pulled out of the parking lot and was on my way.

The first leg of I-64 was a breeze even with the snow leaving a blanket of white everywhere, but when I took the exit to I-295, that all changed within a few miles.

It was like a white-out. The snow was at least five inches deep already and coming down hard. The four lanes were now down to two with double tire tracks marking the way.

Cars had slowed down to adjust to the onslaught of snow, and everybody seemed to be safety conscious of their driving.

I wondered what all these people were doing on the road at two in the morning, but then realized maybe they were dealing with an emergency just like me.

Who else, in their right mind, would be out in this mess unless they had to?

When I heard ice pellets hitting the windshield, I started to panic.

Fortunately, I was close to my exit that would put me back on the last leg of I-64, so I kept my fingers crossed and tried not to hyperventilate. I definitely didn't want to have to pull off to the side of the road to get control of myself. A person could get hit by a car doing that.

Once on I-64 again, the snow had slowed and wasn't nearly as deep. As a matter-of-fact, there were less than a couple of inches on the ground. It was as if the storm hadn't hit this area yet.

I relaxed a little. Maybe I'd seen the worst of it.

I'd been on the interstate for ten minutes and hadn't seen another car. I was beginning to wonder if I was the only one out here, until I saw a car pulled off to the side.

I slowed down to see what was going on and got a quick glimpse of a little old lady wearing a thin coat and a silk scarf tied around her head. She was standing out in the cold and snow beside her car, waving a white hanky at me.

I didn't want to stop, but I couldn't just keep going and pretend I didn't see her. It wouldn't be right.

Besides, the first thing I thought of was my mother. I wouldn't want Mom stranded in this mess with nobody stopping to help her.

I put on my emergency flashers, slowed down, and then pulled over.

I grabbed my coat, jumped out of the car, and then ran over to her, shielding my eyes against the falling snow.

I looked her up and down and then asked, "What are you doing out here dressed like that? You could freeze to death."

"My car broke down and you're the first person I've seen in a while. I need help. Will you help me?"

"Of course I will," I replied while looking over at her car.

She was driving one of those little PT Cruisers.

"I'm sorry your car broke down. What's the matter with it?"

"I don't have any idea," she said, shivering. "All I know is one minute I was driving along and the next the car sputtered, and then died."

I reached over and put my arm around her shoulders to shield her from to cold.

"Come on and get in my car where it's warm, and we'll figure out what to do next."

"Thanks so much," the woman said. "I was getting awfully cold. My name's Grace, by the way."

"I'm Lila."

"Well, Lila, you sure saved me in more ways than you can possibly imagine."

"Just glad I could help."

I walked her over to my car, and once both of us were seated inside and enjoying the warmth blasting from the heater, she turned to me and said, “I guess I picked the wrong time to travel. I didn’t know we were going to get this storm. What’s wrong with those weather people anyway? They never called for snow, until it was too late.”

Looking at her, I guessed Grace to be around eighty years old. She was thin, short and had white hair. Her fingers were twisted in a way that reminded me of my grandmother who suffered from arthritis. I felt so sorry for her, knowing the pain she must endure.

“I don’t mean any harm, Grace, but aren’t you a little old to be out here by yourself? What if I were a serial killer? You never know who you can trust these days.”

“You aren’t a serial killer, are you?”

“Well, no, but you didn’t know that when you flagged me down.”

She grunted as if to blow me off while she dug through her purse. She pulled out a shiny, small handgun and held it up.

“I have protection,” she said with a smile on her face. “I stole it from my son. Unfortunately, I probably couldn’t use it with these crippled old fingers. They give me such a fit sometimes.”

My heart jumped up in my throat. Had I stopped to help a psycho? Was she jerking my chain with that little old lady bit?

“Oh, don’t worry,” Grace quickly said, putting the gun back into her purse. “I’m not just some old psycho you picked up. I know that’s what you were thinking. No… I’m just a runaway.”

“A runaway?”

“It’s a long story,” Grace said. “Perhaps we could talk about it on our way.”

“On our way to where?”

“Well, you’re not going to leave me stranded out here, are you?”

“No, of course I’m not. I thought I could call you a tow truck or something. Maybe I could call your family.”

“I’ve already called my son. He’ll send someone out to pick up the car as soon as he can... or cares to. He'll have to get out of bed first. Sometimes he can be so lazy."

"Okay…"

I thought for a second and then said, "My father had a heart attack and I was on my way to Newport News to see him. He's in the hospital, and I'm kinda in a hurry. Where did you want to go? I can drop you off somewhere as long as it's not too far out of my way."

"Newport News!" she exclaimed. "That's where I'm going. It must be my lucky day after all."

Hmm. Now isn't this a coincident, I thought to myself. Grace said she was a runaway. Perhaps she didn't have any destination in mind and only wanted a ride somewhere… anywhere. Maybe that's why she said she was going to Newport News.

"I don't know what your deal is Grace, but I'll help you if you let me hold onto your gun until we get to where you're going."

"Sure," she replied, pulling the gun from her purse and then handing it to me butt first.

I was impressed that she knew about gun safety by not pointing it at me when she handed it over.

I took the gun and slid it under my seat.

"You know you could get arrested for that," she said. "It's illegal to hide a weapon unless you have a permit."

"That's the least of my worries," I said, looking back at her car. "Is there anything you want to get out of your car before we leave?"

"Yes, everything."

She smiled again.

"I don't have much, only a couple of bags and a briefcase."

"Okay, I'll go get your stuff. You stay here and keep warm."

"Aren't you afraid I'll steal your car while you're gone?"

"You won't, will you?"

She chuckled.

"No, I won't."

We both smiled at that. Grace was a nice person. I hadn't picked up a wacko after all. She was just a little old lady in distress.

"I'll be right back. Don't steal anything," I joked.

Ten minutes later, her things were packed in the trunk of my car, except for the briefcase she had insisted upon holding in her lap.

"What's so important about that briefcase?" I asked as I maneuvered the Toyota back onto the road. "Is it full of money you stole from your son, along with the gun?"

"Don't be silly," Grace replied. "No, it's not full of money, just some important documents."

She changed the subject.

"Tell me about yourself, Lila. We might as well get to know each other. This could be a long ride." She motioned to the snow. "We're not going to be able to go but so fast anyway."

Swirls of snow bombarded the windshield. Visibility was poor.

"It was like this on I-295," I said. "Pretty soon it'll be a white-out."

I glanced over at her.

"The ride could get pretty scary."

"Hey, after seeing what my son has been doing to people, nothing scares me anymore. I'm just glad to be rid of him."

My hands were shaking, but I refused to let go of the death grip I had on the steering wheel. I didn't like to be out in this kind of weather, but I hated driving in it more. My breathing became rapid.

Sensing my anxiety, Grace reached over and put her tiny hand on my shoulder.

"Try to relax, Lila. It's just a little snow. I'm right here with you. Nothing bad is going to happen, I promise."

Her compassion and her kind words were soothing. I relaxed my grip a little, but still kept my eyes glued to the road.

"Okay, you want to know about me," I said. "Well… here's the short of it. I'm a reporter, who wrote a story that put a man out of business, or so he thought, and then he blamed me for his problem. So, he started sending me messages via dead flowers, a headless squirrel, etcetera… etcetera."

"Oh, my God! You've got a stalker! Now, isn't this ironic? You're a bad-mouth reporter with a crazy man after you, and I'm a runaway thief with a snot-nosed son after me. We have so much in common. To quote Tina Turner, 'Ain't we a pair, raggedy man?'"

I laughed at her reference.

"Yeah, I guess we are."

"So, what happened to your stalker? Is he in jail… dead?"

"No, he's still around, but I haven't heard from him since I dropped off the radar. I changed my phone number, traded my car, moved out of my apartment into a small cabin in the middle of nowhere, and did everything I could to keep him from getting to me, well... except change my hair color."

I glanced up in the rearview mirror as if I was checking myself out.

"Maybe I should consider doing that."

Headlights appeared in the distance and were advancing rapidly… too fast in bad weather like this. I was hoping it was just a foolish driver taking stupid risks, but the chill that ran down my spine said otherwise. I tried to suppress my panic.

"I don't want to alarm you, Grace, but it looks like we have company, and he's moving right fast."

Grace craned her neck to have a look and then quickly stiffened in her seat, fear seeping through ever pore in her body.

"What's the matter, Grace?"

"Did I mention to you that my son is dangerous?"

"Oh, Lord, and here I was afraid my stalker had caught up with me."

"Maybe it isn't either one. We could just be working ourselves up over nothing."

Both of us let out a sigh of relief when the reckless driver in a black Dodge pickup truck flew past us fishtailing and sliding all over the road. I was just glad he was now in front of us and not behind us.

"He better slow down or he's going to kill someone," Grace said, still a little nervous from the ordeal. "He scared me half to death. I thought I was going to wet my pants. Oh... I need to go pee."

"The rest area's only a few miles up the road. We'll stop there. I need to stretch my legs and massage my nerves."

I paused for a moment and then remarked, "So, Grace… you stole from your dangerous son, ran away, deserted your car… and now you're traveling with a woman who has a stalker."

"Yeah, how `bout that?"

"We know stalkers are evil and dangerous, capable of killing, but what about your son? Is he so bad that he'd hunt you down and kill you? I'm only asking because I need to know how many bad guys might be after us."

She let out a contagious laugh that I immediately caught.

"I really like you, Lila. You make bad times seem better."

"Thanks for the compliment, but that doesn't answer my question."

"Don't freak out, okay?"

"I'm done my fair share of freaking out. No more. Go ahead."

"I never told you my last name on purpose, and you never asked, but its Madison—Grace Madison. I'm sure you recognize the name from an article you wrote two months ago about my son, Harry."

I sat upright. I remembered Harry Madison and his plan to take over the family business quite well. My article was a harsh write-up of his business practices and his awful treatment of his employees. All facts had been confirmed.

"Don't be afraid, Lila," Grace assured me. "I'm not your enemy. I'm glad you wrote the article. Nobody ever tells me anything. Everyone kept that secret from me. Liars, all of them! I own the company, and I had no idea my son was going to take over, and then kick me out. I might be old, but I'm not stupid. Thank you. I owe you a lot."

She tapped the briefcase in her lap and said, "I got paperwork that's going to send him to jail."

"Holy crap! You're carrying evidence that could get you hurt, maybe killed, and you can't even make a decent getaway. What kind of plan is that?"

"I didn't know my car was going to break down."

"Let's talk about that. How did you know I'd be the one coming to your rescue? I know you didn't set that up. You're not even a good runaway."

"I was lucky. I had no idea you'd be the one who would stop to help me, but I'm sure glad it was you. I was scared when my car broke down. When I saw your face, I wasn't scared anymore. I knew you were someone I could trust. I've read every article you've written. You're a smart lady."

"What was I thinking? I should've kept right on going."

The minute I said that, I realized what an idiot I'd been. Maybe I never should've stopped. I had enough food on my plate without adding dessert, and Grace was definitely the dessert. She was sweet, fun… and trouble. But what could I do?

"You don't mean it. You're not that kind of person."

"Why didn't you tell me from the beginning?"

"I was afraid you might leave me behind."

By the time we reached the rest area, the snow had let up a little and the wind had died down. The snow-covered parking lot was empty except for a big rig at the far end.

After a quick visit to the restroom, Grace and I returned to the car to see a black pickup parked several spaces down. We glanced at each other only for a second before jumping in and locking the doors.

I backed out of the parking space and made a run for it.

Neither one of us knew for sure if it was the same truck, but we were too scared to hang around long enough to find out.

Once we were back on the interstate, I glanced over at Grace and said, "I'm curious, Grace. Why would you call your son and tell him your car broke down if you didn't want him to know you ran away and where you were? I mean, you could've just called a tow truck."

"I lied about that," Grace replied. "I didn't call my son."

"Are you serious? What else have you lied about?"

"It isn't my car."

"Then whose car is it? You didn't steal it, did you?"

"No, I didn't steal it," she said, and then chuckled. "I borrowed it from my housekeeper, Rosie. Oh, don't worry; she doesn't care about the car. I gave her mine to use while I was gone, so she's pretty happy."

"So… you plan to go back home?"

"Sure, I do, as soon as I see my friend in Newport News. He's going to make sure my son gets exactly what he deserves. That's why I have to get these papers to him as soon as possible. When Harry wakes up and finds me gone he's going to have a fit. And he's really going to go crazy when he discovers I've…" Grace paused. "I blocked assess to my accounts. He can't get a dime of my money."

"Well... couldn't you have just faxed those papers to your friend?" I asked. "Sure would've saved you from being out in this dangerous weather."

"No, I couldn't do that," she replied. "These papers are too important. I want to deliver them myself."

Grace Madison was turning out to be a real character. She was headstrong, kind, and determined to set things right. I had to admire her. She had more nerve than I did. She was taking charge of her life, while I was slinking into the background of mine. Maybe I should confront Mike, find out if he's the one, or maybe I'd be better off if I didn't hang around with the likes of Grace. She was giving me false courage, courage I didn't have.

"Have you got any money on you?"

"Why? You gonna rob me?"

"No, Grace. I was just concerned. You need cash instead of credit cards and checks if you don't want your son to find you until after you see this friend of yours. By the way, who is your friend? I'm from

Newport News. I might even know him."

"You do," Grace said. "Joe Stevens. You wrote an article on him a while back."

"I know Joe Stevens!" I said. "He's actually one of the good guys. This is just too weird. Am I going to find out you're a long, lost relative from the wrong side of the family?"

"Lila, you're too much. Once I dump my son, I want us to hang out together. I need to surround myself with people I like and who like me. You do like me, don't you? You know, I can protect you from that guy."

"Yes, Grace, I like you," I replied. "Don't worry about Mike. He's not a problem anymore."

"That's what they all say just before they get murdered."

"Geez, I feel much better now."

"I want you to be realistic, Lila, because if that black truck is following us, it isn't my Harry. His men drive black SUVs with dark tinted windows. You know the kind I'm talking about."

"So you think it's my stalker?"

"Yes, I do, unless you have some other enemy after you. What kind of car does Mike the Stalker drive?"

"I don't know."

"Not good, Lila. You're a reporter. Why didn't you find out? Why didn't you Google him?"

"What?"

"Come on, Lila. Even I know how to get information on people. The internet is the ticket. You should try it sometime."

"I Google. I get a lot of my facts from surfing web sites of people I'm writing about. I was just surprised that you knew what Google was."

"How old are you, Lila?" she asked me.

"How old are you, Grace?"

"I'm eighty-three and proud of it. My mind is still sharp and I'm very active. I work out every day. My only problem is these hands."

"I'm thirty-two and I'm a coward. I let some guy make my life miserable. I'm scared all the time. I was just thinking about how you're so aggressive. You get what you want. You take a stand. I wish I had your nerve."

"You do. You just haven't been cornered into using it. You ran away from your problem. Now me, I would've dealt with it."

"Oh, yeah? And just what would you have done?"

"You'll see. I'll take care of Mike for you. You just get me to Joe's in one piece, and I'll make all your problems go away. It's the least I can do to pay you back for stopping to help me."

"What are you Grace, some kind of gangster? I mean, are you talking about killing this guy, Mike, for me? I never said I wanted him dead. I just want him to leave me alone. Besides, I'm not even sure Mike is guilty. I only suspect him. I don't have a shred of proof."

"You have a gut feeling, and sometimes that's all you need."

"No, I need more than that before I let you bump him off."

I laughed, and then said, "I'm just kidding, Grace."

"Well, I'm not a gangster, but I know people who can fix things. I can have your stalker snatched up and dumped off in some third world country, and nobody would be the wiser. He'd just disappear."

"Now that's a little weird," I said. "I appreciate your offer, Grace, but I think I'll pass. I don't want to be indebted to you. One day you might come to collect, and that's a scary thought."

My cell phone started playing the tune from Psycho.

I snatched it from the console and said, "It just dawned on me that you haven't called me once. What's up with that?"

"Nothing's up," Joshlyn replied. "Daddy's fine. It was just a case of heartburn. He's back home and in bed asleep. Isn't that wonderful?"

"I've been driving for almost three hours in a raging snowstorm, risking my life to get there, and you don't even bother to call and tell me he's all right. Do you have any idea what it has been like for me?"

I quickly took a glance over at Grace.

"Not to mention the encounter I've had."

"You can tell me all about it in the morning. I'm going to bed. I'm exhausted."

"I'll be there in thirty minutes or so. Can't you stay up that long? I've been…"

"I know, but I've been up half the night and I need to get some sleep before the sun comes up."

"Joshlyn, you didn't even ask me about my encounter."

"You sound fine, Lila."

That's my sister. My dilemma was of no consequence to her.

I said goodbye and tossed the phone down.

"Is your sister self-centered?" Grace asked. "I only ask because she didn't seem to care about how you were doing."

"She's a brat."

"I bet it really ticks you off that she didn't bother to call when your dad was out of the woods."

"My father didn't have a heart attack. That's all that matters to me."

"Ah… I see. She's the baby in the family, so you tolerate her bad behavior. I get it. Sometimes we just have to let it slide and go with the flow, huh?"

"I guess you could say that."

It was a little past four and traffic was beginning to pick up. Morning would be here soon, and by then, I'd be at Mom and Dad's house drinking hot coffee. I felt a little more at ease.

The black pickup truck obviously wasn't following us. We could relax and not worry anymore.

"It's quit snowing," Grace said. "Newport News probably didn't get a flake. They rarely ever do. Two inches and the city shuts down. It's kind of funny, isn't it? Just on the other side of Richmond there's a blizzard and here there's almost nothing. Go figure."

"Where am I taking you, Grace?"

"To Joe's house. He lives in Denbigh on the Warwick River. I'll show you how to get to his house when we get close."

"You must really have some damaging evidence in that briefcase to make this trip by yourself."

"Oh, I do," Grace replied. "I have proof that my son's a thief and he's been stealing from the company for years. And that's just the beginning of his illegal activities."

"The Jefferson Avenue exit is coming up next, so I'll have you there in no time. I can't tell you what a pleasure it's been."

"Yeah, I bet."

I put on my blinker, moved over to the exit lane, and then noticed a car on my bumper.

"I wish that guy would…"

Before I could finish my sentence, the car rammed us in the rear end. It slammed us so hard, I lost control of the car.

The Camry fishtailed, slid off the road, down the embankment, and then the back side of the car struck the metal buffer wall.

"What the hell…" I yelled and then looked over at Grace. "Are you all right?"

Grace didn't say anything. All she did was point to my window.

I turned and saw the black pickup truck sitting on the side of the road. The driver had gotten out and was headed our way. Even though it was still dark, there was no denying what he was carrying. He had a gun in his hand.

"Oh, my God, Grace. He's going to kill us."

"Not if I can help it," she replied and then reached down under my seat. "Roll your window down, Lila!"

"What? Why?"

"Just do it!"

I scrambled to find the button and as soon as I did, I pressed it down hard and held it there until it started making a humming noise.

I leaned over and snatched up my phone to call the police when the first bullet hit the back windshield. Another shot hit the hood, and a third missed its mark and hit the metal barrier.

"Where's my gun?" Grace frantically cried. "I thought it was… I got it. Lean back, Lila."

"Are you serious?" I exclaimed. "What are you…"

Grace leaned over against me, stuck the gun out the window, and after struggling a few seconds, cried, "I can't pull the trigger. My darn fingers are too stiff."

"Give it to me!"

I took the gun, pointed it at the guy and fired. The explosion was deafening. The bullet hit him in the leg and he crumbled to the ground.

"You got him, Lila! You hit him in the leg!"

"I was aiming for his chest."

"Plug him again!"

"Are you crazy? I'm not going to shoot him again."

Before I could call the police, I heard the sound of sirens blaring in the distance, and then flashing strobe lights surrounded the pickup truck.

A minute later, policemen were coming to our aid.

"Are you hit anywhere?" I asked Grace, looking her over. "Did you get shot?"

"No, Lila. I'm hole-free. I'm getting a headache and my ears are ringing, but otherwise I'm okay. How about you?"

She took the gun from me and laid it on the dash.

"You don't want to be holding this thing when the police get over here. They might shoot you."

"I think I peed myself," I said.

I looked at Grace as she rummaged through her purse.

"What are you doing?"

"I'm looking for my cell phone. I need to call Joe."

"Call him later. The cops are coming."

"If you don't want to go to jail for discharging a firearm, you'd better let me call him. You did shoot someone."

"But I…"

"Just let me do it. We're going to need his help to get out of this."

She flipped open her phone and called Joe. She told him about being run off the road and that I shot the guy in the leg after he shot at us.

"He's going to call the police chief and take care of our problem," Grace said. "We'll be okay."

"Is there anyone of influence you don't know, Grace?"

"I'll take that as a thank you."

An ambulance arrived on the scene, joining the array of flashing lights. Two EMTs rushed over and gave both of us a quick once-over.

We assured them we were all right, and after seeing for themselves, they gathered their bags and left.

Grace and I had survived an encounter with a madman, and other than a couple of bullet holes, a dented trunk and a smashed quarter panel, my Camry was still intact, and hopefully, drivable.

Now that I knew we were going to be all right, I wanted to know who the driver of the black pickup truck was. I wanted to confront him.

"I have a right to know," I demanded of the officer after introducing myself and Grace to him. "We both do, don't we, Grace? This guy tried to kill us for no good reason."

"I'm Officer Patterson with the State Police," the officer said. "You want to tell me what happened here?"

I hurriedly explained what had happened and then told the officer about the man who had been hounding me for months. I demanded to see if it was him. Then, maybe I'd be able to sleep at night knowing he was locked up.

I didn't mention anything about the possibility of Grace having a posse after her.

"It's not your stalker," the officer said. "It was a woman."

"What?" I gasped. "A woman?"

Grace and I looked at each other and then back at the officer.

"What's her name?" I asked.

"I don't have that information, Miss Jackson,"

"Well, then get it!" Grace ordered loudly and then paused for a second. "Never mind. We'll find out for ourselves."

She looked at me and whispered, "Come on, Lila. Let's go find out who it is that's trying to kill us."

Grace and I started to slip away, but Officer Patterson stepped in front of us and said, "I can't allow you to do that. If you give me a second, I'll see what I can find out."

He stepped away and spoke briefly to another officer.

Grace and I waited with anticipation.

"She must be after you, Grace," I whispered. "My stalker's a man, not a woman."

"Not me," she whispered back. "My son wouldn't send a woman after me. He thinks women belong in the kitchen, because they're not smart enough to do anything else. Besides, Harry doesn't even know I'm gone yet. He's probably still asleep with a stack of my money lying next to him to keep him company. Money is the only thing my son cares about. Oh, if only my husband were still alive. He'd put a stop to Harry's madness. Did I tell you Harry was a thief?"

"A few times."

"I can't believe my son would steal from me."

"The apple doesn't fall far from the tree, Grace."

She started to say something, but hesitated when she saw the officer returning.

"What did you find out?" I asked. "Who is she?"

"Her name's Lucy Harris."

Grace and I looked at each other quizzically.

"Never heard of her," I said.

"Don't know her," Grace added.

"Her driver's license says she's from Charlottesville and the truck is registered to her boyfriend, Mike Grayson."

I gasped.

"Are you sure?"

"I'm quite sure, Miss Jackson."

"Oh, my God! My stalker has been a woman the whole time!"

I looked at Grace.

"Mike's girlfriend! He probably never even knew what was going on. I feel so bad for blaming him."

"She claims you tried to run her off the road and that she was only protecting herself," Officer Patterson said. "Anyway, that's her side of the story."

"That's a big, fat lie," Grace said, agitated.

"Yeah, we know," Officer Patterson replied. "It's obvious she rear-ended you, and we also have an eyewitness to collaborate your story—two of them as a matter of fact." He smiled. "An elderly couple saw the truck run you off the road and then saw the driver shoot at you, so they pulled over and the man called the police from his cell phone." He chuckled. "Gotta love modern technology."

"Are they nuts?" I exclaimed. "They could've been killed."

"I think they know that now. At the time, they were just trying to help."

"We need to thank them," I said, looking at Grace. "They stopped and called the police for us. They probably saved our lives."

"They left," Officer Patterson informed us. "We have their statements and personal information, so we let them go. Lucy Harris is on her way to the hospital and then she's going to jail."

"Well, you have our statements and our information, so are we finished here?" Grace asked. "I'd like to leave, too."

"I'm sorry, but Miss Jackson shot someone," he replied. "I can't..."

"In self-defense!"

A policeman called out to Officer Patterson.

"Excuse me for a moment, ladies. I'll be right back. Don't go anywhere."

"Crap, Grace, they're going to take us to the police station."

"I don't think so," she said.

"You heard the officer. I shot Lucy Harris to stop her from killing us, but do you think that matters?"

"Joe won't let that happen. We're innocent. We didn't do anything wrong."

When the officer returned he said, "You ladies are free to go, but I'm afraid we'll have to keep the gun for now."

"What about my car?"

"I was told to give you a lift and to have your car towed, if that's okay with you."

He looked at Grace.

"Chief Howell was pretty adamant about that."

"Thanks, but no thanks," I said to him, gently taking Grace by the hand. "If we're free to go, we're leaving. Come on, Grace."

"Are you sure?" she asked me. "I mean, your car's pretty banged up. It might not…"

"It'll be fine. It's a Toyota."

By the time Grace and I made it back to the car, some of the police were gone and the others were in the process of leaving. We had refused their assistance, and they had other crimes to attend to.

We were once again on our own, but might still be in a pickle. If I couldn't get my car up the hill, we'd be out of luck. I had turned down the offer of a ride, so a tow truck might definitely be in order.

But I was determined. I wanted to see my father, go back home, and then put all this behind me. My stalker was going to jail, and I had my life back.

"This ought to be fun," Grace said as she slid into her side of the car. "You know the city will bill you if you tear up the ground getting out of here."

"Buckle up, Grace. We're going for a ride."

It was lightly snowing again.

"Better get a move on it," Grace said, encouraging me. "Looks like the blizzard is catching up with us."

"Perfect timing," I grunted. "We gotta get up that hill right now. In five minutes we could be under a foot of snow."

"Yeah, right," Grace joked. "Take it easy. We're in no hurry, right?"

"Right, Grace."

I chuckled to myself.

"I'm so glad you have friends in high places. I thought for sure they were going to arrest me."

"You didn't do anything wrong."

"Now you sound like my sister."

The Toyota roared to life and climbed the hill with little effort. The rear end made a tiny, scratching noise, but that didn't bother me. The car could be fixed. The body was a little worse-for-wear, but otherwise the car ran just fine.

By the time we reached our destination, the snow had stop falling... again.

"So much for the blizzard," Grace said. "Come on, Lila. I want you to meet my friends."

After teasing everyone for hours with snow showers, the blizzard finally hit Newport News, dumping eight inches on the ground.

My dad had recovered from his bout of heartburn, and two days later, I was on my way back home, ready to start all over again. I wouldn't be afraid anymore.

The story about Lucy Harris unfolded. After the failure of his business, Mike Grayson started using more and selling less of his own drugs. His drinking increased, and his relationship with Lucy suffered.

In the meantime, Lucy wanted payback for Mike's decline. She blamed me for everything that had happened.

In the end, she claimed she never meant to hurt me, but you know how that goes. She's going to be out of my hair for a few years, and then after that... well, we'll have to see how it goes.

I still live in the little cabin in the woods and I still write for the paper.

Grace Madison has control of her life again and her son is on his way to prison.

Ever so often, Grace sends a car to pick me up for dinner or to go shopping. She refuses to come to my neck of the woods. She claims it's too eerie out here. After what she's been through, I'm surprised anything bothers her, but I accept her craziness.

Grace and I have remained friends ever since our brief encounter on that cold, snowy night.

The End

The moral of the story: Always carry a gun.